CW01658632

Praise for Tasmina Perry

*'Gripping from the off: sexy, scandalous brilliance, this book is a genuine must-read *****'* – Heat

'Takes you to the most glamorous corners of the globe while keeping you on the edge of your seat' – Glamour

'A gripping, pacy read with a few dark twists I did not see coming. The perfect end-of-summer novel' – Daily Mail

'Well-drawn characters and a twisty plot make this page-turner a must-read' – Good Housekeeping

'Excellent . . . A dark and devious thriller but with all the glamour you'd expect from Tasmina' – Red

'A book to cancel plans for – we were completely gripped' – Closer

About the author

Tasmina Perry is a *Sunday Times* bestselling novelist. Her books have been translated into twenty languages and have sold over two million copies worldwide.

A former lawyer and award-winning magazine journalist, she has edited several national titles including InStyle UK and More.

She also writes psychological thrillers under the pseudonym JL Butler. JL Butler's debut thriller 'Mine' has been optioned by Sony Pictures for development with Original Film.

Tasmina is the founder of Sunflower & Co, a female-focused media company. The team plots escapist stories and creates content from their boathouse office by the River Thames.

This edition published by Sunflower & Co 2022

ISBN 978-1-911297-49-9

* * *

www.tasminaperry.com

facebook.com/officialtasminaperry

instagram.com/tasminaperry

If you'd like to be kept up to date on all the new releases from Tasmina Perry, why not join my VIP Book Club for news on books, giveaways, events and other book recommendations.
www.tasminaperry.com/joinbookclub

The Ivy

A Lara Stone Mystery

Lara Stone
Book 3

Tasmina Perry

Sunflower & Co

Prologue

She had always loved the library at night. Hiding away on the top floor, you felt as if you were floating in space. The absolute silence, the darkness of the book-lined walls that seemed to press in around you and the glass dome above, revealing a black star-streaked Vermont sky, both deprived and heightened the senses.

She came here to read, of course, but lately, she came here to think. She had thought very deeply and had made decisions made that would alter the course of her life; change it forever. She believed those decisions to be right, but still, she knew what a scandal it would cause and how painful it would be for the people she loved.

She took a breath and turned to look at the splendour of the building. Her grandfather had built this place. She'd never known him, but had often heard what a brilliant man he was. What would he think of her now she wondered, as her fingers stroked the spines of a run of leather-bound books, knotty to the touch.

A dark cloud descended over her, a sense of dread that she was about to plunge into the unknown. But at the same time, she felt light, like she'd been carrying a heavy suitcase and had finally put it down.

She stopped; was that a noise? It sounded like her name was being called, but she was alone. It was as if the silence up here was playing tricks on her mind. Perhaps it was time to leave. Everything seemed so overwhelming, the darkness was pressing down from above. No, it was time to go. She turned towards the stairs and she took the first step.

Chapter 1

The boy on the bicycle was wearing tweed. *Of course he is*, smiled Lara. He was handsome, with dark floppy hair, and the right leg of his chinos was tucked into an argyle sock. Hipster trainers, but still... the boy pedalled lazily in front of the taxi, waving them past. From the back of the cab, Lara Stone waved back. It was exactly how she had imagined students at an Ivy League college would be.

She had just arrived from the airport, but so far Benedon College hadn't disappointed. To her left, a scattering of redbrick buildings with ivy crowding around the narrow windows. Preppy students in polo shirts and tea dresses strolled along the sidewalk, all glowing with privilege and intelligence. Beautiful grounds, beautiful buildings and beautiful people. Why wouldn't it be? Perhaps Harvard was the most prestigious American university, or Yale, 100 miles to the south – but Benedon College was certainly the prettiest on the east coast and probably the richest if the grand buildings were anything to go by.

'Is this the place, ma'am?'

Lara smiled again. London cabbies had their charms, but she never tired of being called 'ma'am'.

She pulled a piece of paper from her pocket and read the address.

'If this is 47 Montrose Street, then I think so.'

'This is a pretty sweet college town,' growled the driver, who'd brought her over a hundred miles northwest of Boston's Logan airport. 'Are you a professor here?'

'Well, yes,' said Lara. 'I suppose I am.'

It wasn't quite true, but near enough: she was due to spend the next semester in Benedon giving a series of lectures on modern journalism as a 'visiting fellow'. Lara Stone had no experience in academia, but she had spent her whole working life as an investigative journalist, so she supposed she qualified: just.

'Yep, pretty sweet,' said the driver.

It is, isn't it? Thought Lara as she bumped her suitcase out onto the sidewalk and watched the driver pull away, feeling both excited and terrified. Lara knew she would have to get used to both of those sensations. She looked up at her new home – for the next few months, anyway. The college owned 47 Montrose, a one-storey clapboard bungalow, three shallow steps up to a porch with a huge potted hydrangea, still in bloom. The door was painted a seafoam green, with a polished brass door-knocker and a square frosted window. Beyond cute. Fumbling with the key safe, she finally stumbled through the door into the living room.

'Home sweet home,' said Lara, letting go of her case. To her delight, the interior was just as perfect. It was sparsely furnished, but it oozed 'college academic'. An overstuffed sofa with curly legs, an oriental rug and a huge bookcase, loaded with weighty tomes; it was all clean and neat and slightly worn around the edges, exactly right for a lecturer with their mind on higher things. Not that the description really fitted. Lara could admit she had been surprised to get the invitation to teach at Benedon, but when it came, she hadn't needed to think too hard. Glamour, history and a chance to pretend she was a professor? Hell yeah! Back at boarding school, crowded around the clunky old telly in their tiny common room, it seemed as though every American movie was set on a high school or college campus, where the nerd would win the girl and the jock would get their comeuppance in the final reel. Benedon College was her teenage dream come true.

She crossed to the small dining table; propped up against an earthenware jug was a white envelope with her name written on the front. She pulled out the card and read the invitation inside.

Dean Rosalind Davies requests the pleasure of your company for a Labor Day celebration.

This was exactly what Lara had imagined: cocktail parties and high-brow discussions with brainy professors. Could it be any more perfect? Her phone chirped in her pocket to indicate an incoming text: Alex, her closest friend and a colleague at *The Chronicle* newspaper.

You there yet?

She smiled: checking up on her already. The previous evening when he had come round to her Chelsea houseboat for send-off drinks, he'd been teasing her about the trip. 'What if they ask you questions?' he'd said. 'You know, intelligent questions that need an intelligent answer.'

At the time, Lara had punched his arm and told him he

was jealous, but now she wasn't so sure. Perhaps Alex had been right; it had been a long time since she had been to university. She looked back at her suitcase. More importantly, what was she going to *wear*?

Lara's stomach rumbled, and she suddenly realised she hadn't eaten since she'd grabbed a croissant dashing through Heathrow. She had slept through the in-flight meal and had been far too excited when she had landed in Boston to think about food. But clearly, her stomach had other ideas.

She walked over to the Shaker-style kitchen area and opened the fridge: bare. There were toiletries in the bathroom and a pile of fluffy white towels on the bed, but clearly, food was her responsibility. Fair enough; she grabbed her purse and headed for the door.

The bungalow was not far from Benedon's Main Street, which, in keeping with the rest of the town, was quite lovely. Lara passed a lacrosse outfitters, a Dickensian bookstore with bow windows, and a 'gown outlet' with gold lettering above the door. It was as if Disney had decided to create an 'American College' exhibit at Epcot next to their 'France' and 'China' pavilions. And like Disney World, Benedon was spotless, shiny and pin-perfect. Shady trees, pathways crisscrossing manicured lawns that wouldn't look out of place in a country club. Of course, it wasn't a surprise that the place was so well-kept. Benedon was a private Liberal Arts college with some of the highest tuition fees in the country. If you wanted to attract the fat chequebooks of the well-heeled, it made sense that it should look like a Four Seasons resort transplanted to rural Vermont.

Finally, Lara spotted a deli, sitting on a corner, baskets of shiny fruit stacked up outside like the veggie gardens of Babylon.

Inside, Lara suppressed a grin. Once again, the store

was exactly as it should be. A pyramid of gigantic shiny apples, shelves of brightly-coloured 'chips' and a coffee stand; Lara almost expected Rob Lowe to be sitting in a booth. She grabbed a carton of milk, cream cheese and bagels, then crossed to a silver chiller cabinet next to a board hand-labelled 'Today's Subs', the sandwiches listed below in neat cursive script. But the shelves were empty. Clearly, Lara's confusion showed because a girl behind the coffee counter called out to her.

'Can I help you?'

She was early twenties, with a bleached blonde bob held back with a blue hairclip.

'Do you still have any of the...' Lara checked the menu. 'Pastrami on rye?'

'Subs have finished for the day,' said the girl in a voice that indicated so was she.

'Okay, in that case, I'll just take these.' She handed over the basket. 'And I'll grab a drink too.'

Her eyes scanned the menu board behind the girl, the options swimming before her: Honey and hazelnut oat latte, iced white chocolate mocha, skinny peppermint mocha, toasted cinnamon macchiato.

'Have you got tea?' asked Lara hopefully.

'Youthberry, green tea latte, black tea lemonade,' said the girl in a monotone as she loaded Lara's groceries into a paper sack. 'Rooibos, ginger infusion, Mint and....'

'You don't just have tea? Sorry, I've only just arrived.'

The girl tilted her head.

'Just what it says on the menu, Ma'am.'

Lara wasn't sure that 'ma'am' was quite as well-meant as the cab driver's.

'Be kind, Zoe.'

She turned to see a handsome man with unkempt hair

and a square jaw. He was looking at the server with raised eyebrows.

'Giving the lady a cup of tea isn't so hard, is it?'

Tutting her displeasure, the girl turned to the machine behind her.

'Thanks,' said Lara.

'No need,' said the man. 'In fact, I feel I should apologise on behalf of the nation. You're British?'

'Do I have an accent?' smiled Lara.

'A little. Well, have a great day,' said the man, taking a cardboard cup from the counter. He hesitated, then looked at her again.

'You're not Lara Stone, are you?'

Lara held up her hands.

'Infamous already?'

'No, no,' smiled the man. 'I'm an Associate Professor at the journalism school. We're expecting you.'

He extended his free hand.

'Harry Robbins. Sorry I didn't recognise you sooner. I googled you when I knew you were coming. I found lots of your stories online. I read your story on Jonathon Meyer. Best piece of investigative reporting of the year. No photos of you, though.'

She didn't want to tell him that she paid someone to keep images of her from the internet. She was an investigative reporter, and although she didn't do much undercover work, she found that anonymity could be useful.

'I don't like having my picture taken,' she said. 'I like the newspaper ninja vibe.'

'Welcome to Benedon, international woman of mystery.'

Lara laughed and took a moment to observe him more closely. Harry's eyes were grey, his hair sandy brown, and he was classically handsome; his stubble made him look more like an off-duty actor than an academic.

'So when did you arrive?'

'About an hour ago.'

'I see you've already found the best place for coffee in town.'

'I was just here to pick up some groceries and got tempted by the most comprehensive drinks menu I've seen all year.'

'Usually, this place is packed,' he said, looking around. 'But it's Labor Day weekend, and term starts late this year, so not many students are around yet. Those that are here are probably at the Lake.'

'The lake?'

'Finger Lake, the town's built on the eastern shore, belongs to the college like everything else around here, but it's beautiful. There are kayaks, sailboats, and hiking trails all around it.'

'Sounds idyllic,' said Lara. 'Back in London, I live on a houseboat on the River Thames. Having a lake so close by might stop me being homesick for the water.'

There was a cough, and Lara turned. The server gave her a thin smile.

'One hot tea with oat milk.'

Lara fumbled with her purse. She hated oat milk but thought mentioning it might cause an international incident.

'Zoe put it on my tab,' grinned the man, opening the door for Lara to step through. 'See you in class, huh?'

Lara followed Harry onto the street, tucking her small sack of groceries under her arm.

'So where are you staying?' asked Harry.

'A place on Montrose St. The college sorted it out for me.'

'Green cottage with the porch?'

'You know it?'

'My friend Sanjay lived there last year; a visiting fellow from Delhi. You may have problems with the water heater. If it starts acting up, call me; my dad was a plumber, and I'm just a block away on Floral St.'

'I might just do that,' said Lara, then winced: too flirtatious?

'Listen, have you eaten?'

'Not since London.'

'In which case, how about I show you the best bar in town? It's just down the street: beer, burgers and Benedon bonhomie?'

Lara had wanted to go and check out the campus before it got dark, and it wasn't her style to go off with men she'd hardly just met, but she supposed that, seeing as Harry was a professor, it would be like a semi-official orientation tour. The fact that he was so cute had nothing to do with it.

'Sure, why not?'

* * *

The Shovel didn't look like a bar. It was just a whitewashed box with a plain black door and a discreet neon sign to one side. Back in London, on a warm early evening like this, the doors and windows of a pub would be open, music playing, the lights glowing, and people spilling out onto the street with their drinks. In the States, it was the opposite. Doors were closed, windows covered; the idea was you couldn't see in, to protect upstanding citizens from the temptations of the booze and to hide the patrons' identities, lest the moral lapse of an after-work beer make them a social outcast. But once again, Lara loved it the moment she stepped inside. A dark, long bar with high stools down the left-hand side, tables and chairs scattered across the other. At the far end were booths, a pool table and, yes, a jukebox. Presumably, it would automatically play 'Born to Run' the moment it was switched on.

'Hey Harry,' said the barman, and the professor crossed over, clasping his hand warmly. Harry turned to Lara.

'Lara Stone, meet Buck Wheelan. Buck makes the best martini in Vermont.'

The barman smiled at her. 'Not that there's much competition. Good to meet you, Lara. You working with Harry?'

'From next week, yes.'

'Lara's a big-time journalist,' said Harry. 'If you ever need a lead on a story, Buck knows everyone in town.'

The barman rolled his eyes.

'I know *you*, Harry. That's enough. So what can I get you two?'

'What's good?' asked Lara.

'I say we go with the classics,' smiled Harry.

'Sounds good to me.'

'Couple of Sam Adams and two Shovelburgers,' said Harry, looking to Lara. 'Trust me.'

Buck poured the beer, and Harry led them to a booth; red vinyl seats, chipped Formica table-top, even a bowl of nuts. Lara recognised all the details from a dozen Hollywood movies, but they immediately made her feel at home.

'Are you going to the Dean's party?' asked Lara, thinking about the white card on her kitchen table.

'Not sure. Maybe,' he said, picking a shelled peanut from a bowl.

'Try and come,' she said. 'You're the only person I know.'

'So are you ready for this?' asked Harry, changing the subject.

'American beer?' asked Lara, raising her glass.

'Lecturing. Benedon is a long way from *The Chronicle*.'

'You *have* been googling me, haven't you?' smiled Lara, secretly pleased. 'Well, I've worked at the paper for over fifteen years, and I love it, but it's tough, especially in the investigations department. You see a lot of dark things: greed, corruption, and even murder. I guess I just needed a break from it all.'

It wasn't until Lara said it out loud that she realised how true her words were. Even until a few months ago, she had been unable to think of life outside the newsroom. She had thrived on the pressure, the deadlines, and the joy of getting a story into print. But lately? The truth was, she felt weighed down by it.

'Anyway, my old friend Jenny teaches at Columbia Journalism School. She suggested a visiting fellowship.'

Lara thought back to how a visiting fellowship came on her radar. She didn't post anything on Instagram – part of her social media blackout – but she liked to watch her friends from afar, and she had always thought that Jenny Pearson, a former media editor on *The Chronicle*, had the best work/life balance of anyone in her profession. Over the summer, Jenny had visited Lara in London and told her of the rewards of connecting with students, inspiring and nurturing their talent but then being able to make use of the long holidays to switch off, travel or write the odd feature for one of the nationals. Lara remembered the feeling of envy: 'me time' had never really been in Lara's vocabulary.

'And you came to Benedon instead?' replied Harry. 'Why didn't you go to the Big Apple?'

'I do love New York,' said Lara. 'But honestly, when you're feeling burnt out, I'm not sure Manhattan is the place to be. Besides, I've always loved the idea of the Ivy League. The scarves, the fall colours, the argyle socks...' she added, thinking of the cycling student she had seen on the way in.

Harry shrugged. 'If it was the Ivy League you were after, you should have stuck with Columbia. That's one of the official nine Ivies, even if it is in Morningside Heights. Benedon's only considered a 'baby Ivy': smaller, less famous, but we've got the lake, the mountains, and the Maple trees.'

Buck brought over their food, and they ate without talking. Lara was hungrier than she had thought, plus it was delicious, especially the spicy fries.

'You didn't answer the question,' said Harry when she'd finished eating.

'Which one?'

'When I asked if you were ready for the lecturing.'

Lara looked away. While she had certainly been excited to come over and soak up the atmosphere of an American college, the lecturing part was still a worry. She occasionally gave 'talks' for students at City University, her alma mater, but never anything as formal or structured as a lecture. She already felt like an imposter.

'I'm slightly concerned about the performance aspect, yes,' she conceded, noting how easy it was to talk to Harry. 'In my time at *The Chronicle,* I've walked into burning buildings and grilled politicians from hostile countries, but a room full of super-bright students? That's a whole different thing.'

Harry gave a good-humoured snort. 'Don't worry; the students are usually half asleep. The ones that aren't – just don't let them smell your fear. Besides, we all had to start exactly where you are – and if I can do it, so can you.'

She listened as Harry told her about his journey to

Benedon College. He'd joined the *New York Globe* straight out of college, which was impressive, but Harry felt his timing had been wrong. He joined the profession just as digital journalism was taking off, long-form features giving way to blogs and clickbait, so, becoming frustrated, he had side-stepped into academia.

'I'm not sure it was the smartest move in hindsight,' he shrugged.

'But you get to walk across those lawns every morning,' said Lara. 'You have adoring students hanging on your every word.'

Lara was joking, but she could certainly empathise with Harry's dissatisfaction with the changes in journalism over the past decade; it was something many people in the trade were feeling. And it was partly why Lara had left *The Chronicle* full-time for an editor-at-large role.

'So, who have you been dealing with from the faculty?' asked Harry.

'Doug Bishop. We've only spoken on the phone or Zoom, but he seems nice.'

Harry nodded.

'Did Doug tell you about my symposium?'

'Symposium? What's that?'

Harry explained it was a mini-festival arranged for the first weekend of term, a series of talks he had arranged for the new students, bringing in notable people from the world of media: columnists, broadcasters and newspaper editors.

'We teach the kids an awful lot of theory here,' said Harry. 'But it's just that – theory – and I think we're often in danger of being a little out of date. I wanted to get some more real-time, real-life experience into the discussion. More importantly, I want to fire up these kids. I want to get them looking at people like you, Lara, and thinking, "Damn, that's what I want to do." It seemed the perfect way to kick off the new academic year.'

Lara loved how Harry lit up when he talked about it, his eyes sparkling.

'Will you speak?' said Harry. 'Not the things you'd cover in lectures, the "how-to" stuff'. I'd want you to talk about the colour, the danger, and the excitement of your work at the frontline of investigative journalism. What it's really like, guts'n'glory. I know it's more "performing", as you say, but I know the students will love to hear what you've got to say. I know I would.'

He flashed her a lop-sided grin. Damn, he was handsome.

'No pressure. I'll give you a few minutes to think about it; I'm going to hit the John.'

Lara watched him cross the room, smiling to herself. She hadn't come to Benedon for romance, far from it, but she had allowed herself to indulge in a fantasy about a handsome professor or two – and here was one right in front of her: sexy, clever and charismatic. Was there any harm in it?

Their beer glasses were empty. Despite her jet lag, she didn't want her impromptu night out with Harry to end so quickly, so she got up to go to the bar.

'Hey.'

Lara turned, and a young woman stepped out in front of her. Her eyes were glassy; her expression was confrontational.

'You watch him,' she said, pointing the neck of a beer bottle towards her.

'Watch who?' said Lara, startled by the approach.

'Harry Robbins. The *professor,*' she spat, spittle flying from her mouth. 'Woman to woman, I say stay away from him.'

Lara tried to side-step her. She was drunk. Lara could smell the alcohol on her breath, and engaging with someone who'd had that much to drink was generally not a good idea.

'If you'll excuse me,' she said quickly.

'No, listen to me.' The woman jabbed a finger towards Lara's chest.

'I've seen you two together, and I'm warning you. Woman to woman.' She flashed her teeth in a twisted smile, gums stained with red wine. Lara glanced towards the exit, but the woman was standing between her and the door. She swayed towards Lara, lowering her voice. 'Harry Robbins... is a murderer.'

Lara laughed, then immediately saw that the woman wasn't joking.

'A murderer?' she repeated.

Just then, Buck the barman appeared behind the woman with both hands raised, like a zookeeper trying to herd a tiger back into its enclosure.

'Okay sweetheart, I think you should cool off, huh?'

The girl shrugged him off aggressively.

'Don't you think it's better to warn her?' she slurred. 'Don't you think she should know?'

The girl leant in again.

'Eleanor Campbell,' she hissed, her breath sour. 'Look her up – then you'll see.'

Lara glanced at Buck, who just shook his head.

'Who is Eleanor?' asked Lara.

'Was,' said the woman with feeling. 'Who *was* she? Eleanor was beautiful, and she was my friend. If it weren't for Harry Robbins, she'd be here right now.'

Buck gently put his hands on her shoulders. 'Come on; I'm going to get you some coffee....'

'She needs to know,' said the drunk girl, sobbing. 'She needs to hear.'

He was leading her away when the girl turned back, twisting away from Buck, tears flowing down her cheeks.

'Trust me. Listen to me. Stay away from him. Stay away from Harry Robbins. He killed Eleanor Campbell.'

Her eyes met Lara's.

'He murdered my friend.'

Chapter 2

Lara was already pushing through the door.

'Lara!'

Harry pushed past a group playing pool and dodged around the tables, desperate to stop her from leaving. He'd seen it all unfold as he left the restroom. At first, he'd just thought Lara was talking to Buck, but as he got closer, he'd heard the words. *Stay away from him. Eleanor Campbell. Murderer.*

Crashing through the exit, Harry saw her standing under one of the town's historic streetlamps, just flickering on.

'Lara!'

'Just getting some air,' she said.

'I'm sorry you had to hear all that,' he began, then trailed off, caught between embarrassment, shame and anger. He'd never even met that girl in the bar before, and now she'd dredged up all the innuendo and accusations again. He'd thought all that was over; obviously not.

'It's none of my business,' said Lara, looking back up towards Main Street. Harry could hardly blame her if she wanted to escape from him.

'No, I suppose not, but could you give me a moment to explain?'

Harry wasn't sure why it was so important; he wanted Lara to think well of him, but perhaps he also wanted an outsider to listen to his side of the argument, however futile that was.

'As I'm the only person you know at Benedon right now, I'd at least like you know I'm not the bogeyman.'

There was a whisper of a smile at that, and Harry felt a tug of relief.

'So tell me,' said Lara, turning to walk away from the bar. 'What *was* all that about?'

Harry shrugged helplessly.

'I'm not a murderer.'

'I guessed that much,' she said. Harry glanced up at the English girl in surprise. She was pretty, beautiful, even, with her long dark hair carelessly pulled back, revealing an elegant neck and soulful green eyes, but that wasn't what made her attractive. It was the curl of amusement at the corner of her mouth, the way she looked at the world: wide-eyed and straight on. And the way she had reacted to that scene in the bar. Most women he'd known would be pale, shocked, nervous at least – all of which would be entirely understandable, of course – but Lara looked completely unfazed. Lara Stone was different.

'Eleanor Campbell,' began Harry. 'She is, was a student here. She died in February. Fell from the top floor of the library. Accidentally, deliberately, no one knows for sure.'

There was a moment's silence.

'So who was the girl back there?' asked Lara. 'A friend of hers?'

'I guess so. I hadn't met her before; Ellie was popular. She knew most of the campus.'

The awkwardness was still palpable; it shimmered on the night air.

'Was Ellie a student of yours?'

He shook his head, feeling the familiar helplessness as everything came flooding back. Those weeks following the girl's death: terrible barely covered it. If it had just been a private tragedy, it would have been bad enough, but Eleanor's death had caused ripples that were still spreading, ripples that had all but destroyed his career.

'No, she wasn't my student, but I knew her. Ellie was an English major in her senior year. She had a place to do a Masters at the Business School, but she was interested in journalism. That's how we met. I gave her some advice about a story she was working on.'

Harry saw a little 'v' of a frown on Lara's face.

'But if Ellie jumped or slipped, why did that girl in the bar think you had anything to do with it?'

It was a reasonable question, but hard to answer. Given that he had just been accused of being a murderer, Harry figured he had to try.

'Ellie came to me just after the start of the Spring semester. We talked about journalism, researching, reporting and writing techniques, and we became friends.'

He felt Lara give a tight nod as if things were beginning to fall into place. Like everyone else, she was putting two and two together and coming up with five.

'I can see you've guessed the rest: after Ellie died, a rumour began circulating that she and I had been romantically involved. Apparently, I'd rejected her, broken it off and left Ellie heartbroken. And that's why she did what she did. They blamed me.'

Lara dipped her head and then looked back up. It was almost dark now, and low light threw shadows on her face.

'Was it just a rumour, Harry, or did you have an affair?'

Harry almost smiled. The English had a reputation for being polite and discreet, but he should have known Lara Stone would be more direct. She was a journalist.

'No,' he said firmly. 'We were just friends. Perhaps that girl in the bar didn't think so, but we were. Truthfully, I can understand why people gossiped. We'd seen a lot of each other, so I could see how a rumour might have started. She was smart, and beautiful, I was a young professor. But it wasn't a relationship; it was all about the story.'

He looked away, remembering Eleanor Campbell as she had been.

'Ellie had so much passion for what she was doing, so much passion for life...' he shook his head. 'Such a waste.'

Harry looked up and was surprised to see the glitter of a tear in Lara's eyes.

'Hey...' he said. 'What's wrong?'

She shook her head and turned away. 'I was just thinking about my best friend,' she said, taking a ragged breath. 'She was another brilliant woman, a journalist. She fell over the balcony of her apartment last year. That's what they said, anyway.'

Lara was speaking slowly, as though the memory was painful to recall. Harry knew how that felt all too well.

'Sandrine was a journalist for one of the French nationals,' said Lara.

She spoke slowly, as if even the memory was painful to recall, just as he had found it difficult to think about Ellie's death.

'She was writing a story and I followed it up after her death. It turns out she didn't kill herself; she *was* murdered. And although finding her killer wasn't going to bring Sandrine back, it helped her family and friends make sense of it all.'

'So you're saying I should be a bit more understanding

when people call me a murderer in a bar,' he said with a sad smile.

'When that person is hurting, yes. All that girl cares about is that her friend is gone, and she wants to understand how it happened.'

Harry nodded. He could see Lara's argument, even if he found it hard to sympathise with people who blindly believed the worst.

Lara looked back at him.

'Did Ellie ever write her story?'

'No,' said Harry. He'd read some of Lara Stone's work; he knew she was a great reporter, but there was only so much he could tell her.

'I was going to finish it, but...' he trailed off.

Lara stepped forward.

'You *must*, Harry,' she said urgently. 'Don't let it drop. Sandrine always had a saying: 'ne rien laisser dans le noir': leave nothing in the dark. She believed revealing the truth was more important than anything.'

'Maybe,' said Harry, feeling uncomfortable again.

'Listen, I could help,' said Lara. 'Two heads are always better than one. If only Sandrine had remembered that, maybe she would still be alive.'

He looked at her quizzically, but something told him Lara's emotions were too raw talking about her friend. He could understand that. And besides, there was plenty of time to find out more.

He gestured towards the side street. 'My place is down there; the yellow house with the window boxes. Want me to walk you home?'

Lara shook her head.

'It's fine. But I'll see you at the Dean's party?' she asked.

Harry grimaced. He'd had the invitation but had immediately dropped it in the trash, with no intention of going anywhere near the Dean's residence, not after everything that had happened last semester. But term started on Tuesday, and Harry knew that Lara would soon get scooped up into the whirlwind of campus life; this might be his only chance to get close to her. And he wanted to.

'How about I pick you up at 5.45, and we can go together.'

He held up a finger.

'On one condition.' He let it hang in the air. 'You let me take you out for dinner afterwards.'

Harry watched her face, holding his breath. Finally, Lara smiled, a hint of colour in her cheeks.

'I'd like that,' she said, pushing her hand into her back pocket and pulling out a business card. 'Here's my number.'

'I'll see you then,' he smiled and walked back to his cottage with a spring in his step.

Chapter 3

Her cottage was perfect. Well, perfect for her. Lara couldn't do much about the peeling window frames or the worn rug, but after a little TLC over the weekend, it felt like home. Given Lara was only staying until the Christmas break, she'd decided against sending boxes of her possessions over from Chelsea, but she'd packed enough into her suitcase to get her through the first few weeks and at some point, she'd find a mall to fill the gaps. Meanwhile, she had leased a run-around hire car for the semester, which meant she could load up with cut flowers, cheery house-plants and enough scented candles to banish any hint of dustiness. Taking a glass of wine from the kitchen, Lara walked around the cottage smiling to herself. She loved it all. Mid-century furniture, abstract paintings on the walls, stoneware in the kitchen, a wobbly vinyl table set. There was even a record player and a stack of LPs. She walked over to read the titles: 'Bookends', 'Mama's Big Ones', 'Tapestry'; it was a time warp, but a good one.

Grinning, she pulled out an album and slipped it onto the turntable, dropping the needle with a pop.

'There's only one song worth singing....'

Cass Elliot, a stone-cold classic.

'You've got to make your own kind of music,' she murmured along to the chorus, looking down towards the street where some college kids were strolling along the path. And that was exactly what she wanted for them. Lara hoped these kids would go out into the world and find their own way, maybe even create a brand new counter-culture just like the one Mama Cass and the flower children had created for themselves. Born into an age of social media where shrill outrage was the norm and the ability to get attention seemed to be a valid career choice, young people's aspirations appeared to be getting increasingly narrow: influencer, Youtuber, Instagrammer. It was depressing. Then again, Lara supposed she couldn't criticise. After all, she had followed her father into their glamorous family business, the Avery Media Group. Dad was a newspaper editor, her uncle a publisher; it hadn't exactly required a huge amount of imagination, had it? But being a writer had always felt right to Lara; it fitted her perfectly.

Which was more than could be said about the new dress she was wearing. Lara almost always wore jeans and t-shirts but had packed some smarter pieces for campus life. She stared at her reflection in the hall mirror, shaking her head at the sight of herself in a long black spotted tea dress, an impulse purchase passing a boutique in Chelsea a few days earlier. A sweetheart neckline showed off a simple gold necklace and tanned skin. She only hoped it was appropriate for the Dean's party.

Her phone rang – the distinctive sound of a Facetime call.

'Alex,' she said with a smile. She clicked it on; Alex was sitting forward, running a hand through his dark hair.

'You look tired. Where are you?'

'In the office; where do you think? There's been a big story breaking all week.'

Lara realised with surprise that she genuinely didn't know. She had always been a news junkie but had barely hopped online over the past week; she had been so busy with preparations for the trip.

'What story?'

'Scandal at Number 10. A major donor to the party having an affair with someone linked to a hostile foreign government.'

That was big: Lara felt the old rush of excitement.

'Did we get the scoop?'

Alex nodded.

'James Cannon, actually.'

'I'm pleased; Jim deserves it.'

James had been on *The Chronicle*'s political desk for years, great at the analysis, and well-liked in the halls of power – which was far from common – so getting a front-page splash was great for him. Lara only wished she didn't feel so jealous of the excitement that was going down in the newsroom. *You're here to get away from all that, remember*?

'It's been all hands on deck all week, chasing it down, making sure the story sticks. At least as of tomorrow, I've got the week off.'

Alex rubbed a weary hand over his face. The Facetime image wasn't clear, but she could see how tired he looked.

'Anyway, enough about me,' he said. 'How's the glamorous professor?'

She tried not to smile but couldn't help it.

'Alex, how many times do I have to tell you I'm not a professor.'

'Well, that's how I like to think of you.' He leant forward. 'Look, you're wearing a black gown, aren't you?'

'It's a dress.'

'A *dress*?' laughed Alex. 'Where you off to? A literary salon with Hemingway and Ezra Pound?'

'I'm sure it would be on the cards if they weren't both dead,' said Lara. 'Actually, I'm going to the Dean's Labor Day party. I wasn't sure my biker jacket was going to cut it.'

She'd only seen Alex on Friday night, but still, she missed him, the way she could relax around him, banter, and be herself. Perhaps that was one reason she had gelled so quickly with Harry. His easy-going charm reminded her of Alex.

'Anyway, I just wanted to say good luck for tomorrow.'

The smile faded from Lara's face. In all the excitement of arriving and getting the cottage just so, she had managed to avoid thinking that she would soon have to begin her lectures.

'I'll be honest; I'm a bit nervous.'

'I can see that, but don't forget you're a big coup for them.'

'Me?'

'Lara, in the past year alone, you have broken more big stories than most hacks do in their entire careers. Benedon College should be doing back-flips having you there: you're a rock star of investigative journalism.'

Lara wasn't easily embarrassed but felt herself blush. 'Alex...'

'I mean it, Lar. Maybe you *should* wear your leather jacket tonight.'

The doorbell rang, and Lara glanced at the clock: it was almost five o'clock.

'I should go. Harry's here.'

'Harry?'

Lara flushed again.

'He's one of the professors.'

A pause.

'Is it a date?'

'No, it's not a date!' she said with a dismissive laugh. 'He's one of my new colleagues.'

She didn't know why she sounded so outraged at Alex's suggestion. If she was completely honest with herself, it was one of the reasons why she'd worn her new dress, blow-dried her hair and put make-up on; the flutter of nerves she'd been feeling in the past hour was less to do with meeting new people in an alien setting at the Dean's party, but the fact that she was excited and a little nervous to see Harry.

'Well, have a good time,' said Alex, clearly unconvinced. 'And don't worry about tomorrow. You'll shine; you always do.'

* * *

Harry had seemed on edge when Lara had answered the door. Standing on the porch, hands behind his back, looking smarter than he'd looked on Saturday, dressed in a pale blue button-down shirt and pressed beige chinos. It felt like another classic scene from a teen movie: the nervous boy picking up his date for the prom. She was half expecting him to produce a corsage from behind his back.

Instead, Harry had said, 'Shall we?' and offered her his arm. The Dean's residence was just across campus, and it was a lovely night to stroll.

'So... is there a Mr Lara back home?'

Lara had to laugh: there was no way a Brit would have asked such a direct question without preamble.

'No Mr Lara,' she said, instantly thinking about Alex, how his voice had suddenly seemed more clipped when she'd said that Harry had come to pick her up. 'Not really.'

The truth was that Alex Ford, *The Chronicle*'s deputy

editor, wasn't her significant other, but he was still significant: Lara honestly wasn't sure how else to describe their relationship. 'Friend' seemed too fly-weight for the depth of their bond, and 'brother-figure' didn't cover the crackle of attraction between them. There had certainly been times over the past year when her feelings had veered dangerously towards longing when Lara had caught a glimpse of him, and her heart had lurched. Alex was the only person she wanted to speak to when things went wrong – or even had something funny to share. The previous winter, they'd gone away together to a luxury resort in snowy Sweden, a cabin for two, and Lara had secretly hoped the blissful isolation might push them together. Instead, they had become enmeshed in a story when the retreat's executive chef had been murdered, and the moment had passed.

'So how's the symposium coming on?' she said quickly, keen to change the subject.

Harry sighed.

'Sunday's keynote speaker dropped out this morning. David Bowen from *The New York Times*. It's annoying because he was our biggest name, but I guess that's the risk with booking heavyweight names. They're more likely to drop out because something comes up.'

'So what are you going to do?'

'I've already hit the phones trying to find a replacement, but it's Labor Day, so no one's answering.'

He smiled and shrugged. 'I'll find someone.'

Lara liked that. Pragmatic, unflappable. She guessed that Harry had probably been pretty good in the *New York Globe*'s newsroom.

'I could ask some of my contacts,' said Lara. 'My friend Alex is an amazing speaker; he's deputy editor of *The Chronicle*, so he'd add a bit of heft. It's a long shot because he lives in London, but I know he's got the week off.'

Harry was looking at her, eyes wide.

'You don't mean Alex Ford?'

'Yes. We've known each other since journalism school.'

'Wow,' said Harry, looking impressed. 'Alex Ford is a legend. We use his reporting from Helmand Province in one of our journalism school modules.'

Lara couldn't help laughing. 'I'm not going to tell him that. His ego is the size of Greenland as it is.'

Harry looked excited.

'You really think he might come? I'll have to check with the department to see if we've got the budget to fly him over, but if we can – that would be amazing.'

She thought of Alex, slumped at his desk, worn out from getting that scoop out before anyone else: jumping on a plane would be the last thing he wanted to do right now. In their twenties, Alex would think nothing of jetting off at a moment's notice with nothing but his passport and a toothbrush in his pocket, but they'd all changed a little since then, hadn't they?

They took a left off the high street, down a quiet road fringed with trees. The leaves had begun to crisp and curl, dotting the sidewalk with orange confetti. Lara reflected that these red maples and oaks would soon blaze with scarlet colour, but by the time she left, the branches would be empty and the leaves buried beneath footsteps of snow. For some reason, the thought made her feel melancholy.

'So tell me about the Dean,' she said.

'Rosalind? She presents as scary, but she's charming when you get to know her. But should your paths cross, remember that all the big cheeses on campus are no different from any other CEOs or corporate players. This might be a university, but in the end, the dollar is still king.'

He sounded cynical, but then Lara supposed if she'd

been through what Harry had this year, she might feel the same.

'Is that why you didn't want to come tonight?'

She'd noticed his reticence when she had asked him at The Shovel, a casual shrug, then quickly changing the subject. A small thing, but it had registered.

'I didn't want to go before I met you,' he said and smiled at her.

There was a shimmer of something between them before he looked away.

'Look, I told you about Ellie Campbell,' he said after a moment. 'Students gossiped, the faculty gossiped, everyone made up their mind.'

'Ah, I can see you might not want to see some of those people.'

Harry shook his head.

'It's more than that. The Campbell family put pressure on the Dean to have me dismissed. Outwardly, my colleagues were supportive, but academic office politics can be vicious. It's like the end of Julius Caesar; everyone has sharp knives hidden under their togas. Things got difficult. It made me reprioritise everything.'

Lara saw the pain on Harry's face and felt selfish for having asked him to come.

'I'm sorry, I didn't know. We don't have to stay long,' said Lara.

'Really?'

'Sure. I only want to show my face. New girl on campus and all that. Besides, I thought we were going for dinner.'

The smile was back in his eyes.

'We are. If you're still up for it,' he said in a rush. 'Plymouth Rock is the best place in town. Jack the maitre d' is a friend, so he's got us a table.' Harry trailed off, embarrassed.

‘No pressure, of course,’ he added quickly. ‘I know how important it is for you to meet everyone.’

Lara grinned.

‘I can’t wait,’ she grinned, picking up her pace.

‘Let’s grab a canape, say hi, then get the hell out of there.’

Chapter 4

The Dean's residence couldn't make up its mind. The style was somewhere between Georgian and Nantucket. A square box with high windows and Doric columns framing the double front door, it also had wooden shake siding and shutters. Design-wise, it was confused, but that didn't stop it from being impressive. Not to mention it seemed to be the biggest house in Benedon.

'You like it?' said Harry with amusement as they stood at the bottom of the stairs. 'If you stick with academia, this could be yours in twenty years.'

'Me as Dean? I haven't done my first lecture yet.'

'I don't doubt you could do anything you set your mind to, Lara.'

Lara appreciated the compliment, but right now, she was just worried about going inside. Although they had arrived just a little after six, Lara could hear the bubble of conversation coming from the open door: the party was already in full swing.

Harry led the way, and Lara stepped gingerly inside. Groups of middle-aged people standing in groups, holding wine glasses, talking and laughing, but in a subdued, respectful fashion. The house's interior matched the outside: plain walls in earthy colours – plum, maroon and sepia, with elegant polished furniture, bookcases with glass fronts, and gilt-framed seascapes. If she hadn't been so nervous, Lara would have grinned. In her college teen movie, she would be the rebellious-but-promising protagonist summoned to the forbidding dean – played by James Earl Jones, naturally – for a 'be all you can be' pep-talk.

'This is a lot of people,' whispered Lara, staying close to Harry. 'Is the Journalism school so huge?

He took a glass of wine from a waiter and handed one to her.

'Each faculty at Benedon has a dean, but Ros has been here the longest. She knows everyone, so it won't be just our faculty members here tonight, it will be almost the entire college staff.'

At the far side of the room, a man almost a head taller than everyone else waved in their direction. Harry touched Lara's arm.

'There's my friend Vernon. Come on, let's go and say hi.'

As they approached, Lara could see that apart from being tall, Harry's friend was also very good-looking, with a thick head of dark hair and matching eyebrows that gave his face a serious expression. Lara guessed he was another dean or senior professor – until she saw the dog collar.

'Vernon,' said Harry, gripping the priest on his shoulder. 'Meet our new colleague, Lara Stone. I'm showing her the sights and sounds of Benedon. You're one of them.'

'I'm pleased to meet you,' said Lara extending her hand.

'Vernon Bower, I'm the chaplain here,' he said, his dark eyes twinkling at her. Lara met his gaze, then looked away. *Gosh*, she thought. Was it wrong to fancy a priest?

'If you want to know anything about the college,' said Harry, 'Ask Vernon. He was even a student here, weren't you? Sports scholar.'

'I rowed,' smiled Vernon. 'Many, many moons ago.'

'Really? I rowed at school too,' said Lara. It was a slight exaggeration: Lara had been to the kind of boarding school where messing about on the river was considered a legitimate part of PE.

'Then we'll have to get you back on the water while you're here,' said Vernon. He had a way of making everything he said feel like a proposition. Or perhaps that was just wishful thinking.

'Have you really been here since you were a student?'

'Not entirely. I left Benedon and went off on the hippy trail.'

'Really?' she said, finding it hard to imagine him in Ibiza or Thailand.

Vernon smiled. 'It was more of a spiritual journey. Now I know I was looking for this,' – he indicated his collar – 'but I had a good look around first.'

He had a wonderful voice, deep and resonant. She'd heard the expression that some people made you feel as if you were the only person in the room, but Vernon made Lara feel as if she were the only person on the planet. *His sermons must be awesome,* thought Lara, suddenly feeling hotter than before.

'Well, you can tell the Big Guy Upstairs I'm glad he brought you back to Benedon,' said Harry, clinking their glasses. 'Vern is my best bud on campus.'

Lara stood back and watched them talk. It was nice to see grown-ups just enjoying each other's company: in her world, the media, back-stabbing and bitchiness were far too often the norm. Of course, Harry had shown that the same toxic ambitions could exist here on campus too.

Indeed, since her arrival at the party, Lara had felt glanced at, and then dismissed. She supposed office politics were the same everywhere: people aligned themselves with the powerful, the influential, people who were useful for their careers. Even if they had recognised or identified her as a visiting fellow, she wasn't important, so she was not worth talking to. *Treat it like a job*, she said to herself. If she had been here to get a quote from a Supreme Court judge, Lara knew she would have been fearless, walking straight over and asking about his latest case. But this was more like undercover work or David Attenborough observing an unfamiliar species. She watched the academics interact, swapping gossip, laughing too loudly at each other's jokes, overhearing snippets of conversations about holiday homes and the achievements of their children: no different to the media parties her Uncle Nicholas, Chairman of Avery Media, threw at his London home.

'There's Doug,' said Harry, nudging her. 'I should introduce you to the man who had the good sense to invite you to Benedon.'

Lara recognised the jolly fifty-something immediately. Doug Bishop was one of the professors at the Journalism school, and they had chatted over Zoom in an informal interview which had become a two-hour conversation about the freedom of the press, multi-platform media and the classic investigative journalism movie 'Three Days of the Condor'. In-person, Doug was round like a bowling ball, but his slightly flushed face radiated friendliness and bonhomie.

'Lara Stone, I presume?' he said.

'Lovely to meet in real life.'

Doug gestured towards himself. He was wearing a lemon shirt and red cord trousers.

'Too much?' he asked.

'Oh no,' laughed Lara. 'Just the right amount.'

Doug's irreverent approach had been one of the factors which had persuaded Lara to come to Benedon. She hadn't been at all sure she wanted to join academia when her friend Jenny had first suggested the idea, but once she'd spoken to Doug and felt his passion for the college and his students – along with his enthusiasm for Robert Redford's pea-coat collection – she began to think that a semester on the East Coast could be a fun and potentially fascinating challenge.

'I trust Vernon and Harry are looking after you?'

'They're trying to get me to join the faculty rowing team.'

'Heavens above, no,' said Doug, reaching for a bottle of wine to top up Lara's glass. 'Those rowers keep brutal hours, training every spare hour from dawn to dusk. And what for? Blisters on your hands and thighs like tree trunks. No, my advice would be to take full advantage of the many excellent dining options our little town provides instead. You may observe that I have been doing that for some time. And I would particularly advise getting stuck into this wine. The Dean is something of a wine buff; her cellar is legendary, and she always pulls out the stops for her Labor Day party. Rumour has it there are fireworks at ten o'clock, which is rather exciting, although I'm not sure she should be encouraging such revelry on a school night.'

Filling his glass, Doug raised it in salute to Lara.

'So glad you're here, Ms Stone. I'll be honest; I couldn't quite believe it when you said you'd come. Your story in *The Chronicle*, 'The Yacht Party'? It was nothing short of world-class. A full-on, balls-out investigation writ large. You see it so rarely these days.'

Before Lara could even reply, Doug grabbed her arm.

'Talking of the Dean, I should introduce you. But on the way, let's detour to the cool corner.'

'Hey!' said Harry in mock offence, 'I thought we were the cool guys here!'

Doug just gave him a withering look, but Harry leaned over and whispered in Lara's ear.

'Leave for the Plymouth at seven fifteen?' he said.

Lara nodded gratefully as Doug tugged her away.

'Maybe even sooner,' she called. As Doug led her through the crowd, Lara took in the details of the academics she passed; plenty of linen kaftans and chunky wooden beads, and the women had either dyed their hair in pastel colours or went full grey. Men were big on beards and pocket squares but studied scruffiness still seemed the order of the day as if concern for your appearance might be mistaken for lack of seriousness. They all smiled at Lara, but no one drew her into a discussion of James Joyce.

Doug pulled Lara over to the back of the house, where a woman with brown corkscrew hair and oversized glasses was standing by the window.

'Lara Stone, meet Lizzy Trott, rising star of the Psych department.'

He leaned forward in a loud stage whisper and added, 'Lizzy is the only one of these stiffs you need to bother with.'

Lizzy rolled her eyes. 'Good to meet you, Lara. Doug has been practically doing backflips in excitement over your visit.'

'I *would* have done backflips,' said Doug, 'but I couldn't find a leotard to fit me.'

Lizzy ignored him and turned back to Lara.

'So you're staying at the Montrose apartment? How do you like it?'

'It's perfect.'

'Lizzy asks because those records in your apartment are hers,' grinned Doug.

'Then you've got great taste. I was blasting out Mama Cass before I came over here.'

Richard and Lizzie exchanged a smile as if there were a shared joke between them. If her instincts weren't mistaken, Doug and Lizzy were more than just colleagues.

'So tomorrow,' said Doug more officiously. 'Did you get the schedule?'

'I did,' said Lara, her stomach tightening. 'First lecture at 10 am, right?'

'In at the deep end, but I figured that's the way you'd like it,' he smiled. 'They're mainly first-year students on the Master's programme, so they should be fairly compliant. Still, we should probably have a meeting beforehand to discuss the procedure. I looked at your lesson plans, by the way: very impressive.'

'Thank you,' said Lara. She'd had no idea what she was doing when she dashed them off the previous weekend; she was relieved that she was in the right ballpark.

'How about we meet at 8.15? Come to my office, room 24. I'll have bagels.'

'Okay,' said Lara. Her face must have betrayed her nerves because Lizzy stepped forward and touched her hand.

'Don't worry,' she said. 'Just talk about your life in London, set them fun assignments, and they'll be putty in your hands.'

Lara was grateful to Lizzy for the words of encouragement, but as Doug led her over to meet the Dean, she immediately got the sense that not everyone was quite so enthusiastic to see her there.

Rosalind Davies was standing with two men in suits, and as Doug introduced her, Lara felt the dean's cool, assessing gaze sweep over her. She resisted the urge to shiver.

'Ah, our new visiting fellow from London,' said Rosalind, offering a slim hand. She was an attractive woman with shoulder-length chestnut hair swept back off her face. Lara guessed she was in her mid-fifties, although it was hard to put an age on her; she was slim, and there were just a few lines collecting at the corners of her eyes, but her formal navy cocktail dress with a white collar had a monastic quality that made her look older than she probably was. Rosalind's grip was firm, squeezing Lara's hand as if she was holding a tennis racket.

'I believe it's your first time out by the lake. How long are you with us, Miss Stone?'

'Until Christmas.'

'Only one semester?' she looked around at her companions. 'Let's see if we can persuade you to stay a little longer. Don't listen to anyone who says it's too cold in winter in Vermont.'

Her admirers dutifully gave polite chuckles as Rosalind finally released Lara's hand.

'Well, it's been wonderful to meet you, Lara, but I'm afraid I have to sneak off: our guests are clamouring for my welcome speech.'

She raised an eyebrow in a self-deprecating expression. 'Word has gone out that canapes won't be served until I've spoken. Just a few quick words, I promise.'

As Rosalind melted into the crowd, one of the men turned to Lara and introduced himself: a lawyer named Beale Norris. He was around fifty with thick black hair and a square chin that jutted forward as if in challenge.

'Your first time in Benedon?' he asked. 'Where did you go? Oxford?'

Fit in, assimilate; that was one of the first things she had learned about journalism. People always feel more comfortable talking to people like them.

'My father went to Oxford, my mother to Cambridge,' said Lara. 'Family tradition was split, so I went to City University to study journalism.'

'City? Is that close to Fleet Street?' said Beale, his tone suggesting he was rapidly losing interest in the subject.

'By the time I got to college, all the major newspapers had long left The City. *The Chronicle* and the *Telegraph* are in Victoria, *The Times* and *The Sun* are at London Bridge, the *Mail* is in Kensington.'

'More tradition gone,' said Beale, shaking his head. 'You know, I heard the other day that Bradbury College is getting rid of their print news course entirely. Replacing it with Reporting Data and podcasting majors. It seems as though the newspapers are becoming a footnote in history.'

Lara was about to object when a taller man standing next to the lawyer spoke up.

'I think you'd be surprised how important papers are still, Beale,' he said. 'Sure, social media gets all the attention, but it's like a baby crying: hard to ignore, but the message is always the same. 'Pay attention to me; it's hollow, disposable. Print newspapers still carry a voice of authority.'

Lara looked at the man gratefully.

'That's exactly what I was going to tell the students in my first lecture tomorrow.'

'We haven't met. I'm Arthur,' said the man extending a polite hand. He was tall and upright, the cut of his grey suit marking him as wealthy but not ostentatious. He was older than Beale by a few years. Lara was surprised to find that Arthur had a soft smile and laughter lines around the eyes; more kindly uncle than captain of industry.

'Arthur is a generous benefactor of the college,' said

Beale, his chin raised. 'The Campbell family go back generations at Benedon College.'

An embarrassed silence rang around the group. And Lara knew right then that she was in the company of Ellie Campbell's father.

Chapter 5

Considering the Dean was only planning on saying 'a quick few words,' she kept talking for more than twenty minutes.

Lara knew this for a fact: she had been checking her watch while subtly looking through the crowd for Harry, mindful that it was now well past seven o'clock, and they were due at the restaurant soon. Lara tuned back into the speech.

'...we start this new academic year as we always do at Benedon, privileged that we attract the best young minds of their generation. We are blessed with the opportunity to open our hearts and teach them. To that end, Benedon's first media symposium begins on Saturday, showing our rivals how committed we are....'

When Rosalind finally finished, Lara clapped politely, but she was drowned out by the enthusiastic applause and cheering around her; it was like a curtain call on Broadway.

The guests were all keen for their boss to see their enthusiasm. Lara began to circulate through the crowd, trying not to look too conspicuous, looking for Harry. He wasn't in the main room, but at least the rumours were right – the canapes had started to come out on a succession of silver platters. No wonder the guests were clapping; the Dean had pushed the boat out. There were little cornets of shrimp, delicate summer rolls, blinis topped with quails' eggs and tiny stuffed tartlets. *One couldn't hurt, could it?* reasoned Lara, taking a crispy tempura prawn. Harry had promised her dinner, but if she didn't have something to soak up the Dean's wine, she would never make it.

'Looking for Harry?'

Lara turned to see Doug's friend Lizzy Trott, also reaching for a canape. 'If you are, I just saw him talking to an older lady in the library.'

Lara shrugged. She was embarrassed to be caught out, but at the same time, with Harry's troubled reputation on campus, she didn't want Lizzy to know about their semi-date.

'Just looking for a friendly face.'

The woman nodded.

'Harry's certainly that. Any freshmen who are homesick and having a wobble about being on campus, we send them to Harry.'

Lara wondered what Lizzy was trying to tell her but didn't feel she could ask.

'Well, I'm glad he's come,' said Lizzy. 'Strange to think he won't be here next year.'

Her words caught Lara by surprise.

'Harry's leaving?'

'Didn't you know?'

'No. Why?'

Lizzy paused, her cheeks flushing.

Then Lara nodded, answering her own question. 'The Eleanor Campbell situation?'

'You know about that then,' said Lizzy, looking relieved. She gave a sad shake of the head.

'It was horrible. Not just a student's death but the way Harry carried the can for it all. I don't know how he coped. The gossip was awful, and then when he got passed over for tenure, well...'

'Tenure?' asked Lara. Lizzy gave a little laugh.

'You really do need a crash course in academic life, Lara. Tenure is what every junior academic at this party would kill for,' she said. 'It's a full professorship, a job for life. And Harry was a dead cert; he's done his dues, published papers. He was popular and respected on campus: a shoo-in. But then the Ellie Campbell thing happened, and it felt like Benedon turned its back on him. Once you get passed over for tenure, it's all over,' said Lizzy, drawing a finger across her throat.

Lara took another drink, trying to process it all. She felt hurt, duped. She didn't really know Harry Robbins, but she had thought they'd had a connection. Lara hadn't expected him to tell her his entire life story, but the fact that he was leaving Benedon seemed a big omission.

'So, *was* anything going on between Harry and Eleanor?' asked Lara as casually as she could. Part of her didn't want to ask, but she needed to know.

'I couldn't say,' said Lizzy taking a long slug of wine. 'Doug thinks it's possible. But from a psych point of view, Ellie's final act seemed loaded with meaning.'

'What do you mean?'

'Ellie jumped from the top-floor balcony in the *Campbell* Library,' said Lizzy.

'The library is named after her family?'

'Yes. The Campbells are billionaire industrialists and

local royalty. They paid to have the thing built. They've donated millions to the college over the years.'

Lizzy moved a step closer, lowering her voice.

'Doug heard a rumour that her parents weren't happy about Ellie spending time with Harry, and I guess you can see why: she's their golden girl, and he's a man fifteen years older. But...'

The woman tapped a finger against her glass thoughtfully.

'If Ellie killed herself because Harry had broken her heart, why not take an overdose or jump under a car? Why do it in the family library?'

'You think she was sending a message?'

Lizzy nodded.

'In the trade, we call it a "fuck you" message.'

'But who to?' asked Lara. 'To Harry or the family?'

'Maybe both.'

Lara looked around the room, then checked her watch again; where *was* Harry? What had at first appeared to be a tragedy in which Harry had become entangled now looked like it had many more layers. Lara's journalistic instincts were firing: there was a story here, and presumably, Harry could shed a lot more light on it.

'I felt sorry for Harry,' Lizzy was saying. 'Whatever happened, he was the scapegoat for the whole thing. To be fair to Rosalind, she could have just let him go, but she didn't. You can't imagine the pressure she must have been under from the Campbells and their allies. He was denied tenure, but Ros gave Harry a year to find another position. I know Doug has already written him an excellent reference.'

'Look, I'd better get going,' said Lara. 'Need to prepare for my big debut.'

'Of course,' said Lizzy. 'But listen, I'm in the Psych department. If you want a drink or some female company, hit me up on the college email system. I also swim every day in Finger Lake if you like that sort of thing. In my dreams, I have a little morning wild swimming club but,' she rolled her eyes again. 'I'm surrounded by cowards.'

Lara thanked her and moved off, intent on finding Harry and getting out of there. It was almost 7.30 already; even if Harry was tight with the maitre'd at the restaurant, it was getting very late. Either way, her date with the dashing professor was losing its sheen. She checked the garden where people were standing on the lawn, strings of lights crisscrossing below a twilight sky. No Harry, and no message on her phone.

'Looking for someone?'

Rosalind the Dean touched Lara on the arm, startling her.

'Oh, yes. Harry Robbins. Have you seen him?'

'Harry? I just saw him leave,' said Rosalind.

'Really?' Lara's disappointment must have shown because the Dean

gave her a searching look. 'Sorry, were you together?'

'Oh no, no,' said Lara quickly. 'We were talking about his symposium, and I said I might be able to help him with the guests. Shame he's gone.'

The Dean nodded sagely as if it wasn't unusual for Harry to be a let-down.

'I'm sure he'll catch up with you over the next day or so. I should think he'll make a point of it.'

Lara didn't miss the barb but ignored it.

'You know what? I think it's time I went home anyway, said Lara. 'Jet lag and wine, not a great combination.' As she said it, Lara realised the truth of it; she did feel weary. And if Harry had gone, so what? She imagined tonight's festivities had been more than a little awkward for him: who knew what had happened to make him rush off? She knew almost nothing about Harry Robbins, her conversation with Lizzy had certainly underlined that.

Touching Lara's hand again, Rosalind leaned forward.

'Word of advice about Harry Robbins. I imagine you'll hear various rumours about him while you're here; rest assured, few of them are true, but by the same token, I wouldn't expect too much from that man. He's a fine teacher, but....' She didn't finish the thought: she didn't need to.

'Thanks,' said Lara. 'I appreciate it.'

Rosalind gave her a thin smile.

'The glass ceiling may have cracked, Lara, but it's only a crack. In the meantime, we've all got to look after ourselves.'

You got that right, thought Lara as she turned to leave. *And that's exactly what I'm going to do.*

Chapter 6

Harry dashed along the sidewalk towards home. This was *dynamite*. How could he have missed it? How could he not have connected the dots? For months, he'd wondered why Ellie had played her cards so close to her chest, but now he understood. She had been in an impossible situation, one she was, perhaps, too young to navigate her way out of. The fact that the penny had dropped at the Dean's Labor Day party, well, there was more than a little irony in that.

Stopping under a street lamp, he paused and swore under his breath. Lara.

Damn. He shouldn't have run off without saying goodbye to her, but how could he? She would have wanted to know why he was leaving in such a rush, and a journalist of her experience would have immediately smelled a scoop like an alcoholic could smell whiskey on his breath.

Besides, Harry had never been able to tell a lie convincingly. All writers had their strengths and weaknesses, and Harry's superpower had always been the prose, conjuring up sparkling, persuasive copy. But lie? He couldn't do it. He was far too straight. Harry had been the only kid in high school who had never once cut class or missed an assignment. In college, carded in a bar, he'd handed over his real driver's licence and, startled by his honesty, the bartender had poured him a beer.

He had the urge to at least go back and say goodbye.

Lara Stone. From the moment they had first met at the Main Street deli, he had wondered if his luck was finally changing. Two short meetings with her were enough to know she was extraordinary – exactly the sort of woman he'd been looking for all these years.

He wondered, hoped she liked him too. He'd pitched dinner at Plymouth Rocks, the fanciest place in town, knowing that it sounded like a date, but he was past caring. She was only here a semester. Pulling out his phone, he tapped out a message.

Had to go. Hope you can forgive me. Another time? Hx

He pressed 'send'. He would tell her everything tomorrow, and he felt sure Lara would understand. She was passionate about the story, dogged, tenacious, and driven. You didn't score as many scoops and exclusives as Lara Stone without being completely committed to the job.

He turned and hurried down the street, a nervy excitement brewing in his belly. This was the big one; he knew it. This story could be his passport back into the big leagues. He'd write the story, remind the industry of Harry Robbins' brilliance, and then cherry-pick the best gigs on offer. He'd always liked the idea of working in Europe: London or maybe even Paris. He knew it was a fantasy, but he could picture himself sitting at a table outside a Tabac, scribbling notes and drinking espresso before rushing off to file his copy. As a kid growing up in blue-collar Fenway just outside Boston, he'd devoured 'Scoop' and 'The Rum Diary,' luxuriating in a fictional version of journalism that probably had never existed. But now, it all felt within reach for the first time in years.

A memory popped back into his head. Six years earlier, as a senior reporter in New York, Harry had stumbled across a story about a congressman taking kickbacks to green-light large-scale construction projects. Harry had been seeing an Upper East Side socialite whom the randy Representative had cornered at a party; keen to 'make time' with the woman, the congressman had boasted about his Hamptons beach house and how he'd paid for it, so Harry had set up a sting and got the whole thing on tape.

Standing in the dark street now, Harry still felt his fingers curl into a fist at the memory. Harry had kept the whole operation secret before taking the tape to the *Globe's* features editor Aaron Majors, telling him that he wanted to sit on the story a little longer to shore it up. Two days later, violent food poisoning had forced Harry to take a couple of days off work. In his absence, Majors had promptly run the story with his own name and photo on the byline.

When Harry had complained, Aaron had smiled and shrugged. 'Newspapers are a team game,' he'd said. 'Think of it as a win for the *Globe*.'

Looking back now, Harry could see that was the beginning of the end for him. Disillusioned, Harry's once bright fire for the job had dimmed, and besides, Aaron had done his level best to hasten Harry's exit. Within the year, Harry had accepted a position at Benedon – and Aaron was now editor of the *Globe*. How was that for karma? But maybe this was Harry's reward. When Ellie had first come to him, seeking general advice on investigative reporting, she had always been vague on what story she was chasing. Harry had been intrigued but had played along, hoping that one day she would tell him. After several cryptic, collaborative meetings, he eventually asked her, saying he could not truly help if he didn't know what the story was. But she'd told him she didn't want him getting too deep and that withholding the story's details would protect him. To his shame, Harry had assumed Ellie's dire warnings had been hyperbole, an inexperienced wannabe getting caught up in her own drama. But now he knew. He *knew*.

'Sorry, Ellie,' he whispered, feeling the darkness press in. The campus paths were lit, but it was still lonely crossing campus at night. There was security, sure, but one person's feeling of reassurance was someone else's symbol of oppression. Right now, it felt to Harry that there could be people lurking behind every tree, in every shadow. And given what he knew, it wasn't entirely paranoia.

Do it for Ellie, he thought, turning into Floral Street.

Harry knew he'd let her down like everyone else in her life. But he was determined to set things right as far as he could. He practically ran up the path to his front door, his key rattling around the lock.

'Come on, come on,' he muttered before it slid home, and he pushed inside. Dropping his jacket, he crossed straight to his desk, turned his laptop on, and then went back to the kitchen, pouring a glass of wine.

No, he thought. *No more wine*. He needed a clear head for this. He turned on the coffee machine and went back to the desk.

This was what he had missed; there was nothing like the rush of knowing that you had a hot story on your hands. He flexed his fingers, and then began to write.

. . .

Eleanor Campbell was a poor little rich girl. Privileged, entitled, with a bright red convertible bought for her by Daddy on her 21st birthday. But Ellie was brave. She could have kept quiet, toed the line and done what was expected of her. Instead, she did the right thing – or tried.

Harry was smiling as he typed, the story pouring out of him. Now he had the key piece of the puzzle; the whole thing was clear to him. The challenge was not only to tell the tale but to emphasise Ellie Campbell's role; because now Harry could see that his opening paragraph was true. Ellie *had* been courageous.

Harry grunted with satisfaction as he read his words back, rolling his neck and raising a hand to massage his shoulders. Too much tension, too much pressure to get it just right; too much coffee, perhaps. He stood up, stretching, and opened the French doors to let in the cooling evening air. He shivered – and he knew it wasn't just the breeze.

The truth was, Harry was a little scared. Frightened of finding out he wasn't as good a writer as he thought, finding out that his superiors at the *Globe* were right, that he just couldn't cut it. And now he saw the truth of what had happened here, he was scared about digging too deep. Investigative journalism wasn't for the faint-hearted.

Certainly, it had been much easier to sit back and talk about the nobility of reporting from the safety of a lecture theatre. As an educator, Harry had always thought that George Bernard Shaw's maxim, 'Those that can't, teach…', was insulting. But in the past few months, he'd begun to suspect there was some truth in it. Real-life journalism could be tough. It could be dangerous. But now he could feel its visceral pull. This was his future.

Perhaps getting passed over for tenure was all part of the higher plan. He thought about his first meeting with Eleanor Campbell. Primped and polished, hair and nails just so, Ellie had been the least likely newshound he'd ever met. No one said as much, but Ellie didn't need to be at Benedon: a degree would make zero difference to her assured rise. Eleanor Campbell was on a fast track to wealth and privilege with a spun-gold safety net to catch her should she stumble on the way. But Harry had seen fire in her eyes, brighter than any flame Harry had ever seen in a student. Perhaps it was simply because she didn't need it that Ellie was so utterly free from doubt.

She'd secured a place on the MBA programme at Benedon but had come to him, wondering if it was too late to apply for the graduate journalism school. She didn't have a portfolio, but she had a story.

All she needed from Harry was a little help in 'how' to write it. It was refreshing – no, *inspiring* – to see Ellie's passion. It had forced Harry to see just how far he'd drifted from the lofty principles of truth and justice he professed to hold.

FsssssssooooSHSHHH!

A whoosh, then a delayed 'bang', then a subdued cheer. Harry had always loved fireworks – they'd been popping all over town as soon as night had fallen, but he'd been too busy to go outside to watch them. Watching a plume of golden sparks drift earthwards now, Harry's thoughts turned back to Lara, wondering if she was still at the Dean's party, wondering if she was furious with him for sneaking off, wondering if a bunch of flowers would be accepted as a peace offering. *Probably not*, he smiled. Lara Stone was no pushover – that's why he had liked her from the beginning. And it was why he respected her too. The night he'd met Lara at the deli, he'd gone home and read all her biggest stories. Her scoop about Jonathon Meyer, a secretive financier, had been one of the most powerful and something Lara had said at The Shovel suddenly resonated.

Two heads are better than one – if Sandrine had remembered that, she might still be alive.

The episode with Aaron Majors had stung, but Lara had a point about collaboration. Ellie's story had almost died with her. Harry pulled out his phone and started tapping a message to Vernon.

Hey, it's me. Really need to talk – it's important, are you still at the party?

Some people might think it strange that Harry's first choice to share his news was Father Vernon, but Harry liked the incongruity of it. Plus, it would make for a nice twist in the inevitable movie: liberal professor uses Catholic priest as his confessor. Vernon was a great character, the rebel cleric who loved French New Wave; that's how they had met, at a Truffaut all-nighter. During a break for coffee and croissants, they had fallen into conversation about Polanski and the moral maze of appreciating the art of the creative with problematic beliefs or behaviour. 'I still love *Thriller*,' Vernon had said. '"Billy Jean"'s a classic, whatever MJ has been accused of.'

So no, Father Vernon wasn't a standard priest, but he couldn't be on a campus like Benedon. He needed to span the gulf between the college elders and the activist students.

There was a pause, then a ping.

Back at the fort. Want to head over now? Side door is open.

As always: Vernon had an open-door policy; the church was never locked and was known as a safe space where everyone was welcome, whatever their creed. Over the past couple of years, Harry had taken advantage of it more than most, turning up at all hours to discuss problems and concerns or to shoot the breeze. Or, like now, when he needed to tell someone something. Someone neutral. Someone who would understand the gravity of the situation and be trusted to be discreet. Then again, it was Labor Day. Vernon had done his duty, gone to the Dean's party. The poor man needed a break sometimes. He tapped a reply.

It will wait. See you on the other side.

Turning from the pop and fizz of the fireworks, Harry crossed back to his desk. And he began to type.

Chapter 7

'Shitshitshit,' muttered Lara, running from the shower room, half-dressed, still damp. She twisted her hair into a bun and pulled on her jacket, grabbing her bag. Being late for her first official meeting with Doug Bishop was not a good look. It hadn't helped that she had woken up at 4 am. Partly jet lag, but mostly anxiety, stomach knotted by the absurdity of the whole enterprise. Why on earth was she here, a representative from a *newspaper*, the popular technology of the 19th century, lecturing to a 21st century generation raised on digital media? What did she have to tell them that would be useful in their future careers? She had struggled with it, staring at the ceiling for at least an hour until, despite the raging doubts, Lara had dropped off again, only waking properly when her phone alarm was on its third go-around on the snooze function. She clattered down the cottage steps and onto the street, banging the front door shut behind her.

'You're a rockstar,' she muttered, trotting up Montrose Street. That's what Alex had said the day before. She smiled as the phrase triggered a memory, a story told to her by Beverley, *The Chronicle*'s features editor. Bev had been out at some glittering event in London and had rushed home full of excitement to report the details to her teenage daughter.

'I've just been speaking to Bono,' she'd gushed.

'Who?' the girl had asked.

'From U2,' said Beverley.

'What's that? An app?'

Lara fully expected the same sort of reaction from her students. So many things considered vital to know when Lara had been a student, such as 'stitching', 'GSM' or 'cuttings libraries', were all damn-near obsolete now, consigned to the dustbin of history by the onrush of technology. *Just like me.*

She glanced at her watch as she broke into a trot. It was 8.05. The campus wasn't far. If she knew where she was going, she might make it. Lara had been so busy since her arrival that she'd only had the briefest look around the campus. Doug had told her the room number, but in which building was his office? *Harry would know*, she thought as she approached the corner of his street. But would he be at home? Would he be *alone*?

Lara had tried not to think about Harry's disappearance from the party, but her mind couldn't seem to leave it alone. Had she said something to upset him? Had he been annoyed she'd gone off with Doug? Had he seen her with Arthur Campbell and just bolted?

Lara pulled out her phone, debating whether to call him, but then decided against it and pushed it back into her pocket, sighing. Perhaps it was a sign. She and Harry, they were... colleagues, that was all. Maybe she'd been foolish to think there had been a romantic spark between them, especially after Harry had been dogged by rumours of an affair with a student. It was hardly an ideal start, was it? Yes, Lara liked him, but she didn't know him, didn't know anything about his personal life – and even his professional life was complicated; that much was clear from the Dean's party.

She wavered on the corner of Harry's street, undecided. Deep down, she knew that she was hoping to see him, bump into him in the most casual way, and then they could walk to campus together. Lara shook her head. Was she becoming like her friend Suzanne who, in college, had created all sorts of elaborate scenarios to catch the attention of men she fancied? The 'lost keys', the 'blocked shower', the 'oops! I was sleepwalking': none of them seemed to work. Cursing herself, Lara was turning back towards campus when movement caught her eye at the far end of Harry's street: it was the blink-blink of a police light, a car parked as if it had arrived in haste. Lara felt her feet turning towards it without conscious thought. Pavlovian response: put a bone in front of a dog, they drool. Put a mystery in front of a writer, their ears prick up, and they run towards it.

Closer now, she could see a loose knot of people – neighbours presumably, rubberneckers – standing in the street around a van. No, an ambulance, a uniformed policeman and the flutter of police tape: the unmistakable tableau of a classic crime scene.

'What's going on?'

A girl was standing at the back of the observers, holding a handkerchief to her lips; she looked like she had been crying.

'Haven't you heard?' said the girl. 'It's the professor.'

'Which professor?' said Lara, filled with the powerful sense that she already knew the answer.

I live a block away from you on Floral Street. Harry had said. *The yellow house with the window boxes.*

. . .

She looked around urgently. There were no other yellow houses. No other window boxes. This was Harry's place.

Shit.

On autopilot now, Lara skirted around the crowd and ducked under the police tape, walking straight towards the house. Here was something she could definitely teach her students: the first rule of journalism was 'always proceed as if you're meant to be there'. Confidence would get you through more doorways and across more borders than any passport or laminated ID.

'Ma'am? Hey, Ma'am?'

She turned to face a young uniformed cop, a rash of acne still cursing his neck.

'You can't be in here,' he began, but Lara cut him off.

'This is my friend's house. I have an appointment to meet him here; what's going on?'

'I can't tell you that at this time. Please step back behind the tape.' He was fresh-faced, straight out of the academy, Lara guessed: not good. Experience told her that the newbies were always the most rigid sticklers for the rules. Trying another tack, she reached into her bag and pulled out her press card. Second rule: when challenged, pitch your voice somewhere between authoritarian and bolshy, like you're going to make their life a misery if they don't let you do exactly what you want. 'I'm Lara Stone from *The Chronicle*,' she said, holding up the card. 'I saw Harry Robbins last night, and he specifically asked me to come here and…'.

That got the officer's attention: he held up a hand.

'You saw Professor Robbins last night?'

'Yes, so I really must…' she trailed off as the officer held a radio to his ear.

'Chief, can you come outside? I have someone here who was with Robbins last night.'

A woman strode across from the porch. She was wearing black trousers and a dark trench. A lilac blouse stopped her from looking too sombre, although her expression was still stern.

'I'm Detective Sarah Carter,' she said. 'Can we just step to one side for a moment?'

Lara was aware that the crowd was building behind the police tape, evidently sensing a development. The detective led Lara behind a police van at the side of the house where they would have privacy at least.

'You're a friend of Professor Robbins?' asked the detective.

'Yes. Well, a colleague. My name is Lara Stone. I'm a fellow at the college.'

'You were with him last night?'

'Yes. Please, tell me what's going on. What's happened to Harry?'

There was a pause, and then the woman's eyes met Lara's.

'I'm sorry,' she said. 'Mr Robbins is dead.'

The world seemed to spin. Lara took a half-step sideways, fingers pressed to her lips.

'Dead? How, why? What's happened?'

'His direct family has been notified,' said Carter in a bland monotone. 'Also the Dean of the journalism school. When we know more, we will make a statement....'

'Tell me!' snapped Lara, then squeezed her eyes shut, taking a breath.

'Sorry. Harry was my friend,' she said, her voice more controlled. 'Please?'

Sarah Carter was around her age. Her russet hair was cut short, and she wore little make-up, but she didn't need it: her large brown eyes were her best feature. She looked no-nonsense, but there was compassion; Lara could see it. 'Please,' she repeated.

Carter's expression softened.

'Right now, we are working on the assumption that no one else was involved,' she said.

Lara knew the code – Detective Carter was saying that Harry had taken his own life. Suicide? No. That didn't make sense. She covered her face with a shaking hand.

'Come on,' said Carter, leading Lara out of the view of the onlookers. She waited, giving Lara a moment to compose herself.

'So you saw Harry last night?'

Lara nodded.

'It was the Dean's Labor Day party. We went there together.'

'Was it a date?'

'No. Not really,' said Lara, aware that her hands were shaking. I've only just arrived from London; he was being kind.'

Sarah gave a tight nod as if she was mentally writing it down.

'What time did you leave the party?'

'I left just before 7.30. Harry – I don't know.'

'You came together, but you didn't leave together?'

'We were supposed to go to a restaurant – the Plymouth Rock? – afterwards, but it never happened. Harry left the party without saying goodbye. He sent me a text to say he'd rearrange our dinner.'

'Can you show me?'

Lara fumbled her phone from her bag, her mind whirling. Why hadn't she called Harry back? Why hadn't she spoken to him, talked to him? She should have known how difficult the party would have been for Harry. She should have checked in with him. If only...

She called up the message and handed it to Carter, who read the text and noted the time. '7.29,' she muttered. 'Could I take this?'

'No!' said Lara. 'That is my phone, detective. I can't do my work without it.'

'I realise that, but we're trying to establish Mr Robbin's state of mind.'

'You won't find anything on there. I only met Harry on Saturday. We exchanged numbers; he sent me one message to confirm what time he was picking me up, another to say he'd left the party: that's it.'

Lara watched as Carter flipped through Lara's phone. Seemingly satisfied, she handed it back. Those big eyes flashed again.

'Was there any reason to be worried about the professor?'

Lara thought it over. 'No... No. I can't imagine why he would do something like that.'

'Tell me how he seemed last night.'

Lara gave a soft, sad snort.

'He seemed in good spirits. We met his friend, Chaplain Vernon, and they were joking together, smiling. We discussed the journalism symposium he was arranging, and he seemed very excited about it.'

Lara stopped to think. He *had* seemed that way: positive, looking to the future. It was so easy to second guess how someone had been feeling after the fact, to reinterpret laughter as the tears of a clown. But if Harry was feeling suicidal, he had hidden it well. Lara shook her head.

'No,' she said decisively. 'He *was* happy; he was fun. He seemed to be having a good time, considering...'

'Considering?'

Lara paused. The press and the police were in roughly the same business; finding out what had happened and making sense of it was their basic function, but they were sometimes on different sides. Finding the truth behind a story and solving the case often put them in competition. After all, journalists always wanted to be *first*.

But Lara wasn't in competition here. As Harry's friend, she felt desperately sad and just wanted to help find out why he did what he did.

'Considering he was leaving Benedon,' said Lara. 'I'm sure you'll find all this out, but Harry told me he'd had a difficult time at the college the previous semester. A student died, and people gossiped, saying that Harry had a relationship with the student. Harry told me it wasn't true, but still, he was planning to leave, so it must have been tough being at that party, being judged by his colleagues.'

Lara shook her head.

'Maybe it had been harder than I'd guessed,' said Lara. 'When he cancelled our dinner, I should have called, and checked in with him.'

Carter just looked at her.

'I'm sorry for your loss,' she said. It felt like a dismissal.

'If I need to speak to you again, I assume I can find you on campus?'

'At the journalism school. Let me know if I can do anything else to help.'

'I will.'

As she turned to go, Carter touched her arm.

'Oh, and by the way, Ms Stone? Your press card doesn't work around here.'

* * *

Lara was panting when she reached Doug's office, but he wasn't in the room. She hadn't expected him to be: the detective had told Lara she had informed the Dean, which undoubtedly meant that the whole faculty knew what had happened. Lara continued down the corridor and found a glass door labelled 'Journalism: Faculty Office' – it was ajar, and Lara peeked inside. An officious-looking grey-haired lady with red spectacles hanging on a thin chain looked up from her screen.

'Sorry, I was looking for Doug Bishop?'

It was only then that Lara noticed the woman's eyes were ringed red.

'I don't think Doug will be in this morning; he's with the Sheriff. One of our colleagues....'

'Harry Robbins. I know. I'm Lara Stone, the new visiting fellow. I was just... I heard.'

The woman's expression softened, and she stood up.

'Oh my dear,' she said. 'Welcome, if that's the word. What a day to start.'

Lara could only nod.

'Let's get you some coffee,' she said, stepping across to a machine and pouring a cup. Lara took it gratefully: caffeine was definitely needed right then.

'My name is Mary, Mary Stewart. I'm Doug's secretary: everyone's secretary, really. The rest of the faculty is all in a crisis meeting right now. So awful...'

'Had you known Harry long?'

Mary's face lit up. 'Oh, years. He is, *was* such a lovely man. Always asking after Thompson.'

'Thompson? Who's that?'

Mary laughed.

'He's my dog, my little cockapoo. In fact, Harry gave him his name, after Hunter S. Thompson, the writer? I wasn't sure, but Harry said it suited him because Thompson's so,' – Mary lowered her voice – 'Batshit crazy, always running around, chasing imaginary rabbits. And he was right. It fits Thompson to a tee.'

Mary grinned, and then the smile faded. 'I'll miss Harry. He was a wonderful man. Whatever anyone said.'

Mary looked up at the clock behind her desk. 'Heavens!' she cried, taking Lara's coffee from her hand. 'You'll be late for your lecture.'

'Is it still on?' said Lara with alarm.

'Oh yes,' said Mary, pushing a campus map into Lara's hands and shooing her towards the door. 'Knowledge never sleeps – Harry used to say that. We can't leave the students hanging, can we? Lecture Theatre number four. Chop chop! If you need anything else, just come back here and give Mary a holler, okay?'

'I'll do that,' smiled Lara. Then she turned and ran.

Chapter 8

The room was half-empty but no less intimidating for it. Ninety or so seats raked back like a boutique cinema facing a tiny stage. Lara walked down the steps in the centre, feeling the student's eyes on her, their whispered conversations cutting off the moment she entered.

She took her spot on the low stage, putting her notes on the oak podium, feeling the heat of a creamy spotlight on her face. Squinting, Lara discreetly did a headcount. Thirty. Doug had said there would be around seventy at her first lecture, but she wasn't surprised. As Lara had power-walked across campus, she had seen groups of students standing around, some crying, all in subdued conversation. Attending lectures today probably wasn't anyone's priority.

She ducked out of the glare of the stage light and looked at their faces. They looked young. Apprehensive. She knew how they felt.

'Well, hello, I'm Lara Stone,' she said, hoping they didn't hear the shake in her voice. 'I'm a journalist for *The Chronicle* in London. I've done every kind of work from court reports to sports, but I've specialised in investigative reporting and....'

She trailed off. This was the opening speech she had prepared, scribbled in a notebook on the flight over, imagining a group of starry-eyed students hanging on her every word. But that had been a fantasy even then. Here and now, they weren't interested in her; they weren't interested in their studies – she could see it in their faces. They wanted to know about their professor and what was happening *out there* on their campus. Real life.

'Look, there's only a few of us today. Why don't you all gather on the front rows down here, and we can talk.'

A pause as they all exchanged shrugs and shuffled closer.

'So is it true?' asked a boy with dark floppy hair. 'Was Professor Robbins...' he lowered his voice. 'Was he *murdered?*'

Before Lara could reply, she heard a sob from the second row. A girl with a blue shirt stood up and, with a tight 'sorry', ran out of the room.

'Does anyone else want to join her?' asked Lara.

The room fell silent.

'Good,' said Lara. 'Because we need to talk about this. And running off isn't going to help anyone.'

The boy with dark hair in the front row raised a hand.

'Hey, people are upset here.'

Lara nodded sympathetically. 'I understand how you're feeling...?'

'Brian,' said the boy sullenly. 'Brian Silvinski.'

'Brian, I get you're all feeling shaken up right now. It's the first day of term, a department member has passed away, and you don't know what's happened. Of course, it's going to knock you sideways.' She held up both hands. 'But that's the gig.'

She waited, watching their faces, then started to pace across the stage. Lara was speaking off-script now, but this could be one of the most valuable lessons they could learn.

'Whatever type of reporter you want to be – investigative reporter, TV reporter, crime, celebrity, doesn't matter. Lesson number one is you've got to check your emotions at the door.'

She paused for emphasis. 'It's a sad day on campus today. But as a reporter, objectivity is everything. You have to gather information, present the facts and find the story, whether or not you agree with it, and whether or not you feel involved. We cannot let emotion get in the way of that.'

She paused for effect.

'So, today we're going to do some reporting. We're going to write a news story on the death of Professor Robbins.'

The students looked at each other, suspicious – as well they might.

There was a subdued sarcastic laugh from her left. An athletic-looking boy was glaring at her, his lip curled with distaste.

'Seriously?' he said. 'You're seriously going to turn this into a teaching exercise? Prof Robbins is *dead,* man.'

'Right. And I agree that this is an unusual situation; some of you knew Professor Robbins personally, which makes it tough. But you can't choose the news. I can guarantee you that one day you *will* be dealing with news stories that throw you for a loop: bombings, abused children, social injustice, and horrible corporate malpractice. You'll be angry; you'll be sad; you'll be sickened. Even so, your job is to jump in and get the story. You can't freeze.'

Lara flashed onto a memory: she had been in London at a newspaper party the night of the Bataclan attacks in Paris. Within 10 minutes of the first report coming through, the party had emptied, two dozen men and women heading for the Eurostar. There had been no hesitation, despite the evident danger. They were reporters: they had to get there and report.

Lara clapped her hands, making the students flinch.

'Right then! I am Lara Stone, the new editor of the *Boston Globe*.' She held up her wrist to show them the face of her watch. 'You have 15 minutes. Write me my front page.'

'About Professor Robbins?' asked a pretty blonde girl nervously.

'Do you know another news story that's happening today? Something more important to your fellow students on campus?'

'No, but we don't know what happened,' said the girl. 'No one knows; it's just a bunch of rumours.'

Lara pointed at her.

'Precisely. That's why the world needs reporters like you. To find things out, to pull the truth from the chaos.'

She held up a wrist again. '14 minutes 30. I want a headline and an opening paragraph. The best piece gets extra credit.'

Lara had no idea what 'extra credit' was, but she had seen it mentioned in movies before – and it certainly got them moving.

They scrambled to get laptops and notebooks out. The mood in the room had completely changed. They clearly thought Lara was crazy, but they were smiling at each other; they were engaged.

'When did it happen?' called out Brian. 'Was it last night?'

'I don't know,' said Lara. 'I'm the editor, sitting in my swanky office on Eighth Avenue; you're the reporter on the ground. If you don't know, fill in the blanks for me: that's the skill. And remember, you're not writing this for the editor; you're writing it to be read by Jo Public. She wants – no, she *needs* – to know what's happened.'

Their heads went down again. It was good to see; it was good to give them focus. But this was helping her too. What she said about leaving your emotions at the door was true. The news of Harry's death had floored Lara. She needed time to sit and process it, but there never was time. Even if this was an exercise, she needed to hold her emotions in check and help these kids make some sense of what could be the first tragedy they'd ever encountered.

'One minute to go,' she said to a collective groan. Lara suppressed a smile; it didn't matter what they came up with; the point was that they were trying.

'Come on!' she shouted. '*The Post* is going to scoop us. For those of you using computers, my inbox is 'Lara-dot-stone at the Chronicle-dot-com.'

A girl with curly hair ran down the aisle, tearing a sheet of paper from her notebook. Lara looked at it, then handed it back. 'No byline. You want me to put my name on it?'

The girl squatted down to write as Brian raised his hand and called, 'All yours, chief,' barely half a second before the girl slapped her paper on Lara's desk. The girl – 'Cassie Golden in Benedon' according to her scribbled note – let out a hiss of frustration. This was more like it. Competition was healthy. It was one of the most important traits in a young reporter. And Lara liked Brian's 'chief' – a sense of humour in times of crisis was vital.

'Sending,' shouted someone else. 'Me too.' There were sly grins, and red cheeks as the rest ran down to hand in their work. Blood was flowing. They were engaged. That was half the battle.

'Okay, let's see....'

Lara clicked through the emails and leafed through the

untidy pile of papers on the desk. She could feel the expectation in the room, and hear their muttered conversations.

'These are great, guys,' she said finally. 'I'm going to choose one randomly, if that's okay?'

There was an anxious murmur of assent before Lara held up a sheet.

'Cassie Golden's report.'

She turned and wrote Cassie's headline across the whiteboard behind them in big letters.

PROFESSOR DEAD. POLICE INVESTIGATE CAMPUS SLAYING.

She tapped the board with her pen.

'What do we think of this?'

'It's dramatic. It grabs you,' said a voice on the second row.

Lara nodded.

'But is it too dramatic?"

'Newspapers want sales. Dramatic is good,' said Brian.

'But sales versus integrity, it's always a tough one – what are you prepared to do, what line will you cross?' She turned back to the board. 'What story does "campus slaying," say to you?'

'It was violent,' replied Brian.

Lara nodded.

'But people could get the wrong idea,' said another student. 'It sounds like there's a serial killer on the loose at Benedon.'

'Very good,' said Lara. 'The word "Slaying" is a little too blunt, too emotive. Cassie, full marks for impact, and yes, it sells papers, but we also have a duty to the reader and the victims: to treat them with dignity.

Lara rubbed out "Slaying", replacing it with 'Tragedy'. She turned to face the students.

'One word changes the tone immediately, doesn't it?'

There were nods. They were learning. Lara moved from headlines to writing the story, picking apart the 'Who, What, When, Where, Why and How'. The fundamentals of news story writing had been drilled into her at journalism college, and Lara had never forgotten them. Even when she moved from the news desk at *The Chronicle* to the investigations room, she mentally ran through the checklist before passing copy. The students were now firing questions at her, their faces bright, nothing like the slumped, troubled kids she had found here an hour ago. Lara found she was enjoying it too, so much so that it was a few minutes before she noticed someone else watching from the back row in the lecture theatre. Rosalind, the Dean of the faculty.

'Well done, everyone, that's plenty for today,' said Lara. 'Next time, we'll be looking at the "investigative" part of investigative reporting, so please come to class with an in-depth piece you've enjoyed over the past year. It can be any story from any news outlet – but if you don't know where to start, I can recommend the Le Cache website.'

Lara waited as they filed out, gathering her things. When she looked up, Rosalind was walking down towards her.

'Lara, how are you?'

'First lecture out of the way,' she said, letting out a long breath. 'Only about the second most terrifying thing I've ever done.'

Lara kept her tone light. She'd only spoken to Ros for a few minutes at the party, but it was enough to grasp she was a fairly serious woman, but this morning she looked even more dour. Under the circumstances, she wasn't surprised.

'I'd come to check on you because of Professor Robbins. I know you were aquainted.'

'It's just awful. I spoke to the police at his house.'

'It *is* awful. It's just tragic,' said Rosalind. 'Which leads me to ask: what were you thinking with that lecture?'

'Excuse me?'

Lara looked at the Dean's face and realised that what she saw was not humourlessness or concern but anger.

'That,' said Ros, pointing a long finger at the headline on the whiteboard. 'You asked the students to write a story about the tragedy on campus? You could have traumatised those young people!'

'If they're upset by anything, it was by Harry's death, not by talking about it. And frankly, I doubt anyone in this room was "traumatised", as you put it: there is a big difference between trauma and hearing some bad news.'

Rosalind raised her chin.

'We must protect our students.'

'By wrapping them in cotton wool?' said Lara. 'That was the point of today's exercise. Something terrible happened today, yes, but we don't get to choose the news. And you can't let emotions interfere with the job.'

'*Interfere with the job?* These are students, Lara,' she said, pink spots appearing on her cheeks.

'They are *journalism* students, Ros, and the newsroom is tough. If they can't handle that, news reporting isn't for them.'

Lara tried to keep her anger under control. This was the Dean, after all. She'd noticed the deferential way people had tip-toed around her at her party. But that wasn't Lara's style.

'Miss Stone. You may have noticed this is a university, not a newsroom. They come here to study.'

'But if they can't do the exercise I gave them, they are studying the wrong thing.'

'I think you need to ease off a little.'

'Perhaps, yes,' said Lara, picking up her things. 'But I'm simply doing what I thought I was here to do: preparing young people for their professional lives.'

She turned to point at the headline written on the whiteboard.

'And no-one said it would be easy,' she said, walking up the steps and leaving the Dean standing in the spotlight.

Chapter 9

'So tell me what you see.'

Sarah Carter's voice was little more than a mutter, but it still sounded loud in the house. Crime scenes had that way about them, especially in small, enclosed spaces like Harry Robbins's home; they became instant museums. People spoke in whispers and stepped lightly, especially when, as here, the smell of death was in the air.

She flinched as one of the forensics guys fired off a camera flash; it seemed out of step with the mood.

Sarah guessed that the day before, Harry Robbins's home would have been full of life, the TV on, a kettle boiling on the stove, maybe even the sound of laughter: who knew? But not now. Now it was quiet, the life muffled, shrouded the moment the gunshot echo faded.

'What do I see? I see a cop who needs a cup of coffee,' said a voice behind her.

Sarah didn't need to look at her colleague to know he was suppressing a yawn. Glenn Schultz was the other detective on the small county police force. Born and raised in Benedon, he'd been on the force for nearly thirty years. He was overweight, divorced and a borderline alcoholic: all the cliches, but Glenn had been around the block; he'd seen it all before. And that was exactly why Sarah had brought him along.

'Humour me, Glenn.'

Glenn grunted, reluctantly giving the living room a 360. 'I see a TV dinner by the sink, a half-full glass of wine on the kitchen side,' he said, scratching his belly under his straining blue shirt. 'I see a guy living on his own. Maybe he liked it. Or maybe he was lonely as hell and one night thought, 'Shee-it, what the hell?' Sarah looked up as Glenn made a gun shape with his fingers and mimed pulling the trigger.

'Real nice, Glenn. A lot of empathy.'

She turned, trying to follow Glenn's view of the house, and mostly she agreed. There had been a middle-aged guy living alone, living simply. It wasn't ostentatious, but it felt classy. A high-end sound system, a shiny coffee machine, and bottles of expensive wine in the kitchen, some of which had to have cost fifty bucks. It didn't look like the home of a man in financial trouble. She looked at a framed picture of Harry, his arm around another man as they held up a huge fish. He was handsome, smart, and successful. And he looked happy in the photo—what a waste.

When she'd arrived at the scene earlier that morning, it had been far too late. Harry had died from a single gunshot wound to the head. She was no coroner, but she'd worked enough homicide cases to know that he had been dead for hours, probably between five and ten: it had almost certainly happened the previous night, but none of the neighbours had heard a thing. That was curious. Guns were unusual in Benedon. Before joining the force here five months earlier, Sarah had spent fifteen years in the NYPD, mostly in the city's gritty ninth precinct, so stepping around blood was second nature. But Benedon was peaceful, the only violence in the odd domestic dispute or rowdy student parties.

Sarah walked over to the French doors.

'You noticed these were unlocked?' she said, using her gloved hand to open the handle. She stepped outside into the small yard, where there was a table and a couple of chairs. An old coffee cup sat on the table collecting rainwater.

'I don't think security was top of the professor's agenda last night,' said Glenn as she came back into the house.

Harry Robbins had been sitting in a chair at his desk. The gun was on the floor at his side, a Glock 19, a popular weapon. Its smaller size made the gun standard issue for hoods wanting ease of concealment, but across the land, you'd find thousands of the things stuffed in women's handbags or bedside cabinets. And in Vermont, you didn't even need a permit.

Sarah took out her phone and started taking pictures. The French doors, the desk, the floor. The forensics guys packing up outside had already comprehensively recorded the scene in detail, but Sarah liked to have her own evidence to refer to as she went along.

'Don't you think it's strange?' said Sarah, putting her phone back in her pocket.

'What is?' said Glenn.

'The head wound. Where the bullet entered.'

Glenn looked interested for the first time.

'How so?'

'It was the front of his head,' she said, tapping a finger on her forehead. 'Usual entry point for a suicide is through the mouth or at the temple.'

Doug flipped a hand towards the empty chair.

'So what are you thinking? Mafia hit? Home invasion? One of those CIA black-ops things?'

Glenn was playing the hard-bitten cynic, but Sarah took the point. Harry Robbins's cleaner had found him at 7 am that morning, slumped sideways in the chair, gun cold on the floor.

There was no reason to suppose anything other than the most obvious scenario. Professor Robbins had shot himself: the end – in every sense. Sarah knew the statistics: self-inflicted gunshot wounds were the go-to exit strategy for white, unemployed males determined to take their own life. Harry Robbins fitted the profile perfectly now that Sarah had confirmed the rumour that the Professor had recently been edged out of Benedon.

And yet, she was still here, walking through Harry's house, looking for clues that possibly didn't exist. No forced entry, no sign of a struggle, nothing out of place. And yet...

Glenn sighed.

'Look, I feel bad for the dude, but I think you're over-thinking this. Guy shot himself – how and why, it doesn't matter, he's still dead. It's real sad, but it happens.'

Sarah nodded; she knew she was wasting her time here. Glenn was experienced, but he was also counting down the days to retirement and would take the path of least resistance every time. Then again, what did Sarah have? Nothing. She was wasting her own time too.

'We all done in here?'

Sarah turned and saw Sheriff Roscoe stride inside. He was sixty-one, tall but overweight, with clipped grey hair and a penchant for light-coloured suits he imagined made him look like Henry Fonda in '12 Angry Men'. Until two years before, Roscoe had managed a successful chain of out-of-town hardware stores and seemingly ran for election to Sheriff to improve his social standing.

'What are we waiting for?' said Roscoe, spinning a

finger in the air in a gesture of impatience. 'Let's wrap this up.'

Even if Glenn resisted hard work, he was still a good cop. Sheriff Cal Roscoe, on the other hand, had two settings: macho and sexist. Sarah didn't mind the former so much; law enforcement was a tough profession. But their little police force was 20 strong: only three women were on the payroll, and even that seemed to irk Roscoe. Or maybe it was just Sarah he didn't like.

'We still need to locate Mr Robbins' computer,' said Sarah. 'And I want to check out his movements yesterday after the party at the Dean's residence. I'll get Brin to knock on some doors.'

The Sheriff shrugged. 'Fine, just have the report on my desk first thing tomorrow morning.'

Sarah flexed her jaw muscles, once again marvelling at a system which would put a man with zero experience in law enforcement in authority above her. But that was the situation and she had to live with it.

'I think it might take a little longer than that,' said Sarah.

Roscoe gave a small shake of the head. *Uh-oh,* thought Sarah. *Here it comes.*

'Why?' he asked. 'It's pretty clear cut what's going on here, Sarah. This Robbins guy is caught banging one of the students, so he gets turned down for his full professorship, right? He goes to the party, and he's faced with the dream of what he could have had. Realises he's screwed up his life – not to mention that poor girl's – so he comes home and boom!'

'But why go to the party if he felt that guilty?'

Roscoe waved a hand as if to dismiss petty things like logic and evidence.

'Who knows? Maybe he'd had a drink. Maybe he

sobered right up when all eyes were on him. We'll never know. So let's not waste any more time on this.'

'With respect, sir, this is still a *suspected* suicide. It needs to be investigated properly.'

Roscoe turned to Glenn.

'Give us a minute, huh?'

Flashing a look at Sarah, the other detective scuttled away. She could hardly blame him; confrontation wasn't Glenn's thing.

'Look, Sarah,' began Roscoe, turning up the disdain a couple of notches. He might as well have said, 'now see here, little lady…'.

'This is a college town. It's a safe place; we don't want to make people think otherwise. I understand that the professor sent the priest a text message, "See you on the other side." Now, what's that if it isn't a suicide note?'

A jolly sign-off, a pop culture reference, an in-joke, thought Sarah. It could be anything.

'I have yet to speak to Father Vernon,' she said, fighting to control her temper. Roscoe's condescending smile did nothing to help.

'Sarah, I know you may miss the big city,' he said. 'I know that in New York, on any given day, you probably had double homicides, bomb threats and a death cult ready to throw themselves off the Empire State building. But things work differently here.'

He said it as if he was explaining the local customs to the big city girl, but Cal Roscoe knew full well that Sarah was from the Benedon area too. In fact, Sarah had been to the same school as Glenn, albeit fifteen years later: Apparently, 'Dumptruck' Schultz was still thought of as the best quarterback the Benedon Bears had ever had. Yes, Sarah had left town for the big city police department, climbing the greasy ladder via vice and robbery, but Sarah understood only too well how 'things worked' for people like Cal Roscoe. Reputation, status and the outward appearance of civility mattered more than things like justice and truth. Hell, she was surprised that Cal hadn't been to the Dean's party himself, schmoozing with the trustees, the real power behind the town.

'Bad things happen everywhere, Sheriff,' she said.

'Not here,' said Roscoe firmly. 'This is Benedon. There hasn't been a serious assault in two years or a big robbery in five. This isn't *The Wire*. I get that things might not seem too exciting after NYC, but don't look for things that aren't there.'

He looked at her.

'And that's an order, Sarah.'

Chapter 10

Lara's office was tiny. Barely thirty feet square, there was just enough room for a desk, two chairs and a filing cabinet, but that afternoon, Lara had been grateful to have anywhere she could close the door and shut out the drama of the day. The crying, red-eyed students, the academic staff who were practically vibrating with the tension of trying to hold it all together. And that was without TV news crews camping out on the lawns, pointing cameras and fingers. Dean Rosalind Davies had issued a short statement, requesting that students and staff respect Professor Robbin's privacy 'and that of his family at this difficult time'. She was really sending a message: 'don't tell tales out of school', but it was too late. Lara had already seen headlines such as 'double death on campus' about the 'disgraced professor with the troubled past'; one even went with 'sex scandal suicide'. Lara felt strangely detached from it all, as if none of it related to the man with whom she had planned to go for dinner less than 24 hours ago. Hiding out in this little cupboard was also a reaction to Lara's terse showdown with the dean; in hindsight, not her best strategic move. The smart play would have been to have apologised, deferred to Rosalind's greater experience and taken the slap on the wrist. But right then, Lara had still been reeling from the news; it hadn't occurred to Lara that the rest of the Benedon staff – the Dean included – would have felt the same. After all, they had worked alongside Harry for years. Lara had barely known him.

Lara was just closing her laptop when she heard a ping: an incoming email.

Not all of us froze, chief. Brian.

Attached was a link to the *Boston Morning Post* website.

'Benedon Professor dead. Campus in mourning' read the headline.

Frowning, Lara scanned down the text. At the bottom of the page, she spotted it: 'pictures by Brian Silvinski'.

Lara grinned. 'Not bad, Brian,' she whispered to herself. 'Not bad at all.'

She looked up as she heard her office door creak open.

'Here you are.'

Doug Bishop squeezed through the door of Lara's office, causing the filing cabinet to wobble. Doug was a big guy, and the room was the size of a coffin, but after some effort, he managed to close the door.

'Hi,' he said, pulling that 'Isn't this awful?' face everyone had been using. 'I haven't seen you all day. I was worried.'

'Thanks, but I'm fine. Well, not fine, but you know what I mean.'

They fell into a gloomy silence, another key move everyone was making that afternoon.

'Sorry to abandon you on your first day,' he said. 'I've

been at the Sheriff's office, speaking to the Dean, getting hold of Harry's family. Everything is just so...' His voice faltered, and Lara reached out a hand.

'How about going down to The Shovel?'

Doug shook his head.

'Thanks, but Harry loved The Shovel. Feels a bit raw to go there.'

Lara could empathise. Sitting in that booth eating fries under the red neon glow felt like a lifetime ago.

'So how was the first lecture?' asked Doug.

'Better than I'd hoped. There weren't many there, but those that came seemed to enjoy it. I think we connected.'

Doug looked at her meaningfully.

'I believe Ros spoke to you.'

'Yesss...' said Lara. 'She had a slightly different view. She felt my first session wasn't appropriate.'

She recounted her confrontation with the Dean.

'I feel terrible, Doug,' she said truthfully. 'The Dean had only come to check on me, and I gave her an earful.'

Doug gave her a sympathetic smile.

'It's hard to know how to react at times like these. And Ros spends so much of her life living in fear of lawsuits; cleaners slipping in puddles, and listeria outbreaks in the canteen. The latest threat is sensitive students who've had their feelings hurt.'

'I didn't mean to upset anyone. It was just... Harry was the elephant in the room. We had to talk about it.'

Doug nodded, then shivered. 'Lara – why did he do it? I worked in the next office from him for three years and I never thought, for one moment, he could do that.'

Lara looked at him for a moment.

'What *did* he do, Doug?' she said in a low voice. 'I mean, you've been to the Sheriff's office.' Perhaps it was unhealthy to dwell on the specifics, but she was a journalist: the devil was in the detail.

'Apparently it was a gunshot wound,' said Doug, his voice faltering. 'Around midnight. I don't know much more, I got the feeling that neither do they until the autopsy is done.'

A gun? Lara could barely believe it. Guns were so alien to her, but then this was America. But Harry... he'd been so liberal, so smart, she just couldn't imagine him walking into a store and buying into some *Dirty Harry* fantasy. Lara was quickly learning that she had never really known the man.

'So,' said Doug, letting the word roll out slowly. 'Did Harry mention the symposium to you?'

Lara nodded. 'It's happening this weekend, right?'

'Uh-huh. I guess it seems uncaring to talk about it now, but it was one of the big topics at the faculty meeting earlier today.'

Lara waited. She had a feeling that this was the real reason Doug had come to see her.

'The Provost thinks we should nix it.'

'What? No!'

Doug nodded ruefully.

'Ros thinks we should can it too. She believes it's insensitive under the circumstances, but I disagree. The symposium was Harry's baby, it was important to him and the best thing we can do for him now is ensure it goes ahead. It's what Harry would have wanted.'

'Absolutely,' said Lara, remembering how passionately Harry spoke about it at The Shovel.

'I'm glad you agree. Because I've persuaded Ros that we should carry on, but it's conditional.'

'Conditional on what?'

'On someone taking the reins. The event is in four days' time. It's a big deal for the university. To Ros and the

Provost, the reputation of the college is paramount. We can't put on an event that reflects badly on the department. I agree with Ros on that. There can be no mistakes.'

'I'll do it,' said Lara. 'That's what you were about to ask, wasn't it? For Harry?'

Doug nodded sheepishly, but he didn't need to use emotional blackmail; Lara wanted to help, both for Harry's sake, but also because she thought the initiative was a good one. The best thing any college could do was to connect the students with the reality of their chosen industry as soon as possible. That was exactly why she had refused to back down to Rosalind after her lecture.

Doug leaned over and handed her a neatly-folded piece of paper.

'Here's the schedule. And there's another catch: Harry was due to speak three times over the weekend, so you'll need to fill the holes in the timetable.'

Lara gave it a glance, then nodded, unconcerned. This was her bread and butter as a journalist: hitting the phones, arranging interviews. The challenge would be finding people who would come to Vermont on such short notice, but if there was one thing Lara knew about hacks, it was that they loved to talk about themselves.

'Point me in the direction of his notes and contacts, and I can make a start on it tonight.'

Relief was written all over Doug's face, and Lara was glad to be able to ease his burden. He had enough to deal with right now. They all did.

'We haven't got his personal computer, but he had a desktop computer in his office. The IT team are trying to access the symposium files from that now. I'll collate everything we can retrieve and drop them off at your place later. But first, there's somewhere we need to be.'

Doug gave a sad smile and nodded towards the window

where the sky was darkening. Lara peered through the glass; she could see golden teardrops moving across the lawns outside.

'It's a candlelight vigil. For Harry. The kids have arranged it all.'

Lara felt her heart jump, a strange flutter of pleasure, anxiety and melancholy. She was moved that the students cared enough, but she wasn't entirely sure she was ready to face Harry's passing in such a public forum. And honestly? She wanted to keep him for herself, for a little while longer, at least.

'We should go,' she said, looking up at Doug uncertainly. 'Right?'

Doug smiled softly as if he had been sharing her thoughts. 'Right.'

He cocked out his arm for her to link, and they walked outside onto the flickering lights of the Square.

Chapter 11

Sarah's first thought was how pretty it all looked. On the paths that crisscrossed the vast square of lawn at the heart of the campus, hundreds of students were sitting in groups facing the college chapel, many holding candles, each one lit for Professor Robbins, their voices subdued, respectful. Sarah did not consider herself sentimental – she was a cop, after all – but it was hard not to be moved. Not all of the mourners had known Harry Robbins personally, but his death had hit the campus hard. One of their own had died suddenly, and while there had been no official announcement of the suicide, that was the assumption here at the vigil, adding to the sombre mood.

Sarah had spent the afternoon interviewing various members of the faculty, which had felt more like community service than detective work: no one had any useful information, so she had wasted valuable time reassuring them that yes, it was an isolated incident and no, it wasn't likely to impact on the college. Looking around the darkened lawns, Sarah felt only sadness. If her talks with Professor Robbins' colleagues had told her anything, it was that no one knew him at all. He was 'smart', 'respected', and 'good at his job', but no one had been to his house, no one seemed to know much about his life outside work, and almost no one had even spoken to him at the party. And only Rosalind, the Dean, had even noticed when he had left.

Which was why Sarah was here. Officially, she was on duty: crowd control and general visibility being the vague brief, but really she hoped to gain more insight into the elusive Harry Robbins.

Not that there was much information here, either. Students walking side by side, girls wearing college sweat-shirts, boys in Benedon hoodies or plaid shirts, all either holding hands or with arms draped across one another's shoulders. Casually dressed, sure, but they could all have been heading to a funeral. The hastily xeroxed flyers circulated around campus had spoken of a 'celebration of Professor Robbins' life', but there was little evidence of that. Eyes downcast, comments muted, this was collective grieving.

All of which made Sarah wonder: why? Twenty-four hours ago, if you'd mentioned Harry Robbins, many of these kids would have smirked and said something smart-assed like Glenn Schultz: how he'd been 'banging a student', but now Harry Robbins was something like a saint. Nothing like death to polish your halo.

Just then, Sarah zoomed in on a couple on the far side of the lawn coming out of one of the college buildings. Lara Stone, with the big guy, Professor Doug Bishop, one of the academics she had interviewed that afternoon. Sarah took a minute to watch Lara walk towards the church. The woman had such natural confidence and poise. She had that air of having dressed in a hurry but still looked gorgeous and glossy, as if she had just stepped out of a Ralph Lauren advert. Certainly, Lara Stone looked like the sort of woman who would have gone to Benedon College – or somewhere like it – herself. Doug Bishop saw her approach first and nodded respectfully.

'Mr Bishop, Ms Stone,' said Sarah, stretching out her hand.

'Impressive turnout,' she said, looking around the vigil.

'It seems the kids do care,' said Doug in a low voice. 'I mean, it's sometimes hard to work out whether the students actually enjoy our lectures or are just turning up because that's what their parents have paid for.'

A girl walked past holding a hand-painted sign reading, 'We always loved you, Harry.' Sarah nodded towards it.

'Was Professor Robbins still popular after everything that happened?' she asked.

'Not everyone listens to gossip and rumour,' said Doug. 'Before all that unpleasantness, Harry was very well-liked. Still is. *Was*,' he corrected himself, shaking his head. 'It's so hard, isn't it?'

Sarah watched as Lara Stone gave Doug's shoulder a reassuring squeeze. Doug looked away, then hurriedly added, 'Oh look, there's the Dean. If you'll excuse me, I need to speak to her.' He walked away, fumbling out a handkerchief, leaving Sarah alone with Lara.

'What a day,' said Lara quietly.

'A long day, too,' agreed Sarah, nodding towards the students sitting on the lawns. 'But tonight, the message is loud and clear, I think. Harry was a popular man. Did you know Harry before you got to Benedon?'

Lara shook her head.

'I wish I had. I bumped into him just after I arrived, and

within twenty minutes, we were sharing a burger at The Shovel. He was that kind of guy, you know? Kind and welcoming....'

'You shared a burger?' said Sarah, too eagerly. 'Was it a date?'

Lara gave a polite laugh.

'Figure of speech, detective. We each had our *own* burgers. But if you're asking if I was attracted to him, then sure. Harry was funny, and good-looking, but I'm only here for a semester. I wasn't looking for a boyfriend.'

'So nothing happened between you?'

'No,' said Lara firmly, pressing her lips together. Sarah knew she had over-stepped the mark, but then that was part of her job, to push witnesses and suspects, see how they reacted.

'And you still can't think why he would just leave the party?'

'No.'

'Did you argue?'

'I am a journalist, Miss Carter,' said Lara impatiently. 'A good one, I think. I want to work out what happened to Harry as much as you, possibly more so because he was my friend. I have spent all day thinking about last night, wondering what I could have done or said to change things.'

'And?'

'If I think of anything, I'll be sure to let you know.'

Sarah watched her go, threading through the crowd. A lot of detective work was done on instinct, and gut feeling, and Sarah was inclined to take what Lara had said at face value, despite her defensiveness. She imagined the attraction with Harry had been mutual, but Sarah had already checked out Lara's version of events: she had only arrived on Saturday.

There was a squeal of feedback, and Sarah turned towards the chapel. Up on the steps by the church doors, a microphone was being set up: Sarah had already been briefed that Father Vernon was going to address the mourning students. *Now, this should be interesting,* she thought; unlike Lara Stone, the priest had known Harry Robbins for years.

The noise from the crowd simmered down to almost silence. Sarah took a moment to admire the beauty of the campus – the white spire of the chapel, the forest green ivy that twisted its way up redbrick buildings. Growing up in the small town of Windsor, just three miles south of the campus, Sarah had dreamed of being one of the beautiful people who came to Benedon College. But it had always stayed that way: a dream. The tuition fees were astronomical, and while Sarah was good at the lateral thinking needed for detective work, it didn't get you very far in the examination hall. Ironically, both her parents had worked at the college. Her father was a security guard, and her mother was a cleaner on campus, so Sarah would often hang around the college or sit in Clayton's, one of the diners on Main Street, making a milkshake last for hours as she waited for their shifts to end. By the end of high school, Sarah had scraped enough points for community college, but compared to the Ivy-clad dream of Benedon, it was drab and unexciting. So Sarah had packed her bag and joined the New Jersey Police Academy, assuming she would never be back. *What is it they say about assumptions?* Thought Sarah with a twisted smile.

She looked up as a tall man approached the microphone and tapped on it. Even without the long robes he was wearing, Sarah would have recognised Father Vernon; she had seen him around Benedon. He was hard to miss.

'Thank you all for coming,' said Vernon. 'These are terrible times and terrible circumstances that bring us here. But...' He held up both hands, indicating the crowds gathered in front of the church steps. 'Look at us; we are gathered here together, united in our grief and our love for

Harry Robbins, a man who has given so much to this college and so much to so many of you out there.'

He was good at this, thought Sarah. Public speaking was a big part of his job, but given his close friendship with Harry, it must have been hard for him. Very hard.

'We must mourn,' he continued. 'But we must also remember why we loved this man. Remember what he gave to us, what we can use – and what we can pass onto others, just as Harry passed on his wisdom, friendship and love to all of us.'

The priest's voice cracked on the last word, and he quickly turned away, walking back inside the Chapel, followed by spontaneous applause and cheering. As it died away, someone started playing an acoustic guitar, and the students began to sing raggedly at first, and then with more force.

'Knocking on Heaven's Door', thought Sarah. Not too subtle, especially the line about the gun, but then the BPD hadn't released that detail yet. Sarah turned her head, hearing a gentle sobbing from a young woman with bobbed blonde hair, wearing a purple coat, standing under a tree. She didn't want to intrude, but then she reminded herself that these were just kids, 19, 20 years old, most away from home for the first time. She pulled a package of tissues from her jacket pocket.

'Here,' said Sarah.

The young woman's eyes flashed with fear.

'I'm sorry,' she gulped, hardly able to speak through her tears, then shook her head and backed away. 'I'm so sorry.' Stumbling on a tree root, she almost fell, recovered herself and began to run.

'Hey, wait,' said Sarah, following as the girl disappeared into the crowd. She picked her way through the knot of people, taking care not to knock over anybody with a candle.

She was sorry? What about? Something about the way she had said it, the look on her face.

'Hey!' snapped a girl as Sarah bumped into her.

Sarah held up both hands in apology, disentangling herself, losing sight of the girl in purple, but she kept moving in that direction, dodging around groups, stepping over people huddled on the floor. She caught a flash of pale blonde hair crossing the lawn beyond the Chapel, but it was all shadow when she reached the edge of the vigil.

'Dammit,' Sarah muttered, turning in a full circle. She was alone. The girl was gone.

Chapter 12

Lara left the campus through the main gate, a sweeping arch that looked like a mini Marble Arch or a baby Arc de Triomphe. It had been a mistake to go to the vigil; she knew that now. Emotions had been too high, the atmosphere too charged. She was glad so many people had been there for Harry; Lara only wished he could have seen it. He would have appreciated the irony: his reputation was destroyed by one student, but he was rehabilitated by the love of the entire student body.

Even so, Lara couldn't stay. What she had said to Sarah Carter was true: Lara had spent the day agonising over what she could have done or said to change the outcome. Coulda woulda shoulda: a pointless game unless you had a time machine. But still, she turned over every detail again and again. If only she'd called him back after the text. If only she'd not spent time talking to the Dean or Lizzy. If only they'd spent the night together. But... 'If only' always meant that you were too late.

Lara picked up her pace, looping back along Benedon's Main Street, passing the red neon of The Shovel. They'd both laughed so much sitting in that booth; there had been no hint of what was coming. Or had there? Had she missed something vital?

Stop it, said a voice in her head. When you're going through hell, keep going. That old saying – she wasn't sure who had said it, maybe Churchill - had always been one of her favourites because it was proactive: forget the self-pity, keep moving forwards. And she already had a direction, the one that Doug had given her: The Symposium. If she could do anything to honour Harry it would be to make his conference as brilliant as it could be. Doug hadn't been joking when he said that Harry's absence would leave a big hole in the schedule. Not only was Harry doing three of the talks himself, he had been down to be a moderator on another three. And Harry had already mentioned to her that a key speaker had pulled out.

'Alex,' she said out loud, stopping and pulling out her phone. For a moment she hesitated; it was after dark in Vermont, which meant it would be well past midnight in London, but Alex was a night owl. She dialled his number. He picked up on the third ring.

'Professor Stone,' he said warmly, a smile in his voice. 'How was the big date?'

Lara didn't speak. She had held it all together all day, but now, hearing Alex's voice, she could feel everything peeling apart.

'Are you okay?' Alex's jokiness was immediately replaced by concern.

'No,' she said, her voice so quiet it almost floated away.

She leaned against the trunk of an oak tree, her palm pressed against the rough bark. At the end of a branch, she could see the leaves curling and turning brown at their tips.

Everything's dying, she thought. Everything.

'Lar? Please speak to me. I'm here.'

Alex knew her too well. Even over sketchy reception, he still could tell something was wrong.

'It's…' she took a long breath. 'It's been a tough day.'

'What's happened?' His voice was soft and empathetic. How she wished she could feel his arms around her now.

'My colleague, my friend Harry, passed away last night.'

'That's the guy you went to the party with? Lar, I'm so sorry.'

'It's just a bit of a shock,' she said, wiping the tears from her face with her sleeve.

'What happened?'

'It looks like he took his life,' she said bleakly. It hurt to say it out loud.

'What can I do?' said Alex.

That made her feel better: Lara knew he meant it.

'There's one thing….'

She gave him a breakdown of the symposium and how she'd been tasked with organising it.

'You want me to come?' he said. No hesitation, no ifs or buts: Lara grinned, despite herself. Of course he would come.

'I know it's super last-minute,' she said. 'But if there is any way you could come, it would mean a lot, especially as I told Harry about you on Saturday and he knew your work. He even used it in his lectures.'

She was babbling, but she suddenly knew she needed Alex by her side. She was kick-ass reporter Lara Stone, but even superheroes needed someone in the Batcave.

'I'll be there,' said Alex decisively. 'Darius will moan, but whatever it takes, I'll come.'

'Thank you,' she said with a surge of affection and hung up. She looked up at the waving branches above her, instantly feeling better, calmer. Sometimes it was enough to know that someone was in your corner, that you weren't alone. Standing there, she could hear the singing from the campus. It didn't seem quite so sad somehow; something of Harry would live on in the symposium.

She started walking again, not wanting to go home, to face an empty house without any of the familiar comforts of home. Even in the dark, Benedon was impressive; every house seemed to have been sketched out by some romantic artist: clapboard siding, fold-back shutters and the little balconies on the roof they called 'widow's walks' where wives and mothers used to pace waiting for the return of the fleet. It was a town with melancholy built into its fabric. Lara had once been to Nantucket, the island community off the coast of Massachusetts, and it had the same time-warped feel. But pretty though it was, now Benedon was too quiet and lonely. Considering this was still mainstream America, you hardly ever saw cars on the streets; the campus had been laid out before Henry Ford's internal combustion revolution.

Lara supposed the town planners had expected students to ride a horse to classes; there were certainly still cast iron boot scrapers next to some of the exterior doorways. Lara began to feel the darkness pressing in. There were too many shadows and not enough people. She supposed all the pedestrians she would normally have passed were still on campus. Thinking about Harry again, Lara turned into Floral Street. Lara had convinced herself that she had been wandering aimlessly, but that was a lie. It was as if her regretful feet were taking her back to Harry's place.

Now, the street was empty: the rubberneckers, the emergency services, they were all gone. Lara walked slowly past the house: even the yellow police tape had gone. That was quick by any measure. The street was peaceful and still.

But… there was a light on in Harry's cottage. She blinked, unsure if it was an illusion or just wishful thinking. Had the past 24 hours just been a nightmare?

'It's not true,' she whispered aloud, then jumped as she saw a woman come into view, silhouetted in the light. Lara realised this was the first time she had considered that Harry might have a wife or a girlfriend. He'd asked her out, so she'd assumed that he was single, but she'd assumed a lot of things about Harry Robbins.

Suddenly Lara wanted to know; she felt the urge to go and knock on the door; but what would she say? 'Hello, I saw Harry yesterday, and now I want answers?'

Before she could untangle her thoughts, the front door opened, and a woman stepped out onto the porch. She was around fifty, with dark grey-streaked hair tied up in a bun. In a plaid shirt and jeans, there was something efficient and practical about her, possibly helped by the fact that she was carrying a wooden box of tools: Lara could see the handle of a saw poking out. Just then, the woman looked up, their eyes meeting.

'Oh, hello there, I…' stuttered Lara, aware she must look half-mad standing in the dark street. 'I was passing. My name is Lara Stone. I was a friend of Harry's.'

The woman hesitated before she spoke.

'I'm Marie. Harry's sister.'

Lara felt relief, then immediate sadness. He had a sister; another thing she didn't know about him. And another person with a broken heart.

'Marie, I'm so sorry,' said Lara awkwardly. 'I was with Harry last night. I wish I could have…' she trailed off, not entirely sure what she wanted to say, but the woman was looking at her with more interest.

'You were with Harry yesterday?'

Lara stepped forward into the light from the porch. At

least that way, Marie might see she wasn't some weird stalker.

'Yes, we went to the Dean's Labor Day party together.'

Marie put the toolbox on a wooden bench to the right of the door. She looked at Lara for a long moment.

'Do you want to come in?' she said, not waiting for a reply. Lara held her breath as she stepped inside Harry's house. It looked similar to her place – a one-storey cottage with a big opening living space, doors leading to a bedroom and bathroom and what looked like a study. There were wide French doors along the back wall, and a brass ceiling fan gave it the elegant feel of a gentlemen's club. Marie led Lara through to a small but chic kitchen area with brushed steel appliances and white metro tiles on the walls, expensive-looking bottles of wine lined up like sentries in front.

Marie turned to fill the coffee jug.

'Did you know that when something like this happens, the family has to clean up?' she asked, not looking at Lara. 'Once the forensics have done everything they need to do, the sheriff hands it back to you. And then you....'

She paused, head down. 'And then you've got to get down and scrub.'

'I can help,' offered Lara, but Marie shook her head.

'It's done,' she said. 'But it was tougher than I thought it was going to be. I'm a nurse; I see a lot of things. But I guess when it's your brother, things are different.'

Lara leaned across and gently took the pot from Marie.

'Here, let me make the coffee. At least I can do that.'

'It's fine.'

'No. I insist.'

Lara opened a cupboard above the shiny espresso machine and found a connoisseur's dream of coffee accessories and vacuum-sealed beans. Of course, Harry wouldn't be an instant coffee man. Happily, Lara knew her way around the space-age machine, having spent a weekend working as a barista for a 'real life' story a few years earlier. She set the whole thing going, then looked for cups. Next to the carefully stocked beans and filters, there was a shelf of coffee mugs; finally, Lara smiled. It was a mismatched collection of what were clearly favourites. An 'I've been to Yosemite' mug with the outline of a grizzly, a Boston Red Sox mug: World Series 2018 – presumably a good year – and, surprisingly, a chipped and stained 'property of New York Globe' mug. She took down two at random and poured Marie a cup.

'So you're British,' she said, sipping.

'I'm lecturing at the college this semester. I live in London usually. I only got to Benedon on Saturday.'

Marie leaned against the kitchen units, one hand massaging the other.

'So, you weren't dating Harry, then?' Marie's voice had a note of surprise.

'No,' said Lara with an embarrassed laugh. 'He was the first person I met here; he showed me around, then arranged to take me to the Dean's party on Monday. He was... kind.'

Marie gave a sad, knowing smile. 'Sounds like Harry. And how was he?' The last word disappeared in a sob, the flat of her hand pressing against her mouth as if to keep it in.

Lara felt terrible. Powerless to stem this woman's pain, powerless to help in any way. And worse, she didn't know what the woman wanted to hear. She went with the truth.

'I didn't know Harry, but he seemed happy. He was excited about the symposium, the lecture series he was arranging. We'd arranged to go to a restaurant in town after the Dean's party, but he left without saying goodbye. I didn't think anything was wrong. I assumed he left because... well, Ellie Campbell's father was there.'

'God, Ellie Campbell,' Marie said. 'That was a witch-hunt, a knee-jerk response to a stupid rumour. And it destroyed his career.'

'I heard they refused him tenure because of it.'

Marie scowled. 'Harry was so smart. Even as a kid, he was streets ahead in his classes, it was like his brain worked faster than everyone else's. Turning him down for tenure was their loss,' she said harshly, then seemed to realise what she had said. 'But now it's ours.'

Lara hesitated to ask because she didn't want to add to the woman's fragile emotional state, but she had to know.

'How did Harry take it? The tenure thing?'

'Just like Harry: he didn't like to show weakness to the outside world. But he was hurt, badly hurt. Benedon gave him a year to "find another situation" as if they were doing him a favour.'

She sighed. 'I know he'd been applying for job in newspapers, but he was finding it tough. According to Harry, they want cheap kids who'd trawl the internet and rehash stories on zero-hour contracts.'

Lara could understand that frustration. It was a depressingly familiar story. There were still a few experienced old hands at *The Chronicle* but more and more columnists were now online stars with copy as vacuous as their fictional lives, and any writers with interesting opinions were being quietly eased out, pre-empting any potential online backlash.

'Did Harry talk to you about Ellie Campbell?'

'Never mentioned her once,' said Marie. 'And we talked every week.' She shook her head, clearly mystified.

'When she died, everyone was pointing fingers at Harry, saying it was his fault. But Harry was hilariously indiscreet about his girlfriends – to me, at least. If he'd been seeing her, I'd have heard.'

'How lovely to have been so close,' said Lara with a hint

of envy. She'd never had that sort of family relationship. Her parents had died when she was young, and she'd been shunted off to live with her Uncle, Aunt and cousin Charlie, but the English boarding school system had put a swift end to any chance of developing a sibling relationship with Charlie.

'We probably shouldn't have been so close,' said Marie, picking up on the mood. 'I was fourteen when Harry was born, almost old enough to be his mum, but I saw him every month, and spoke on the phone whenever we could. He told me stuff, you know – too much sometimes, so I know that Ellie girl wasn't even his type. A rich, blonde, cookie-cutter WASP? Never. Harry liked clever brunettes.'

Lara felt the woman's incisive gaze on her. 'Like you,' she said.

Lara felt uncomfortable and turned away, concentrating instead on a framed photograph on the far side of the kitchen. She quickly realised it was Harry as a student, looking fresh-faced and preppy with his arm around an attractive woman – a younger version of Marie.

'Happier times,' said the woman.

Suddenly Lara felt as though she was intruding; she wasn't even sure why she had come inside – this was Marie's place now, somewhere still alive with her brother's memory. Lara was torn: she knew she should go, but she'd never get a better chance to gain some insight into Harry's life. She could see a desk and some bookshelves through a doorway to the left. It looked like a classic men's den with a leather wingback chair and abstract art on the walls.

'That's Harry's study?'

Marie raised a finger.

'You might not want to go in there. I scrubbed the wall, but I couldn't get it clean. Next time I'm in Target, I'll have to get some paint.'

Lara knew what she was saying, but still, she stepped inside, forcing herself to be professional, trying to picture Harry in the swivel office chair. Where had he kept the gun? she wondered. In his desk drawer? Had it been that easy for him, had he just reached in and... She stopped and frowned.

'Did the police take anything?' she asked, turning back towards Marie.

'Not that I can tell, although I haven't been here for a few weeks, so I couldn't be sure. I know they took some journals away because they asked permission, not that I had much choice in the matter.'

Lara looked at the desk. One thing was missing: a computer.

'Has the detective spoken to you?' asked Lara.

'Sarah Carter? Yes, I got the grilling this afternoon. She was very polite, but I felt I was being interrogated. If I didn't know better, she sounded like she was accusing me of something.'

Lara turned back.

'Accusing you of what?'

'I'm not sure, but she asked when I last saw Harry, whether I saw him last night. Luckily, I have an alibi: I'm a nurse at Brigham Hospital. I have about a hundred witnesses who can swear to my whereabouts.'

An alibi? That was a strange word, thought Lara. Why would Sarah Carter care about anyone's movements if this was a cut-and-dried suicide? Hadn't she said, 'We're not looking for anyone else? Lara gazed back towards Harry's desk. Marie saw her thinking.

'What's up?' she asked.

'Sorry,' said Lara. 'It's just that I'm British; we don't have guns, so I find it hard to imagine Harry owning one. That probably sounds naïve to you.'

'Not at all,' said Marie with feeling. 'I work in ER, and I wish we had the same regulations you have in England. Harry was the same: he was liberal, anti-NRA, and anti-anything to do with guns. But...'

She shook her head. 'Maybe he felt unsafe for some reason, but honestly, I'm staggered he would even have something like that in the *house*.' She spat out the last word as if she was angry, but then Marie let out a gulping cry and buried her face in her hands. Lara went over and put her arms around her, feeling better that she was there to console the woman. They stood that way for a while before Lara felt around in her bag to hand Marie a tissue.

'Thanks,' said Marie, taking a heaving breath. 'I think I've stayed here too long, but....' She didn't have to finish the sentence. When she left, it would be closing the door on Harry forever.

'Where are you going back to?'

'Lowell,' said Marie. Lara had never heard of it; then again, she didn't know this part of the world. Just Boston and Salem because she had read *The Crucible* in school.

'How far away is Lowell?'

'Just a couple of hours.'

Lara imagined the grief-stricken woman driving along the dark, winding freeway, eyes glassing with tears.

'Why don't you stay in Benedon tonight? You're welcome to stay at my place if you don't want to stay here. Or there are a couple of good hotels in town. I can call and make a reservation.'

Marie shook her head.

'That's good of you, but Harry's got a 15-year-old niece who's devastated; I've got to get back for her. It was nice meeting you, Lara. I'm glad Harry had people around him like you.'

'Like me?' she said, surprised.

‘People who cared about him. In the end, that’s all that matters, isn’t it?’

Marie barked out a laugh and blew her nose again.

‘Listen to me; I sound like James Stewart in *It’s A Wonderful Life*,’ she said. ‘It’s hokey, but there's some truth to it. “No man who has friends has wasted his life”, or whatever the quote was. Harry always had friends: that was the one thing he was good at.’

Lara waited out on the street as Marie locked up the house, then waved to her old station wagon, which beeped its horn as Marie indicated and turned the corner. Then she was gone.

Lara walked quickly back to Montrose Street. It was cold now, and the dark had a strange hollow echo Lara found unsettling. Lara picked up her pace; she’d been warned that the Vermont weather could be unpredictable in the Fall when the harsh winds from Newfoundland could send the mercury plummeting in minutes. She definitely hadn’t brought the right clothes, and besides, she didn’t like the slant of the shadows at this time of night. She practically ran up the path to number 47 and, in her haste to open the door, almost dropped her keys. Pushing inside, Lara tried to close it behind her.

‘Hey,’ she said; something was catching under the door jamb. A piece of paper. She bent and pulled it free. It was just a piece of folded white paper with two words written on it. *Harry knew.*

Chapter 13

Living with your mom sucked. That wouldn't be news to any teenager in America, thought Sarah, but it was much worse when you were a grown woman.

Today that was going to change. Sarah looked down at the forms on the kitchen table, the endless paperwork required for admission to Beauville care home. There were copies of her mother's birth certificate and driver's licence, a medical history, a list of current medications, proof of employment and income, and a declaration of Sarah's power of attorney. It reminded Sarah of the triplicate forms the desk sergeant used to book a felon into the station house lockup.

'Sarah!' She flinched as her mother called her from the bedroom. Sarah looked at the clock above the stove.

'Give me a minute, Mom!' she shouted back. Not that Colleen Carter had much grasp of time these days. If living with your mom sucked, watching her destroyed by dementia sucked even more. She looked down at the paperwork again. According to the brochure, Beauville was 'a residential care experience tailored to individual needs', but everyone involved knew what it was. It was a prison for old people, and no amount of carefully crafted marketing hooey could hide Sarah from the guilt.

Sarah picked up her pen and scribbled her signature at the bottom of the form. *There.* It was done. The moment she had been dreading had arrived.

'You've got to soldier on,' that's what her mother had always said whenever Sarah had found something tough. Don't whine, don't feel sorry for yourself, get on with it: an old-school approach to life where your expectation of happiness was tempered by the reality that some blows couldn't be avoided. Sarah didn't need anyone to tell her that the world could be brutal, she had seen enough of the dark side working vice and homicide in the big city, but at the same time, it was hard to watch. So damn hard.

Ding-dong.

Sarah frowned as the doorbell rang; she wasn't expecting any visitors. Beauville had offered to send their mini-bus to collect Colleen as part of a 'comprehensive pick-up and settling-in service' that involved taking new residents and 'small personal items up to two feet in diameter' to the care home, but Sarah had turned it down, not least because of the $500 fee.

She ran to the door and opened it—an unfamiliar woman, forty-something, dressed in a navy trouser suit and a fixed smile.

'Leanne Birch. Windsor Realtors. We have an appointment,' she said. The smile inched wider still. Sarah looked at her watch.

'The appointment was 8 o'clock *tonight,*' said Sarah feeling panicked.

'It's 8 am, I believe,' said Leanne, her expression becoming just a little more steely. Sarah hesitated, wondering who had made a mistake, but whatever; the real estate agent was here now. It was going to be more awkward than she had intended, but she had to get the ball rolling on this.

'Come in, come in,' sighed Sarah, waving her through.

'It's so cute,' said the realtor as she walked into the hallway.

Sarah tried for a smile; it was one way to describe the Carter family home. On a corner plot on the intersection of two quiet roads, the house was not grand compared to the beautiful, well-kept clapboard houses in Benedon or the other tonier towns in the county. Her mom's place was well-lived in and, truthfully, poorly maintained ever since Sarah's dad had passed away six years earlier. But look past the peeling window frames, the house had some strong selling points: original hardwood floors, two working fires and a good-sized garden full of mature plants and shrubs.

'When are you looking to move?' asked the realtor, her eyes always moving, surveying, assessing, no doubt already deciding on an asking price.

'As soon as possible,' said Sarah going into their kitchen. 'My mother is going into a care home.'

Leanne nodded. Sarah didn't need to spell out the objectives here.

Something had to pay for the Beauville care home, and a cop's salary, especially in a small-town backwater like Benedon, would not cut it.

'Sarah! Have I got a visitor?'

Slow, unsure footsteps came creaking up the stairs.

'My mom,' said Sarah apologetically. She hadn't wanted Colleen to see or hear any of this, hence arranging for the realtor to come that evening after her mom had safely moved to Beauville. 'This is a little delicate. Do you mind just waiting here?'

Sarah hurried out to meet her mother in the hall. In her day, Colleen Carter had been a vivacious and attractive woman, but the disease had withered her from the inside, draining the life force from her, drip by drip. Colleen was barely seventy-five but looked like a strong breeze would blow her away.

'Who is it?' said Colleen, peeping into the kitchen.

Sarah tensed; her mother was already on edge this morning. Sarah had tried to explain the reality to her again: she couldn't stay here and was moving into a new home. It hadn't gone well. Some days Colleen seemed to understand everything, but today wasn't one of those days.

'It's just a lady who wants to look at the house.'

Sarah expected outrage or tears, but Colleen went into the living room and sat in her chair by the television, lowering her tiny frame onto the brown velour cushion. It was as if Leanne was not there.

'Would you like a glass of water, Mom?'

'Sure, thank you, honey.'

Sarah quickly crossed to the kitchen and returned with a glass, waiting as her mother took it in her thin hand. Colleen's eyes stayed fixed on the blank TV screen.

'Do you want to watch something?'

'We can watch something together. When you've done your homework.'

Sarah smiled and touched her arm, then returned to find the realtor, who had disappeared from the kitchen. Sarah found her upstairs, peering into the closet in Sarah's bedroom.

'Is this the master?'

'This is my room, actually.'

It was only by looking at it through Leanne's eyes that Sarah could see that her old teenage bedroom must now look like the smartest space in the house. The week she'd moved in, Sarah had done her best to revamp it; a modern room for a modern woman, covering the yellow primrose walls of her past with fashionable chalky cream. She'd bought a new Nordic-style bed, some framed prints, and crisp white sheets that made her feel as if she was staying in a hotel, not returning to her mom's tired, sagging home.

'Three-bed, three bath, good street, nice aspect,' said Leanne pulling back the curtain to look outside. 'It's got potential. Yes, I think this should move quickly.'

Pouting her bright red lips, Leanne told Sarah her valuation. It was a decent six-figure number, but Sarah still felt her heart sink. It wouldn't last long.

'Fine,' she said, 'But on one condition....'

Her words were cut off by a crash coming from downstairs.

'Sarah! Sarah, here!'

Sarah took the stairs two steps at a time.

'Mom, what is it?' she called, rushing back into the lounge.

Colleen was standing, the velour cushion on the floor, her eyes wide – staring into the corner where shattered glass lay in sparkling pieces.

'It's here again!' Colleen hissed. 'Get it out of here; you know I can't stand the filthy things in the garden.'

'The cat?'

'Of *course* it's the cat digging up my roses again. Get it out, get it out!'

Suppressing a sigh, Sarah opened the French windows onto the yard and waited until her mother relaxed, her clenched fingers unfurling, the lines on her face relaxing. Sarah knew the drill by now. There had been no cat. Her mother had been seeing the phantom memory of Lupin, a stray tabby who would scratch at their back door begging for scraps decades before. It had been happening more and more recently, although this was the first time Colleen had thrown something. Broken glass aside, Sarah supposed it was a fairly benign delusion. The doctor had told her that people suffering from cerebral damage often had terrible visions of intruders, people stealing from them, and dead relatives coming back to settle scores. The human mind was a complex place, and dementia had the power to open some doors better left firmly locked. *Be grateful for small mercies*, Sarah told herself. *It's only a cat.*

Sarah put a reassuring hand on her mom's shoulder, ushering her back into the chair.

'You didn't need to throw the glass,' she said firmly. 'It was only Lupin.'

'But I turned around, and he was just there,' said Colleen, her voice retreating into a dramatic whisper. 'I can't have him sneaking through the doors and creeping up on me like that.'

'Well, he's gone now.'

Colleen looked up, a blank but untroubled smile on her face.

She had forgotten the cat. Lupin had disappeared as if he had never been there. Then Sarah stopped, a thought slipping into place like a lost piece of a puzzle.

And suddenly, Sarah could see it, unfolding like a movie in her head. Harry Robbins at his desk. Typing, reading, maybe some soft classical music playing in the background. He was busy, distracted, until he heard a noise – the noise of someone coming into the house through the French windows. Sarah turned as if she was Harry sitting in that expensive-looking swivel chair. Then she raised her hand and pointed a finger at the centre of her forehead.

'Well, I'll be damned,' she said.

Chapter 14

Eight thirty AM. Lara had only just set foot on campus when her phone began buzzing insistently. 'Dammit,' she muttered, pulling it out. Lara might have ignored it on any other day, but she knew this could be one of her potential symposium speakers calling her back.

'Lara Stone,' she said as brightly as she could. Lara didn't feel bright. She had been up half the night, first puzzling over the mysterious note pushed under her door – *what* did Harry know exactly? And who wanted her to know? – then, starved of sleep, Lara took advantage of her wide-eyed jet lag to email dozens of prospects who might fill the glaring gaps in the symposium's schedule.

'Lara, darling. How are you?'

Lara stopped and let out a silent scream. Darius Allen, editor-in-chief of the *Chronicle*. He hardly ever called her personally, and she couldn't remember him using a term of endearment such as 'darling'. Lara was immediately on guard.

'Darius. What a lovely surprise,' she said, knowing the ironic tone would be lost on Darius.

'Alex has been telling me all about your exciting adventures across the pond,' gushed Darius. 'Isn't Benedon just wonderful? When I was at Oxford, one of the girls on the Isis team was over from the college in her Junior year. Terrible business about that professor, mind you. I thought about running a small item in the foreign news section but felt it was too morbid. We went with the invasion of Bishkek instead.'

Lara wasn't sure whether she was supposed to comment on Darius's sharp editorial choice, but he ploughed on before she could speak.

'Talking of Alex,' said Darius. 'He mentioned that you'd invited him to speak at Benedon's media symposium.'

'That's right,' said Lara warily. 'I'm helping out with the programming. Alex's warzone experience is second to none, and the "Foreign Correspondence" module here at the college is popular.'

'Darling, that might well be, but you do know everyone wants to be the editor-in-chief.'

The penny dropped with an almost audible 'clunk'.

'Wait, you want to speak?' said Lara.

'I don't do many keynotes, as you know; don't have the time, however much they pester. But when Alex went into his spiel –inspiring the next generation of journalists, yadda, yadda – I thought, Darius, you have to do this.'

Lara's heart sank. Despite the tragic circumstances, Lara had been enjoying the distraction of organising the conference and was looking forward to spending time with Alex, but to have to babysit a diva like Darius? It didn't bear thinking about.

'Darius, I'd love you to speak,' she said, 'But it's such short notice, and with Alex away too, I'm worried whether there will be enough senior management at the office?'

'Bless you, Lara, still thinking about the smooth running of your alma mater,' said Darius indulgently. 'No, Ed and

Toby are perfectly capable of manning the ship for a couple of days. Besides, I can fly in on Saturday and then get the red-eye out on Sunday evening. I can even do the closing speech and still catch the 10 pm out of Logan.'

'You do know our budget is very limited,' said Lara, already knowing it was hopeless trying to divert him.

'Airmiles can cover the flight, and seeing as it's you, we can waive my speaking fee just this once, so you'll be saving a substantial amount of money there....'

As he chattered on unabated, Lara closed her eyes. It was one of Darius's unique talents, asking for something he wanted and making it seem like he was doing you a favour. Clearly, when he'd heard that Alex was going to speak, Darius couldn't stand to let his deputy have all the glory. Lara knew there was no point in appealing to logic; the only hope was to work on Darius's vanity.

'Darius, can I be frank?' said Lara. 'I think you're too big for this.'

That stopped him.

'You do?'

'You're one of the most famous editors in the world.'

'Well, yes...'

'My point is that I fear your presence may over-balance the programme. It's like having Pele turn up at a kids' 5-a-side football game.'

There was an audible intake of breath.

'I can see that...' he said. The man's ego was monstrous.

'Lesser speakers will be in your shadow,' pressed Lara.

'But how are they to learn?' he interrupted. 'If they never see the best, how can they raise their game? No, I appreciate you thinking of the other speakers, but I'm thinking of the *students*. Moulding young minds is my priority; it always has been. And do you know that Simon Routledge got an MBE for that half-arsed equality foundation he set up? Such cobblers...'

So that was it. Darius was angling for letters after his name and wanted to use the symposium to launch his campaign for a knighthood. Well, it would be painful to have him at Benedon, Lara consoled herself that Darius Allen was second to none on self-publicity. Crowing about his keynote triumph on social media would be fantastic PR for the event – and Lara wanted it to be a success for Harry's sake.

'I'll send you the details,' she sighed.

'Splendid. And tell my driver I'll be bringing a trunk.'

He hung up, and Lara burst out laughing. It was either that or cry.

* * *

The library was magnificent, a triumph of classicism – or neo-classicism- as the building couldn't have been more than 50 or 60 years old. Even so, it was carved from white stone with Corinthian columns and wide steps leading up to double doors with the words 'Sinclair Campbell Library' carved above. Inside, it was all hushed calm: wood-panelled walls and polished shelves, but the eye was naturally drawn to the centre of the building and the staircase.

Lara took a sharp breath as she looked up towards the domed roof. The stairs coiled up through the building like a snake, a bone-white spiral giving out onto all five floors. It reminded Lara of the Guggenheim Museum in New York. It was designed to impress you not only with its beauty but also to be a physical manifestation of power. Well, it was working.

Lara had headed to the library as soon as she could, but the morning had been taken up twisting arms and finalising details for the symposium. To her surprise, the story of Harry's death had spread in media circles, and it had been relatively easy to flesh out the schedule, landing two big names, an editor from *The New Yorker* and a columnist from a cutting-edge tech magazine *Platform* who would chair a debate about spanning the gap between print and digital: Lara was looking forward to that one.

But Lara knew she had something else to do. She couldn't say why exactly, but even before the note had been pushed under her door, something felt wrong about the whole thing. Harry's sudden exit from the party, Sarah Carter's 'alibi' questions, and Marie's baffled reaction to the gun. Each taken on their own, they were nothing, inconsequential. But together, they formed an itch at the back of Lara's mind that she just needed to scratch. The library seemed to be the best place to start, as it was here that it had all started to go wrong with the death of Ellie Campbell.

'Pretty impressive, huh?'

Lara turned to look into a pair of brown eyes peering out from under a dark fringe.

'Brian?' she said. The student from her lecture the previous day. He was standing there awkwardly; an overloaded courier bag slung over one shoulder.

'Hey, congratulations on the scoop,' said Lara. 'Excellent instincts snapping those pictures – but sending them off to the *Post*?'

She circled her thumb and forefinger in the 'OK' sign. 'That was smart.'

'Well, you did say being first is everything.'

'I did.'

Lara didn't point out that Brian had almost certainly sent his pictures of the scene outside Harry's *before* her lecture. But that only showed that Brian Silvinski had all the right instincts to become a fine journalist.

'Anyway, I enjoyed the lecture yesterday; we all did,' he said. 'Although... I saw the Dean listening in. Hope everything was okay.'

Lara smiled. Brian would be an excellent journalist: he hadn't missed that detail either.

'The Dean was just checking in on us all,' she said noncommittally.

'But what's happened to our lecture tomorrow? We got a note to say they were being rescheduled.'

So that was it: the students had assumed that Lara Stone had already been relieved of her duties.

'No, I've been just pulled off tutorials and talks until next week because I've taken over organising the symposium.'

Brian smiled with apparent relief.

'Cool. So it's still going ahead? It's good that the Prof's thing will live on. Plus, you know, I'll be networking like hell.'

Lara held up a finger.

'Hey, that's a great idea. I should add a meet-and-greet thing for the speakers and the students.'

'Don't tell anyone else, though,' he said with a wink. 'Don't want the others getting in on my action.'

'Are you a first or second-year Brian?'

'Second year.'

'Have you started looking for jobs yet?'

'Sure. I did a great internship with the *Sun-Herald* over Christmas.'

'Really? That's impressive.'

Brian laughed.

'Nothing like you, chief. I googled your career – now that's impressive.'

Lara shrugged modestly.

'I had an easy start. My family is in the industry.'

Brian shook his head.

'Everyone needs a break, sure. But you succeeded because you're an amazing reporter.'

Lara was grateful for his words, but Brian was in the minority. No matter how many front-page stories she wrote or awards she won, there were always whispers of nepotism. Lara Stone was part of an elite newspaper dynasty: her father had been one of the great editors of the Eighties, and her uncle was the Chairman of Avery Media. People assumed Lara had strolled into the *Chronicle*, whereas in reality, the 'jobs for the boys' accusations had worked against her, and Lara had needed to fight twice as hard to climb the career ladder.

She looked up towards the library stairs again. Would it have been the same for Eleanor Campbell, she wondered? Or would her father, Arthur have just handed her the keys to the kingdom?

Brian followed her gaze. 'You know about it, the accident last year?'

Lara nodded.

'I can't walk past without thinking about it,' said Brian. 'I used to love that top floor. You can see the whole county from up there, but not many students go there now, knowing how easy it is to fall.'

Lara looked up towards the top floor: sunlight shone down into the central shaft, dust motes twinkling. God, it was high. She forced herself to look at the marble floor beneath her feet, half-expecting some terrible stain. There was nothing to mark the spot, but standing there, Lara was still overcome with sadness. Right here where she fell, it didn't seem to matter whether Eleanor Campbell had been heartbroken or depressed or anything else. The simple, awful fact was that her life had ended here – a terrible, tragic full-stop.

'Did you know Eleanor?'

Brian shook his head.

'No, not my crowd, but I see her brother Brandon in the gym sometimes.'

'Her brother is at the college?' said Lara in surprise.

'Senior year. Spanish Studies, although I think he spends most of his time on the football pitch. Anyway...'

Brian thrust something at her: a paper he'd pulled from the bag on his shoulder.

'What's this?'

'*The Ivy*, the Benedon student paper. Thought you could mark it for us.'

Lara looked down at the front page: Campus Mourns at Midnight Vigil.

'That was fast.'

'No flies on us, coach.'

'Us?'

'Well, me.' Brian gave an ironic half-bow. 'I'm the editor, although that might be overstating it. I'm also writer, designer, copy-editor and the dude hitting the phones trying to persuade Kelly's Farm Feed to advertise. We're a little short-staffed.'

'In that case, I'm even more impressed.'

Brian grinned and dumped his pile of papers onto a table near the entrance.

'Maybe wait until you've read it,' he said.

She watched Brian leave, then took the stairs to the first floor and then the second, marvelling at the endless rows of neatly stacked books. Words had always been important to her; how could they not when her father and uncle were both newspapermen? But books had become Lara's sanctuary after her parent's death in a boating accident. She'd gone to live with her uncle at his vast Cotswolds estate, where she would sneak into Nicholas's study and borrow from his collection: Dickens, Christie, Updike, Conrad; anything escapist, anything with a story where all the threads tied up at the end. Not like real life, where things were messy and unknowable. Lara stopped at a shelf and took out a book at random: *Smile or Die, A History of Self-Help*. Interesting. She flipped to the introduction and began reading, then clapped it shut. *Concentrate,* she scolded herself. You're not here for fun.

She took the stairs, climbing higher and higher until she finally reached the top floor. It was a circular space with a domed glass ceiling. The whole area was like a mezzanine with the middle scooped out, like a polo mint.

The walls were lined with leather-bound books with thick yellowing pages – Lara had done her homework and knew that the oldest volumes were kept up here. There were just a couple of students here, squirrelled away in one of the booths that punctuated the rows of shelving. It was flooded with light up here, but as Lara approached the edge, she could imagine how dark and eerie it would have been when Ellie Campbell died. She gripped the rail as she peered down to the ground floor. *Damn.* No one could have survived that fall.

Focus. What was she looking for up here? What indeed? Lara desperately wanted to follow the thread of that mystery note: 'Harry Knew'. Putting aside whatever knowledge Harry supposedly had, Lara was just as interested in who had sent the message. What did *they* know, and why did they want Lara involved? Sadly, she had zero information to go on, so in Lara's experience, it was always best to start with the background. Something was happening in Benedon, that was clear – and as Lizzy had pointed out, this library seemed to have a significant role in the story. Lara looked around at the shelves. Somewhere in here, there was an answer. But what was the question?

Lara walked back down the stairs and approached the librarian's desk; a studious-looking lady looked up.

'Do you have an archive of local papers here?'

'We keep the last three months of newspapers in physical form', said the woman nodding towards a shelf of leather folders. 'If you want anything further back, we can set you up on the microfiche. I can show you how it works.'

'Oh, I know how it works,' smiled Lara. 'I seemed to spend half of my life on these things back in London.'

'Really? In London?' said the woman. 'I thought we were the only ones who hadn't gone fully digital.'

'I rather like microfiches.'

'Between you and me, I think the old ways are sometimes the best.'

After a brief refresher on how to use the machine – essentially a giant magnifying glass built to read floppy celluloid sheets – Lara settled down with a box of them, each sheet holding about 100 pages scanned from *The Benedon Examiner*.

Lara agreed with the librarian that some institutions had been too hasty to get rid of microfiches in the name of technological advancement. Google had its place, and most media outlets had comprehensive digital archives of all their stories, accessible at the push of a button. But microforms and microfiches allowed you to read and see stories just like they had been printed on the day of release. It allowed you to see a story in context, side-by-side with all the other news. Was it a big story or a small story? Had it been buried amongst bigger news, or did it have an impact?

Lara tried to concentrate as the headlines from the county whirled past. 'Council funds new sports field: pictures', 'Student festival brings art show', 'Crop report: early spring announced'.

Lara skimmed back through the dates until, finally, she

came across the *Examiner*'s front page for the day after Ellie died.

'Local Girl Tragedy: Heartbreak For Family. No one needed telling which family.

Tuesday PM: The body of a young woman was discovered in the Sinclair Campbell Library. The victim was named Eleanor Cordelia Campbell, 22, a student at Benedon College. Benedon PD was called to the campus at 9.55 PM along with emergency service personnel who attended to the victim at the scene but were unable to revive her. Ms Campbell was declared deceased at the Mercy Hospital later that night.

'A tragic incident,' said Sheriff Roscoe. 'Our thoughts are with the family.'

It was workmanlike reporting; although possibly they were being extra careful, given Ellie's identity and the high chance of upsetting powerful people. Lara flipped on through the subsequent issues, but surprisingly there was almost no coverage. Just one follow-up a week later at the bottom of an 'any other news' column.

Benedon PD declare tragic library incident closed.

Detective Glenn Schultz says it was an isolated incident and they are 'not looking for anyone else in relation to the death of Benedon College student Eleanor Campbell.'

Then, a week after that:

. . .

A memorial service was held Sunday for Eleanor Campbell, beloved daughter of Arthur and Eliza Campbell, at the St. Saviours church on the Benedon campus. The Dean and Damian O'Rourke, Mayor of Boston, were among the mourners.

Lara scanned back and forth either side of the date, but that was all she could find. There had been no news features, no comment and no report on any inquest; perhaps there hadn't been one.

Lara leaned back in her chair, massaging her neck.

'Didn't find what you were looking for?'

The librarian who had helped her pushed a cart of books past.

'Is it that obvious?'

The woman smiled kindly.

'Anything I can help with?'

Lara glanced around to check that they weren't overheard.

'I wanted some background on the Campbell family.'

'Ah. I did wonder why you wanted the February archives,'

There was a flicker of disapproval as she said it.

'I'm Lara Stone, by the way,' she said quickly, holding up her ID laminate. 'I'm the new visiting fellow at the journalism school.'

The librarian's expression changed again—this time to sadness.

'Poor Mr Robbins,' she said. 'The department must be devastated.'

Lara nodded.

'It's a difficult time for everyone.'

'I'm Marjorie Clark, chief librarian,' said the older

woman, extending a hand. 'I'm always glad to meet a new fellow. Last year we had guests from Delhi, Rio, Tokyo and Rome. I don't travel as much as I used to, but meeting the fellows is a wonderful way to learn about the world.'

She raised an eyebrow at Lara. 'Tea?' she asked.

'Tea would be lovely.'

Lara followed the woman down to a small office area and watched with amazement as she produced a box of Yorkshire Tea.

'You make real tea?'

'I spent a year on secondment to the British Library,' said Marjorie. 'We all used to eat in Frank's Caff around the corner on Gray's Inn Road. I've been trying to replicate Frank's tea ever since.'

Lara smiled to herself, another lesson for her journalism students: never judge a book by its cover.

'I suppose you've been up to the top floor,' said Marjorie, clicking on a kettle. 'Most students go to look, but not many stay up there. There's been talk of raising that railing; it hasn't happened yet.'

'Why is this place called the Sinclair Campbell library?' Asked Lara.

'Because that's who paid for it,' said Marjorie simply, taking a biscuit from a pack and placing it on the side of a saucer. 'A gift to the college from the founder of the Campbell empire.'

Lara nodded. She knew something about philanthropy; her own family was involved. Her Aunt Olivia especially liked nothing better than writing cheques to have her name appear on brass plaques or to secure places on an influential charity board or committee. In Lara's view, it was less about philanthropy and more about status and social positioning. In some cases, it was even about immortality: the prestigious music venue Carnegie Hall in New York was donated to the city by steel tycoon Andrew Carnegie, his name living on long after his death. She expected more than an element of that with the Campbell library.

'Where did the money come from?'

'They make things. Building materials, lubricants, chemicals, synthetic dyes, cosmetic ingredients. Nothing particularly glamorous but things which quietly make an awful lot of money,' said Marjorie, reducing her voice to a whisper.

'But at least they do good things with it,' she added. 'The Campbells have always had a reputation as a good employer and, as capitalists go, they are genuinely philanthropic.'

'The library, you mean?'

'Not just the library. They built health clinics and helped out workers with housing and welfare long before anyone had invented corporate public relations. I'm talking back in the forties when it would have hurt them financially – but they still did it.'

Interesting, thought Lara. A rich corporation with a selfless social agenda? Now that would be news.

'So, did you know Eleanor?'

Marjorie sipped her tea and shook her head.

'It's a library; we like silence, so you don't get to chat with the students. But she came to the library a lot. More so in those last few weeks. She spent many, many hours alone in those stacks. I thought it was odd because she usually came in with the shiny people.'

'The shiny people?'

'The beautiful crowd. Lately, they think it's cool to look clever.'

Lara sat forward.

'Did you ever see Eleanor in the library with Professor Robbins?'

'You mean, do I believe the rumours?'

Lara let her silence answer the question.

'The answer is no. No, I never saw them together. And no, I don't believe Harry Robbins was the sort to have an affair with a student.'

Lara nodded, wanting to ask more, wanting to know why Marjorie was so sure. But she didn't want to alienate the woman and reminded herself that she was just here for background. All she knew was that things didn't quite fit.

'Any idea what Ellie was studying all that time?' Lara thought of the neat labels above the shelves. That at least might give Lara a sense of whether Ellie had been simply doing her degree assignments or whether she had been looking at something else. Something to do with her story.

'Do you remember which section she was in?'

'Sorry, no. As I say, as long as they're quiet, we don't pay attention to where they go.'

Disappointment must have shown on Lara's face.

'What's wrong?' asked the librarian.

'It's just that I spoke to Harry the weekend before he died, and he told me Ellie was working on something important. Something significant.'

Marjorie put down her cup.

'There is one way to find out what she was doing.'

She turned to a computer on a corner desk. The old-fashioned monitor was cluttered with a pot of pens, a framed photo of three small children and a bright green pottery cat. Lara stood behind Marjorie, watching as a list of titles came up on the screen.

'What's this?'

'The books Eleanor Campbell checked out of the library.'

Lara's eyes opened wide.

'Isn't this... private?'

'Oh yes,' said Marjorie turning to her. 'Privacy is one of the principles librarians hold most dear. We believe anyone should be free to read anything they want. We took on the government over it,' she added with pride.

'You did?'

'Oh yes, back in the 1960s, the FBI began monitoring reading habits after they discovered Lee Harvey Oswald had checked out a book about a guy who assassinated a senator. It was an outrageous affront to civil liberties and free speech, so the librarians of America reacted by destroying borrowing records straight after the books were returned.'

Lara looked at Marjorie, grasping the point.

'But these are the books Ellie borrowed before she died. They were never returned.'

Marjorie frowned at the anomaly. 'I doubt they're coming back now. Shame.' She hovered a finger over a key.

'I'll clear the record – it's the least I can do for that poor girl.'

'No, don't!' said Lara, turning back to the screen, trying to read the titles of the books, but it blinked off. Just then, there was a mechanical grinding sound. Marjorie reached across to a printer, then looking meaningfully at Lara, dropped the print-out of Eleanor Campbell's reading list into the wastepaper basket.

'Whoops,' she said. 'Oh well, I imagine someone will come and clear that away soon.'

Then she turned her back on Lara and walked away, back onto the library floor.

Chapter 15

D*amn. I need coffee.* Sarah rubbed her eyes and looked down at the map. Hemsley, next exit, assuming she hadn't gone completely delirious. Sarah felt like she had been driving all night. She had been on the road less than an hour, but after the intense morning, settling her mom into Beauville, Sarah felt it was midnight, not midday.

The guilt hit her the moment she had left the nursing home. Sarah had slipped off without even saying a proper goodbye, telling herself it was best that way. Her mother had gone to look around the rose gardens with Eileen, another new joiner at Beauville, and the two had seemed quite happy with their random, disjointed conversation about birds, cars and the actor Elliot Gould. The care home manager had indicated that it might be a good time to leave, but as soon as she was on the road to Hemsley, Sarah couldn't shake the feeling that she was a terrible daughter for abandoning her mother like that.

'Stop it,' she told herself out loud, determined not to let herself get maudlin. This was for the best. Moving back to Benedon was only meant to be temporary, and working such long hours, Sarah couldn't look after her mother's needs. Colleen had been lucky to secure a place at Beauville, having been waiting for a spot to come up for months. 'Like gold dust', the manager had said.

Sarah turned at the next intersection, ducking her head to look at the buildings. Hemsley was five times the size of Benedon, but what it had gained in girth, it lost on style. Sure, they had a small business district with eight-storey office blocks, but compared to the perfectly formed grandeur of the campus, their county cousins looked boxy and cheap. Where Hemsley did score, however, was the St John's Hospital, a state-of-the-art complex covering most of the west of the town. If you got sick in Benedon, this was where you came. It was also where the county medical examiner had set up their local outpost; it was why Sarah had come. She pulled into the underground car park and left the cruiser in the reserved section: there had to be some perks for being a cop. She followed the signs to the mortuary. In the basement: no big surprise.

Sarah tapped on the glass door and held up her badge; a silver-haired woman in a white coat looked up and buzzed her in.

'Detective Carter, come on in,' said the woman. 'I'm Annie Campion, the assistant medical examiner. We haven't met before, have we?'

'No, I only came to the county a few months ago.'

'That explains it. Besides, we don't get a whole lot of business from your part of the world.'

That much was true. Sarah had re-checked the records, and there hadn't been a genuinely suspicious death in Benedon in nearly a decade. Certain fatalities – gunshot, puncture wound, poison – would trigger an autopsy, but only if the local law enforcement felt it was justified. And while there had been firearms-related deaths in Benedon, they had all been hunting accidents. It seemed the college town was as peaceful as it looked. Most of the time, anyway. Annie directed Sarah to a chair.

'Now, how can I help? It's rare I get a visit in person from a detective.'

Sarah hesitated. It was a risk sharing sensitive information with a stranger, not to mention a huge deviation from department protocol. For all she knew, Annie Campion could be best buddies with Sarah's boss Sheriff Roscoe, who would certainly be furious if he knew Sarah was here. But then Sarah desperately needed another pair of eyes; someone detached from the politics of the college. She took a breath.

'I'm here about Professor Harold Robbins.'

Annie nodded. 'Ah, yes. Sad business.'

'Yes, it was. And I wanted to ask your opinion on a couple of things?'

'Really? I got the impression Roscoe thought this was pretty straightforward.' The older woman threw Sarah a conspirator's smile. 'Of course, he always says that. You think differently, huh?'

'There's nothing cut and dried,' said Sarah. 'But I wanted to talk it through with you, see if it all adds up.'

'Second opinion, hmm? Well, that's what we're here for.'

Annie pulled out her laptop and opened a file.

'I've got another meeting in twenty minutes, so I can't show you the body, but I should have enough on here to talk you through it all.'

Annie bent forward, peering at the screen as she opened a set of images: photos from Harry's study and close-ups of the body.

'Cause of death GSW. Single shot, centre forehead... horizontal trajectory, exit rear centre,' she murmured.

She clicked on another image. 'Blood spatter corresponds as does bone fragmentation... bullet traverses....' She looked at Sarah. 'Did you find the bullet?'

'Buried in the wall. Calibre fitted the gun.'

'Gun left at the scene?'

'Yes, on the floor, right-hand side of the chair.'

Annie nodded and began to zoom in on the shots of Harry's face, concentrating on the area around the bullet hole. Sarah didn't consider herself squeamish, but it was still hard to look. The only thing that made it tolerable was that it stopped looking like a person after a while.

'Sheriff Roscoe believes this was self-inflicted. I'm guessing you don't share his view.'

'It's my job to consider everything,' said Sarah, still looking at the images. Finally, Annie sat back, lacing her hands behind her neck.

'Okay, first of all, I'm guessing you want to know about the placement of the wound.'

Annie *was* sharp. She had focused on the thing that had been bothering Sarah the most. Why would Harry shoot himself right in the centre of his head?

'Yes, don't most suicides shoot themselves here,' said Sarah, pointing to the side of her head.

'That's statistically correct, yes,' said Annie. 'But we still see all kinds of unusual things. Shooting themselves in the heart, blowing a leg off with a shotgun. When people are in such emotional despair, ...' She raised both hands in an 'anything can happen' gesture.

Annie looked back at the photos.

'I'd be more concerned about the distance.'

'The distance?'

'In gunshot suicides, we usually see contact wounds.' Annie used her pen as a gun barrel, pressing it against her temple. 'They are often determined and don't want to miss. In a contact wound, you would see more soot and gunpowder residue around the wound.' She used the pen to touch the screen. 'This definitely wasn't contact or close range. The muzzle didn't touch the skin.'

Sarah sat forward, feeling that she was onto something.

'How far away was the gun?'

Annie tapped a pencil against the desk.

'We can approximate from the stippling.'

'Stippling?'

'The pattern of soot or gunpowder residue around a wound. Judging from that, I'd say between 12 and 30 inches from the body.'

'But why would Harry Robbins do that?' asked Sarah. 'I mean, why hold the gun so far away?'

Annie shrugged.

'Now you're into psychology, detective, not my field. But I suppose if the victim wasn't sure – shaky – he could have used two hands to steady himself, pointing the gun back towards the face. That might also explain the central entry wound.'

Annie looked at Sarah, examining her face. 'You're considering homicide?'

Sarah liked how the woman cut straight to the chase. 'I just want to know if it's possible.'

Annie laughed. She had soft grey eyes lined at the corners. 'When you've done this job as long as I have, you know that anything is possible.'

Slowly, Sarah recounted the revelation she'd had sitting with her mother. She re-enacted the scenario, which had Harry Robbins sitting at his desk, hearing a noise behind him, turning around in his chair and... bang. She was relieved to see Annie Campion nodding thoughtfully.

'It's plausible,' she said. 'What are forensics saying?'

Sarah hadn't had their report yet. When the assumption was suicide, you weren't a high priority: no flight risk.

'No results yet, and there were no witnesses. Late at night; no one heard or saw anything.'

'So, what makes you think this could be homicide?'

What was Sarah supposed to say? An unlocked French door, a theory spinning off a dementia patient's hallucination. It sounded thin. Very thin.

'A hunch,' she said honestly. 'No real evidence.'

'Well, I would work on that,' said the older woman not unkindly. 'And as quickly as you can.'

'Quickly? Why?'

'Because if an intruder shot Professor Robbins, single shot to the head, no witnesses, zero evidence left at the scene, that sounds like someone very efficient and very motivated.'

Despite herself, Sarah felt her stomach drop.

'Benedon's your town, Detective,' said Annie, closing her laptop. 'But I wouldn't want someone like that running around if it were me. Especially if he – or she – gets the idea that you are out there looking for them.'

Chapter 16

The college chapel was the highest point of the campus, even taller than the library tower. Lara stopped at the bottom of the path, taking a moment to look up past the big clock up to the spire, a single finger pointing to the heavens, which today were a vague pastel blue, washed with fish scale clouds.

Lara blinked hard. Her eyes were dry and scratchy from staring at a computer screen for most of the day, helping Doug go through Harry's notes for the Benedon Symposium. Considering Harry had been doing all the symposium organisation and administration himself in just a few weeks, he had done a brilliant job, but there was still much to be done. Lara had spent hours confirming travel arrangements, liaising with speakers in four countries, and ensuring Darius had a suitably grand suite at the nearest hotel. Dimly, Lara was aware she might be using all this activity to avoid thinking about how she felt, but whenever she was working, she couldn't stop her mind from drifting back to Harry and what had happened to him. Lara pushed open the big wooden doors and stepped inside the chapel.

'Hello? Father Vernon?' Her voice sounded hollow

inside the stone walls, and she suppressed a shiver. Lara didn't like churches, never had, not since her parents' funeral, aged twelve. Her Uncle Nicholas had insisted she sit in the front pew, three paces from the twin coffins: 'show the world you're strong, Lara,' he'd said. But Lara hadn't felt strong; she had felt bereft, crushed like an earwig under a heel. She had wanted to throw herself on those coffins and scream out her grief. Instead, she had listened mute while the vicar spouted his platitudes, and then the next month, she'd been shipped off to boarding school. It didn't take a psychiatrist to join the dots and work out why she now felt unsettled. Lara walked down the aisle, the heels of her boots tapping against the flagstones.

There was no denying that churches were haunting places, all those tombs, cloisters and dark shadows. *Blind spots*, thought Lara. Just like Harry's story. Everything seemed to be out in the open, but there was so much missing from the picture; pieces of the jigsaw that were not yet out of the box.

Harry's death hadn't just upset her – it had troubled her. Harry owned a gun, yet his sister Marie had been adamant that he hated the things: he'd died alone at home, yet the detective was looking for alibis: and Ellie Campbell had been researching something in secret, something she had presumably shared with Harry. That was the problem. Lara didn't have the full story about anything.

It was why she was here. Father Vernon Bowen had been Harry's best friend. Surely his closest confidant could fill in some of the blanks?

She looked up as she heard footsteps.

'Father?'

Despite his height, Vernon moved with the grace of a big cat. He looked more like a campus athlete than a chaplain, but his handsome face was creased in a frown.

'Lara?' He said with a note of surprise.

'Yes, we met at the Dean's party.'

'Of course, I remember. You were with Harry.'

'Yes,' she said, her voice thick.

Without hesitation, Vernon stepped forward and put his arms around her.

'Come on, come through to the vestry,' said Vernon, leading Lara through an arched doorway. Lara had been expecting to step into a room just like the church: grey stone walls and slate floors; instead she stepped into a cosy lounge: carpet on the floor, soft pink paintwork and a couple of squashy sofas facing a fire.

'This is nice,' said Lara, immediately more at ease.

'I try to make it welcoming,' he said, sitting down opposite Lara. 'The chapel can be chilly in the winter. I've always ensured the students feel comfortable coming to the chapel 24-7. Kids tend to have their biggest crises in the middle of the night.'

'Do they?'

'Sure. Poor romantic choices, and unfinished term papers. Too much vodka, that's the big one.'

Lara smiled as she thought back to her student days, dive bars in Soho, dancing at the Union, and cocktail parties back at her Fleet St apartment. Vodka cranberries; she used to love those.

The priest leant forward.

'How are you, Lara?'

She knew what he was saying. How are you coping with Harry's death? Instead, she started telling him about the Symposium and how they had people flying in from all around the world for it.

'I didn't ask how the faculty was,' said Vernon kindly. 'I asked about you.'

'Well, I came here to talk about Harry,' she said. 'I want to talk about Harry.'

She felt her voice shudder. All the emotion she had been trying to hold in for the past 24 hours felt ready to burst out into the open.

Lara wasn't religious, wasn't Catholic, and hadn't ever taken confession, but right now, she felt as if she could tell Vernon anything.

'Good speech yesterday. At the vigil,' she said.

'Was it? I can't even remember what I said. You know you train for this sort of thing. Funerals, counselling. But nothing prepares you for when it's personal.'

Lara nodded.

'You knew Harry better than anyone. Was he depressed?'

Vernon let out a long breath.

'Not to my knowledge, not in the way you mean anyway, although that whole thing with Eleanor Campbell was a dark time, certainly.'

'I heard a lot of people blamed him.'

'Yes, they did. I guess people wanted to make sense of it and pointed the finger at Harry.'

That was what she had told Harry herself when the girl at the bar had called him a murderer.

'Did he blame himself for her death?'

Vernon rubbed one of his knuckles with his fingertips.

'He was devastated when she died, certainly. Harry cared about the students and spent some time mentoring Ellie in her last weeks. But blame himself? I'm not sure.'

'So, they weren't having an affair?'

'He said he wasn't,' said Vernon, his gaze steady. 'And I believe him.'

Lara couldn't imagine anyone lying to a priest, particularly this one.

'His sister said that Ellie wasn't his type,' she said with a hint of relief. Vernon smiled.

'And I'm not sure Harry was Ellie's type either.'

'You knew her?'

'A little. She sang in the choir in her first couple of years at Benedon. I'd often see her at a service.'

Lara was trying to picture it all. Back in the investigations room of the *Chronicle* she had a huge whiteboard on which she would pin pictures of suspects and players, maps, photos and hastily written notes. She would build the world she was investigating. Lara wasn't sure how Ellie Campbell's death was connected to Harry's, but she felt sure that there was some causal effect somewhere. If she wanted to make sense of Harry's death, she had to understand why Ellie died.

'Was Ellie in good health?'

Vernon looked puzzled.

'You said you knew her a little bit. Had she been to the doctor? Was she ill or worried about getting ill?'

Vernon still looked perplexed.

'I'm the college priest, not the campus physician. Why – do you think she was?'

Ellie's lending record at the library revealed she had a stack of medical books on loan. She wasn't sure if it was relevant, but as an experienced journalist, Lara found that if you poked around long enough, something would dislodge and help more of a picture come into view.

'It seems Ellie was interested in oncology,' said Lara. 'The study of cancer. I wondered if she was ill or if anyone in her family was.'

'No, not that I'm aware of.'

Lara felt her shoulders sag. She knew she had pinned too much hope on coming here.

'I just don't understand it, Vernon,' she said. 'We'd

planned to go out. It felt like a date; I thought Harry was excited about it.'

'Don't torture yourself, Lara,' said the priest. 'I feel the same way. Harry was fine at the party. And then he wasn't – and I don't know why.'

Lara thought back: how Harry's hand had brushed against hers as they walked down Floral Street, how he had excitedly told her about the cocktail menu at Plymouth Rock and the gin he liked from a local distillery on the other side of Finger Lake. Did his mood change once they'd got to the Dean's house? She couldn't remember.

'It must have been so hard for him at the party,' she sighed. 'I could tell he didn't want to go, but I persuaded him to come. I didn't know he'd been refused tenure.'

'I thought he was over all that,' said Vernon, his voice low.

'Harry was certainly upset when he was passed over for tenure. It was the injustice of it that bothered him the most. Harry always had such a strong sense of fair play. Ros Davies had said he could stay another academic year while finding another position, but at first, Harry just wanted to leave Benedon. But then, over summer, we went kayaking together in the Adirondacks, and he changed his mind.'

'You went canoeing together?' said Lara in surprise.

'Kayaks,' he said with a smile. 'It's different.'

It was hard to imagine a priest on holiday. Then again, she guessed that the clergy might need regular breaks more than most. Weddings aside, you often dealt with the bad parts of life: illness, loss, death, holding people together just as he was helping her now. She didn't envy him his day-to-day.

'We spent days kayaking around Lake Champlain. It's big, like an inland sea and stretches past the Canadian border. It was perfect; camping by the lakeside at sunset, cooking fish on the fire.'

Lara found she could picture it; both Harry and Vernon so handsome, athletic and vital. In her vision, Vernon was emerging from the lake in just his trunks for some reason. She felt her cheeks flush.

'Before the trip, Harry was down,' said Vernon. 'But I think spending all that time in nature gave him strength and perspective because Harry had made a decision by the end. He went to see the Dean and pitched her the idea for a media symposium. It was smart: giving something back while also making new contacts. Plus, he believed in the project.'

'So he was happy?'

'Perhaps not happy exactly, but things felt like they were turning a corner for Harry. He was full of beans on campus – and I know he was excited to meet you.'

Lara felt good about that, at least. But even so, she still couldn't get away from the facts: Harry had disappeared from the Dean's party, and then a few hours later, he was dead.

'Something made him leave the party, Father. What can it have been?'

She knew she was asking the question to herself as much as to Vernon. He spread his hands in a gesture of helplessness.

'I don't know. I left straight after the Dean's speech. That must have been about 7 pm. I don't really enjoy those academic get-togethers, and I had a service to prepare for. And anyway, I thought you two were going on to a restaurant.'

Lara thought for a moment.

'Arthur Campbell, Ellie's father, was at the party. Do you think they argued?'

‘I doubt it. Harry saw him and was trying to avoid him. They didn’t speak, certainly, whilst I was there.’

‘What about Mrs Campbell, Ellie’s mother?’

Vernon shook his head.

‘She won’t have been at the party. Eliza Campbell has psychogenic mutism.’

‘Psycho what?’

‘She’s mute. Someone who stops speaking after psychological trauma. Hasn’t spoken since Ellie’s funeral.’

Lara made a mental note to look into the condition.

‘She’s a very glamorous woman,’ continued Vernon. ‘You’d always see her at Benedon events, but not anymore.’

‘Did Harry say anything to you? Anything at all that made you worry?’

Vernon pulled out his phone and passed it over to Lara, showing her their text exchange.

‘This was from the night he died?’

Vernon nodded.

Something I need to tell you – it’s important, are you there?

Sure. Want to head over now? Side door’s open.

It will wait. See you on the other side.

Lara felt her scalp prickle. ‘See you on the other side...’ she looked up. ‘Why would he say that? Was this his suicide note?’

Vernon gave a sad smile.

‘At the time, I thought nothing of it. It was just a

running joke between us, the agnostic and the cleric: the idea that one of us had to be wrong. That way, the other one could spend eternity feeling smug. But... who knows, Lara? Something was troubling him.'

'What did he want to talk about?'

'I don't know,' said Vernon. 'And I'll spend the rest of my life wishing I had called him back to find out.'

Chapter 17

Sarah bumped through the doors of the station house holding a cardboard tray of take-out coffee like a waitress, trying not to spill a drop. Faces looked up; cops could smell roast beans at one hundred paces.

'All right, don't drool,' she said with a smile. 'My need is greater than yours.'

In actual fact, Sarah felt remarkably chipper. Caffeine always worked wonders when she was tired, but her conversation with Annie Campion at the hospital had given her much more of a boost. She felt more clear-headed, more energised. It was as if she had scented her quarry and was on the hunt. Admittedly, she was no closer to the 'who' or the 'why', but she felt her meeting with the medical examiner had given her a little of the 'how' and more importantly, it had given her the green light to pursue her theory, however crazy it might sound.

Sarah walked down to the detectives' section – nothing fancy, just two desks in the far corner of the building. She carefully placed the tray on the edge of Glenn's desk.

'Coffee?' said Glenn gratefully. 'Man, I could kiss you.'

'Less of the "man",' said Sarah, handing him a cup. 'And a rain-check on the kissing too.'

She dropped a paper sack in front of him.

'Doughnuts?' said Glenn, looking up suspiciously. 'Why do I get the feeling I'm being manipulated?'

'You're too cynical to be a detective,' said Sarah.

'Where the hell have you been, anyway?' said Glenn, biting into his doughnut. 'It's three o'clock. I've had to cover for you half a dozen times. Told Roscoe you were on that truck theft thing, but he wasn't happy.'

'I've been settling my mom into the care home.'

'I thought you said it would only take a couple of hours.'

'Well, it didn't.'

She looked around: this part of the station was practically empty, and there was little chance of being overheard, but she still lowered her voice.

'Listen Glenn, you worked on the Eleanor Campbell case, didn't you?'

All the way back from Hemsley, Sarah had been thinking about Harry Robbins. If the professor had been murdered, she had to consider possible motives.

She didn't know much about the professor's life but did know the final few months had been mired in a scandal about Eleanor Campbell.

'Ellie Campbell? The student who killed herself? Not sure you could call it a case. The chick did a swan dive off the balcony.' Glenn bared his uneven teeth. 'Real messy.'

Sarah pulled up the chair next to Glenn's. 'Run me through what you remember.'

Glenn had already finished the first doughnut; he carefully licked the sugar from his fingers.

'Anything odd about it? Anything that didn't fit?'

'Nah. It was a cut'n'shut. Poor little rich girl gets depressed, jumps off the stairs: goodnight Vienna.'

'You say it was ten at night? How did she get in?'

'Campus library is open 24 hours a day, but it was almost empty that night. No witnesses. Just the librarian who found the body.'

Sarah fell quiet, taking this all in. She checked that no one was eavesdropping, then turned to the real business.

'I think we need to get forensics back to the Robbins house.'

'It's already been done.'

'I know. But it didn't look that thorough to me.'

Glenn recoiled. 'Thorough? What were you expecting? Cadaver dogs and a SWAT unit?'

'They only did the inside, Glenn. Nothing outside the property, especially in the backyard area. We need them to sweep the whole perimeter.'

'Why?' said Glenn, finally putting his doughnuts down, leaving a trail of sprinkles down his blue shirt.

'When we were at the Harry Robbins place yesterday, you said something about a home invasion?'

Glenn sipped his coffee and frowned.

'I did?'

'You weren't being serious, but you got me thinking. Remember the French doors were unlocked when we went round on Tuesday morning?'

Her colleague nodded.

'So *why* weren't they locked?'

'Who knows? I'm always forgetting to lock my gun cabinet. And I'm a cop.'

Sarah ignored him, still following her train of thought.

'Harry left the party between 7PM and 7.25PM,' began Sarah. She'd spoken to the college chaplain who'd been with Harry until seven o'clock, and Lara Stone got a text from him at 7.29 which suggested he'd gone by then.'

'Assuming he didn't detour, he was back home by 7.45.

It was still warm at that time on Monday evening. Let's say he opened the doors to let in some fresh air. Even if he closed them later in the evening, why didn't he lock them?'

'Because obviously, he had other things on his mind.'

'Someone could have walked in, Glenn.'

He frowned.

'You think this was a robbery?'

'There was no computer on his desk, none in the house. Pretty odd for a professor.'

Glenn's hand rasped at his chin.

'But why stick him up with a gun for a five-hundred dollar laptop?'

'I bet he was an Apple man.'

'Still. Why not just wait until he's asleep and burgle the place?'

Sarah shrugged.

'Maybe the shooting was accidental. Then he grabs the computer and runs?'

Glenn was shaking his head.

'Brin did door-to-door on the Prof's street. No one saw anything or anyone, especially not a gunshot.'

'Nothing they *thought* was a gunshot,' Sarah corrected. 'People heard bangs all night, it was Labor Day: folks were setting off fireworks all over the place. Even at the Dean's house.'

'Sure, maybe,' said Glenn, without enthusiasm. Sarah knew she was losing momentum. Glenn was not the most proactive detective she had ever met, but she respected his opinion and agreed that the 'armed robbery' scenario was weak. In South Central LA, maybe, but not in rural Vermont.

'I spoke to the medical examiner this morning.'

'So that's where you've been,' he said with a little grunt of discontent. 'Why go all the way to Hemsley?'

Sarah waved it away. 'The doc said the distance between the gun and the wound was unusual for a suicide. She said someone else might have shot Harry.'

Glenn still didn't look convinced. 'Sarah, this is a smart part of the world. Plenty of students with money; you've seen the designer bags and the fancy cars around campus. I don't buy it that some hood would break into a teacher's house and kill him for some junk when they could take some WASP's $50,000 jeep.'

'But maybe this wasn't a theft gone wrong. Maybe someone was targeting Harry.'

'Dude was a professor, not Al Capone.'

'But you heard the rumours about the Campbell girl's death. People were blaming him. They were angry with Harry Robbins.'

Sarah was already picking up her phone, punching in the number for the forensics team. She knew they were overstretched and returning to Harry Robbin's cottage wouldn't be a priority, but Sarah had a secret weapon. Steve Kirk on the lab team had asked her out for a drink not long after she'd arrived back in Benedon, and although she'd turned him down, it was time to call in a favour.

'Steve, it's Sarah Carter. Call me back, could you?'

Glenn was shaking his head, looking unimpressed.

'Roscoe won't be happy, Carter.'

'Roscoe's never happy, Glenn,' she said. 'Look, humour me. If it's not suicide and not robbery, what are we left with?'

Glenn rubbed a hand over his face.

'Accident? And murder, I guess. But who wanted to kill him?'

'A lot of people disliked him for the Ellie Campbell thing.'

Glenn see-sawed a hand uncertainly.

'Maybe. But six months on, why suddenly get all het up?'

'That's what I want to find out. Who'd have a grudge against Harry? Ellie Campbell has a brother, right?'

'Yeah, he goes to college here; he's some big-time jock.'

'Well, I doubt he was happy with Harry Robbins.'

'Sarah, come on. Some kid being pissed off and upset doesn't make him a murderer. And you've got that truck theft to look into.'

Sarah picked up her coffee and stood up,

'The trucks can wait. I'm going to find Brandon Campbell.'

Glenn looked appalled.

'You're kidding? You can't point fingers at a Campbell and not expect trouble.'

'I'm willing to take my chances,' she smiled. 'And Glenn? Do me a favour, and don't eat all the doughnuts.'

* * *

Like everything else at Benedon, the football field was exactly like the movies. Bright green grass, with the logo of the Benedon Bears – a grizzly clawing a ball – etched into one end, an outsized scoreboard with blank spaces for 'down', 'qtr' and 'ball on', whatever all that meant. Sarah had never really followed football, she had always preferred track and field. It made her an outsider in the locker-room atmosphere of the station house, but then she was already an outsider being unburdened by the curse of testosterone.

Even so, Sarah did appreciate the spectacle of football, the blaring music, and the marching band. Even here, during afternoon practice at a small college, there were cheerleaders whooping and high-kicking on the sidelines, adding atmosphere to the players' drills. More chance of snagging a boyfriend, too, she guessed.

Sarah climbed up into the bleachers and watched the practice. Down on the pitch, a line of players in full armour and helmets took turns to charge at another line of players who would then converge and block. Then they would stop, do a load of high-fives, and do it all again. As far as Sarah could see, this was mostly what happened in the game anyway. But how it happened, that was interesting. The police academy had a lot of modules on law but hardly any on anthropology; Sarah had always thought it was a glaring oversight.

Human behaviour was the same everywhere; that old cop maxim that everything came down to sex and money. People were depressingly predictable; you just had to watch out for the patterns. And even within the rigid confines of this game, there were leaders and followers, generals and soldiers. Even from this distance, it was easy to see that Brandon Campbell was one of the leaders. He was the archetypical American jock: tanned, square-jawed and handsome. But crucially, the other players all looked to him for instruction and approval; he was the general on the field. A high-five or a wink from Brandon Campbell was what everyone wanted, both boys and girls.

For a moment, she thought about Glenn's warning against messing with the Campbells. Sarah might have lived in New York for fifteen years, but the Benedon area was still home. And growing up in these parts, everyone knew the Campbell name and that they were the big dogs in town, but that didn't put them above the law. Maybe in Benedon, they were happy to accept the simplest explanation – ashamed teacher commits suicide – but that wasn't how she operated. She might work in small-town Vermont, but Sarah was still a big-city cop. New York police work was messy, complex, and tough. Sarah's philosophy was always to keep pushing whoever was in the way.

Finally, the practice broke up, and the cheerleaders ran across to give the players more encouraging whoops and delicate hugs. Sarah made her way down to the field.

'Brandon?' she called out.

He peeled away from his admirers and jogged across to her.

'Sarah Carter,' she said, pulling out her badge. 'Benedon PD.'

'Brandon Campbell,' he said, extending a hand. His accent was crisp, almost British. If he was on guard, he didn't show it. He had the confident, easy manner of someone brought up in the finest schools.

'I saw you in the stands,' he said. 'Do you like college football?'

'Never been into team sports. The javelin was my thing.'

He raised an eyebrow with just a hint of flirtation.

'And how can I help you, Miss Carter?' he said.

'You cut straight to the chase,' said Sarah with a smile. 'I like that.'

'Life's too short. I guess I've learned that recently.'

'I'm sorry for your loss, but I'm investigating the death of Harry Robbins.'

Still, he looked unrattled.

'Yes, that was awful.'

Sarah must have shown her surprise.

'You thought I'd be happy he was dead because he broke my sister's heart?'

'Are you?'

'I lost my sister, Miss Carter, but I'm not heartless. So, no. I'm not happy that a professor took his own life.'

Either he was telling the truth, or he was in practice for a life in politics. He was certainly smooth enough for it.

'When did you last see Harry Robbins?'

'I didn't see him. Well, maybe occasionally, around campus. But not since last semester.'

'Did you go to the Dean's party?'

Brandon frowned. He was exceptionally handsome, and when his eyebrows knitted together, he looked like a moody male model.

'Why would I want to go there?' he said, perplexed.

'Free drinks, fireworks?'

'With people, like, fifty years older than me? Seriously, that's not my idea of a good night out.'

'So where were you on Monday night?'

'It was Labor Day; I went down to the lake with some friends. I stayed the night at Lisa's, my girlfriend's place.' He nodded towards a blonde in a cheerleader's outfit, still loitering at the edge of the field.

'If you speak to my parents, I'd appreciate it if you didn't tell them that. They still haven't quite grasped that their kids aren't kids anymore.'

Sarah nodded; she had no interest in stirring up trouble, not unless she had to.

'Can I speak to Lisa for a moment?'

Brandon gave that frown again: *why are you bothering me with these trivialities?*

'Hey, Lise!' he shouted, beckoning her. The cheerleader trotted over, her ponytail swinging from side to side.

'Everything okay?'

The girl was beautiful. Corn-coloured hair, skin so smooth and flawless it didn't look real and a slim yet curvy body. *If only I had legs like hers*, thought Sarah. If only she'd *ever* had legs like Lisa's, she figured she wouldn't be driving a ten-year-old Landcruiser or worrying about balancing her bank book at the end of the month.

'Lisa? I'm Sarah Carter, Benedon police. I was just wondering if you could tell me where you were on Monday night?'

'Have we done anything wrong?' said Lisa, looking anxiously at Brandon.

'No, I'm just asking everyone.'

Lisa curled her ponytail into a bun, using practised fingers to make a tight ball.

'There was a party by the lake,' she said. 'I was there with Brand and maybe twenty friends.'

'How long did you stay there?'

'Late. Maybe midnight? We built a bonfire.'

She turned to Brandon.

'Is that the problem? We made sure we put it out, didn't we, Brand?'

'And then what?' prompted Sarah.

'Then me and Brand went back to my place. I'm over at Sutherland House.' She winced. 'I'm not, uh, supposed to have friends stay over.'

'No problem,' said Sarah, turning to Brandon. 'Can you give me your friends' names? The ones you were at the lake with.'

Brandon and Lisa looked at each other again; then Brand rattled off

a list of names. Sarah pretended to write it down in her notebook, but she knew this was a dead end. Brandon wasn't defensive, just a little irritated and keen to get back to his friends. He hadn't snarled at Harry's name or gloated over his passing. Plus, Lisa had confirmed where he was on Monday night. Together, it didn't lend weight to her half-assed theory about the vengeful brother: she hated it when Glenn was right.

'Can I go now?' asked Lisa, pulling down her tiny pleated skirt.

'Sure,' said Sarah, turning back to Brandon as she walked away.

'This might seem like a dumb question,' she said. 'But were you and Ellie close?'

His expression was softer now.

'I guess. We were pretty different. Ellie was smart, she was allergic to sports,' he smiled. 'But there was only fifteen months between us. We used to get pushed around in this double buggy or put in a play-pen together like twins. Maybe we weren't close, but she was always there. And now she's not.'

'You said Harry broke her heart. Do you think that's why she did it?'

He looked away toward the horizon where the Benedon skyline bled into the Vermont mountains beyond, a smudge of grey and ochre in the distance.

'I don't know,' said Brandon quietly. 'Wish I did.'

'Were they dating?'

'She was spending a lot of time with him, and I told her to be careful. It wasn't smart to date a professor, but Ellie always walked her own line. If she got an idea in her head, you couldn't shift it. Like, she was all set to do an MBA, then she wanted to switch to a journalism masters? My parents weren't happy about that, but she wouldn't change her mind.'

'They were angry with her?'

'More disappointed, I guess.

He dipped his square jaw and then looked up again. 'My mom hasn't spoken since Ellie's death, did you know that? I don't know if she felt guilty that she and dad were pressuring Ellie to drop the journalism thing. It's easy to blame Professor Robbins, but I think it was a lot of things altogether.'

'It often is.'

For a moment, Sarah thought back to her last days in New York. At first, it had seemed clear-cut: dirty cops on the take? Of course, she had to report them. But when the fallout came, so did the sleepless nights. Her doctor had prescribed pills, and Sarah had blamed her boss's betrayal, but deep down, she knew it was more than that: her mother's dementia, the thought that she would soon be alone with no family to lean on. Thirty-nine years old, no partner, no house, and she had just pressed self-destruct on her career. Yes, sometimes things all came at once. She handed Brandon her card.

'Thank you for talking to me,' said Sarah, feeling a pang of sympathy. Brandon stopped and tucked his helmet under his arm.

'No, thank you,' he said. 'You know, after Ellie died, no one in my family spoke about her. Like everyone was ashamed or something, like they wanted to pretend it never happened.'

Sarah nodded, wanting to say more, but just then Lisa shouted, bouncing on the spot impatiently and beckoning to Brandon.

'You go,' said Sarah. 'And thanks again.'

'Hey, any time,' said Brandon, and ran away across the field.

Chapter 18

Alex bent over the map spread out on the passenger seat of his hire car. He peered through the windscreen. On the flight over he'd read a feature about Vermont. Apparently, its name was derived from French, *vert* and *mont*, meaning green mountain. But right now, all Alex could see was pitch black. He certainly couldn't see anything that matched what he saw on the map – hills, lakes and towns with English-sounding names – Windsor, Plymouth and Reading. Perhaps he should have spent more time paying attention in cub scouts, but Alex had been far more interested in chopping things up and setting fire to them. And perhaps he should have given more than three seconds of thought to it before he had said yes to Lara and booked a flight to Boston.

'Come on over, join my symposium; it will be fun,' he said out loud.

Alex didn't even know what a symposium was: some sort of conference? He hadn't bothered asking because it was clear that Lara needed his help. Harry Robbins, whoever that was, was dead, and Lara needed a friend. That much he could do.

Alex took a swig of the coffee he'd picked up at the airport and winced: cold, but he drank it anyway. The past few months had been unusually stressful, and he'd been desperate for a break. Darius was a mercurial boss, prone to changing his mind, and there was pressure from upstairs to make more money. The latest financial wheeze was dressing up paid content as editorial – which Alex had fought hard against. But again and again, he felt he was losing an uphill battle. In pursuit of survival in the digital age, newspapers were getting grubby and Alex wasn't sure how much more he could stand. A vacation was long overdue, if only to help him get some perspective on where to go next.

'Yeah, and where *are* you going?' muttered Alex, staring back into the darkness, wondering what was out there – Bobcats? Wolves? Bears? He used to enjoy the feeling of being lost. The happiest days of his professional life had been as a war correspondent dashing off into the wide unknown, not knowing what would happen in the next few minutes, let alone the next 24 hours. The bombs, the minefields, and the high drama had been fun, of course, but Alex found he missed the one thing foreign correspondents never told you about: the gratitude of the locals who understood you had made the effort – risking your life – to come and tell your story. Their story. That was what he missed: meaning.

Sighing, Alex picked up his mobile phone and tapped away, trying to send Lara a message.

Where are you? I am in a dark, dark forest, and the last shop I saw only sold fertiliser. Any advice gratefully received. Ax

. . .

He pressed send, surprised to see a single bar on his phone; maybe it could squeeze his message through. Immediately there was a 'bing'.

Picked you up on radar, guiding you in now. Lx

Alex laughed out loud before picking up her next message, which contained more detailed instructions to her house. It seemed he'd been going in the right direction all along. He started the car and, after another twenty minutes, he found himself approaching a picturesque town – all white clap-board and stars and stripes hanging over porches – exactly how you might imagine an American college town to be.

Finally, he pulled into the street on Lara's instructions and yanked on the handbrake outside number 47. Looking up at the window glowing amber in the dark, Alex felt a flutter in his chest. There she was: Lara. He could see her in silhouette as she pottered about the cottage. Was she tidying up for him? A pang of affection gripped him. She'd only been gone a few days, yet he knew right then how much he missed her.

Alex had gently tried to dissuade Lara from coming to New England. What the hell did she want to leave London for? Lara had money; she had a stylish houseboat in Chelsea Wharf with fairytale views of Albert Bridge. And she had a dream job too. As a roving reporter for the *Chronicle,* she'd been liberated from the day-to-day grind of office life, working from home most of the time, immersing herself in whatever story gripped her. So, when Lara had announced that she was taking time out to spend a term at Benedon, Alex couldn't help but take it personally. She wasn't just leaving London. She was leaving him.

'Alex?'

He looked up, and Lara was standing by the car, a finger tapping on the side window.

'What are you doing sitting in the dark?'

He laughed and jumped out. He opened his arms, and Lara stepped into his embrace, holding him tight. Alex didn't say anything, just held on until he felt the tension in her slowly let go.

'You okay?'

She nodded, then squeezed him once again before letting go.

'I can't believe you came,' she said.

'Yes, you can,' he smiled.

'I suppose I can.' She crossed her arms around herself, 'Come on then, let's get you inside. I'm guessing you've only brought a toothbrush and a giant pot of hair gel?'

'Au contraire,' said Alex popping the boot and pulling out a slim silver suitcase. 'I travel like an executive now.'

'Fancy,' she said, and they both laughed.

Lara's house was bohemian and very American; Alex spotted both a Mr Coffee and a waffle machine on the kitchen counter. And yet, it still felt like her place; it felt familiar.

'This place is like something out of *Little Women*. I always had you down as an Amy March type.'

'Wasn't she the crazy one?' said Lara, pushing his shoulder.

'You're right. I meant Jo; wasn't she the strident writer?'

'Hey! I'm not sure that's much better. Anyway, the house belongs to the college.'

'They're letting you stay here for free?'

'I have to pay rent. But it's cheap.'

Alex slipped off his jacket and sank onto the worn but comfy sofa.

'Welcome to college life,' said Lara, handing him a glass of red wine. He raised it in salute.

'Here's to their newest professor.'

Lara clinked her glass against his.

'You're a lecturer too now, remember?'

'Kind of. But I can't believe you invited Darius,' groaned Alex.

'I told you; he invited himself. Darius never knowingly lets an opportunity pass by to talk about himself and his glittering career. And he can't let you get one over on him.'

'I don't think Darius is threatened by me,' said Alex.

'I wouldn't be so sure.'

For a split second, Alex felt a glimmer of hope that Lara might have heard something. After all, Lara's uncle was the chairman of Avery Media and her cousin Charlie was the *Chronicle*'s managing director.

But Lara pointed to a copy of a media paper she'd left on the coffee table: 'Avery Media profit warning', read the headline. 'Print newspapers on the wane'. It was just more of what Alex already knew: it was time to jump – and soon.

But he hadn't come all this way to talk shop, and in the soft lights of the cottage, he could now see how pale and tired Lara looked.

'I'm sorry about your friend,' he said. 'What happened?

She took a ragged breath and filled him in on the whole story. It was more complex and dramatic than Alex had been expecting; some meet-cute with the professor in a deli, a screaming girl in a bar accusing him of murder, a dead student he'd been accused of having an affair with, a glamorous party at the Dean's house and then the shock of Harry's suicide the following morning.

Lara didn't seem to know many more details but didn't need to: the poor man had blown his brains out with his gun, and Alex could tell she was devastated.

'Bloody Hell, Lar. That's awful; I can see why you're so shaken up.'

Lara didn't say anything for a few seconds.

'Alex, it doesn't feel right.'

'I know. It's tragic.'

'No. It just feels like... like it's happening again.'

Alex knew what she was getting at. A year before, their friend Sandrine had been found outside an apartment block in London, an apparent suicide. He examined her face; she couldn't be blaming herself, could she?

'I was with Harry the night he died,' she said. 'He was happy; he was looking forward to the future. Yes, the rumours about this Ellie girl had rocked him, but he wasn't defeated by it all.' She paused and looked at him with those large green eyes. 'Why would he kill himself? And how did he have a gun? Harry was a liberal professor!'

'Nearly a third of all Americans say they own a gun, Lar. It's not unusual out here. It's commonplace.'

'But I spoke to Harry's sister, and she was adamant that Harry hated guns.'

'She's grieving.'

Lara went to her desk and returned with a piece of paper.

'So what do you think of this?' she asked, thrusting it into his hand. 'I found it on my doormat last night.'

'Harry knew,' he said, reading it aloud. 'Harry knew what?'

'I'm not sure yet.'

He heard the last word: 'yet', and he knew that look of steely determination. He resisted a sigh. Although Alex was a journalist, he didn't *always* want to look into the hidden meanings behind everything. Sometimes he just wanted to switch off.

'I think there's more to Harry's death than people think,'

insisted Lara. 'I know that Sarah, the police officer in charge, is asking a lot of questions.'

'I don't doubt she is. It's her job.'

'Ours too.'

Alex softened. He could tell this was important to her.

'Look Lar, I'm not just here for the symposium; I'm here to help you however I can. If there's something off about Harry's death, we'll find it together, okay?'

'Thank you,' she whispered fiercely. 'Thank you for coming, and thanks for understanding.'

Alex paused.

'You know, it sounds like the best thing you can do for Harry right now is to make this symposium the best thing the college has ever done.'

She nodded, her eyes sparkling.

'There's so much to do. It's not just the symposium, there's a party on Saturday night at The Boathouse, and now the Dean is talking about a cocktail reception on Sunday night.'

'And Darius,' smiled Alex. 'Don't forget Darius.'

Lara groaned and clapped both hands over her face.

'Anyway, I think I'd better get my head down before I fall,' said Alex, pushing himself up.

Lara's eyes opened wide. 'I'm so sorry. I've been so excited to see you; I keep forgetting you've travelled across the Atlantic just to get here.'

'It's not quite the five-minute Uber ride it usually is.'

They both smiled. Alex's apartment was just a mile or so away from Lara's houseboat. On balmy evenings, when they weren't working, they'd regularly text each to ask if they wanted company, and within minutes would be having supper together or strolling down the King's Road to catch a movie. Suddenly those days seemed a long time ago.

'You're in the study; I've made up the sofa bed.'

His smile faded, fighting down a niggling feeling of disappointment. But that was stupid, wasn't it?

'I've missed you,' he said.

'Have you really?'

'Well, no.'

She picked up a cushion and threw it at him, laughing.

'Still, I'm very glad you're here,' said Lara in a soft voice. Then she turned and walked into the bedroom, closing the door behind her.

Chapter 19

Alex was jealous; there was no other way to describe it. Lara had left the house early with a to-do list a foot long for the symposium. She'd insisted that she didn't need his help, that everything 'was in hand', so Alex had spent the morning strolling around the campus and the college town, soaking up the atmosphere, trying not to grin too widely every time he saw another Ivy League cliché: the students with their polo shirt collars popped up, rusty bicycles casually leaning against a spreading tree, a pretty girl just lying on the lawns reading Faulkner. Lara was getting to spend a whole term here, immersed in this amazing theme park as a visiting fellow, a legitimate lecturer, with one of those dangly lanyards, an ID card with her photo on it saying 'STAFF'. The whole scene was a world away from the London media scene he'd left behind, where everyone was becoming more competitive and on edge with each passing day, everyone desperate not just to get promoted but to safeguard their jobs. The days of office camaraderie, when everyone would pile down to the pub after work, seemed to be a distant memory. Suddenly Benedon felt like a very good lifestyle choice indeed.

Alex circled back to Main Street and stopped at the door of the College Deli, wondering whether to go in. It was a warm morning, and he could just bet they would have rows and rows of Dr Pepper and bright green Gatorade in chiller cabinets. Why wouldn't they? Everything else about this town was so classically American.

He imagined Lara and Harry here just days earlier, flirting over cream cheese and lox bagels, like a scene from a Nancy Meyer movie and felt a knot in his stomach, this time a real case of the green-eyed monster.

Yes, Alex knew it was wrong to feel jealous about a dead man, but still, he had felt decidedly uncomfortable the night before, listening to Lara talk about the handsome, tragic professor. Worse still had been their Facetime call on the night of the Dean's party when she'd cut it short to see Harry. Alex had been under no illusions: it was a date, whatever Lara had said. Lara had been in Benedon for two minutes, and she'd been whisked off her feet by a man in tweed. That hurt.

He sighed to himself. Alex knew that if he was jealous, he only had himself to blame; he'd had plenty of time and opportunity to tell Lara how he felt. What had held him back was that he didn't *know* how he felt. The only thing he did know was that it was complicated.

Alex shook his head and turned away from the store. He didn't need a coffee. He needed a real drink. Glancing at his watch, he saw that it was only 11.30. He hadn't had a drink before lunch since his days in the field. Working in Kandahar and Mosul, when you fell asleep to the sound of gunfire and woke up to the smell of rubble and dust, made it easy to reach for a drink, whatever the hour.

Like a mirage in a desert, a sign for The Shovel appeared in front of him as if by magic. It was another American classic. Neon sign, black painted door, all that was missing was a row of Hells Angels bikes lined up outside. The bar looked grittier than everything else he'd seen in Benedon town – perhaps that was why he liked it, he thought as he pushed inside.

The place was quiet; a few stools were still upturned on tables at the far end of the bar. He wasn't surprised. He suspected the place had just opened, even if it was a Friday.

The bartender walked over, flipping a bar towel over his shoulder just like in the movies.

'What can I get you?'

'Can I have a pint of the Sam Adams?' said Alex, nodding towards the beer on tap.

'This size okay?' said the barman holding up something slightly smaller than a UK pint glass.

Alex smiled. He'd been to America dozens of times, but he still couldn't get the hang of the fact that they generally only sold beer in bottles.

'From England?' said the man, glancing up as he poured the amber liquid, tilting the glass to get just the right amount of foamy head.

'That's right.'

'You here for the Symposium?'

'My friend is organising it.'

The barman's hand wavered.

'You're a friend of Harry's?'

'No – sorry. Lara Stone. She's helping out.'

He didn't know how much the man knew. Benedon was a small town. He figured that everyone knew everything, but still, it was right to be sensitive. The barman put the beer in front of him, and as Alex took out his wallet, the other man shook his head.

'On the house,' he said with a sad smile. 'Harry Robbins was a good buddy of mine. The last time he was here was with Lara on Saturday night.'

'I was sorry to hear about him,' said Alex. 'Lara speaks very highly of him.'

'He was a great guy.'

Alex looked around the place, noting the cased vinyl on the walls – The Ramones' *Rocket to Russia*, REM's *Automatic for the People*, Led Zep IV and *Pet Sounds*. Someone had good taste. In an alternative universe, Alex had always wanted to own somewhere just like this. On all those late nights at the *Chronicle* office, he thought about it more and more: what he would have on the jukebox, which beer he would have on draught, what food he would serve. That part was easy: burgers using meat from farms he knew in Cumbria and an excellent ploughman's using cheese he had sourced himself.

'Name's Buck,' said the barman, offering a hand.

'Alex. So this is your place?'

He nodded. 'My ex-wife said I was mad for buying it. What do you want a bar in a college town for? Most kids aren't 21. It was the one thing she was right about.'

Alex took a sip of his beer. It was good. It reminded him of the local bitter they served in the Lake District pubs where he had grown up.

'Where I'm from, we'd get served in our local from about 16. By the time I got to college, I was sick of beer.'

'Maybe I should emigrate,' laughed Buck.

Alex nodded. Back home at this time, the pubs would already be busy.

'It's not always quiet though, right?' said Alex, looking up over the froth. 'Lara told me there was a bit of shouting here on Saturday.'

'You mean the business with Jenny Price?'

Alex nodded as if he knew what he was talking about. He was fishing for information because he was curious, and Lara hadn't gone into too much detail. He knew her professor friend had been accused of being a 'murderer', which was a serious accusation. Lara was usually a good judge of character, so of course, it had piqued his interest.

'I thought all those rumours had died down, but Jenny had had too much to drink that night,' said Buck, shaking his head. 'It took two of us to get her in a taxi. She threw up all over the back seat. Cabby is chasing me for the clean-up fee for some reason. I'm tempted to ban her from The Shovel, but Jenny's a good kid underneath. And she was a good friend of Ellie's, so I guess I'll cut her some slack.'

'Ellie. Was she the girl who died? I heard the rumours.'

Alex was vaguely aware that any sane person would not be asking too many questions about the recently deceased friend of a gnarly barman who looked like he could snap Alex's neck just by looking at him, but Alex was a newspaperman: curiosity was an occupational hazard.

Alex watched as Buck seemed to weigh up whether to answer the question or to grab a baseball bat from under the bar. Happily, he chose the former.

'A lot of people thought Harry was responsible for Eleanor Campbell's death, that he broke her heart. Look, Harry was my buddy. He wasn't an angel, but he was a straight-up guy.'

'So why did everybody believe the story?' asked Alex.

'Dunno. I saw Harry and Ellie in here a couple of times, and it always looked platonic to me. Working in a bar for as long as I have, you get to read people pretty well. But the rumours?' He held up his hands in a shrug. 'I guess it was a story that just gathered speed because it was better gossip that way. It was tragic and dramatic. Like what's-her-name: the chick who drowned in that pre-Raphaelite painting.

Alex looked up. 'Ophelia?'

'Nah, Lizzie Siddall.'

Buck smiled at Alex's reaction. He'd obviously walked

into a trap: who would expect a barman to know John Everett Millais's famous painting, much less the tragic story attached to the model in the picture?

'How do you think I ended up as a barman in Benedon?' Buck grinned. 'I was an English lit major here. A long time ago – but I'm not exactly run off my feet here most days. I get a lot of time to read.'

'So, who is the girl? This Jenny, I mean.'

'She works at the Playhouse, Benedon's theatre.'

Buck gave him a shrewd look.

'If you see her, tell her the taxi company is chasing me for the clean-up fee.'

* * *

The theatre was at the other end of Main Street. For a small town, the road seemed to go on forever. Every few minutes, a car would whip past; this was America, of course – nobody walked – but it hadn't seemed worth going back to get the hire car. Plus, Alex had had a drink at the bar and didn't want to fall foul of the local cops on his second day in town. Anyway, it was a fine day for a walk, giving him time to think.

Alex had googled Harry Robbins back in London as soon as Lara had called and told him about his death. A quick search had thrown up a decent amount of local coverage about the tragic professor, and the allusion to a background scandal hadn't escaped Alex's experienced journalistic eye either. But as soon as he'd left The Shovel, Alex had searched Ellie Campbell too, to learn about her death – a fall from the top floor of the campus library named after her grandfather, a pioneering industrialist who had been one of the wealthiest men in the state. The whole thing had enough tragedy, glamour, mystery and drama to go straight into the pages of *Vanity Fair* magazine.

As Alex walked, the town thinning out, a voice in his head told him this was none of his business. He was off-duty. On holiday. Knackered. For a moment, he let his mind drift to where he should have been that week. A four-day trip to Norway with his mates, Tim, Anil and Dan, where they had a schedule of drinking and hiking all planned. His friends hadn't been surprised when he'd bailed out at the last minute. It often happened – nights out cancelled when a big news story came in, birthday celebrations missed when he couldn't escape the office or was out of town.

But now, Alex felt as if he was back out in the field and could feel the rumble of excitement that came with it. As the son of a newsagent, Alex had always wanted to be a newspaper editor, but reporting was where his heart lay. The travel, excitement, the frisson of danger, the thrill of unearthing a story until, sometimes, only you had the full picture. And he was feeling it right now, striding towards the Benedon Playhouse.

From the front, the theatre looked like a large Dutch Colonial house, with neat brickwork and a pitched roof, but at its rear was a huge architectural box, presumably the auditorium. There was a billboard outside advertising the latest show – *Oklahoma*, but the place appeared shut.

Alex peered through the double doors into the darkness of the lobby. No: the box office had a light on. Alex walked in just as a woman in a red blouse came from a back room holding a stack of popcorn boxes.

'Hello there,' said Alex, turning up his British accent a few notches. In his foreign correspondent days, Alex had discovered that playing the bumbling posh Hugh Grant kind of character seemed to open the most doors. It didn't work in Afghanistan, however; perhaps *Four Weddings and a Funeral* hadn't been big in Kabul.

Today, however, he was rewarded with a wide smile.

'Do you want tickets for tonight's show, honey?' asked the woman.

Alex shook his head. 'I've only just arrived in town, and I'm a little lost. I'm trying to find Jenny Price; I understand she works here?'

'Well, your timing's good, hon. Jenny's on her break right now – my guess is you'll find her across the road in the diner.' She pointed through the doors. 'Can't miss it.'

She was right: it was pretty obvious. It was a classic diner with red checked tablecloths and rustic trappings: there was even a waggon wheel nailed to one wall. You could even smell the bacon. It was a little early for lunch, so the diner was fairly sparse, two old guys and a twenty-something wearing a red blouse just like the one worn by the lady in the theatre.

'Jenny Price?'

'Yes?'

'Hi there,' he said. 'Sorry to bother you. My friend Buck at The Shovel told me I'd find you here.'

The girl looked up at him through her thick, blunt fringe – bangs; Alex corrected himself: when in Rome...

'You know Buck?' She said uncertainly. 'Is this about the taxi?'

Alex slid into the booth.

'He did mention it, yes.'

'I'm so embarrassed. But they want a hundred bucks for the clean-up fee. I just haven't got it.'

'Is the pay not good at the theatre?'

Jenny shrugged

'I only work at the box office, sometimes backstage. I

want to be an actress, but you've got to start somewhere, right?'

'Well, it's more than just 'somewhere'. It's a beautiful building,' he said.

'The college owns it. Same as they own most places around here.'

She took a French fry off her plate and dipped it into a small metal pot of ketchup.

'So what did Buck say? I'm guessing this isn't a blind date.'

The girl's voice had a flirtatious note, and his younger self would have flirted back.

'He said that you were friends with Ellie Campbell.'

'Yeah, so?' said Jenny, her guard going up.

'I heard that there was trouble at the bar on Saturday. You attacked Harry Robbins and his friend.'

Jenny sat forward, patting the air.

'Will you keep your voice down,' she hissed. 'I come here all the time.'

She took a deep breath.

'I did not attack Harry Robbins or that woman he was with,' she said in a more measured voice. Alex wasn't surprised she was a wannabe actress. Jenny could switch emotions rapidly.

'But I did have a lot to drink. I said a few things to Harry and his new girl. Buck put me in a cab home... that's all.'

'You do know Harry Robbins is dead?'

'Everyone knows,' she said quietly. 'And yes, I had issues with the guy. But what happened was still sad.'

She tilted her head and looked at him.

'Are you a cop?'

'No. I'm trying to help Harry's friends understand what happened.'

Jenny pushed her plate to one side. It was clear she

would rather Alex simply disappear. He tried a different approach.

'You and Ellie were friends?'

Seeing Alex wasn't going to leave, she sighed.

'We were roomies in the first year. I studied drama and graduated last summer, the same time Ellie was supposed to graduate.'

'What was she like?'

'Ellie was cool. Generous. This place is full of rich kids, but Ellie made me feel included even though I wasn't one of them. I'll always be grateful for that.'

'And how was she then? Just before she died, I mean?'

Jenny stared across the road towards the playhouse, her expression mournful.

'I hadn't seen her so much in the last couple of years. I was in a lot of plays, and I mainly hung out with the theatre crew. I guess we're cliquey. But I'd still see Ellie every now and then, and we'd talk when we did. That's how I got to know about Harry.'

'She told you she was in a relationship with Harry?'

Jenny pursed her lips.

'Not exactly, but I could tell. It was "Harry this, Harry that".'

She glanced up at Alex. She must have seen that Alex wasn't convinced, so she pressed on.

'Look, at the time I was seeing this guy. He had money and wanted to take me away for a couple of days somewhere fancy. He asked where I wanted to go, so I asked Ellie because she was the most stylish person I knew. She always knew the best shops and restaurants. She recommended a place in Maple County: The Blackberry Inn. She said she'd just been, said it was very romantic.'

'You think she went with Harry?'

'*Obviously,*' said Jenny. 'No one would go all that way for anything else.'

Alex was trying to remember everything Lara had told him the previous evening.

'Jenny, you called Harry a murderer. Why?'

The young woman looked around, then over to the bar where the two waitresses were deep in conversation. Even so, she lowered her voice.

'The last time I saw Ellie was a couple of days before she died. And she'd changed.'

'Changed how?'

'She was dark, like miserable, something heavy on her mind. I'm an actress, you know. I'm *sensitive.* I have amazing intuition, and I could tell something was wrong.'

'You could tell what?'

'That creep had dumped her; he'd broken her heart. And the next thing I knew, she was gone. It's obvious, isn't it?'

It didn't seem obvious to Alex at all. Harry Robbins had been cast as the evil professor who had manipulated a young, beautiful student, and Jenny's intuition aside, Alex wanted more proof.

'Is there anyone who might know more about Ellie and Harry's relationship?'

Jenny sat back in her seat.

'Why don't you just let it rest?' she said. 'I told you what I know, and nothing will bring them back.'

'Please, Jenny.'

The girl sighed dramatically.

'I guess you could try Julia,' she said reluctantly.

'Julia?'

'Julia Bevan, Bowen. Something like that. She and Ellie were good friends. I saw them hanging out together in those last few weeks.'

‘Do you know how I can get in touch with her?’

Jenny shook her head.

‘I think she was doing an English master’s. Not seen her around since last semester, though.’

She glanced up at the clock.

‘Listen, I've got to go back to work.’

Alex stood up and pulled two fifty-dollar bills from his wallet.

‘Here,’ he said, placing them on the table. ‘Taxi clean-up charge is on me,’ he said, turning to walk out. He knew Hugh Grant would have been proud.

Chapter 20

Lara loved the way the early morning light spread across the kitchen table. Filtered through the curling leaves outside the window, it formed a dappled canvas that gave the room a reflected glow. She sipped her coffee and smiled. There were some advantages to getting up early.

It was the day of the symposium, barely 8 AM and already, Lara had been in conversation with Michaela O'Brien, the Irish war correspondent, who had been stuck in Halifax due to fog. Predictably unflappable, the woman had told Lara she would 'commandeer a trawler' rather than miss her slot at the symposium. Word about the event was spreading; Lara's inbox that morning was clogged with messages from journalists: both offering their services and wanting to run stories on the conference. What had begun as a neat little idea to help Harry Robbins find a new job was threatening to spread far beyond the borders of Benedon. Which almost made the lack of sleep worthwhile.

'You're up early,' Alex came out of the study, pushing a hand through his bed hair. 'I thought I was the one with jet lag.'

Yawning, Alex stretched, his T-shirt riding up, showing

a strip of warm skin. Lara tried not to look or notice how cute he was. But she did.

'The symposium seems to be having the same effect on me,' said Lara, rubbing her eyes. 'I'm no longer sure what day it is.'

'I'll tell you what day it is,' said Alex, miming a drum roll. 'It's Symposium Day!'

Lara groaned. 'You don't need to tell me. Next time I tell you I'm organising an event, shoot me.'

She stopped, realising what she had said, but Alex reached over and squeezed her shoulder sympathetically. 'Hey,' he said with a sad smile, his thumb stroking her collarbone for a moment, her skin tingling where he had touched it. Lara looked up to meet his eyes, but Alex had gone, pottering towards the little kitchen.

She moved to get up. 'Do you want me to make some eggs?'

Alex waved a hand.

'I'll do it. You've got enough on your plate – no pun intended.'

'Well, there's coffee in the pot.' She didn't add that it was the second pot she had brewed already that morning. It felt like she had pure caffeine running in her veins: she'd also stayed working at the college until nine the previous evening. Taking on the symposium had seemed entirely manageable when Doug had suggested it the night of the vigil, but the event had grown into an admin nightmare, coordinating all the speakers and their various needs. Luckily, Lara had been ably assisted by faculty secretary Mary who was super-organised and calm when Lara was scattershot and given to shouting at the computer.

'Scrambled or boiled?' asked Alex.

'Scrambled.'

She watched him crack eggs into a bowl and whisk

them. She was glad he was here. Glad he'd stayed at the cottage. There had been no discussion about it; they'd both assumed that Alex would stay at Lara's while he was in Vermont – a hotel wasn't even mentioned. They'd shared living spaces before; in their twenties, they'd travelled together to Greece, Sicily, and Peru, bunking up in cheap B&Bs, tavernas and hostels. Later, when Alex was posted abroad, she'd gone to visit him, and stayed at his apartments in Berlin and Beirut, but somehow it had not felt like this, the easy domesticity.

For a moment, Lara allowed herself the fantasy of herself and Alex as a couple. She looked over at him, theatrically spinning a frying pan and banging it down on the hob. *But was it just a fantasy?*

'When does Darius arrive?' he asked.

'This afternoon. Can you believe he's already complained about his hotel before he's even set foot in it? I tried to tell him there's no Four Seasons in Benedon and that the Lakeside Inn is good enough for the mega-rich parents who come to visit their progeny, but....'

'But it's Darius,' smiled Alex. 'Well, savour the moment. We have about five hours before he gets here, and the real moaning begins.'

Lara sipped her coffee.

'I'm sorry for abandoning you last night.'

The plan had been to take Alex to The Shovel for drinks and a Shovelburger, but then Doug had thrown another spanner in the works: he needed Lara to help with the Saturday night party – an after-hours symposium event for speakers and VIP guests. So on top of dealing with the speakers, she had been tasked with dealing with the catering staff and ordering flowers for the tables. If Lara made it through this experience in one piece, she felt sure she could easily organise next year's Glastonbury festival.

'No worries, I quite enjoyed just chilling here on my own last night,' said Alex, pouring himself a coffee.

'Did you work on your speech?'

Alex waved the whisk carelessly. 'It'll be fine.'

Lara looked up. She knew Alex too well; 'It'll be fine' was delivered in such an off-hand manner it meant he was being evasive. She turned in her chair, open-mouthed.

'You haven't written it, have you?' she exclaimed.

'Look, I had a couple of beers and started watching *Game of Thrones*,' said Alex. 'I've never seen it before, and I just got sucked in. Sean Bean in a wig is just...mesmerising. And you never know when a dragon will turn up and burn everyone to a crisp.'

'Alex! You're speaking in like three hours!'

'I'll wing it.'

Lara threw her hands up in exasperation, then, shook her head, laughing. Of course, Alex would be fine. She'd seen him do off-the-cuff talks and speeches, and they'd been brilliant. He was a natural – funny, insightful, and charming. No, he'd be great. Plus, Lara was aware the poor guy needed a break. Alex worked at the *Chronicle* office until midnight most nights, and his personal life had shrunk to almost zero. At college, Alex had been the most cultured person she knew, reading 'important' books, going to gigs or the Curzon to see foreign movies. If he wanted to spend a few hours catching up on the pop culture he'd missed, then Lara wouldn't complain.

'So I spoke to Jenny Price yesterday.'

His tone was casual, but Lara sat up in her chair.

'Jenny Price?'

'The girl who called Harry a murderer on Saturday. I went to The Shovel for a drink, and Buck told me she works at the theatre in town. So I went up and spoke to her.'

'You did? What did she say?"

'They were roomies in freshman year. She couldn't confirm if Harry and Ellie were dating and didn't properly explain why she called Harry a murderer.'

'You did all that?' said Lara, eyes wide.

'It was before I discovered *Game of Thrones*.'

Alex put the scrambled eggs onto two plates and served them with thick chunks of sourdough bread and some salsa that he seemed to have whipped up from nowhere. He joined Lara at the table.

'Anyway, Jenny told me about another friend of Ellie's. Julia. A closer friend, it sounds like. I did a bit of digging around on social media. It looks like Julia left Benedon and lives in Boston now. I have her parent's address.'

Lara put her fork down.

'Alex, why did you do that?'

'Because I have a psychiatric disorder and can't stop working.' He looked up and grinned at her. 'I don't know. You said Harry's death didn't feel right, so I thought I'd ask around.'

Lara laughed.

'You might be one of Britain's top newspaper executives, but you're still a bloody good reporter, Alex Ford. I genuinely hold no grudges that you beat me to Student of the Year at college.'

She meant it and was grateful for what he'd done, but somehow, it made her feel bad too. Perhaps she should have spoken to more of Harry and Ellie's friends herself.

'You're a decent cook too, Ford,' she said. Her breakfast was delicious; Lara hadn't thought the cottage's tiny kitchen was capable of such a gourmet feast.

'Actually, there's something else I wanted to talk to you about,' he said. 'I had a call from....'

Just then, Lara's mobile began to ring.

'Dammit,' she muttered, jumping up to grab it. 'Hold that thought; I'm waiting for a call from The Boathouse.'

But it wasn't The Boathouse; it was Doug Bishop.

'Lara, we've got a problem with the party tonight,' said Doug down te line, 'The champagne hasn't turned up.'

'None?'

'Not a drop. Every local supplier I've spoken to can't get any until Monday.'

Lara bit her lip, refraining from asking the obvious question, '...and this is my problem how?' Harry had originally conceived the VIP reception on the lake as his own personal networking event, but Ros Davies had been extending the guest list all week. Now it was a party for 200 speakers, staff and local dignitaries, and that required a whole new level of organisation – and efficiency was not a core trait in the Benedon Journalism department.

'Couldn't organise a piss-up in a brewery' was the phrase which had often sprung to mind over the last few days. Lara stopped: *actually, that's not a bad idea.*

'All right, forget the champagne,' she said decisively. 'Apparently, there's an amazing local distillery around here. Ask Buck at The Shovel if he has a contact. Get as many bottles as they can spare, then send Mary to get lemon juice, eggs and soda water. Anyone can serve up fizz: we'll give them gin fizz.'

'Okay, good idea,' said Doug uncertainly. 'But eggs?'

'Trust me. The egg white gives it a thick foamy head; it's very theatrical – right up your street, I should think, Doug. Oh, and we need syrup to make it sweet – tell Mary to get maple syrup. We'll pretend it comes from local trees. Hey, maybe it does.'

She hung up. Sometimes all people needed was someone to tell them what to do. 'Crisis averted,' she said.

'Is there anything you can't do?' smiled Alex.

'Ask me that on Sunday, after the symposium,' she said. 'Now, what did you want to talk about?'

'Doesn't matter,' said Alex, getting up. 'You've got work to do, and I've got dragons to get back to. But first...' He pushed his plate towards her. 'I think someone needs to do the washing up.'

* * *

The noise in the main auditorium was huge, like an orchestra tuning up. Benedon's biggest lecture theatre was an impressive semi-circle of raked-back cinema seats and polished oak panelling, but it had been created to maximise the acoustics from the stage. When everyone sat around chatting, as now, the conversations and laughter were amplified threefold. Peeking out from her position backstage, Lara was more than pleased to see the place almost full and buzzing with anticipation. A few hours ago, checking the seating plan in an empty room, she had been sick with nerves. What if no one came? What if no one cared? What if modern journalism wasn't the fascinating topic Lara, Doug, and Harry had believed it was?

But clearly, she shouldn't have worried. Not only had there been a queue trailing down the auditorium steps when they had finally opened the doors, but the mix of the audience was also encouraging. Students were allowed to come for free, but there were plenty of older faces, people not from the college, *real* people from the wider community who had paid for their tickets. From the looks of anticipation, it seemed as though they were excited at the prospect of listening to 'a load of hacks wittering on', as Alex had

memorably put it. She turned to see Rosalind Davies approaching. Despite herself, Lara tensed. It was like being back at school and seeing the Headmistress beckoning you over. She knew why Ros was here, of course – the Dean had called Lara the day before, insisting on making the opening speech. Obviously, Rosalind had changed her mind about the importance of the upcoming symposium. Lara guessed that the brisk ticket sales might have helped sway her.

'Quite the turnout, Miss Stone,' smiled Rosalind as she approached. At the Labor Day party, the Dean wore a staid dress, her hair wound in a tight bun. Today, her hair was glossy and blow-dried, and she was wearing a silk blouse with a bow at the neck; the look was somewhere between Diane Sawyer and Julianne Moore.

'I've seen today's schedule,' said Rosalind briskly. 'All very impressive. You should be congratulated, Lara, especially your keynote speaker: how did you persuade Darius Allen to come at such short notice?'

I was begging him to stay on the other side of the ocean, thought Lara, but instead, she just shrugged modestly.

'Of course, I know Darius already,' said Ros. 'We were in Davos together a few years ago.'

'Really?'

Lara couldn't imagine what the dean of a small east coast college was doing at the annual meeting of the World Economic Forum. Darius, however, she wasn't at all surprised.

'And we have a full house,' Ros continued. 'So nice to see so many people interested in the media arts.'

'Yes, we're all surprised but pleased,' said Lara. 'Harry would have been proud.'

Rosalind's smile took on a sickly aspect.

'Yes, I'm sure.' She paused. 'I wanted to have a word about that before we started.'

'About Harry?'

'Yes, you may have noticed that there has been some police activity around the campus over the past week. They are investigating the circumstances of Professor Robbins' passing; that is only right and proper.'

Lara waited. She had a feeling this was all leading up to something.

'But we don't want to dwell too much on the circumstances of Harry's death, do we? It was tragic and heartbreaking, of course, but I'm not sure it's helpful to remind today's guests about it. His reputation is at stake here. As is ours.'

Lara looked at her, aghast.

'I can reassure you that if Harry is mentioned, which as the founder of the event, he should be, it will be in glowing terms,' she said.

'Of course. I fully expect that there will be discretion and sensitivity across the board.'

Rosalind paused, pulling a pained expression.

'I am more concerned about the presence of Detective Carter. It has been noticed that you have been in conversation with her.'

'Yes, I spoke to her the morning we found out about Harry, as I'm sure you did.'

'That's not what I'm talking about.' The Dean's eyes met Lara's.

'I'm talking about today's guest list. I notice that Sarah Carter is on it.'

Lara nodded. The detective had called her the day before and asked if she could attend the symposium. Carter had said it might be helpful if the police and the media *understood* one another. Lara guessed she was still nosing around but didn't think it was a problem for her to come along. After all, she could buy a ticket.

'What's wrong with that?' asked Lara.

'What's wrong is that we don't need unwanted interference.'

‘I just think she wants to listen to a few talks.’

‘I doubt that very much,’ said Rosalind, her lips tight and thin.

‘It will be fine, Ros,’ said Lara with as much reassurance as possible.

‘It better be,’ said the Dean. ‘The last thing I want is for any of the distinguished guests to think that the college is being investigated for any reason.’

Ah, thought Lara. *That* was where all this had been going. Rosalind wasn’t worried about dragging Harry through the mud; she was concerned about the college’s worldwide reputation. She didn't want journalists from France and England going away with the impression that the campus was swamped with cops looking for murderers or asking difficult questions about the alleged wrongdoings of the staff.

‘You keep an eye on her? Am I understood?’

‘I hear you,’ said Lara. Although she very much doubted whether anyone would be able to keep the detective out of any event she chose to attend.

Evidently satisfied, the dean inhaled sharply and stepped out onto the stage. There was a ripple of polite applause as she took the podium like a seasoned politician.

‘Thank you for coming to the inaugural Benedon Symposium,’ she said. ‘I’m sure you’re all as excited as I am to get started on our packed programme of talks, workshops and panel debates, but first, I wanted to give you some background on how the symposium came about.’

Lara waited, wondering how she would handle ‘the Harry question’.

‘The idea for this brand-new initiative began in a faculty meeting when we’d fallen into a slightly heated discussion about the future of journalism. Twenty years ago, the internet had barely got going; there was no such thing as social media and newspapers were still hugely influential. Was that still the case, I wondered? And more to the point, would it still be the same when our students go out into the world? So, I thought, why not bring that discussion out into the open? Why not discuss those questions with the people making the media today? Why not bring different generations together and see if they can inspire each other? Well, that was the vision – and now this is the reality. Please join me in welcoming all of our speakers, and together let's make this an event to remember!'

Lara stood there as the applause swelled. It was unbelievable. Ros hadn't mentioned Harry once; she had hijacked the whole thing. Lara had expected self-aggrandisement and back-patting, but without saying it out loud, the Dean had implied that she had thought up the symposium and brought it into being single-handed.

She's got some brass balls; that's what Alex would have said.

Lara realised she had underestimated Rosalind Davies' ambition. If *she* wasn't going to protect Harry's memory, thought Lara, it was down to her. And that meant making the symposium as good as it could possibly be.

Chapter 21

Sarah filled the vase from the tap in her mom's little en suite bathroom and carefully arranged the tulips she had brought. Her mother's bathroom was nicer than the one at the Carter family home. It looked like an expensive hotel with a cream sink, gleaming tiles, and a walk-in shower with a grey slate floor. A *very* expensive hotel staying at the Ritz-Carlton might be cheaper. Sarah had to read the price list in the Beauville brochure twice before it sank in. *The price of freedom* – literally.

Sighing, Sarah carried the vase back into the living room. It was warm and cosy, with pale green painted walls, cream curtains and two framed prints. Sarah placed the tulips on a table next to her mum's bed. Colleen had always loved flowers.

'I have to go now, Mom.'

'Why?' said Colleen bluntly. 'Sick of me so soon?'

The doctors had warned Sarah that people with dementia could lose their empathy and even become cruel. But having a doctor explain it to you didn't make it any easier when it happened.

'Sorry, mom, but I have to work.'

'Work?' sneered Colleen. 'Is that what you call it?'

Sarah took a deep breath. 'Mom, you might not think....'

'What your *dad* does is real work, taking twelve-hour shifts on campus security, keeping those pampered rich kids safe through the night. He does long hours, hard hours, in all weathers.'

'Mom, please.'

'And you should try walking in *my* shoes once in a while, young missy, scrubbing floors and washing windows until your hands sting with the cold.'

Sarah had never heard her mother speak like this; before the disease, Colleen had always boasted about Sarah's achievements. She had been inordinately proud to see her daughter succeeding in a man's world.

'And why is homework suddenly important to you?' snapped Colleen. 'At that parent conference last week, Mr Baxter said you'd been slacking off again. He said your math division was like a 5-year-old had done it.'

Sarah knew it was the dementia talking, but it was still strange to hear, like stepping through a doorway and finding yourself twenty years in the past. There was some truth to it, too: Sarah was never a particularly good student, especially in Mr Baxter's class, whom she had loathed. A few years ago, after scraping her way through the police civil service exams, Sarah discovered she had mild dyslexia. But then, if Sarah had been more academic, perhaps she would never have joined the police and never would have found the thing she was best at.

'Will you listen to the audiobooks I bought you?' said Sarah, keen to change the direction of the conversation.

'What audiobooks?'

Sarah went over to the sideboard and held up the CDs.

'I got you some Debbie Macomber, Nora Roberts, some Danielle Steel. You used to like all those.'

'I don't like reading,' said Colleen, still grumpy.

'Well, you used to. And you don't have to read them; you can listen to them. All you need to do is pop them in the machine.'

'I don't know how,' said her mum, sullen and truculent. It was as if they'd swapped roles: Sarah, the exasperated mother; Colleen, the teenager, prone to sudden mood swings.

Sarah glanced at her watch, eager to get away. She had an appointment out of town, and it wouldn't look good to be late.

'Just wait there,' she said. 'I'll see if I can find someone to help.'

Sarah walked into the corridor and down to the first office, knocking on the doorframe. 'Hi, I wondered if you could help my mom, she's in room eight?'

A carer looked up from some paperwork. She was about Sarah's age, with at least 50 pounds on her, but she had a round jolly face with a mass of curls sticking out in all directions.

'Sarah Carter?' said the woman. 'Is that you?'

Sarah frowned. The woman looked strangely familiar... then Sarah's eyes widened in recognition.

'Heather?'

It *was* her. Heather Harris had been in her year at school, living just a few blocks from their house. They had been quite close at elementary school, playing with Heather's collection of plastic horses in her sand pit and riding their bikes out to the lake.

'What are you doing here?' said Sarah, surprised at how pleased she was to see a friendly face from the past.

'I work here,' said Heather. 'Have done for five years now. And what about you? I heard you moved to New York to join the police?'

'New Jersey at first. But yes, I was NYPD for a while.'

'You came back to look after your mom, I guess?'

Sarah pulled a face. 'That was the idea, but I don't seem to have done a very good job of it.'

Heather shook her head. 'Uh-uh,' she said. 'Don't you go beating yourself up. You brought your mom to Beauville, which is just about the best place she could be. Trust me, I know.'

It was all coming back to her now: she remembered her mother telling her that Heather had gone into nursing. Sarah couldn't remember why she hadn't stayed in touch with Heather, or any of her other school friends. When she had left Benedon, she hadn't looked back. Scorched earth.

'So, do you still have family here?'

'You remember Dave Miller, on the junior high football team?' asked Heather.

'Sure, I remember,' she lied. The name rang a bell, but that was all. For the life of her, Sarah couldn't put a face to the name.

'We got married,' grinned Heather, waggling her ring finger like a newlywed.

'No way!' said Sarah, feigning enthusiasm. 'He was a hottie.'

Heather gave a modest shrug. 'He's a bit more cuddly now, but he's still my Dave.'

'Do you have kids?'

'Four.'

'Wow.'

'Don't I know it, those puppies run me ragged. But they're worth every minute.'

'I bet,' said Sarah, feeling the small talk running out, and she really needed to get out of there. 'Look, I brought my mom some audiobooks, but I'm not entirely sure she will be able to work the CD player. Do you think you could...?'

'Surely I will,' said Heather. 'I might sit with her and have a listen to them myself. Are you coming back later?'

Sarah felt guilt again; did people visit their parents more than once a day?

'I'm not sure. Cops are supposed to do regular hours like everyone else, but it never seems to work out that way.'

'I get that,' said Heather. 'You can't be in the middle of dealing with a live bank robbery and go, "shift's over, boys, let's all go home!"'

'No. Not that we get many bank robberies around here.' Sarah had to think for a moment, unsure whether Benedon even had a bank anymore.

'Listen, you should come and join us on Monday,' said Heather. 'We have a regular bowling night. Maybe you could bring your husband. Or your wife?'

'I'm in Benedon on my own,' said Sarah awkwardly.

'I'm sorry,' said Heather, seeming genuinely sad. 'Divorced?'

Sarah shook her head, feeling even worse.

'Nope. Just married to the job.'

'All the more reason to come down to the bowling alley one of these weeks. It's a great stressbuster.'

'I'll definitely try.'

'Well, good seeing you, Sizzle,' said Heather with a wink.

Sarah was sure she was still blushing when she reached the car park. *Sizzle*. She hadn't been called that since eighth grade. She put the car into drive and pointed towards Wilmington. Wasn't it strange how things turned out, the different paths people took? Heather with her bowling team and her full-time job caring for other people's families. But Sarah could see it suited her to a tee. Heather had always been a nice girl – no faint praise intended – and had always been family-minded. Hadn't she had four siblings herself? It was no surprise that Heather had never left town, either: this was her world, the Windsor county everywoman. Blue-collar, two cars, a giant BBQ grill in the backyard. But happy, which was more than Sarah could say about herself.

She turned onto the highway, heading west, still thinking about their conversation. Why had she felt so ashamed to admit to Heather that there was no husband or boyfriend in her life? Not even an ex-husband; that would at least have implied some grand passion in the past. Of course, Sarah hadn't been completely chaste. There had been Mike back in the city. Kind, funny Mike, with the dancing blue eyes. The only cop she had ever met who didn't like baseball and one of the few she could call wholly honest. Which was, of course, why she had sacrificed him when everything had fallen apart. When she had fled.

Angrily, Sarah stepped on the gas, the big V8 engine growling and responding, grey asphalt disappearing beneath her tyres. Another perk of the job: no one was going to stop you for speeding. Swearing to herself, she eased off, dropping back to sixty. No sense in going through all that to end up dead in a ditch. Then they really would have won.

Sarah barked out a cynical laugh at that. Because, of course, they *had* won, there was no other way to describe it.

Working vice, it was routine to raid crack houses, nightclubs, and anywhere the bad guys might choose as an HQ. Most of the time, it was a wash-out, just part of the endless game of hide-and-seek they all played. But sometimes, those raids struck gold. Sometimes they got lucky and found money, drugs, and even on one occasion, an old master oil painting stolen from the Upper East Side.

And, of course, most of the time, they bagged it and tagged it, then hit O'Reilly's, whooping and toasting the TV as NBC ran the news. Most of the time.

But that winter night hadn't been most times – and Sarah had felt it when Tony Mankowitz called her out into the corridor. 'Who'll know?' he'd said. Jimmy and Carl were on board, he'd said, a four-way split: get yourself a new car, a nice vacation. And at that moment, standing by that splintered door, Sarah's career was over. She'd gone to the Captain, who'd gone to the chief. And somewhere along the chain of command, they'd done the math: one good cop is better than three dirty cops, sure. But weighed against the good name of the department? It just didn't stack up. It was an election year, and the last thing they needed was another police scandal. So Mank and the others were quietly moved – oh, the irony! – to fraud, and Sarah was left with a choice: transfer or resign, which was no choice at all. So, she grabbed the lifeline of a job here in Benedon, telling herself – and Mike – that she had to go because of her mom, which was half true. But only half.

After just a few minutes, she turned off the freeway, bumping down onto a county road, then into a forest of yellow and orange, the leaves of the trees not yet the deep scarlet they would become in just a few weeks, but still glorious like a shimmering golden fleece. Finally, she saw the estate entrance, just a gap in the trees, bookended by two stone pillars. It was a surprisingly low-key marker, but the drive was just as Sarah had expected, winding away from the road through perfectly-tended parkland dotted with colourful shrubs. And then there it was, the house rearing up through a gap in the trees.

'Now that's more like it,' she said. In Benedon, they

called it 'The Compound', an ironic nod towards the Kennedy clan and their walled-off power base in Hyannis Port out on the Massachusetts coast. The Campbell family home was no Camelot-style castle: a two-storey colonial mansion in the style of Deep South plantation houses with an open porch that ran all the way around, set among trees and well-tended gardens. But there were no walls, no fences, no guard house or visible CCTV; you could drive straight up to the front door. As a law enforcement officer, the lack of security made Sarah jumpy. Even her mom's house had an alarm.

Sarah got out of her car, feeling a little out of her comfort zone. She had never had reason to come out here before; she didn't move in social circles as the Campbells. The Sheriff flattered himself that he was part of that rarefied world, although Sarah suspected Roscoe's invitations to dinner were more about keeping law enforcement on side than how much they enjoyed the Sheriff's repartee.

'Miss Carter?'

A middle-aged woman in what Sarah imagined was a housekeeper's uniform met Sarah at the top of the stairs.

'*Detective* Carter, yes,' she said, pulling out her ID and flashing her badge. 'I have an appointment with Arthur Campbell.'

'Of course, if you'd like to follow me?'

She led Sarah through the cool entrance hall and along a corridor lined with paintings in ornate frames. 'Mr. Campbell is out back in the stables.'

'The stables, of course,' muttered Sarah, taking in an antique clock and an oriental vase sitting on an ornate sideboard, feeling even less happy about the building's lack of security. The corridor ran the length of the building, and to her right, she could see a conservatory with sofas facing the bay windows with an incredible view.

They crossed a long terrace, taking some steps down through a gap in a clipped hedge. In front of them was a long stable block across a cobbled courtyard, like a set from a Western movie.

'Mr. Campbell is with the ponies.' The maid gestured towards a pair of double doors at the centre of the building. Inside, Sarah found a middle-aged man in riding gear – jodhpurs, boots, jumper and gilet, brushing the mane of a chestnut horse.

'Ah, Detective Carter, I presume?' he said, patting the horse's neck and putting down his bristle brush to offer her his hand.

'I'm Arthur Campbell. Sorry for dragging you down here, but if Nelson doesn't get properly groomed, he'll be grouchy the next time we're out. They say elephants have long memories, but I'm sure horses hold grudges even longer.'

He looked Sarah up and down.

'Do you ride, detective?'

'A little,' said Sarah, not wanting him to get the upper hand so soon in their exchange. On a rare vacation to South Carolina five years previously, Sarah had signed up for a riding course, imagining herself galloping along a beach, hair flying. The reality had been rather less boho, bouncing around a covered arena in endless dizzying figure-of-eights, being shouted at by a Germanic woman.

'That's excellent news,' said Arthur. 'I have just the mount for you.'

'Oh no, I'm not dressed for it,' said Sarah, indicating her sensible trouser suit and flat shoes.

'Nonsense, we can find you a pair of boots. Giuseppe!'

Before Sarah could object further, Arthur's groom had led Sarah to the back of the stables where her horse, Sherpa, was snorting and stamping its feet.

Great, she thought as the groom adjusted her stirrups. *How do I get myself into these situations?*

'Hi there, Sherpa,' said Sarah, patting the horse's neck and muttering into his ear. 'I'm Sarah. We're going for a ride.' Sarah kept murmuring sweet nothings and stroking his mane, hoping the beast would treat her gently when it came time to ride.

'Shall we?' Arthur led his horse from the stable by the reins. 'We'll walk down to the Meadow and mount up there. Now, how can I help? I assume you didn't come all this way just for the exercise?'

Sarah took a deep breath. Eleanor's death had been a delicate matter even before Harry Robbins' suicide, but the implication of any connection between the two tragedies could be a flash point.

'I'm investigating the death of Professor Harry Robbins. I'm sure you heard that he was found at his home on Tuesday?'

Arthur nodded solemnly. 'I did.'

'When was the last time you saw him?'

'Saw him or spoke to him?'

'Both?'

He shrugged, then sat up a little straighter in the saddle.

'I saw him at Rosalind's party. We didn't speak. We spoke briefly at my daughter's funeral. He had the nerve to show up.'

'What did you discuss then?'

'He gave his condolences. I accepted them. I didn't have to, but I didn't want a scene. Things were emotional enough that day. I haven't spoken to him since.' Arthur looked at Sarah. 'Which begs the question, why do you want to talk to me?

'Harry's was a sudden death, and I'm looking at every angle, Mr Campbell. I'll be frank; I'm at a loss to explain it.'

'Suicide is hard to understand, Detective.'

He didn't need to add that he had almost certainly spent the last few months struggling with that question.

'I agree, but I'd like to understand if I can. Professor Robbins had no money worries, no issues with depression we know about....'

Arthur looked at her.

'That we know about. It is my experience that some kinds of depression are like that. The sufferer hides it from their friends and family.'

'Experience?' said Sarah.

'I'm sorry?'

'You said you had experience with depression.'

He looked at her.

'Eleanor, Detective,' he said tersely. 'I know what the grapevine is like in Benedon. It can't have escaped your notice that there were rumours surrounding my daughter's mental state before she passed.'

'And...?'

Arthur nodded sadly.

'I can confirm that there had been brief periods when Ellie would have a black cloud hovering over her.'

'Was she on medication?'

'Periodically. Although I couldn't say what, you'd have to speak to our doctor.'

'And was it for depression?'

'It was,' said Arthur. 'But an affair with an older man didn't help.'

Sarah looked at Arthur in surprise.

'So Ellie and Professor Robbins *were* dating?'

'Apparently,' he said impatiently. 'Look, I still fail to see where this concerns my family.'

'I'm simply trying to establish the Professor's movements and state of mind. So you didn't say anything to him at the Labor Day party at the Dean's residence?'

'No.'

'If Mr Robbins was driven to suicide by guilt, he might have tried to apologise to you....'

Arthur laughed bitterly. 'That would require a conscience.'

Sarah felt as though she was intruding on the family's grief. This tragedy was still a deep open wound for the Campbells – it was foolish to think otherwise.

'Thank you for your time, Mr Campbell,' she said. 'If you don't mind, I'll take Sherpa back to the stables. But before I go, could you give me a quick rundown of your movements that night?'

He gave a soft sigh.

'I went to the party with my colleague Beale Norris. We left together at around 8 pm, then popped into another Labor Day event at my Country Club. I can give you all the details if you want to corroborate that. But I don't see... it was my understanding that Professor Robbins had taken his own life?'

'Yes, that appears to be the case, and there's no suggestion that anyone else is involved. I'm just collecting facts.'

Arthur shook his head sadly.

'Good luck with that, detective. It's been my experience that some things are unknowable.'

Sarah walked Sherpa back, handing the horse over to the groom after whispering a word of thanks into the animal's twitching ear.

She retraced her way back up to the house, pausing on the terrace, looking at the manicured grounds. She sighed, wondering what she had hoped to achieve here. A confession that the Campbell clan had conspired to break Harry

Robbins and push him towards suicide? Even Sarah could see that was unlikely. And why would they? Arthur had disliked Harry and blamed him for his part in Eleanor's death, but that was very different from forcing Harry towards the edge. Had the Campbells ruined Harry's career; put pressure on the college to ease him out? Probably. Could they have hamstrung his finances or piled legal troubles on his shoulders? Easily. But was Arthur so vengeful after all this time that he would kill Harry Robbins for the death of his daughter? It was possible but unlikely. Grief made people do the strangest things, but from this visit, it looked to Sarah like the family had their hands full just getting through the days.

As Sarah began walking back through the house, she suddenly had that strange sixth sense that she was being watched. She turned and standing there in the sunlit conservatory Sarah had spied earlier was a familiar-looking middle-aged woman with silvery blonde hair. It was a moment before Sarah realised why she thought she recognised her: this woman looked like an older version of Eleanor Campbell.

'Mrs Campbell?' called Sarah. 'Eliza Campbell?'

The woman didn't respond, but her red-rimmed eyes fixed on Sarah's in an intense glare.

'I'm Detective Carter. Could we have a word?'

'No!' The shout made Sarah jump. Sarah saw Brandon Campbell appear from a door behind his mother. He whispered something urgently into his mother's ear, then strode across the room and closed the doors behind him, blocking Sarah's view.

'What do you think you're doing here?' he snapped, face flushed. All the grace and good manners he exhibited at the sports field had gone.

'I'm here to speak to your father,' said Sarah, 'And I was wondering if I might ask your mother a few questions too.'

'No, you can't,' he said. 'My mother is not well; she is in no condition to speak to anyone, especially not the police.'

Sarah pressed on.

'I just wanted to ask about the Labor Day party and where she was when Harry Robbins died.'

Brandon snorted.

'Do you think my mother could help you with any of that? She hasn't spoken since the funeral – I thought I had made that clear.'

He had said something similar at the football field, but Sarah hadn't believed that Mrs Campbell was mute.

'It wasn't a turn of phrase,' said Brandon, as if he was reading her mind. 'My mother doesn't speak. So, as you might imagine, she wasn't at the party. She hasn't gone anywhere for a very long time.'

Sarah made a mental note to check, but she suspected he was telling the truth. After losing a sister, she could understand Brandon wanting to protect his mom, but still... a mother who hadn't spoken for six months? That was strange.

'Please, Detective Carter,' said Brandon, his tone softening. 'My mom's so fragile right now. We've been through enough in this family and now it feels like we've lost her too.'

Sarah saw his eyes glisten, and suddenly she felt bad. Brandon Campbell's situation wasn't that different from hers – they both had moms who were physically present but also heartbreakingly remote.

Sarah looked back at the conservatory door and thought of arguing. She sensed that the Campbells weren't telling her something, but maybe Brandon was right: there had been too much upset for one day.

'Sure, thank your dad for me,' she said and walked back onto the drive.

She slid into the Landcruiser and fired up the engine. Then again, maybe a little upset wouldn't do any harm. When you kicked a bee's nest, sometimes you got stung, and sometimes you got honey – but either way, you always created a hum. 'Let's see which way they go now,' said Sarah, putting the car in drive. 'Let's see if they bite.'

Chapter 22

'Of course, today it's the Gaza Strip, tomorrow it's going to be Iran or the Central African states, all of them dominos waiting to fall,' said Darius, stroking the lapel of his pale blue suit. 'When the world is run by Wall Street and the Hang Seng when policy is dictated by people who profit from war, how can we possibly even dream of world peace?'

Lara had stopped listening to Darius ten minutes ago. The man had been holding court at the 'after-show' party as if he were John Pilger himself. Pontificating about the situation in Palestine, giving on-the-ground anecdotes as if he had spent the last six months on the frontline dodging mortar shells – when in fact, he'd spent the majority of the time at his manor house in Sussex. Lara wasn't sure Darius had ever been to the Middle East – he preferred cocktail parties to foxholes.

Lara murmured an 'excuse me', then wandered away and helped herself to a Gin Fizz: the cocktails had certainly been a success. In fact, the whole first day of the symposium had gone amazingly well. Alex's talk on the politics of the newsroom had been a particular triumph, vividly evoking the crazed energy of the 'news rush' with anecdotes about royal babies, terror attacks and sex scandals. Even though he sometimes dismissed newsprint as a 'thing of the past', after Alex had finished, Lara knew that everyone in the auditorium still wanted to be a part of it - and how much Alex still believed in it.

Legendary American writer Francis Barbier had given a change of pace straight after Alex's talk. With snow-white hair and a desert-lined face, Barbier's voice was barely a whisper but drew the attention as he quietly told a hushed audience the story of being kidnapped in Colombia and held in the jungle by rebel forces. Befriending one of his guards, Francis was offered the possibility of escape but instead chose to have the young soldier smuggle a report of his capture to the AP office in Bogota, written on the back of a soup can label. When Barbier finished his story, the applause was so deafening that Lara had to put her fingers in her ears.

Lara tried to imagine Harry here. Imagined how much he would have enjoyed it. She accepted how difficult it must have been for him in his final few months, but if only he could have seen this, seen what he had created—seen the fire in the students' eyes, and the queues outside the door. Perhaps, just perhaps, he might have reconsidered.

'Can I help you with anything else this evening?'

Lara turned to see Mary. She was beginning to think of Mary as 'her assistant', but after tomorrow, Lara would be back to a plain old 'visiting fellow', and Mary would be back to being Doug's secretary. Lara could admit she would miss the craziness of the past few days, their frantic planning and ball juggling.

'You've done more than enough, Mary,' smiled Lara, touching her new friend on the shoulder. 'I genuinely don't think it would have gone half as well without you. And I think our gin fizzes were a hit.'

'I see that policewoman is here,' said Mary, looking down her nose and over her glasses.

She nodded across the room to where Sarah Carter seemed deep in conversation with Alex. 'I saw her on the symposium guest list, but the *VIP party*? I guess with a badge, you can get in anywhere.'

'Speaking of which, could you do me a favour?' said Lara, lowering her voice.

'Shoot.'

'The guest list for the Dean's Labor Day party. Could you get it?'

'I'm sure it won't be too hard. Caroline, Ros's secretary, owes me a favour. I watered her tomato plants for two weeks when she was in Italy last month.'

'I'd be grateful.'

Lara turned away, realising she needed some fresh air. Lara walked towards the windows that looked out onto the lake, skirting around the groups formed around the speakers, each with their own little fan club of guests and Benedon academics. That had been one of the best things about the symposium for Lara; how the whole faculty had engaged with the VIP visitors, genuinely interested to hear about the practical application of things in modern journalism.

Bifold doors opened on a balcony; a wide wooden deck strung with fairy lights swaying gently in the breeze. Leaning on the rail, she looked down at the dark water, the reflection of the warm white lights rippling and fracturing in front of her.

'Don't jump.'

Lara jerked back and spun around. Vernon was grinning down at her.

'Bloody hell, you scared me,' she said. 'I almost *did* fall in.'

'Well, I would have felt duty-bound to jump in after you.'

'You'd only be doing it out of *duty*?" she laughed. 'What kind of holy man are you?'

'I mean, I could leave you there if you'd prefer,' the priest dead-panned.

'As it happens, I'm a strong swimmer,' retorted Lara. 'It's the 21st century, you know; I don't need a man to save me.'

Vernon held up both hands.

'Okay, okay, I apologise unreservedly for *almost* making you fall into the lake. And I promise that if you do fall in, I won't try to save you.'

'Fine.'

'Fine.'

They both burst out laughing. It was good to be able to let off steam after all the pressure of the planning. After Harry.

Vernon joined her at the rail, both looking out towards the distant shore where the white disc of the moon was reflecting off the water.

'Harry would have loved this,' said Vernon.

'He would,' said Lara.

'Actually, Harry would probably have been inside drinking gin and trying to get a job at the *Chronicle*,' corrected Vernon.

She laughed again. 'Right now, Darius would probably give him one. I've never seen him so upbeat.' She looked across to where her boss was laughing with Ros Davies. The Dean looked like she was enjoying herself for once too. Perhaps she and Darius should get together – they could slap each other's backs for all eternity. Lara briefly scanned the crowd looking for Alex – and Sarah Carter – but they both had gone.

'This is a very fancy boathouse,' she said, looking back at the beautiful cedarwood building behind them. 'Back in London, most boathouses are a bit rickety.'

'They call this place the Boathouse, but really it's just an entertaining space for events like this, schmoozing donors, visiting guests, parents and so on.'

'So where does the real rowing action take place?' she asked.

'Down there,' said Vernon, pointing to a brick building fifty metres away. 'Come on. Let me show you.'

Lara hesitated.

'It's getting dark.'

The priest held out his hand to Lara, palm upwards.

'Don't worry; I know my way around.'

Lara glanced back towards the party, where Alex was still talking to the policewoman, then shrugged. *What the hell.* Life was too short to hang around waiting for someone to come and save you.

Lara placed her hand in his. 'Lead on,' she said.

Chapter 23

Sarah rarely went to parties. Back in New York, the few she'd been to had been of the BBQ-and-brews variety, never one like this, full of socialites and intellectuals. In fact, Sarah had never even been to The Boathouse before. She had seen it glittering like a jewel on the edge of the lake from a distance, but this wasn't usually a place for the likes of her. Not unless she was investigating a break-in.

So what was Sarah doing here? If she was off duty, then why was she at the symposium after-party in the first place? For the same reason she had gone to the vigil. Because she was hoping for a break. Sarah's instinct told her that something was wrong in this case. Two suicides months apart, a powerful family, a respectable college with a vested interest in staying that way? She could be reading far too much into this, but she didn't think so. Something just wasn't right. It was just a matter of waiting and watching. Eventually, something would click; it always did.

Standing at the bar, Sarah watched Rosalind Davies, the journalism school dean, work the room. The woman was a born politician, flitting from group to group, listening intently, nodding in agreement, and then sharing a polite joke before moving on again. That was the point of parties like this; not to socialise or have a good time, but to make a connection and leave a good impression. For people like the Dean, this was just a business meeting with added canapes. It was all a long way from the Benedon Sarah had known as a kid, seeing it from the other end of the telescope. Sometimes, when her dad did his patrol on a white golf buggy, he would let Sarah perch on the back seat. She'd watched the professors and the students disappear behind the ivy-clad walls and had fantasised about what they did after the lessons finished. But she didn't imagine this, something so glamorous and magical.

Her phone rang. It was a number she didn't recognise: not work then. She stepped out into the lobby, where it was quieter.

'Carter, is that you?'

Sarah almost jumped. She hadn't heard that voice in so long.

'Mike?'

Mike Walsh, her friend from the Ninth Precinct. Well, 'friend' didn't quite cover it. They'd been on a handful of dates a couple of years earlier and decided they were better in the platonic zone. Or rather, Sarah had.

'Don't sound so surprised.'

'I am. Your number didn't come up.'

'New phone.'

There was a pause.

'Are you at a party?'

'Work thing at the college,' she said.

'You've gone all fancy, huh?'

'Still a beer and pretzel girl.'

She heard Mike snort down the line.

'Sarah, you were *never* a beer and pretzel girl.'

The silence hung heavy on the line, and Sarah had to

check the screen to make sure that the line hadn't disconnected.

'So, what's up, Mike? Just checking up on life in the sticks?'

'I was wondering if you'd heard the news?'

'News?' she said, suddenly more interested.

'Mankowitz, King, and Franklin. They're going down.'

At the names, Sarah's heart skipped a beat. Her former colleagues; the ones who had ruined her career.

'They're going down? What do you mean?'

'They're all suspended pending trial: internal affairs caught them red-handed in a sting. After you blew the whistle, Mank obviously thought they were untouchable. He was wrong. IA got them on tape conspiring to lift a case of unsigned credit cards straight from the factory. Dumbasses.'

Now Sarah's heart was beating. It was beating hard.

'Sarah, this time they're going to jail. You were right.'

'I know I was right, Mike. The *Commissioner* knew I was right. Everyone just wanted to turn a blind eye.'

That wasn't fair, but she was past caring. Mike had believed her, and he had supported her, but Mike had been as powerless as everyone else. The NYPD hierarchy had decided to sweep it all under the carpet, and Sarah Carter was just collateral damage.

'Well, it sounds like someone did listen after all,' said Mike. 'I guess they've been watching them, waiting for them to do something this stupid.'

Sarah was finding it hard to process it all.

'You should call the Captain,' said Mike. 'He always liked you. There's no reason you couldn't walk straight back into that job.'

Hope flared in Sarah's chest but then died almost immediately. She had gone over and over this in her mind so many times, but there was no way back. She'd been right about the dirty cops, but in that precinct, Sarah would still be seen as a snitch.

'Thanks Mike, but I can't come back. You know why.'

'It's got to be worth a call. Plenty of people around here think you're a hero, Sarah.'

She felt her eyes water, emotion swelling in her chest. She'd pictured this moment, walking back into the station house, everybody stopping to clap and applaud. That's how it would work in the movies, but in real life? Sarah couldn't go back on the street, kicking in doors, never quite sure if her buddies would be right behind her, always unsure if they fully trusted her.

'Thanks for the call Mike; it's great to hear your voice. Been too long.'

'That's the other reason I'm calling. I might be up your way next weekend.'

'What? Why?'

'My buddy Joey T, you remember him? He lives in Vermont now. He's bought himself a boat, and we're going fishing.'

Sarah let out a laugh.

'You fish now?'

Mike chuckled.

'I'm getting old. But why don't you join us? I'm not sure we'll catch a damn thing, but we can kick back and raise a few brews; what do you say?'

'Maybe,' said Sarah. 'Have to see how things fit together.'

She wasn't exactly sure why she was being resistant. For so long, she had wanted to get this phone call, but right now, the NYPD just felt like a piece of her past.

'Hey,' said Mike. 'Should have asked: how is your mom?'

Mike had always been thoughtful.

'Mom's good and bad, I guess. Just moved into a care home.'

'Full time? That's good – well, tough for you, but you know I had the same thing with my dad? In the end, if it works, it works.'

Of course, she knew what Mike was really saying. Nothing was standing in Sarah's way anymore; she could return to the city. Not the same precinct, perhaps, that bridge was burned, but could she go across to anti-terror or the gangs unit? For one moment, she allowed the fantasy to grow. Her old life was within reach once more, just as she had wanted it to be.

'Thanks for letting me know, Mike,' she said. 'And give me a call when you're passing through, yeah?'

'Sure. I'll do that.' She could hear the disappointment in his voice, but she couldn't give him anything more. She hung up and walked straight across to the bar: she was trying to stay sober, but if ever there was an excuse for a cocktail, Mike's phone call was it. But no luck: the bar was unmanned. She turned and scoured the room. Maybe she could get one from one of the roaming wait staff. Sarah stepped towards one of them and then felt a 'click' of recognition. It was *her* – the girl from the vigil. The one wearing the purple jacket, the one who had been sobbing. *Damn.*

Sarah quickly made her way across.

'Hi. Do you have any of the gin cocktails left?'

'Yes, we do,' said the girl, holding up a jug.

'Okay, why not?' The girl filled Sarah's glass, and Sarah raised it in salute.

'It's been a great day,' she said. 'Such a wonderful tribute to Harry Robbins.'

She watched the girl's face. Micro-expressions, that's what they called them at the academy: slight ticks and movements of the face. A clenched jaw, a flared nostril.

They were fleeting, but they revealed the true feelings of the respondent. When Sarah mentioned Harry's name, the girl's eyes widened, and her mouth turned down. Surprise, sadness, maybe even distaste.

'Did you know him?' asked Sarah, putting her cocktail down without even taking a sip. There was some sort of whipped egg floating on the top of it. Sticking with Pepsi Max was safer.

The girl's eyes flicked towards the bar, but Sarah was standing between her and an exit.

'Harry was my professor, yes.'

'That's right,' said Sarah. 'I saw you at the vigil. You looked upset.'

'We all were,' said the girl. 'He was my teacher. He was wonderful.'

'Oh, were you close?'

In all this time investigating this case, Sarah had yet to form a complete picture of Harry Robbins. He was indistinct, an enigma. That often happened when someone had died suddenly because people tended to reassess them and reframe them as heroes or villains. It could make it tough to get a handle on what they had really been like. One thing was sure though; Harry Robbins had been accused of sleeping with a student. Maybe it was true, maybe it wasn't, but it wasn't out of the realms of possibility. If it had happened with Ellie Campbell, it had probably happened with other students too. And maybe it had happened with this girl.

'Sorry,' said the girl, moving to get past Sarah. 'I need to get back. I'm working.'

Sarah stood back to let her pass.

'Sure. And I'm sorry for your loss.'

The girl just gave a tight nod and hurried away, around

the bar and out of the door at the back. Sarah walked over to one of the other waitresses.

'Who was that? The waitress with the blonde hair?'

'Oh, that's Meghan. Why, is there a problem?'

'No, no problem, I just think I've seen her somewhere before.'

Sarah pulled out her badge and flashed it, then put it away again.

'So are all the waitresses here Benedon students?'

'Yes. I study Fine Art. There's a group of us who do all the events. It's pretty well paid.'

'Meghan too?'

The girl shook her head. 'This is Meghan's first time.' A dark-haired waitress walked past, and the girl waved her over.

'Hey Susie, you know Meghan. This lady is a police officer.'

'Sure. Megan's in Franklin, my house,' said Susie.

She saw Sarah's confusion and explained: 'We don't have dorms at Benedon. We live in houses, like sorority houses, without any of that hazing stuff. Is Megan in trouble?'

'No, I just saw her at the vigil. I was worried about her because she was so upset.'

Susie and the other girl exchanged a look.

'She's been distraught all week. Meghan was in love with Professor Robbins. I mean, *seriously* obsessed with him,' she said, rolling her eyes. 'When she found out we were working at the symposium party, Meghan wanted in. She begged me to get a gig tonight so she could bump into him. When he died, Meghan didn't want to do it anymore, but I'd put myself out to get her this job tonight, so I told her this morning, "you've got to come."'

'Listen do you mind going and getting her for me?' said Sarah. 'I just want to ask her a couple of questions.'

Susie nodded and headed for the door. She was only gone a couple of seconds before she came back.

'Uh, sorry, officer,' she said. 'But she left her apron on the counter. She's gone.'

Chapter 24

Lara and Vernon walked out into the open air, the night sky above them like parachute silk pricked with holes. Lara turned her face up towards it.

'Now that's impressive. We don't get night skies like that in London.'

'But you have fish and chips, right?'

'Yes, and that makes up for it completely.'

She looked across at the priest.

'So, did you make it to the symposium? I didn't see you on the guest list.'

Vernon pointed to his dog collar.

'This thing is a bit like a police badge; people just let me in without asking for a ticket. So yes, I was there, and I loved it. I've always been obsessed with the news. When I was a kid, I used to love Tin Tin.'

Lara frowned.

'Tin Tin? The Belgian cartoon fella?'

Vernon gave her a sideways look. 'You do know that Tin Tin was a reporter?'

'Really? I had no idea. I thought he was a meddling kid who hung around with a sailor.'

It was fun talking to Vernon; he was one of the few people with a sense of humour around here.

She followed Vernon down a path towards the long dark building he'd pointed out from the balcony.

Vernon took a set of keys from his pockets and slid back a door with a shudder. Lara stepped inside.

'Wow, you weren't joking; this is impressive.' They were standing in a passageway between high shelving units; on either side were racks of long thin boats stacked on top of each other. Even in the low light, she could see their gleaming hulls and the polished oars.

It was another example of the power of money. Each one of these boats probably cost more than a family car – and there were dozens of them.

'So how come you have the keys?'

'Coach Wilson was my mentor here – he's still in charge of the rowing team. He lets me come down and take one out whenever I like.'

Lara walked along the rows, trailing her fingers along the side of one of the carbon fibre racing shells.

'Do you row or do you scull?' asked Lara, trying to sound like she knew what she was talking about. That was about all she remembered from her days on the water at school. If you rowed with one oar, you were rowing, when you had two oars, you were sculling.

'I scull; it's faster,' said Vernon.

He knocked his knuckles against one of the boats, giving a hollow sound. 'But I prefer to train with a partner: double sculls.'

Lara found herself thinking of Vernon's shoulders as he reached forwards and pulled back. Why was she thinking about a priest's muscles? She had obviously had far too much of that gin.

'Let's find somewhere to sit.'

They walked out of the lakeside doors onto a narrow deck. There was a bench near the shore, and they sat down side-by-side, looking out at the dark, lapping water.

'So why did you come to Benedon, Lara?'

'The college called me.'

'No, I mean, *why*? Why now? Why here? I've googled you; it turns out you're one of the most accomplished investigative reporters in the world. So why step off the treadmill so suddenly?

'I guess I wanted a change,' she said vaguely. 'What about you?'

'Ah. That's a long story.'

Lara looked up towards the balcony of the luxe Boathouse.

'I think we have time. Everything's running smoothly upstairs.'

It was true: the symposium had been a success, and so had the party. She could still hear the hubbub and the laughter coming from the open terrace doors, but Lara had been running on empty for days; she hadn't been able to relax for a moment since she'd arrived. Frankly, she could do with a lie-down, but sitting in the dark with a handsome priest would do for now.

'I did my degree here,' said Vernon. 'I came on a rowing scholarship.'

'I didn't know the college had a divinity course.'

'I studied astronomy and philosophy,' he said.

'Brainy and brawny,' laughed Lara. 'But why rowing?'

'I grew up near Washington, on the Potomac River. My pops rowed every morning, and no surprise: he encouraged me too. Physically I was built for it. You need to be tall to be a rower. But I enjoyed the discipline, the focus too.'

'So when did the church become a thing?' asked Lara, then cringed at the question. 'Sorry, is that a bad thing to say? Aren't you supposed to be hit by a bolt of lightning or something?'

Vernon gave a low laugh.

'My parents were fairly devout Catholics, so that helped. But I guess it started with a girl,' he said, reaching down to pick up a pebble, which he threw into the water, ripples spreading in dark circles.

'I fell in love when I was a student here. In my senior year, I got engaged to a girl I met on my first day.'

Lara looked across.

'You were *engaged*?'

'For a while. The wedding was planned for the summer after we graduated, and then – pow! – it was over.'

'You called it off?'

'She'd been sleeping with a friend of mine. A really good friend. The guy I rowed with in the men's pairs, actually.'

'Ouch. But how did you get from that to this?' Lara touched her throat, where he wore his dog collar.

'About the same time, I tore a ligament in my knee, so a serious competitive career was over for me. She broke my heart, I broke my knee. There was nothing more for me here.'

'I'm so sorry.'

He waved a hand, dismissing it.

'It was for the best. After I limped over the line to get my degree, I went travelling. India, Cambodia, anywhere life was cheap.'

Lara looked at him, finding it hard to imagine him in Thailand, a stoner on the beach.

'I realised pretty quickly that I was lost, directionless. And then, I met a missionary in Africa. We became friends. Before I knew it, I was at a seminary in Kentucky. Three years later, I was ordained, and a short time after that, I heard Benedon was looking for a chaplain. I guess this place still held happy memories.'

Lara could understand that. She had chosen to live on a narrowboat docked on the Thames because some of her most cherished times had been with her parents on their boat. Given that they were killed in a sailing accident, some people thought that choosing to live on a houseboat was strange, but the water was where she felt closest to them.

'The guy who did the lecture about the newsroom was great, by the way. I saw you with him earlier. You seemed pretty cosy.'

'Alex is my best friend. We went to journalism school together, and both ended up at *The Chronicle*. You know he didn't even write that speech? He wings it, and he's completely brilliant.'

Lara was glad that it was dark as she found herself blushing.

'Harry wondered if there was someone back at home,' said Vernon with a smile.

'He did?'

'I saw him on Sunday afternoon. He was in a great mood. He said he'd met someone at the deli.'

'Harry said that?'

'He was struck by you.'

'Well, Alex is not my boyfriend.' Lara wasn't entirely sure why she said it, but right then, it seemed important.

'But you do love him?'

Lara thought about his question for a moment.

'Everyone I love dies,' she said. 'My parents were killed in a boating accident when I was 12. I went to live with my grandfather, who died soon after that, which is how I ended up being brought up by my uncle. My best friend was murdered last year when she was investigating some very bad men – and they came for me too. They didn't get me, but they killed my cat.'

'Your cat? Man, how low is that?' said Vernon.

'It's fucking low.'

Lara grimaced: 'Sorry, sorry for swearing.'

'It's OK,' said Vernon with a chuckle. 'What was his name?'

'Dingo.'

Vernon made the sign of the cross, then looked up towards the sky.

'Via con Dios Dingo,' he said softly. With anyone else, Lara would have assumed that he was taking the mickey, but with Vernon, it felt like a solemn moment.

'And now Harry's dead too?' said Vernon. 'I guess that's what you're thinking?'

'I didn't know Harry well, but yes, he died too. So if you want to know why nothing has ever happened between Alex and me?' She held out a hand in a 'there you go' gesture. 'You know I tell the journalism students to check their emotions at the door. But it's hard, you know. To be that tough.'

Vernon gently touched her shoulder and waited until she turned her face towards his.

'None of that was your fault, Lara. I know you may not hear it through all that pain, but it's not your fault.'

'Thank you,' she said.

She put her head on his shoulder, enjoying the release of being so honest with someone. Vernon smelt good, and warm - but then she was a bit drunk.

'Do you miss it?' she asked.

'Miss what?'

'Sex.'

She felt the chuckle deep in his throat.

'Have you always been this blunt?'

'You say that like it's a bad thing: blunt is my superpower. In my early days at the Chronicle, the features desk sent me to interview celebrities, but the PRs complained because all the actors and TV presenters thought I was too intrusive.'

Vernon laughed.

'What did you ask them?'

'Oh, you know: "Why did you cheat on your wife?" "Why was your movie a flop?" I just asked the questions I wanted to know the answers to.'

There was a pause. Somewhere out in the darkness, Lara could hear something splashing about in the water. Fish? Mermaid?

'In answer to your question, I'd be lying if I said it's not difficult sometimes,' said Vernon. 'A few months after I was first ordained, Lucy, my ex-fiancé, came to see me and said she had made a terrible mistake. That... well, that was tough. But now? I have no regrets. The pluses far outweigh the minuses.'

Lara nodded, her head still against his shoulder.

'In answer to *your* question, I came to Benedon because of Alex.'

Vernon didn't say anything, letting her continue.

'I needed some distance. Over the past year, things have begun to feel complicated between us. I don't know how he feels about me. Truthfully, I can't quite work out how I feel. I did know that I felt stuck, like I couldn't move forward with my life. I couldn't take it anymore, so I decided the best thing to do was to get away from him.'

'But he dropped everything to come to the symposium, didn't he? It sounds like it's not that complicated for Alex.'

'Maybe,' she said, looking up towards the balcony. She saw a shadow shift, but it was just the fairy lights in the wind.

Chapter 25

Alex was watching the woman's mouth move with detached fascination. He had never seen lipstick so shiny and red; it was like fresh gloss paint. It reminded Alex of the highly polished bodywork of Darius's midlife Ferrari. Perhaps that was the idea.

'...And, of course, fake news has become such a concern to everyone, hasn't it?' the woman said, as Alex tuned back in. 'Wasn't that what you were saying in your talk, Mr Ford?'

Alex had a vague idea that this woman was a socialite or the rich wife of a college benefactor, but he had spoken to so many people over the past 12 hours they were all starting to blur into one.

'Yes and no,' said Alex, aware that the whole group was now listening. Darius, Dean Rosalind, Doug, the flamboyant professor and a few others keen to be seen.

'My point was that a broadsheet newsroom only deals with *real* news,' said Alex. 'We just don't have the time or inclination to produce anything fake.'

'But your news still goes through a filter, am I not

correct?' said Rosalind. 'Journalists are still human and open to influence wittingly or unwittingly.'

'Yes, of course,' said Alex. 'But we do our best to report as honestly as we can, and to do that, we have to nurture balance from the top down.'

Darius preened at the compliment, as Alex had known he would, but the truth was that Darius rarely wasted his precious socialising time on anything as trifling as the news. Theoretically, Alex was supposed to run the front page past him every day, but in practice, Darius was usually coming back from a long lunch or on his way out to dinner when it came to press time.

'But the fascinating thing is that the newspapers continue to have influence despite dwindling circulations,' said Doug. 'And that's an encouraging thing for our students.'

Alex saw Darius's jaw tighten at the mention of shrinking sales.

'It is nice that people are still listening,' said Alex, trying to change the subject. 'And we shouldn't lose sight of the fact that it's a huge privilege for us to be able to report the news freely. That isn't a given in many parts of the world.'

There were solemn nods all around.

'You're talking about censorship, of course,' said Ros. 'But do you ever find yourself self-censoring?

'You mean not writing the story because it doesn't fit our agenda? No. We write what we see in front of us.zAs my colleague Lara said to your students earlier this week, Ros: 'You can't choose the news.'

There was a titter of polite laughter around the group from everybody except Rosalind, who clearly didn't find that little anecdote amusing, but Alex couldn't resist: Lara had told him about her first lecture, and he would have done exactly the same.

'But we do choose the news. We choose the agenda; we shape opinion,' said Darius.

Everyone stopped and looked at him.

'Or rather, *I* do,' he said grandly. Darius turned to the group as if he were lecturing to them, his adoring students.

'Within any newspaper, there is a tension between the journalist and the editor. Journalists write the news, but we don't have room for *everything*.'

He chuckled at the absurdity of the idea.

'So the editor chooses what goes into the paper and decides what goes on the front cover. And therefore, the editor picks which stories are the most important. Sometimes I choose not to run a story at all. Maybe even a story which would sell a million papers.

'Really?' said Doug, clearly fascinated. 'Why would you do that?'

Darius held up an imperious finger, and Alex could imagine him posing for a statue.

'Timing,' said Darius. 'Imagine we had an exclusive about a political scandal—something of the size of Bill Clinton and Monica Lewinsky. But then there is a terror attack – another 9/11, for example – it would be pointless running the political story, wouldn't it? It would lose its impact.'

Darius looked directly at Alex. 'Am I not right? We don't fake the news, but we curate it and set the agenda.'

Alex reluctantly nodded.

'Of course, we're lucky,' said Darius with a growing smile, 'We live in a time when politicians can't seem to keep it in their pants, which means I'm never short of headlines to choose from.'

As laughter bubbled around the group, Alex excused himself. All this newspaper talk was just a reminder that he had some hard decisions to make and wanted to forget all that, at least for now.

He grabbed a drink and headed for the balcony, leaning on the rail as he looked out over the dark open space of the lake. With the moon's shimmer on the water, the lake looked more like an ocean stretching into infinity.

Alex took a long swallow of his cocktail and was turning back to go inside when he saw movement to his left. Two figures in front of a building down by the water, entwined together. Alex smiled to himself: at least somebody was finding love tonight. Just then, the moon edged from behind the cloud, and Alex saw the shine on the hair of the woman below him. It was Lara, pressed up against a man with dark hair. He slid away from the balcony, not wanting to see more, feeling a sickness all the way to his stomach. He left his glass on a table and walked back inside, heading towards the lobby. If there wasn't a cab, he'd walk. *Run.*

'Leaving already?'

Alex looked up. It was the detective; what was her name again? They had chatted briefly earlier, just standard small talk: how do you like our campus? Isn't it a lovely setting? The symposium's a wonderful initiative for young people; I enjoyed your talk. Alex had had half a dozen almost identical conversations that night.

'I'm tired: it's been a long day,' said Alex.

'I can imagine. Going back to the hotel? I should imagine there's an after-after-party there.'

The woman was good-looking, with short hair. Sexy in an I-carry-a-gun kind of way, but Alex just wanted to leave.

'I'm staying with my friend,' he said. 'She's a lecturer here, she helped organise the symposium. She lives locally.'

The policewoman nodded.

'Yes, Lara Stone. I met her.'

Alex remembered Lara telling him about meeting the detective at Harry's place the morning of his death.

'So why are you here, officer? Are you here on official business?'

'Nah, I'm casing the joint,' she said. 'The moment they lock up, I'm coming back and moving in.'

'It is pretty spectacular,' smiled Alex, looking back towards the windows. 'But it'd be a nightmare to heat.'

'Maybe you're right. You'd need a ladder to pull the drapes too.'

She looked at him.

'So d'you want a ride?'

Alex couldn't help laughing. 'I take it you're offering me what us Brits call "a lift"?'

'Sure,' she said. 'Just that.'

Alex smiled.

'Will it be in a real police car?'

'Yep. No playing with the radio, though.'

Chapter 26

Sarah sat in the car, still stunned. She couldn't believe she'd offered that hot British editor guy a lift back home. Such good-looking men usually intimidated Sarah. She didn't meet many of them, but when she did, they were typically self-important jerks. But Alex's lecture had been genuinely fascinating. Funny too. Sarah had only gone to the conference to get a feel for Harry Robbin's line of work, but by the end of Alex's talk, she was almost ready to quit police work and join the local newspaper.

Sarah took a breath, wondering if she had come on too strong, but then figured it was too late to worry about it. Being a cop, she could explain it away as community service in action, and besides, Alex had seemed more interested in Lara Stone than anyone else at the symposium.

His mouth had pinched when Sarah asked why they weren't leaving together. You didn't need to be a detective to work out that Alex and Lara were probably more than friends.

Sarah got out of the car and walked towards the college rooming house, checking her purse. It only contained her ID wallet, some wipes, a pack of gum and her service weapon. Sarah didn't seriously think she would need much firepower to deal with a house full of young women, but it was department procedure to have it on you at all times. Then again, Sarah remembered what girls that age were like. They could be vicious when they wanted to be.

The lights were on, so Sarah pressed the bell. A girl with perfectly blow-dried hair opened the door on the security chain.

'Jimmy's Pizza?' she frowned.

Sarah flashed a smile and held up her ID. 'Guess again,' she said.

The door closed. She heard some hissed conversation, and the door opened again.

'How can we help you, officer?' said Miss Blow-dry robotically. Everyone had heard that phrase on TV and thought it was the only way to speak to the police.

'I understand a girl named Meghan lives here,' said Sarah. 'Could I speak to her?'

'I think she's in her room. Shall I get her?'

'No need,' said Sarah, stepping into the entrance hall. 'Just show me the way.'

In Legally Blonde, the sorority houses looked like a Beverley Hills mansion, but Franklin House was more like a cheap hotel with individual rooms off a central corridor. Most of the doors were open, and Sarah glanced inside as she passed. Warmly lit, plenty of colourful bed linen and posters of musicians on the walls: just like her days at the dorm at the Academy. It was funny; at the symposium, everybody talked about how technology had made modern society accelerate to lightspeed, but if you looked more closely, things didn't change that much. Blow-dry Girl stopped at a closed door with a '7' painted in the centre.

'This is it,' she said, her voice low. 'Should I... tell her you're here?'

Sarah suppressed a smile: that was another legacy from the TV cop shows. Cops never knocked on TV; they always kicked the door in.

'I think I can take it from here.'

Sarah rapped briskly on the door.

'Meghan?' she called.

There was shuffling, and then the door opened a crack.

'Me again,' said Sarah, flipping the badge and stepping inside. Compared to her housemate, Meghan's hair was a mess; her eyes were bloodshot and red-rimmed too. It didn't take much detective work to guess she'd been lying on the bed weeping. Sarah left the door open; the girl was skittish enough as it was.

'You're not in any trouble,' said Sarah soothingly. She wasn't sure about that, she was waiting to see what the girl had to say for herself, but for now, it paid to play good cop.

'I just need to ask a few more questions: why don't you sit down?'

The girl perched on the edge of her unmade bed, glancing towards the door. Sarah pulled the girl's chair from her study desk and positioned it strategically between her and the exit.

'I just wanted to continue our conversation before you ran off. Now, why was that? Why did you run, Meghan?'

'I didn't feel well,' said Meghan, looking at the floor.

'Your friends were worried.'

'I'll bet they were,' sneered the girl.

Okay, so they weren't BFFs. Susie wouldn't be asking Meg to do a waitressing shift again.

'You were telling me about Professor Robbins,' prompted Sarah. 'How you admired him.'

Meghan didn't respond, her hair hanging down and hiding her face.

Sarah tried another tack: 'So you're studying journalism?' she turned to look at Meghan's desk, which was covered in textbooks and files. And there, propped up on a shelf, was a framed picture of Harry Robbins, smiling at the camera, his arm around a young woman. *This* young woman, Sarah realised: Meghan.

'Gosh, where was this taken?' she asked, picking it up.

Meghan's eyes flared with alarm, then anger. Finally, she looked down at her hands again.

'The last day of last semester. Harry... Professor Robbins took me out.'

Sarah looked more closely at the photo; she recognised the background. The counter at Jimmy's Pizza on Main Street. For college girls, Jimmy's was the place to be.

'Just the two of you?'

The girl shot Sarah a look of pure spite. *If looks could kill...* thought Sarah.

'He took the whole class, actually,' said Meghan, raising her chin defiantly. 'Professor Robbins was very generous that way; he wanted everyone to feel as comfortable with him as... as I did.'

'So you two had a special relationship?'

'I know what you're implying,' said Meghan. 'But you're wrong – they were all wrong about Harry. You think he was some predator praying on impressionable young girls? It wasn't like that. Harry was just an amazing man, and they hounded him....'

'To his death?'

'Yes,' said Meghan. She was quietly crying now. 'They hounded him to his death.'

It was worth bringing the purse, after all, thought Sarah, pulling out a packet of tissues and handing them to the girl.

'You've never heard of Professor Robbins having a relationship with any of the students?'

There was a pause.

'Not the students, no.'

Sarah looked up sharply.

'Harry had a relationship with someone else? Who?'

But Meghan didn't seem to be listening.

'They were all so pious, weren't they?' she muttered.

'Pious?' Asked Sarah. 'Who was pious?'

'The college – Benedon,' she said. 'Spreading the rumours about Harry, letting those disgusting insinuations circulate, when all the time they knew the real truth.'

'What truth Meghan? What did they know?'

'That Harry wasn't having an affair with Ellie Campbell.'

Meghan turned her pale face towards Sarah, her eyes wet and bleak. 'Because Harry was screwing the Dean.'

Sarah looked at her, not sure she had heard correctly.

'The Dean? Are you saying Harry Robbins was having an affair with Rosalind Davies? How do you know?'

'Because I saw them. I saw Harry going into her house. I know he stayed the night.'

'The whole night? How do you know that, Meghan?'

The girl gave in to sobs, pressing Sarah's tissues to her eyes. When she looked up, the young woman looked frightened.

'Meghan, you can tell me. You're not going to be in trouble.'

'I saw him go into the Dean's house,' said Meghan quietly. 'I saw Harry and Dean Davies together through the window. I couldn't believe it. I waited to see how long he would stay. I waited a long time.'

'When was this?'

'The week Ellie Campbell killed herself.' Meghan's lip curled in distaste. 'And then that hypocritical bitch Ros pushed him out. And everyone's surprised that....' She let out a sob. '...that Harry did what he did.'

Sarah felt for the girl, she felt the urge to put a consoling arm around her, but that was another department directive in this new enlightened age: no physical contact that might be misinterpreted. Instead she thanked her and turned to leave; Sarah was fairly clear about what had happened here. Meghan was obsessed with Harry Robbins; perhaps she was even stalking him. She'd followed him to the Dean's house and watched all night until Harry emerged the next morning. She could only imagine the hurt Meghan must have felt. But could Meghan have harmed Harry Robbins in return? Sarah wasn't sure about that. She wasn't sure Meghan could hurt Harry in any way.

Sarah walked back out into the corridor. She was not entirely surprised to find a clutch of Meghan's housemates whispering to each other in the corridor. Sarah beckoned the Blow-dry Girl over.

'Listen, Meghan's a little upset. Could you stay with her?' she asked. 'Check that she's OK tonight?'

'Is Meg in trouble?'

'No, quite the opposite: she's been helping me with my case. I need her looked after. Can you do that?'

The girl's eyes lit up.

'Like the witness protection programme?'

'Not quite,' smiled Sarah thinly. 'But it's important.'

On her way out, Sarah would call the college; these days, they had an active counselling team who were on call 24/7, but in the meantime, she was sure that Meghan's housemates would fuss around her like she was a celebrity. Sarah headed for the door. She needed to get some sleep. And tomorrow, she had other places to be. Someone had some questions to answer.

Chapter 27

Sarah was waiting outside the lecture theatre as the crowds streamed out, pulling on their coats. Smiling faces, people chattering, excitedly discussing the lecture: 'Didn't you think that point he made about the internet was exactly...' 'I never trusted the government before, but after this...' '...how can you put the genie back in the bottle?'

It was day two of the Benedon Symposium, but the excitement was still high. According to the sign next to the entrance, the lecture that had just finished had been by Ben Danson, 'ex-FBI, New York Times tech columnist and author of *Careful Where You Click: How Your Internet Searches Could Get You Blacklisted*.

Sarah guessed that the man in the tweed jacket was Ben Danson. He had an overcoat draped over his arm and a battered leather briefcase. He certainly fit the profile of 'brainy ex-spy'. The big clue was that he was walking between Doug Bishop and Rosalind Davies, sycophantic smiles pasted on both of their faces.

The Dean's smile slipped the moment she saw Sarah, replaced by a look of irritation. Sarah could hardly blame her: who wanted the police roaming about in the corridors while paying guests were watching?

'Miss Davies,' said Sarah mildly. 'Would it be possible to have a word?'

Without looking at Sarah, Rosalind turned to her guest. 'It was a wonderful talk, Mr Danson; thank you so much for giving us the benefit of your expertise. Doug will show you to your onward transport.'

Then Rosalind turned and began walking along a path across the lawns. Sarah trotted to catch up.

'Another success for the symposium, it seems?' she said.

'Save me the small talk, officer. What do you want?'

Sarah tried not to smile.

'Why so hostile, Ms Davies? I'm simply doing my job, and right now, my job is to find out why one of your colleagues is dead. I would have thought that that was something you would like to assist with.'

'Harry Robbins shot himself, Miss Carter. It's a tragedy but hardly a mystery. And right now, I have other concerns; most particularly, I have to get on with the smooth running of the university. I fail to see how this constant harassment is helping Harry Robbins or the work he began here.'

'Harassment,' repeated Sarah. 'That's an interesting choice of word because there is strong evidence to suggest that Mr Robbins was driven to suicide.'

Rosalind stopped.

'Driven to...?' she gasped, her face paling. 'That's just preposterous. Who would want to do that to Harry?'

'That is what I aim to find out.'

'Well, of course, you will have the full cooperation of the college.'

'That's excellent news, Rosalind,' smiled Sarah. 'Because I regard you as a vital witness.'

'Me? How so?'

'Because you were having an affair with Harry Robbins.'

The jab hit home. Rosalind flinched, taking a half-step backwards on her high-heeled shoes, her face a mask of surprise.

'Well, that's just ridiculous.'

She was fast; Sarah could give her that. In a few seconds, Rosalind had assessed her options and decided to go on the offensive.

'You deny it?'

'Categorically. And should you choose to repeat such unfounded accusations, I should have no hesitation in seeking legal remedies.'

'Not unfounded, Mrs Davies.'

Sarah used her marital title deliberately. She pulled out a notebook and flipped it open, making a show of reading out her scribbled notes.

'I have two witnesses, who saw Mr Robbins at your house,' she said.

One, thought Sarah. *A stalker named Meghan, who was pretty unreliable.* But then Ros didn't have to know that.

'I also have CCTV footage from a camera on your street.' That was an out-and-out bluff, but experience told Sarah that nobody ever noticed security cameras, even when they were pointing straight at them. She looked at Ros.

'I have clear images of Mr Robbins entering your house, time-stamped and dated. He does not leave until the following morning.'

She watched as Rosalind re-evaluated her options: should she continue with denial? Perhaps go for some believable explanation, an extended faculty meeting that went on all night?

'My private life is none of your concern, detective,' she

said. 'Harry Robbins and I were both consenting adults. How we choose to spend our evenings is our own business.'

'Exactly right,' said Sarah. 'Right up until Professor Robbins was accused of having an affair with a dead student. Then I have to ask myself why you didn't come out in support of your boyfriend. Why didn't you say, 'He wasn't in a relationship with Ellie because he was in a relationship with me?'

Rosalind lifted her nose into the air.

'We were no longer together at that point.'

'He dumped you?'

A flash of fury crossed her face.

'It was mutual. And I don't have to justify my romantic choices to you.'

'Unfortunately, you do,' said Sarah. 'Because to me, this looks bad. Harry Robbins rejects you....'

Ros began to object.

Sarah held up a hand. '...Harry rejected you, so you reject him back. As part of the faculty election committee, you could make sure that Professor Robbins was denied tenure, using the accusation of Harry's dalliance with a student, something you knew to be untrue.'

'Harry could have been carrying on with Ellie Campbell, too, for all I knew.'

'But you turned him down because you were slighted, didn't you, Dean? No other reason.'

Her nostrils flared like the thoroughbred horses she had seen at the Campbell stables.

'I do not have to justify the committee's decisions to you either, Officer. No laws have been broken.'

Sarah held her gaze.

'But a man was,' she said, letting the words hang in the air.

'Harry Robbins was broken, wasn't he? His career was

ruined, his reputation in tatters, and he was betrayed by someone he trusted – maybe even loved. Is it any wonder he turned that gun on himself?'

As Sarah had anticipated, Rosalind Davies lost her temper.

'How dare you?' she yelled. 'How dare you accuse me of such things? Nobody was more devastated by Harry Robbins' death than me – but I don't exist in isolation, detective. My feelings sometimes have to be put to one side, and I have to look at the bigger picture.'

'What bigger picture?'

'The health and the reputation of the institution. I am one of the most senior staff members at Benedon, and I will do my best to maintain its place in the world.'

'At any cost?'

Rosalind formed her face into a sneer.

'It's easy for you to see things in black and white. It's easy for you to condemn me and say I should have supported Harry when he was accused of seducing a student. But what you fail to understand is it doesn't matter.'

'It doesn't matter?' said Sarah. 'Rosalind, if you knew he wasn't having an affair with Ellie Campbell, you should have given him tenure. That sort of vote of confidence might have shut people up.'

'Don't be so naïve.'

'Is it? They believed the worst of him because you let them.'

Ros gave a hard shake of her head.

'Benedon could not, *cannot,* be associated with sex scandals. Which parent would send their children here? I merely did what I had to.'

'That defence has been used to excuse some of the worst crimes in history, Ros.'

This time, the Dean didn't rise to Sarah's bait.

'Leaders have to make hard decisions,' she said, tight-lipped. 'Sometimes they have to choose the good of the many over the few.'

For a split second, Sarah felt transported back to New York, the office of the Commissioner of Police. He had used those same words, the same argument when he told Sarah that they wouldn't be prosecuting the dirty cops on her squad. The institution was more important than the individuals, he had said. Sarah Carter and Harry Robbins were just inconvenient problems to be brushed aside. Suddenly Sarah felt sickened by the whole thing.

'Thank you so much for your time, Dean,' she said. 'You have been extremely helpful.'

She began to walk away from her, but when she turned to glance back, she saw that Rosalind Davies was standing where Sarah had left her, standing quite still and yet completely off balance.

Because that was exactly where Sarah needed her, unbalanced, rattled, frightened. Rosalind Davies was on the hook, and Sarah had only just begun to reel her in.

Chapter 28

Alex hated to admit it, but Darius had been the star of the Benedon Symposium. In a packed auditorium, Darius had delivered his keynote speech with passion and verve. Standing at the back with Lara's colleague Doug, he had watched practically open-mouthed as his editor had delivered an outrageous polemic about how newspapers were more vital to democracy than parliament or the US Senate. He had argued that newspapers did three things: they set the agenda, they offered true balance to a debate, and they held the powers that be to account. 'People trust us more than they trust any of those sweaty idiots in suits' was just one of the sound bites that brought on spontaneous applause. Alex supposed it took someone with Darius's deranged ego to sell such a self-serving position. Either way, it had worked: Darius received a five-minute standing ovation from the gathered students and townspeople.

'He's so good,' said Doug, still clapping with enthusiasm as the applause refused to die down.

'He's never going to leave, is he?' said Alex, leaning over to Lara.

'As soon as the clapping stops, he needs to be gone,' said

Lara glancing at her clipboard. 'He's on the last flight to London out of Logan airport, but even so, he's going to have to hustle.'

'I didn't mean Benedon. I meant he's never going to leave the *Chronicle*.'

His friend looked at him, understanding.

'Alex, your time will come,' said Lara. 'And when it does, you'll be the best editor there ever was.'

'Damn, we've got to go,' said Doug, looking at his watch. 'Darius over-ran by fifteen minutes, and drinks start at the Dean's house at six.'

'Are you sure you don't want to come?' said Lara, turning to Alex. She'd asked him to the symposium finale – a cocktail party hosted by Ros Davies, several times, but Alex knew he would be left standing about while Lara ran around sorting out every last detail of the event, just as she had been doing for the past 72 hours.

'Much as I like Doug,' he whispered, 'I'm still officially on holiday, so I think I'll give it a miss.'

She grabbed his hand and nodded.

'I'll be as quick as I can. Literally in and out.'

He knew she meant it, but he also knew it was out of Lara's control. He gave her a sympathetic smile; she was just doing her best.

'Well, make sure you're at the Shovel at eight. I'm holding you to it, okay? Now I'd better go and stroke Darius' ego.'

Down at the front of the stage, there were students actually handing up symposium programmes for Darius to sign; he was lapping it up, oblivious to the idea that any of them might be doing it in an ironic way.

Alex went over to join the crowd.

'A success, yes?' said Darius.

'It was genuinely bloody good,' replied Alex.

Darius nodded; *of course* it had been good. 'I'm so glad I made the effort to come this weekend. You know, many editors end up in academia, masters and principals of colleges. Another ten years and honestly, I wouldn't mind it.'

God help them all, thought Alex, leaving Darius to his fan club, walking out of the building and onto the campus. It was only just past five o'clock, but the light was dimming, and the sky was streaked with the peach and dove-grey stripes of sunset. He'd been surprised at how much Darius's keynote speech had affected him. Plenty of people in the office considered Darius a figure of fun; he was pompous and vain and his work ethic was certainly questionable.

In the three years of being his Deputy Editor, Alex had convinced himself that Darius had a short-shelf life for all those reasons. So when job offers had come, Alex had always turned them down, believing that the editor's job at the *Chronicle* was just within reach. But after tonight, Alex knew that he was kidding himself. What he'd said to Lara was true: Darius was going nowhere. Darius loved his job and the status that went with it.

Alex pushed his hands into his pockets and turned onto Main Street, his thoughts preoccupied with what he was doing with his life; it was something he came back to more and more these days. He had a smart apartment in Chelsea, a top-of-the-range Tesla, plenty of friends, a full head of hair and a six-pack. But professionally, he'd stagnated, and his personal life – well, he didn't want to dwell on that.

He was so deep in thought that he almost bumped into someone coming out of the deli. As he quickly stepped back, he realised it was the detective from the party, Sarah Carter.

'Oh hey, Alex,' she said, 'You heading home?'

‘Killing time, actually. Lara is running around at some cocktail party.’

Sarah flashed him a smile.

‘Well, I’m just coming off duty. If you’re hanging around, do you want to grab some food?’

Alex hadn’t eaten since breakfast, and his stomach had started rumbling. ‘You read my mind,’ he said. ‘Where’s good?’

‘You can’t come to Benedon and not go to The Roll.’

‘The *Roll*?’

‘Come on. I’ve got my badge, so we’ll get a table.’

* * *

The Lobster Roll restaurant didn’t need a menu: everything was explained by the big blue and white sign above its striped awning. You could have a lobster roll, a crab roll, or if you were feeling adventurous, a bowl of fish chowder. Oh, and you had a choice of beer: the local ‘Conehead’ brew in a bottle or no beer at all. The menu was limited, but it was excellent, and the setting was spectacular, just far enough off campus to have a view of the lake. And it was still warm enough to sit at the outside tables with the sun still half an hour from sinking into the water.

Sarah was surprisingly good company, talking openly about her experiences at the sharp end of policing in New York. To a film buff like Alex, it sounded both familiar and glamorous, imagining all of Sarah’s stories as neon-lit and backed with a wah-wah funk soundtrack. Sarah insisted it was gruelling and gritty, but Alex had grown up on *Starsky And Hutch*; he knew better.

‘So why come back here?’ he asked.

Sarah looked out across the water. ‘My mom. She has

dementia and needs full-time care. But it's tough; I feel guilty all the time.'

'You shouldn't,' said Alex. 'At least you're here; at least you're engaging with your mum's needs. I should be back home looking after my dad, but I constantly seem to be able to find excuses.'

'Where is your dad?'

'He lives in the Lake District in the north of England, which I suppose is roughly equivalent to Vermont, if a little more compact. Terry's retired, and he's on his own. He had plenty of friends around him, but at the same time....'

'You feel that you should be there helping.'

'Exactly. Terry's very proud and independent, so he'd never ask, but you're right; the guilt is always there, nagging away at you.'

Sarah took a sip of her beer.

'The funny thing is, before the dementia, my mom was always clear that she wanted me to go out into the world and do my thing, whatever it took. Career, relationships, travel, whatever: she wanted me to follow my dreams. And you know what? I think she meant it.'

Alex nodded. 'My dad's the same. I guess as a parent, you want your kid to go off and spread their wings, and be all they can be rather than hanging around for your sake. That's parental love. You want what's best for them, not you.'

'You got kids?'

He shook his head.

'What about you?'

'No. Cops aren't known for their stable relationships. Mainly because we only ever hang out with other cops.'

He signalled to the waitress for two more beers. Sarah didn't object, which he took to be a positive sign.

'So what case are you working on now?' asked Alex.

He'd been dying to ask and felt sure that Sarah was far too professional to reveal anything, but that was before she had told him a story about a vodka-fuelled teenage fumble in a Jacuzzi, so Alex figured she might have loosened up.

'Harry Robbins' murder,' said Sarah, taking a swig of beer.

Alex stopped, amazed.

'His *murder*?' he said, looking around to check that they weren't being overheard. 'Wasn't Harry a suicide?'

Sarah looked away as if she'd said too much.

'You're right; all the evidence says suicide,' she said, wiping her mouth. For a moment, neither of them said anything.

'What do you think happened, Sarah?' Alex prompted. 'I know you can't reveal much....'

She gave a low laugh. 'Alex, I can't tell you anything.'

'Why?' he said. 'I'm a journalist, but I'm on holiday, so I have no professional interest in this story.'

'Case...'

'Okay, but I have no professional interest in Harry's death. I just want to help my friend make sense of it.'

He looked at her, trying to meet her gaze.

'You don't think Harry killed himself, do you?'

Sarah looked away and shook her head. Hundreds of police officers had stonewalled Alex down the years, but he wouldn't let it happen this time.

'Sarah, I can guess what life is like for you here in Benedon. A small team, two, maybe three detectives? This isn't the NYPD. And believe it or not, I'm good at this. Maybe I can help.'

Sarah gave a quiet, low laugh as if everything he had just said was true.

'Okay. Harry was in a relationship with someone at the

start of the year, but I don't think it was with Ellie Campbell.'

'Who was it?'

'There's a student who was a little fixated with Harry.'

His interest was piqued. 'Harry had a stalker? You think they targeted him?'

Sarah shook her head. 'This girl took one of his classes, and developed intense feelings for him. It seems like she followed him one night. Right to the Dean's house.'

Alex opened his eyes wide.

'Harry was having an affair with Ros?'

'It seems that way. I checked it out. Ros is married, but her husband David was at a conference in Italy the week Harry spent the night at her house.'

'Wait, you're considering a link between Ros Davies and Harry's death?'

'You have to consider everything. And when you do, you realise that Ros had a motive.'

They were speaking in hushed tones how. The Lobster Roll was a laid-back place, but still the sort of restaurant you might find a faculty member having a Sunday supper.

'Ros Davies is a hot bet for the Provost of the College when it comes up next year,' said Sarah. 'The current Provost is Edward Barker. His term of office finishes next year but the appointment process starts shortly.'

Sarah's eyes were shining now. She reminded Alex of Lara when she was excited about a story.

'Harry left the Dean's party suddenly,' said Alex, thinking out loud. 'Perhaps Ros had said something to him, made a threat?'

'It's possible.'

'Do you think she's so ambitious she'd actually silence him?'

Alex saw Sarah frown and rub a hand over her mouth; a classic poker tell. 'I think I've said enough.'

Alex was about to speak when the waitress interrupted. 'You guys want anything else?'

Alex glanced at his watch. Oh crap: it was past eight. He'd been so engrossed in Sarah Carter's revelations that time had run away from him. 'Just the check,' said Alex to the waitress.

Sarah laughed and shook her head.

'You pump me for information and then leave me? I feel used.'

Alex felt embarrassed, knowing how it looked.

'It's not that. I gave Lara a hard time for abandoning me for the symposium, now I'm late to meet her.'

Alex tucked some bills under his half-full bottle and left the restaurant, heading back towards The Shovel.

'When do you go back?' asked Sarah, stopping under the soft sodium glow of a street lamp next to the bar.

'Tomorrow, sadly.'

'Are you going to come back?'

'I hope so,' he said. He knew he shouldn't be flirting with a cop, but then maybe he'd one too many beers.

'Next time, dinner is on me.'

Alex saw the flush in her cheeks, the slight tilt of her head and he stepped towards her. Then he heard a swoosh, the sound of a door opening, and music from the bar. Lara was standing on the pavement.

'Oh,' she said. 'I'm not interrupting anything am I?'

Alex immediately realised how this might look; how it *was*.

'No, no, I was just coming in to find you,' he stuttered.

'Sure,' said Lara in a tone that said she didn't believe him, then nodded to Sarah.

'Detective Carter,' she said formally.

The two women gave each other frosty nods.

'Well, I should be going,' said Sarah.

'Do you want to join us for a drink?' Lara said it graciously but Alex could hear the tight snap in her voice. He imagined Sarah could too.

'No, I really should go,' she said, giving Alex just the hint of a smile.

'You folks have a fine evening.'

And Alex watched her disappear into the night.

Chapter 29

'So, are you seeing Sarah again?' Lara banged the pan down onto the sink a little too hard, water and suds sloshing everywhere.

Alex was sitting at the kitchen's small table.

'Given that I'm flying home in ten hours, probably not.' His tone was weary, annoyed. There had been an brooding atmosphere between them all morning.

'Shame,' said Lara, scrubbing at the detritus of congealed egg from their breakfast two days before. 'You seemed to be getting on really well.'

She had tried to say it generously, but it came out as a cutting remark. She reminded herself that she was not Alex's keeper. He had kindly travelled 3,000 miles to plug the gaps in the symposium schedule, a trip that he had cut into his holiday time; of course he deserved a night out, even if it wasn't with her; yes, even if it was with another woman. Lara knew they should have talked about Alex's impromtu dinner with Sarah Carter when they'd gone back into The Shovel. Instead, she had completely glossed over it, talked about the symposium's success and Alex's But it wasn't the thing that was making her chest feel tight.

'Look, I bumped into Sarah on Main Street and we were both hungry,' said Alex. 'You can hardly blame me for trying to find something to do when you went off to the Dean's party.'

'I invited you to the party!' Lara protested.

'I told you, I didn't fancy it.'

'But you fancied dinner with the sexy detective?'

Lara knew she sounded childish, but she couldn't seem to help herself. Alex held up both his hands.

'Can we just leave it, Lar? I'm not giving you a hard time about that bloke at the boathouse.'

'What bloke?'

She saw Alex frown.

'Dark-haired hunk, down by the lake? That one you were all over.'

For a moment she had no idea what he was talking about. And then the penny dropped.

'You mean Vernon? *Father* Vernon.'

'Father?'

'He's the college priest, Alex!'

Lara felt herself blush. It had been entirely platonic with Vernon, but had it looked more than that to other people? Had it looked like that to Vernon himself?

'I didn't think that sort of thing was allowed,' said Alex. 'You know, by the church.'

Lara was still inwardly wincing. 'It isn't allowed. And anyway, we were just talking.'

Alex's expression softened into a smile.

'A priest?'

'Yes. He was Harry's best friend.'

Lara came down to the table to sit opposite her friend.

'Look, I'm sorry. I hope you had a lovely time with Sarah,' she said. It wasn't entirely honest, but she forced it out anyway. 'I just thought you'd rather go out with her than hang out at The Shovel with me.'

'You know that's not true. And anyway, I only went with Sarah because I thought you'd rather hang out with your college lot.'

'That *really* isn't true.'

She looked up at him.

'I'm sorry Alex, I've been a terrible host.'

He waved a hand.

'Ah, I knew the deal when I came here. I knew how much you had to do. And I only came to help, remember? I never expected you to spend every waking minute entertaining me.'

Alex picked up the coffee pot and poured Lara a cup; it felt like an olive branch.

'So, Ros Davies was having an affair with Harry?' she asked.

Lara was shocked when Alex told her what Sarah had confided over dinner. It was another of the issues they should have discussed at The Shovel, but Lara had been unsettled by what it said about Harry. She'd genuinely liked Harry and thought he liked her too, but now it seemed as though Harry liked lots of attractive women on campus.

'Does Sarah really think that Ros might have murdered him?' she asked, wrapping her hands around the mug, somehow needing the warmth.

'I think she's considering it, yes. Harry left the party abruptly, didn't he? It's possible he and Ros had words.'

Lara tried to think back to that night. She remembered how Ros had stopped her on the way out and warned her about Harry. Looking back, she'd been testy, on edge.

'But the Dean? A murderer?' she said out loud. The woman was ambitious, sure, but a killer? Lara's mind was already whirling; after the distraction of the symposium, she felt she could turn her focus back onto Harry. She was annoyed with herself for believing that Harry's death was a straightforward suicide – or, more accurately, annoyed with herself that until this point, she hadn't questioned it enough.

'If Sarah is open to the idea that Ros Davies – or anyone - could have murdered Harry, then she must think murder is possible,' said Lara, thinking it through. 'Perhaps she saw evidence of an intruder; perhaps forensics have suggested that the gunshot wound wasn't self-inflicted.'

'Makes sense,' agreed Alex, glancing at the clock. 'But I should go and pack. I need to get the hire car back before I check in.'

Lara looked at him, a thought forming.

'Is there any chance of a lift?' she asked.

'To where?'

'Boston. I should speak to Eleanor Campbell's friend Julia. If you can drop me near the airport, I can find my way in.'

She saw Alex's sceptical look, but Lara still believed that Harry's death was connected to Ellie Campbell's. She wasn't sure in what way, but if Sarah Carter was still on the hunt for answers, it felt like Lara should keep digging too. Alex looked at her, holding her gaze just a moment too long.

'I'll take you all the way.'

'Alex, you'll miss your flight. She lives in Back Bay.'

He stood up. 'We'd better get moving then, hadn't we?'

Chapter 30

Sarah leaned against her car and took a bite of her sandwich. *Damn.* A meatball sub – was that what they called it? She peeled back the bread and looked inside. It had all the right ingredients: meatballs, lettuce, cheese, and some unspecified red sauce, but it was bland, tasteless. Back in the Ninth precinct, they'd eaten at Larry's, a near-legendary sandwich truck parked half a block from the station house. Technically, it was a parking violation, but who would give Larry a ticket when he made the best damn sandwiches in NYC?

Hell, she missed Larry's. Disgusted, Sarah re-wrapped the sandwich and dropped it back through the car window, turning to pick up the coffee she had left on the roof. Lunch in The BPD parking lot; *the glamour of it all.* Glenn suggested they go to the Lobster Roll, but Sarah had been slightly embarrassed to show her face back there so soon after her boozy tete-a-tete with Alex Ford. Besides, she had far too much work to do, because Sarah did not believe that Harry Robbins had killed himself. Was 'murdered' the right word? Assassinated? Or did you have to be a president or a king or something to be assassinated? Either way,

Sarah desperately needed to prove that someone else had been there that night. The medical examiner's hunch wasn't enough. A motive for Ros Davies wasn't enough. So the forensics team were back at the professor's house collecting more evidence, but so far, there was no news from them.

Sarah heard the car before she saw it, tyres complaining as it entered the parking lot at speed. Turning, Sarah immediately recognised Sheriff Roscoe's shark-grey Escalade, the middle-aged man's muscle car. It slid to a stop, rocking on its springs as Roscoe jumped out, making a beeline for Sarah.

'You have a problem with me?' He shouted at her as he closed the gap. 'Are you deliberately questioning my authority? What makes *you* so special?'

Sarah took two steps back, splashing herself with coffee.

'Whoa, whoa,' she said. 'What's going on? I'm just having my lunch here.'

'Screw your lunch,' hissed Roscoe, jabbing a finger at her. 'Where do you get off ordering another Goddamn forensic search of Harry Robbins' house?'

Ah. She supposed she should have expected this.

'I had received information that suggested the victim's gunshot wound was inconsistent with suicide,' said Sarah as calmly as she could. 'So I felt it was wise to look into the theory that another actor was present on the night of the death.'

'You felt it was *wise*?' said Roscoe. 'Wise is not a word I would use to describe you, Detective. Arrogant, disrespectful, insubordinate – those fit you perfectly, I would say.'

'I can understand your feelings, Sheriff Roscoe....'

'You can understand them, can you? And can you understand how I felt being informed while on a *weekend away* that my Chief of Detectives had ordered an extremely expensive series of forensic tests when our spending for the year is already twice over budget? And it's only *September*, Carter!'

Sarah looked at Roscoe with disbelief. Did he really think that budgets were more important than results?

'Of course, the tests are expensive,' she said, 'But I'm confident we'll get something conclusive very soon.'

It wasn't entirely true; however much Sarah impressed upon the lab guys the need for urgency, forensics operations were still painfully slow.

'I don't give a rat's ass about your confidence,' snapped Roscoe. 'The fact is we didn't need any more tests. This investigation is over.'

'As I said, Sherriff, I have received new intel that suggests....'

Roscoe pushed his pink face closer to Sarah's. '*Over*, detective. I believe I gave you an order.'

Sarah stood her ground.

'And *I* believe I'm better placed to assess whether a serious crime has been committed and what response is required.'

'Do you?' said Roscoe with a cold glare. 'Because it seems that Glenn Schultz might be "better placed" to handle this particular incident.'

'With respect, Sheriff....'

'Respect?' He barked out a laugh. 'What kind of respect have you ever shown me? What kind of respect have you ever shown this town, Sarah? Because you make it very clear that your big city cop ways are much more important than the well-being of Benedon and its citizens.'

Sarah frowned.

'I don't see how investigating a violent death is disrespectful to anyone.'

'You don't, huh? Well, I received a phone call from the Dean of the Journalism School this morning.'

Sarah's heart sank. *Ah, crap.* Of course, Rosalind Davies would have called her buddy the Sheriff. Roscoe caught her reaction and smiled with satisfaction.

'She tells me that you waylaid her on campus and – in full view of students and VIP guests – made a series of unsubstantiated claims about her private life and....'

'She admitted to it,' cried Sarah, but Roscoe merely shook his head, dismissing it.

'And,' he continued, holding up the finger, 'And you accused her of dishonesty and professional under-handedness.'

Well, yes, thought Sarah. That part was true, at least.

'Rosalind Davies was having an affair with Harry Robbins,' said Sarah. Roscoe just shrugged.

'And how is that any of our business?'

'It's our business because Harry Robbins knew she had lied to the tenure committee, putting the Dean's career in danger and creating motive.'

Roscoe's lip curled.

'Motive for what, detective?'

'For Harry Robbins' murder,' she said.

'Murder?' he snorted. 'It seems this so-called murder is only in your mind, Carter. The damn teacher shot himself in his Goddamn head: end of story.'

Roscoe peered at her as if he was examining a particularly distasteful bug.

'I thought we'd had a conversation about this already,' he said. 'I thought I'd been very clear that I didn't want you investigating this business any further.'

Sarah gaped at him.

'So, you're taking your orders from Rosalind Davies now?'

Roscoe's face immediately turned red. If he'd been a cartoon, flames would have been shooting out of his ears.

'I'll pretend,' said Roscoe, his voice low, 'that I didn't hear that.'

Deep inside, Sarah knew it was unwise to keep poking a growling bear, but then he'd already pointed out that 'wise' didn't fit her.

'Maybe that's the problem, Sherriff,' she said. 'Turning a blind eye to things that might be inconvenient for your friends at the Country Club.'

Roscoe slammed a hand down onto the roof of Sarah's car. She flinched and stepped back. Maybe that *was* too much.

'You think you're above us, don't you, Sarah?' said Roscoe, advancing on her. 'You think our small-town ways are backward, don't you? But like it or not, Benedon College is right at the heart of our community. It brings in money; it provides jobs; it gives us continuity. You might not approve of it, Carter, but I make no apologies for trying to keep us all on the same page.'

'And I make no apologies for trying to do my job. Even if it upsets the people you think you need to keep "onside".'

Roscoe tipped his head to one side.

'You find it hard to make friends don't you, Sarah?'

Sarah swallowed.

'What's that supposed to mean?'

'You don't think I know about what happened in New York? Don't you think I would have done a thorough background check on my new Chief of Detectives? I heard what happened at your precinct. Loyalty is not one of your strong suits, is it?'

Sarah bristled. What did this red-faced hick know about what had happened to her in Manhattan?

'Loyalty to dirty cops? No.'

'But not everybody in your precinct was dirty, were they? There were plenty of good cops there, but you were prepared to blacken the name of the entire department. And all because you were convinced *you* were right.'

'You don't know anything about it.'

Roscoe's eyes flashed with triumph.

'Don't I, Sarah?'

He looked at her for a long moment, then closed his eyes, seeming to tire of the conversation.

'Take the day off,' he said, waving a dismissive hand, 'Take the week off if you have to, but I don't want to see you wasting any more time on this crap.'

His eyes met hers.

'Let me see if I can be crystal clear: I'm shutting this down and putting you on the truck theft case. And if you've got a problem with that, take it up with our personnel department.'

He turned back towards his car, the door still open. 'Oh, and Sarah? *I'm* the personnel department. I do all the hiring and firing around here,' he said with a cruel smile. 'Maybe better bear that in mind.'

Chapter 31

Boston wasn't what Lara was expecting. She'd thought it would be a combination of *Good Will Hunting* and *Cheers*: snow on the ground, neon shamrocks and chunky dudes in leather jackets who said 'Howyadoin'?' But from the passenger seat of Alex's hire car, Boston looked just like any other modern American city: a distant high-rise business district, strip-malls offering five-buck nail 'therapies', car parks and gas stations. She was disappointed; it was a long way to come for more of the same.

'You need to get off the freeway and follow the river down there,' said Lara.

The tension that had shimmered between them that morning had disappeared. If Alex was interested in Sarah Carter, Lara realised there was little she could do about it. But at least Lara knew she had his friendship and support; this trip into Boston alone proved it. And a friendship this strong was no small thing. When Lara told Father Vernon that everyone she loved died, she meant that she was terrified of losing Alex. For years, she hadn't wanted to risk a relationship with him, because if it ended, she knew she might lose Alex forever. But lately, when she saw him with another woman – whether a serious relationship, like his last girlfriend Alicia, or someone as casual as Sarah, she knew that once Alex settled down, what they had together would also change. It had to.

'Thank you,' she said quietly.

'What for?' said Alex.

'For being there. For being my friend.'

'I know you're obviously devastated that I'm going back to England, but there's no need to get so sentimental.'

He said it light-heartedly, but suddenly it felt like they were in the Autumn of their friendship. Lara felt emotion well behind her eyes.

'I was just...' she began, but Alex reached out and took her hand.

'We always will be,' he said, squeezing gently as if he knew what she was thinking. Alex always knew. That was something, wasn't it?

'According to the map, this is Back Bay,' said Alex as they turned into a smart residential area with tall red-brick townhouses and manicured hedges.

'Nice area,' said Lara taking it all in. It reminded her of the back streets of Chelsea, except with wider roads and more coffee shops.

'All I know about Boston is from movies, like that one where Leonardo DiCaprio went undercover in the Irish mafia. He was sexy as hell back then.'

'I think you mean *The Departed*. That was set in Southie, the mean streets of Boston. Back Bay's more of a Gucci handbag sort of place.'

He slowed the car down at an amber light.

'So this girl we're looking for, Julia?' said Alex. 'What do we know about her?'

Lara smiled, glad that they were back on track.

'Very little. She was a good friend of Eleanor Campbell's, a grad student in the English department. I got Brian, one of my students, to look into her. Julia's a bright girl; she did her undergraduate studies at Yale and came to Benedon to do a Masters. Then dropped out.'

Alex steered the car into a grid of streets made up of grand four-storey red-brick houses with clipped box trees on the steps and neatly tended window boxes. Alex pulled up at the kerb next to number 36. Wide steps with a brass handrail led up to a double-wide door with a stone carving of an eagle perched right above.

Alex whistled. 'Now that's the kind of place the real Leo DiCaprio would live.'

Lara got out and walked up to the door. She had been watching closely as they had cruised these streets; the rash of bells next to some of the doors showed they had been subdivided into apartments, but not this one—only one bell, with the name 'Bowen' beneath it. Lara pressed. Nothing. She tried again.

Just then, the door opened, and a fifty-something man in Lycra bumped an expensive bicycle onto the steps.

'Hello, I'm looking for Julia,' said Lara.

The man peered at Lara over his wire-framed spectacles.

'Julia's at work. And you are..?'

'Lara Stone,' she said, ramping up her accent. She had the vague notion that Bostonians were often Anglophiles. 'I'm a lecturer at Benedon; I thought I'd pop by and see Julia.'

The man's manner immediately changed.

'Oh, how lovely to meet you,' he said, juggling his bike to offer Lara a hand. 'I'm Alan, Julia's father. I'm afraid Julia is at work. If you can call being a shop assistant 'work'.' He said her job title as if it were offensive.

'Could you direct me?'

'It's called 'Source', three blocks away on Newbury.'

He paused, looking troubled again.

'When you see her, could you try and talk some sense into her?

'Sense?'

'The new semester has just started, hasn't it? We were hoping Julia would return to finish her Masters, but no. If you could do anything to help her get back on track...?'

'I'll try,' said Lara.

'I'd be so grateful,' said Alan meaningfully, before bumping down the steps. Lara watched him go, feeling like she'd just been offered a bribe. Some people truly believed that money could solve any problem.

As Lara and Alex walked across to the shopping area, she took a moment to enjoy the sunshine – the leaves on the Bostonian trees were still green and looked crisp against the bright blue sky. 'Source' was easy to find, wedged between a cupcake bakery and an optician selling designer frames. It had a small shop front with houseplants and coffee table books in the window. It was edgy and fashionable, although from this distance, it was unclear what sort of shop it actually was.

'Can you go in?' whispered Alex. 'I find places like this intimidating.'

'Alex, you've walked across minefields in Afghanistan.'

'This is worse,' he said. 'Much worse.'

Grasping Alex's sleeve, Lara led the way inside, where the achingly cool vibe continued: three dresses hanging on a rack like paintings, a shelf of artisan ceramics and a pedestal displaying beauty products in brown medicine bottles.

Julia was the only assistant in the store. Lara wasn't surprised – she doubted the shop had many customers. The girl's brown hair was tied back from her lean, oval face. She had pale skin, big eyes and a small mouth heavily painted with dark lipstick. In an oversized jumper and jeans, she looked every inch the rich hipster, a Brooklyn blue-stocking who was probably writing poetry behind the counter.

'Julia?' asked Lara.

The younger woman nodded.

'How can I help?'

'My name is Lara Stone. I'm a visiting fellow at Benedon. This is my friend Alex.'

Julia folded her arms across her chest, immediately defensive at the mention of the college.

'Did my dad send you?' she asked, tilting her head.

'We met him a few minutes ago, but he didn't send us.'

Lara hesitated. The girl was nervy, but they had come here for a reason.

'We're here about Harry Robbins.'

'Professor Robbins?'

Lara had expected more hostility, perhaps even anger like Jenny Price, but Julia's face showed little emotion: Lara realised that she didn't know.

'Julia, he died last week.'

'Harry Robbins is dead?'

She looked at Lara, eyes wide. Then abruptly, Julia walked to the front of the shop. At first, Lara thought she was about to flee, but instead, she flipped the open sign to 'closed'.

When she walked back, Lara saw her hands trembling.

'I'm sorry, I'm just in shock,' she said. 'I left Benedon a few months ago. I haven't stayed in touch with anyone. What happened?'

'Apparently, he took his life.'

'Apparently?' said Julia, her eyes darting from Lara to Alex and back.

The younger woman was definitely on edge now. All colour had drained from her face.

'Was Harry a friend of yours?' asked Alex.

'We had a mutual friend,' she said, looking down. 'I only met him once or twice. But my friend thought highly of him.'

'Your friend was Ellie Campbell, wasn't it?'

Julia nodded warily.

'That's right.'

Lara paused, unsure how to approach this. *When in doubt, use the direct approach*, she reminded herself.

'Julia, Harry was my friend too, and I'm trying to work out what happened to him.'

Julia gave a tight nod of solidarity. That was a good start.

'The police are working on a theory that Harry was depressed – guilty because of everything that happened to Ellie.'

Lara used the word *are*, but it should have been *were*, assuming Sarah was now considering Ros as a suspect.

'Harry had nothing to be guilty about,' said Julia quietly.

'Are you saying they weren't dating?'

As Julia shook her head, a tendril of hair fell loose on her pale face.

'Nothing romantic ever happened between Harry and Ellie.'

Lara looked at Alex.

'Are you sure?' she asked.

'Pretty sure. Because Ellie was in love with me.'

Lara stopped, shocked.

'You and Ellie were together?'

Julia nodded, her eyes damp.

'We kept it quiet, just between us. Her parents are conservative; so are mine.'

She took a ragged breath.

'In those last few months of her life, Ellie was finding herself, her true self. Not just her sexuality, but what she wanted to do with her life too. All her life, she'd been told her destiny was a strategic marriage and taking the reins of the Campbell empire. But she didn't want any of that.'

'Was that why Ellie was trying to switch onto the Journalism Masters programme?' asked Alex.

Julia nodded.

'She went to work for the family company in the Christmas holidays last year - and hated every minute of it. The corporate grind, the pursuit of money. It just made her angry, so she came back to college wanting to be a journalist and went to see Professor Robbins. The next thing I know she was working on a story.'

'Harry mentioned Ellie's story,' said Lara, 'But he said she wouldn't tell him the details.'

'She wouldn't tell me any specifics either. She kept it very close to her chest. That upset me. I was her girlfriend, but she said it was best not to know.'

'Didn't you have any idea?'

Julia's mouth twitched into a bleak smile.

'She kept saying it was big. Really big. This wasn't just a story that was going to get her on the Masters programme, she was convinced it was big enough for the *Boston Globe*. All I know is that something in Maple County was at the heart of it.'

Lara and Alex glanced at each other.

'Maple county? How do you know that?'

'An author we both love was coming to college. We had tickets to hear her speak. But on the day of the talk, Ellie pulled out, said she wasn't coming, said she had to go to Maple County instead; it was very important for her story. That's what she said.'

Julia pulled a pained face and looked away. 'We argued about it.'

Alex stepped forward.

'Jenny Price said she had gone to some place called The Blackberry Inn in Maple County,' he said gently. 'Does that sound right?'

'All I know is Ellie was gone for 24 hours. I guess she stayed the night at that inn.'

Julia took a breath, but it stuttered in her chest.

'And a couple of weeks later, Ellie was dead.'

'Why do you think she did it?'

Julia pressed her fingers to her eyes to stop crying.

'I don't know. Maybe it was me. Our relationship. Ellie was trying to walk her own line, but with the weight of expectations in a family like hers, it was...difficult.'

She looked at Lara, tears rolling down her face. 'I tell myself that she fell.'

Lara pulled out a tissue and handed it to her.

'You left Benedon afterwards?'

Julia nodded.

'There were too many bad memories. I couldn't stay.'

Lara looked around the shop.

'Do you like working here?'

Julia dabbed at her eyes and gave Lara a thin smile. 'In the past week I've sold two cheese plants and a candle. When I got to Yale, this wasn't where I saw myself in five years.'

Lara pulled out a business card.

'Listen, this is my number and email address. I'm a visiting fellow at Benedon all semester. If you want to talk, here's where you'll find me. I lost someone very dear to me last year. I'm in Vermont because, well, I'm trying to find my way through it all too.'

Lara felt Alex's hand on her shoulder.

'We should go,' he said softly. When they reached the door, Julia called out.

'Thank you,' she said, waving the card. 'You know, I might call. I do miss Jimmy's pizza.'

Out on the street, Alex was already on his phone.

'There's only one Blackberry Inn in Maple County. It's in a place called North Bend.' He held up his phone, showing Lara where the town was on the map: around 70 miles northwest of Benedon. 'I wonder what's there that's so important?'

'I'm going to find out,' said Lara decisively. 'I need to get myself back home and pick up the car. I think there's an Amtrak train part of the way...'

Alex cut her off by rattling his car keys in the air.

'...Or I've got a car three streets away?'

'Alex, you have to get to the airport.'

'Maybe, but not today,' he smiled. 'I'm not back in the office until Thursday. And besides, we haven't really hung out together, have we?'

Lara couldn't help grinning.

'You want to hang out?'

'Don't sound so surprised.'

'How about we hang out at the Blackberry Inn?'

'I thought you'd never ask. Come on,' he said, looking up at the sky. 'If we push it, we'll get there before dark.'

Chapter 32

It was the smell. Floor polish, hotdogs, over-heated fluorescent lighting, and undercutting it all, the unmistakable reek of the deodoriser they sprayed into the rental shoes. Big Ed's Bowl-A-Rama smelled just like every other bowling alley in America. Not that Sarah had been to them all, but it sure looked – and smelled – like they all bought their carpet and vinyl fittings from the same off-the-peg catalogue. They all seemed to have the same menu, too: nachos, hot wings and corn dogs—a balanced American diet.

'You want a burger or something?' asked Heather. 'Dave's going to get some onion rings.'

'No thanks,' said Sarah, 'I ate before I got here.'

She registered Heather's disappointment and quickly added, 'But I'll take a beer if you're heading to the counter.'

Dave nodded cheerfully. 'Sure thing. Think we'll all join you.'

'Can always fit in another brewski,' smiled Heather, winking at her husband. Sarah appreciated the effort Heather was making, even if her relentless friendliness sometimes set her teeth on edge. It had certainly been kind of Heather to invite Sarah to her regular Monday night 'bowling thing' along with Dave's best friends Martha and Bobby. Martha was a nurse 'up at the clinic', and Bobby sold tyres at Karl's SuperParts just off the Highway.

And then there was Nick. Sarah knew she should have anticipated that Heather might invite Nick or someone like him. Single, inoffensive, keen. Just what any unmarried woman in her thirties was looking for, right?

'So, Heather tells me you've moved back in with your mom,' said Nick, leaning across the vinyl-topped table.

Sarah flashed him a wry smile. 'For now,' she said.

'I think it's great that you came back to support her. It's tough, I guess, but it's family, you know?'

Nick was a nice guy. Cheerful, well-meaning; Sarah supposed Nick might even be considered a catch. He was an accountant at a company that specialised in pool-cleaning products and drove a late-model Subaru. He was a little pudgy, but that was easily done when onion rings were on the menu. No, what made Sarah uncomfortable was that Heather clearly thought that Nick was her level.

Sarah thought back to her night at The Lobster Roll with Alex Ford. Alex was gorgeous, worldly and successful, and he'd gotten a standing ovation talking to a packed auditorium at the college. Maybe she'd been kidding herself that a boyfriend like Alex was even a possibility. Perhaps she had been punching way above her weight, and anyway, it was only a few beers, barely a date.

'Hey Sarah, you're up,' called Heather.

Groaning, Sarah made her way to the stand and selected a medium-weight ball, avoiding the bright pink 'ladies' ball' on principle.

Cradling the bowl to her chest, she looked down the lane, muttered a small prayer and swung.

‘Steee-rike!’ shouted Heather with delight as the pins collapsed with a satisfying ‘thunk’. ‘You’re a natural!’

Sarah hadn’t mentioned that the Ninth Precinct had a league of its own; bowling was a very ‘cop’ pastime: competitive, blue-collar, and they served Bud in plastic glasses. The perfect trinity.

‘Just beginner’s luck,’ she shrugged.

‘Sure,’ smiled Heather, seeing right through her. ‘So, how’s your mom doing? How’s she liking the new place?’

The real answer was that Colleen Carter did not like the new place at all. Sarah had been visiting daily, and her mom had been tetchy and unsettled, constantly asking Sarah when she could go home.

If she was honest, that was part of the reason why Sarah had agreed to Heather’s invitation; she wanted to talk to somebody – and who else was she going to ask? Glenn?

‘I guess it takes a little time to get used to it?’ said Sarah.

Heather put her hands on her hips and let out a long breath.

‘Sure,’ she said. ‘And you know, sometimes it just isn’t the right fit.’

‘Really?’

‘I wasn’t lying when I said that Beauville is one of the best care facilities in the State,’ said Heather. ‘But that doesn’t mean it's going to be right for everyone.’

She looked over to where Dave was laughing with Nick.

‘Did you know Dave’s mom lives with us?’

‘No,’ said Sarah with surprise.

‘We thought about bringing her to the care home, but Barb – that’s Dave’s mom – she’s the kind who needs familiar surroundings. She grew up in that house and raised her family there. To her move away from that right now, when she's that's the most vulnerable?’ Heather shook her head. ‘We wanted to avoid that.’

'Is it difficult having Barb there with you 24/7?'

'Sure. Almost impossible at times, and Dave and me, we've had our troubles over it. But in the end, what's right for Barbara is right for Dave – and what's right for Dave,' she held both hands palm up. 'That's always going to be right for me.'

Sarah saw the melting look of love that Heather shot across to her husband. Dave's hair was thin, and his bowling game certainly needed a lot of work, but even so, Sarah couldn't help but feel a little jealous. Even through the tough times, Heather had Dave. And she had Martha and Bobby, and she had their four kids. It wasn't anything spectacular, but it was more than enough for Heather.

But it wasn't enough for Sarah. Her confrontation with Roscoe that afternoon had only underlined that. Roscoe represented all that was wrong with Benedon: small-minded and unforgiving of anything that didn't fit a narrow mould. If Sarah stayed here, she feared she might drown.

'What do you think of Nick?' asked Heather.

'He's nice.'

'But not for you, huh?'

'Maybe not.'

Heather shrugged, ever the pragmatist. 'You win some, you lose some. Talking of which, I'd better go pick me up a spare, or the girls' team is toast.'

She watched Heather walk across to select her ball: the heaviest one on the rack.

'Watch this, losers!' she called, swinging the ball between her legs. It thumped down onto the polished lane and, with an ominous rumble, trundled towards the pins.

'Go on, baby!' shouted Dave.

'You got this!' yelled Nick.

Slowly drifting towards the gutter, Heather's ball

veered to the right at the last moment, sending the pins flying like they'd been hit by a grenade.

'YESSSSSS!' howled Heather, throwing her arms in the air. Sarah looked around; it seemed the whole of the Bowl-A-Rama was on its feet, applauding and whooping, genuinely revelling in Heather's victory. Just then Sarah noticed her phone was buzzing and pulled it out, striding out to the relative calm of the entrance lobby.

'Sarah, it's Steve in forensics. We've done a sweep of the property.'

'And?'

'And we have shoe-prints, and we have DNA.'

If Sarah hadn't had a phone in her hand, she would have whooped louder than Heather.

'We got quite a large sample,' said Steve. 'Whoever it was possibly cut themselves.'

When Sarah ordered an external search of Harry's house, she hadn't been optimistic; it had been days since the incident and any variables could have contaminated the scene. But the forensics team had outdone themselves. There are multiple shoeprints in the flower beds at the rear and an actual blood sample on the fence outside. If someone had cut themselves in Harry's yard, they might only have needed a Band-Aid. But to the forensics boys, this was Christmas come early.

'Of course, it could be Harry Robbins' blood.'

Sarah understood that, and there was a bigger problem too. It was all very well getting a DNA sample, but it needed to be matched to a DNA sample from a suspect or matched to someone already on the CODIS DNA database.

'Great work Steve,' she said. 'Tell me when you've built a profile. Then can you run it through CODIS?' she asked.

'The lab's pretty quiet at the moment, but it might still take a little time, OK?'

'Beers are on me if you can make it as quick as you can. And by the way, Steve, if you speak to Sheriff Roscoe, try to keep it quiet.'

'If I do, can we upgrade beers to dinner?'

'You're on,' she said, and stepped up to bowl again.

Chapter 33

'Now *this* is America,' said Alex as they came down through the valley and passed the sign for North Bend: The Jewel of Maple County. 'This is more like how I had imagined it to be.'

'Actual buildings, you mean?' said Lara with a wry smile.

'Maybe I've been living in London too long,' said Alex, 'But all that open space back there was making me feel spaced out. I don't think we've seen a wall for two hours.'

Benedon hadn't exactly been Hong Kong: the church spire in the centre of the campus was by far the tallest building, and it was rare to see anything above two storeys in the rest of town. But as Lara and Alex had left Boston and headed towards Maple County, the houses had slowly got smaller and more distant until there was little but farm shops, then scattered farms, then nothing but open agricultural land for miles and miles; crops stretching to the horizon, with only the occasional windmill or marching line of pylons to break up the nothingness.

Adding to the mood, the further they got from the urban sprawl, the harder it was to get any pop music on the radio, so Alex had flipped to a country and western station. Mercifully, Alex didn't know any country and western songs, so he couldn't sing along. For the most part, they sat in comfortable silence, the windows open, just listening to the rush of the wind and the hiss of tyres on asphalt as the cowboys and cowgirls crooned about their lost loves. Lara tried not to dwell on how it related to her own situation.

North Bend wasn't a metropolis, but in the twilight, Lara could see that it was more like an overgrown village centring on a single long main street. It would have been the dictionary definition of a 'One Horse Town' had it not been for the big high school they'd passed on the eastern edge; a low modernist 1970s library and a scattering of other municipal-looking buildings dominated by a floodlit baseball field surrounded by bleachers: presumably home to the famous 'Hornets' whose logo covered every surface. But here in the centre of town, Alex was right: Main Street was almost a shrine to Americana. Al's Diner, Plimpton's Hardware Store, a sporting goods store called Cody's that seemed to specialise in 'bow hunting', whatever that was. There was even a 1920s-style deli with a sign that read 'soda fountain'. It was twee, but Lara immediately liked North Bend. It wasn't pretending to be anything other than itself; that was refreshing in the 21st-century digital whirl.

'What was Ellie Campbell doing in a place like this?' said Alex, peering through the window to take the town in.

'Blackberry Inn is up to the left,' she said, glad her phone had a signal again. 'There, see the sign?'

Set back from the road, it had a shingled pitched roof, with four chimneys, a porch with a swing and shutters painted pale blue; it was like Hansel and Gretel's gingerbread house reimagined by expensive interior designers.

Alex pulled the car into a slanted bay right outside, and

they walked up the steps into the warm lobby, which smelled of raw pine and woodsmoke.

'Checking in?'

A sixty-something man walked up to the check-in counter. He was wearing a check shirt and a waistcoat. Pinned to it was a polished brass name badge that told them his name was Cliff.

'We have a reservation. Mr and Mrs Ford?'

Lara tried not to react to her new title. Alex had called the Inn from a gas station on the way over, but she didn't know what he'd said to the proprietor.

'Mr Ford, you got the last room. The cottage,' smiled Cliff, fetching some keys from a rack behind him. 'We get so busy around here in the Fall, but you got lucky tonight.'

He slid a form across to Alex, and he began to fill it in.

'Your first time with us?'

'We're over from England. It's our first time in Vermont.'

'Honeymoon?'

Lara gave a nervous laugh.

'No.'

Cliff nodded. 'That's how we ended up in these parts. I used to live in New York. Didn't meet my wife until I was 42, I was working so hard. We came up for our honeymoon and decided to relocate here by the end of the trip.'

'I'm not surprised you wanted to stay,' said Lara, looking around the lobby, taking in the ceiling fan, the oriental rugs on the floor and the sweeping oak staircase. It was hard not to feel like Scarlett O'Hara just checking in. 'It's beautiful.'

'And the leaves are starting to go. We have a Basswood in the garden that is already turning red. I'm Cliff, by the way. Here to help in any way I can. Breakfast is served in the conservatory in the morning. You must try our blackberry muffins made from fruit from the garden. Or we can bring it to your room,' he added meaningfully.

'I can't think as far ahead as breakfast,' smiled Alex. 'Where do you recommend for somewhere to eat now? It's been a long drive.'

Cliff glanced at his watch.

'We've got a great place in town, but it's closed on Mondays. The diner takes last orders at 6.30 pm, so you've just missed that too. But we do room service. My wife's cooking, but if there's a better home chef in the state, I've yet to meet them.'

'Sounds good,' said Alex and Lara in unison.

They followed Cliff out of the main house and into the garden. It was almost dark now, but it was softly lit with fairy lights, and the path was lined with hurricane lamps.

'This place was built in 1914,' said Cliff as they walked towards a small one-storey cottage. 'It used to be the summer house of a wealthy Boston family, and this carriage house belonged to their butler.'

He twisted the brass key in the lock, and the gush of warm air as he opened the door made Lara sigh.

'Wood-burning stove, logs, coffee and home-made cookies over there by the love seat. *House Beautiful* said we were one of the East Coast's top ten romantic inns. We'll take that.'

Lara drank in the other details – a French-style bed laden with cushions, a claw-foot bath with big brass taps by the window, a soft-grey sofa in front of the fire.

'We'll get the food over as quick as we can,' said Cliff, handing over the key. 'There's a storm coming tonight, so I expect you'll want to hunker down.'

They let the door click behind them.

'Do you think he noticed we had no bags?' whispered Lara.

'I'm sure he's used to it,' said Alex, helping himself to a biscuit. It's one of the East Coast's top ten romantic places. I'm sure plenty of people swing by for impromptu sex.'

As he said the word 'sex', Lara had to look away. She could talk about most things with Alex, but she suddenly felt embarrassed in this cosy, intimate space.

He bent down by the stove and used the logs, kindling and matches to light it. Within a few minutes, the room had an amber glow, and the only sound was the crackling of the wood.

'So. This is what we know,' said Lara, sitting cross-legged on the sofa, facing Alex.

'Lar, maybe we should do all this tomorrow,' said Alex, lying back and sticking a cushion under his head. 'This is nice. We should enjoy it, especially after the week you've had.'

'How can I leave it, Alex?' she said urgently. 'I went out with Harry and a few hours later, he was dead. We should make sense of Harry's death for his sister and his college friends, but I need to find out what happened so I can make peace with it myself. Otherwise, Harry becomes someone else I couldn't save.'

Alex nodded. He knew better than anyone how badly affected Lara had been by the death of her friend Sandrine the year before. The circumstances had been similar and Lara had almost sent herself mad, wondering what she could have done to save her friend. They had solved the case together, but that was little consolation; she would much rather have her friend back. So that was why Lara was so desperate to find out if she could have saved Harry from his hopelessness.

There was a drinks trolley by the fire. Alex reached over and poured himself a bourbon.

'Want one? We need something stronger than coffee.'

Lara took the tumbler from him and let the golden liquid slide down her throat. 'So Harry left the Dean's party without telling anyone. That same night he died of a gunshot wound, even though his sister says he was anti-guns and didn't own one.'

Back at the *Chronicle* or in the study on her houseboat, Lara would have written all this down on her whiteboard, but tonight, they only had each other to chew over the facts and speculations and come up with a theory.

'Some people think Harry was depressed because of the death of Ellie Campbell. Rumours said they'd had an affair. But Ellie Campbell was gay.'

'That doesn't necessarily preclude a relationship between Harry and Ellie,' said Alex.

'But it's not likely.'

Alex nodded in agreement.

'Vernon was Harry's best mate. What did he say about Harry's state of mind?'

'He said he'd been down over the summer. Not depressed, maybe a little blue. Harry wanted to leave Benedon, but after a kayaking trip, he changed his mind. He came up with the idea of the symposium to help get back into journalism. According to Vernon, he was in good spirits. Happy.'

She didn't add that Vernon had also said that Harry was happy because he'd met a girl. Her. Lara stood up and started pacing the room.

'Meanwhile, Sarah Carter doesn't think it was suicide. But it was Ros, not Ellie, that was having the affair with Harry.'

Alex sat forward, resting his arms on his knees. Lara had seen him like this in executive meetings of the *Chronicle* many time before, clear-headed and methodical.

'So if we're looking for a reason for Harry's death,

perhaps that's it: he was upset about Ros. Hard to believe, but it was her party, remember - and Harry left suddenly. Perhaps she said something to him that affected him and pushed him over the edge.'

Over the previous few days, Lara knew that she had elevated Harry in her mind to the perfect man. Funny, charming, clever. But Lara thought one of the most revealing things about a person was the company they kept. Her cousin Charlie, for example, was a vain and shallow man, and his friends were a bunch of frightful bores. On the other hand, Alex's friends were smart, down-to-earth and fun. QED, it wasn't easy to believe that Harry was so in love with Ros that it pushed him over the edge.

There was a knock on the door and Cliff came in holding a tray.

'BLTs and French fries. Marina made the bread this morning, and the bacon is from a farm just down the road. I practically know the pigs, although I probably shouldn't be saying that.'

He put his hands behind his back.

'So, how are you enjoying the cottage? We always say that our guests arrive as strangers and leave as friends.'

Lara had already noticed that the personal touches were important to the Blackberry Inn. Calling guests by name, everything homemade and home spun.

'We love it, Cliff,' she said. 'In fact we came here because someone we know came here a few months ago.'

He perked up. 'Really? Who?'

'Eleanor Campbell. Ellie. Do you remember her?'

'Of course, I remember,' said Cliff, nodding solemnly. 'We're a small place. She was the girl who died, wasn't she?'

Lara nodded.

'I read about it in the paper. I didn't realise she was a *Campbell* Campbell.'

'Did she come here with someone? A man called Harry?'

Cliff shook his head.

'She came alone. She took Emily Dickinson, that's our smallest room in the eaves. Why do you ask?'

Lara felt a flutter of excitement. After all this time, this felt like a breakthrough.

'Well, we were wondering why she came to North Bend.'

Cliff took a moment to think about it.

'You're right; we're not popular at that time of year and the reason I remember Eleanor so clearly was she was our only guest that night. I don't know how well you know this part of the world, but it gets very cold around here in winter. Lots of snow. Marina thinks we should just shut down from January to April, but we get some skiers passing through on the way up to the resorts, so I like to keep it open. But still, it's not the time most people choose to come to North Bend. If I remember rightly, though, she was visiting someone local. At one of the farms.'

Lara and Alex both looked at each other.

'Can you remember which one?

Cliff folded his arms across his chest as if deep in thought.

'She asked us for directions,' he said, nodding. 'I think it was somewhere past Sugar Dew Farm. That's where we get our cheese from. I think this place grew sweetcorn. I didn't know it.'

He pulled his phone out of his pocket and started tapping.

'Yes, that's it: Heckfield Farm. It's a twenty-minute drive from here. Can't imagine why she wanted to go to a sweetcorn farm in February, but there you go.'

He clapped his hands, brightening.

'Well, I'd better get back into the house. Did you hear that thunder? The rain is coming.'

* * *

At least the fire was roaring. Outside, the rain was clicking on the windows, the thunder rumbling in the distance. Alex and Lara settled down on cushions on the floor, backs against the sofa, legs stretched out in front of them towards the glowing logs.

'These are great chips,' said Alex, popping a French fry into his mouth.

'Yes, I just wish he hadn't told us about the pigs.'

'We should visit this farm tomorrow,' said Alex thoughtfully.

'But Cliff's right. What do you think Ellie wanted with a sweetcorn farm in winter?

'Maybe we just think about that tomorrow,' said Alex with a yawn.

The fire popped and hissed as the rain found its way down the chimney and every now and then, the sash windows would rattle with a gust of wind.

'Filthy night,' said Alex, taking another sip of his brandy.

Alex gave her such an intense look, she had to look away.

'Do you think you could live here?' he asked after a while.

'I *am* living here.'

'I mean, full-time. In America.'

Lara shook her head. 'Not sure. I mean, spending a semester in Benedon is a wonderful experience. Well, it would have been if the circumstances were different, but I'm not even two weeks in, and it's made me realise how much I love London. I miss the houseboat. I miss Chelsea and the West End. I miss getting on the motorbike and heading out to the countryside. And believe it or not, I miss you.'

'You miss me?'

She laughed and flung a cushion at him.

'Don't make me say it again.'

She paused.

'What about you?'

Alex thought for a moment.

'You know when I was at primary school, the teachers would let you work on a "topic", and you got to choose their subject? Most kids chose something like dinosaurs or whoever the latest pop star was. I always chose "America" because everything in America was cool. Cartoons, bubble gum, cop shows, Clint Eastwood. I remember doing a whole thing on the Grand Canyon. I couldn't believe it was over a mile deep. Years later, when I went to Arizona, I discovered that the Grand Canyon isn't even the biggest canyon in the world. There's one in Peru that's almost twice as deep, but then that's another of the reasons I love America. They're brilliant at marketing.'

'Well, your school sounds more fun than mine was,' said Lara. 'I think the only project I did was Greek and Latin translations.

'I bet you loved it.'

Lara shrugged. 'I wasn't hugely happy at school. All girls' boarding schools can be cliquey and competitive. I wish I'd had you there as a friend.'

'We wouldn't have been friends,' said Alex.

She looked across, preparing to be offended.

'Why not?'

'Because I would have fancied you something rotten.'

'Oh yes, and what changed?' she smiled.

'Nothing,' he said softly.

Something shifted in the atmosphere. It felt like the charge in the air just before a storm.

His hand reached across the rug and touched hers, softly as first, until Lara's fingers were intertwined in his. Lara knew she could pull away, *should* pull away. But she didn't want to. Nerves, excitement, and desire gripped her. Her eyes closed as she could feel his warm breath on his face.

'Alex, we shouldn't….' she murmured. Lara didn't know why she was objecting because this was exactly what she wanted.

'We should have done this long ago,' he said.

And then his lips were on hers, their kiss deepening in intensity as they fell back onto the rug. Alex pulled his t-shirt over his head. His body was better than she remembered from the few times they had gone swimming together, his firm, tanned chest, a scrub of hair. He lowered himself onto her, her heartbeat speeding up as he pressed down on her, kissing her lips, her throat and the side of her neck.

'The bed,' she whispered. They scrambled to their feet, each shedding their clothes as they went. In his haste, Alex helped to unclip her bra, and she gasped as his hand rolled over her nipple. Over the years, she'd had idle thoughts about what Alex would be like as a lover, but this was incredible, better than she could ever dream of. Finally, they sank back on the mattress. The rain was beating down hard outside, but Lara could hardly hear it. She moaned as she felt his mouth move across her body, then back up, across her belly, her breasts and back to her lips. One firm but gentle hand parted her thighs, and then he was inside her - in that moment, she was gripped by such joy and desire that she forgot to breathe. She came before he did, a searing pulse of ecstasy so strong that she cried out. He followed her, bucking and then collapsing on her sweat-sheened body, they fell silent, just listening to the sound of the rain and their regulating breath.

'I think that was worth the seventeen year wait,' smiled Alex turning over to face her, and they both burst out laughing.

Chapter 34

Just for a moment, Alex kept his eyes closed. Warm, safe, contented; this was where he'd always wanted to be, and he knew it now. He held his breath as Lara stirred beside him, her leg entwined with his, her naked hip against his. He didn't want to wake her; he wanted this moment to last. Because there was no going back now. For years they'd pretended that there was no attraction between them, but now they couldn't hide it. Not that he wanted to: not for a second. That night had been hands down the best of his life, everything he'd hoped it would be and more.

'Hey,' murmured Lara, turning over.

'Hey yourself.'

As he waited for her to say something else, he felt a flutter of nerves. For all he knew, he could have been feeling all these emotions by himself. Lara had always been hard to read, and he had no idea what was coming next, a cough, a grimace then, 'Last night... it was a mistake.'

But instead, she smiled and kissed his shoulder. Then kissed his neck and then moved her lips so they pressed against his.

'You know what?' she said, a sly grin on her face. 'I think we need to do that again.'

Her hands moved under the sheets, and Alex groaned, torn between his desire and what he knew he had to do. This was everything he'd ever wanted, and yet...

'What's wrong?' she said, pulling back. Lara's instincts had always been sharp. He pushed himself back on the mattress, sitting up.

'Lar. We need to talk.'

She closed her eyes and pulled a pillow over her face.

'Oh, God.'

'No, it's not that, seriously,' he said. 'No regrets, no second thoughts. I'm so glad this happened. *So* glad.'

'Then what?'

Alex shifted uncomfortably.

'I need to tell you something.'

'This isn't the bit where you admit you're gay or secretly married, is it?' Alex could still hear the quaver in her voice.

'It's something I tried to tell you at breakfast the other day.'

Alex took a deep breath.

'I've been offered a job, an editorship.'

She sat up.

'What? Alex, that's amazing!'

He watched the tension in her face melt. She was beaming now. Lara sat up and the covers slid down, revealing her perfect breasts. Seeing his expression, Lara snatched the sheet back up, covering herself.

'Control yourself,' she said with a flicker of a smile. 'Okay, so which paper?'

'That's the problem,' said Alex. '*The LA Globe*.'

He saw something cross her face – disappointment? Resignation? – then it was gone. Instead, Lara grabbed his hand.

'Los Angeles. Gosh. Alex, this is an amazing opportunity. *The Globe's* like the west coast *Chronicle; they're* really strong on reportage. Jim Cavanagh's there, isn't he?'

Alex nodded, his excitement rising with hers. 'And Annie Franks; there are some good people.'

He hesitated, and she looked back at him more sharply. She knew him too well.

'Alex, you have to take it. Bite their hand off.'

He tried to form his face into a smile, but it didn't quite get there.

'What's the problem?' she asked more softly.

'It's you.'

She gave a nervous laugh.

'What have I got to do with it?'

She was reacting exactly as he had expected her to: selfless, happy and encouraging. And it was killing him.

'You have everything to do with this Lar, because....' He gestured towards her and the bed. 'Because of this.'

'Don't be stupid,'

Alex threw up a hand. 'Don't say that. Please don't say it didn't mean anything. Because it did, to me at least.'

Lara's face softened.

'It did mean something, you big idiot. And it still does. But you can't build your whole life around one night, however awesome it was.'

Alex looked at her sideways. 'You thought it was awesome?'

'Yes,' she said, blushing. 'I did.'

Lara grabbed Alex's t-shirt and pulled it on. Then she sat cross-legged on the bed.

'This is massive, Alex. It's what you've always wanted.'

You're what I've always wanted, he wanted to say, but the words got stuck in his throat. Lara was strong, and independent. The strongest, most independent woman he had ever met. Perhaps she could cope with some half-formed, long-distance relationship, but he wasn't sure he could. Not now. Not with her.

'Maybe it is, but this is a job on the other side of the world.'

'Exactly, in one of the biggest cities in America. Alex, you said it yourself, you've always loved America, and you'll be the editor of a major newspaper read by a million people.'

'Half a million.'

'Still, it's one of the most plum editorships in the world. You know how rarely they come up.'

She was right, of course. The higher up the ladder you went, the fewer opportunities there were. There were possibly fifty agenda-setting, big-circulation newspapers in the world, and when you took out the non-English speaking titles, it was a small pool if you wanted to be the editor of a heavy-hitter. People could spend ten, or twenty years in the top job, not shifting.

'How did it happen?'

He gave her a brief run-down of how the job offer had come about. It was nothing more complicated than a US headhunter contacting him and asking if he was interested. Alex already knew David Lyons, publisher of the *LA Globe*, having met him the previous year at Cannes Film Festival. David had flown to London to meet him and hear his ideas. A few days later, he got the offer of a job.

'Have you accepted it?'

'No. Not yet. I wanted to discuss it with you.'

And this was the real reason why he'd come to Benedon. Of course, he wanted to support her at the symposium, particularly at a difficult time, but he also wanted to tell her about the *LA Globe* and he wanted her to give him a reason why he shouldn't take it. He wanted her to say that she had always loved him, and no job was worth not being together.

'Don't turn it down for me,' she whispered.

'Why?'

'You don't have to do it forever, and in the meantime, LA isn't that far. You know money isn't a problem for those transatlantic flights and I'm only in the office a couple of days a week now.'

Alex's stomach sank, knowing his worst fear was coming true. Lara hadn't offered to move out to California to be with him; she hadn't said, 'We can make this work.' No suggestion that their night together changed anything.

She took his hands in hers. 'I'm so proud of you. I always knew you'd get there.'

'I think you're more excited about this than I am.'

'That's because I know you better than you know yourself. I know how much you want this.'

'So you think I should take it?'

'You should definitely take it.'

Lara moved forward and cupped her hands around his face. 'You are amazing, Alex Ford.'

She kissed him full on the lips, then suddenly sprang up and ran to the bathroom, giving him just a tantalising flash of her buttocks as the t-shirt moved. She closed the door, then opened it again, her face peeking out.

'Come on, chop-chop, we'd better get ready. They start early on the farm.'

Chapter 35

Lara closed the door and slid back against it. She covered her face with her hands.

Oh God, oh God, oh God, she thought. *What have I done?*

Last night... it had been everything she had ever wanted. Romantic, passionate. Perfect. The sex had been incredible, but it was more than that. It was a connection, a sense of home and belonging, that had made her realise how much she loved him – and was in love with him. And she had felt his love for her coming back just as strong.

In fairy tales, what happened last night was where the story ended. You found your soul mate, your Prince Charming – there was some fancy wedding with a golden carriage – and you lived happily ever after.

But then he had told her about the LA job, and everything had changed. This was Alex. The one person she couldn't risk losing, not after she had lost so many before. Kissing him last night had been a huge spin of the wheel; everything stacked on red. And right now, it looked like she was going to lose it all. Now, in the blink of an eye, he was leaving her.

Los Angeles. The other side of the world. And it was true that she could go there once a month, stay a week. A long-distance love affair fuelled by love and air miles. But she knew how this all worked in reality. Alex was a workaholic – he always gave 110%. Lara knew enough about US media to understand that the *LA Globe* editorship was a turnaround job. Sales were declining, so who better than a charming Englishman to persuade advertisers to keep supporting them? A charming Englishman who was brilliant at the editorial side too. She imagined him hitting the ground running, going into the office blazing with ideas, energy and focus, a general at the head of his troops. It would be a brilliant appointment for them and the perfect opportunity for Alex.

But working long stressful hours, would he want his girlfriend popping over every two minutes? What would start as a romantic reunion would quickly become an unwanted distraction.

'Should we go down to breakfast or have it sent up?' he shouted through the door.

'We'll go down. I won't be a minute,' she trilled and reached up to turn on the shower to keep up the pretence that she was getting ready for the day, not freaking out. She sat on the edge of the bath, hunched over, running her hands through her hair.

What a mess.

For as long as she'd known Alex, he had always wanted to be a newspaper editor. It had been his childhood dream. He loved America too, remembering how his eyes lit up the previous evening. Alex deserved to be the editor of a big paper like the *LA Globe; it* was perfect for him in every way; it was his destiny. So how could Lara stand in his way? When you loved someone, really loved someone, you did what was best for them, not you.

Lara couldn't see which way to turn.

She knew that if he took the job and she stayed in London, their fledgling relationship couldn't, wouldn't last. Of course, she could go with him, but she hated LA and would have to scale back her work. She might even end up resenting him.

And if he didn't take the job – he would resent her. Alex had been deputy editor now for over three years and it was definitely time for a change, especially when you were ambitious and turning forty was on the horizon. So how could Lara stand in his way?

Lara pressed a hand against her chest as her heart fluttered, remembering that perfect night. It had been fantastic. Lara had loved Alex before, of course, as a man, friend, decent human being, but lying there together, their bodies and hearts in complete sync, she didn't think life could get any better.

And then you woke up, she thought cynically.

She stepped under the scalding water and began scrubbing herself harder than she needed. How could things change so quickly? How could she go from searing happiness to whirling confusion in the blink of an eye?

Tearing back the shower curtain, Lara wrapped herself in a towel and wiped an angry hand across the mirror. She looked blotchy, and pale, her mouth an upside-down 'U': a picture of disappointment and pain.

'Come on, Lara Stone,' she whispered to herself. 'Game face on.'

She *did* know Alex Ford better than he knew himself; if she showed how she was feeling, he would stay in London, stagnating at the *Chronicle*. And she couldn't do that to the man she loved. She poked at her mouth with two fingers, pushing the corners upwards.

'Smile,' she whispered. And she reached for the door.

Chapter 36

The farm was beautiful. That was the first surprise. For some reason, Alex had imagined it as a desolate place. Instead, Heckfield Farm was lush and sparkling after the rain, surrounded by vast green fields, their arrow-straight rows stretching into the distance.

Right by the entrance gate was a wagon, the front stacked with baskets of vegetables: carrots, cabbage, broccoli and kale. 'Help yourselves!' read a hand-chalked sign, 'Honesty box at back'.

Alex bumped into the yard and they parked by a low red building he presumed was a barn. It didn't look like anyone was home.

'Hello?' called Alex. No answer.

'We should have called ahead,' said Lara. 'They'll all be out in the fields, doing... well, farm things.'

Alex nodded. He hadn't really wanted to come to the farm. He'd wanted to stay at the Blackberry Inn and talk about the future. The publisher of the *Globe* had sent him an email overnight, pushing him for a decision, and he knew he had to make it soon. But he knew all this – the circumstances behind Harry's death – was important to Lara.

Personally, he couldn't see where the dots connected, and he wasn't even sure they should try. At the back of his mind, there was even a nagging thought that Harry Robbins had meant more to Lara than she was letting on. That was why she was happy to chase all over Massachusetts and Vermont to work out the depth of connection between Ellie Campbell and Harry. It was perhaps why she seemed unwilling to commit to him – because she was in love with someone else, even if he was a ghost.

Somewhere in the distance, he could hear the sound of coughing. 'Sounds like someone's around.'

Alex called out again, and a man walked out from the barn. He looked like a farmer: plaid shirt, worn jeans and scuffed Redwing boots, wiping his hands on a bandana.

'You here for the potatoes?' he asked. 'We're all out, sorry. Everyone's after the reds this year. But we got plenty of beets.'

'No,' said Lara. 'We're not here for the vegetables.'

The man eyed them suspiciously.

'How can I help you folks, then?'

'Is this your farm, Mr...?'

'Miller, Jake Miller. And it's my daddy's farm, well was before he passed on, God rest him.'

'I'm sorry to hear that, Mr. Miller,' said Lara. 'Recently?'

'Last Fall,' he said, a hitch in his voice. He pressed the handkerchief against his mouth.

Great, thought, Lara. You've been here a minute and already reduced the man to tears.

'Are you Elmore's people?' asked the farmer, his voice rasping. 'You don't sound like you're from round here.'

'We came over from Benedon College,' said Alex.

Shaded by the curved baseball cap bill, Lara still caught the flare of Miller's eyes. Alarm or anger?

'I can't talk to none of you people,' he said. 'I'm going to have to ask you to leave.'

A woman walked out behind Jake. She was older, with grey hair tied back in a bun, and her face was lined by a life outdoors, but she moved with assurance.

'What's going on, Jake?' she asked.

'More folks from the college,' said the man, pointing to them with his chin.

'More folks?' Asked Lara. 'Do you remember talking to our friend Ellie Campbell? It was around six months ago.'

'She was here, yes,' said the woman. 'About GreenGo.'

'Mom, no!' said Jake. 'We can't.'

Alex saw a look exchanged between mother and son, but Jake shook his head decisively.

'We can't talk to you,' he said. 'All that's over and done...' his words dissolved as his chest began heaving, and Lara realised that he hadn't been using the bandana to stifle his grief; he was using it to cover a heavy cough. He bent over, leaning on the barn as his shoulders shook.

'Do you need help, Mr Miller?' said Alex, concerned, looking up at the old woman.

'He'll be fine,' she said. 'Just needs a glass of water and to go and rest. Jake go. I'll deal with this.'

Jake Miller must have been in his late forties but he still nodded in front of his momma and went inside.

Mrs Miller looked back at her with sad, brown eyes.

'She's dead, I know.'

'Then you understand how important it is for us to talk to you.'

'We can't.'

The woman shook her head sadly.

'And there's one thing we've learned is that you can't ever bring anyone back with words.'

'Mrs Miller, what did Ellie come here for? What's GreenGo?'

'Please, I think you should leave. My husband's gone. I can't cope with much more.'

'What happened to your husband, Mrs Miller?'

Her eyes were pooling with emotion.

'I wish I could tell you, but I can't.'

Lara stepped towards her.

'You can tell us,' she said with quiet authority.

The woman glanced back towards the barn, then in a low voice said: 'Go see Elmore Jones, a lawyer in North Bend. He knew Ellie. He'll tell you all you need to know. But you didn't hear that from me.'

There was a noise from the barn, and Jake Miller stood there, his hands on his hips.

'Come on, mom. I need you inside.'

She raised her hands, waving them back towards the car as if she were shooing cattle back through a gate. Jake stayed where he was, coughing into his bandana.

'Speak to Elmore,' she said, then turned back to the barn.

'We will,' said Alex quietly, as he and Lara got back into the car.

Chapter 37

'Brian, it's Lara Stone.'

'Miss Stone. Hello' said her student Brian Silvinski, clearly shocked to receive the call. Her student had been one of the helpers at the symposium, and Lara still had the volunteers' numbers punched in her phone. 'I just wanted to say that the symposium was amazing. And I was so glad to help out and….'

'Brian, I need your help again. Are you busy today?' Lara glanced up as she stood on North Bend's Main Street, watching as Alex chatted to a pretty young woman in a floral dress. Usually, Lara smiled at how women of all ages seemed to fawn all over Alex Ford, even when he asked for directions, but she was now irritated.

'Sure, what can I do for you?'

'I've got a list of names. Party guests. I'd like you to give me a potted profile on each of them.'

'What for?'

Brian was smart. He asked all the right questions, but she had an answer prepared.

'It's always important to know who is at your party so that you know what to ask when you're introduced to them.'

'I hear you,' said Brian. 'So, is there going to be another party?'

'Maybe,' she said vaguely. She trusted Brian but didn't want him to know that the list of names was from the Dean's Labor Day party. Mary, Doug's secretary, had got them for her as a favour, and she didn't want her to get in trouble. 'Can you get that to me as quickly as possible? Make sure you include pictures as a visual prompt. And try and keep it to yourself, huh? I'm not sure the other students will be too happy thinking you're my research assistant.'

Alex was walking back towards her, pointing up the street. 'Elmore Jones Attorneys. He's in the Red House with the clock.'

It was a good description: turn of the century, red brick building in the style of a courthouse from a John Ford western movie. Perhaps that's what it had been built for.

Crossing the street, they found the front door to the red building was wide open, giving onto a cool reception hall. The name Elmore Jones was on a brass plaque in the lobby, listing about another dozen names.

'Hello?' called Lara, pushing open a glass door with 'Elmore Jones' stencilled onto it. There was a small reception – a desk with no one behind it. Lara rang the brass bell by the pencil pot. 'Anyone here?'

A middle-aged man came out of the back. Shirt sleeves rolled up, he was slightly crumpled, but he had a look of efficiency.

'I'm looking for Elmore Jones.'

'You've found him.'

He offered her a big hand.

'My name is Lara Stone. I'm a visiting fellow at Benedon College. I'm also a journalist at the London *Chronicle*. This is my colleague Alex Ford.'

Elmore raised a brow.

'The London *Chronicle*, huh? You're a long way from home looking for stories.'

'Sometimes stories find you when you're least expecting him.'

'What do you want to speak to me about?'

'The death of Ellie Campbell and Harry Robbins, a student and a professor at Benedon.'

She didn't expect the names to register, but the smile faded from Elmore's face. He walked past Lara and closed the door behind them.

'I think you'd better come into my office.'

They followed him through a door into a surprisingly large room, more like a 1950s den than a lawyer's office, with leather chairs and a wet bar in the corner. 'Excuse the mess,' said Elmore, distractedly moving papers from one pile to another. 'We don't get many visitors; most of our work is done in the field; literally in our case, given this is a farming town.'

Elmore settled down behind his desk and took a second to look them over.

'I was expecting a visit from you.'

'You were?'

'Not the London *Chronicle* specifically. Someone more local. Although I'm not sure anyone but the big boys have the budget for investigative reporting these days.'

He took a sip from the coffee cup on his desk.

'So, what do you want to know? I should point out before we start that the people you're dealing with have unlimited budgets to shut us down.'

Lara's heart bumped: she immediately knew they were on the right trail.

'Ellie Campbell was writing a story. We know it was a story involving Heckfield Farm. We know Ellie came to see you about the story. And few days later, she was dead.'

Lara was careful not to say too much more. Elmore was a lawyer, and she couldn't be sure how much he knew or whose side he was on. The way Jake Miller, the farmer, had asked, 'are you Elmore's people?' suggested hostility, but then Miller's mother had sent them this way.

Elmore took a sharp intake of breath.

'Ellie Campbell. Smart girl. Brave too.'

'Brave?'

He sat back in his chair.

'How much do you know about AgriCam?' he asked.

Lara shook her head and looked at Alex, who seemed equally puzzled.

'You know about the Campbell family, right?'

'Big-time industrialists,' said Lara. She'd researched them and knew their list of interests spanned from dyes to refrigerants.

Elmore nodded. 'AgriCam is a division of Campbell Industries. Agrochemicals. Pesticides, herbicides, fertiliser. Many farms out here use GreenGo, that's AgriCam's wonder brand.'

'I saw that logo a lot on the drive up here,' noted Alex.

'You will have done. GreenGo is a fertiliser. This is farming country; agriculture is our main industry. GreenGo is the best pesticide anyone's used in a generation. It can increase crop yields by up to 20%, which may not sound a lot to you, but in farming circles, that's a miracle product right there.'

Elmore's face turned serious.

'A few weeks after Christmas, a young woman comes to see me. Ellie Campbell. Did you know that Ellie was the anointed one who was supposed to take over from Arthur Campbell as Campbell Industries CEO? Her daddy was training her up, so she'd spend her vacations interning at their various divisions. She spent a few days over the Christmas vacation working at AgriCam's head office.'

Lara could feel her journalistic instincts tingling. This was the answer; this was where it all hinged.

'Ellie had discovered that GreenGo was far from being a miracle product.'

Elmore rolled his chair across to a grey steel filing cabinet and pulled out a thick bound document, dropping it onto his desk with a thump.

'GreenGo is a relatively new product,' said Elmore, keeping one hand over the file. 'AgriCam didn't roll it out nationally at first. They started right here, in Vermont, five years ago. People loved it. The increase in yield and the fact that it didn't appear to degenerate soil quality. Then farmers around here started getting sick.'

'There's a link to GreenGo?' asked Alex, pre-empting the lawyer.

'Well, of course, the fertiliser went through rigorous testing. But mistakes were made. GreenGo has low toxicity to humans, but only for the normal man in the street. Lots of farmers around here use boom sprayers to apply pesticides and herbicides. It seems if you sit in a tractor with GreenGo blowing about, breathing it in for a few years, it's gonna do some damage. We've seen a significant uptick in cancer and respiratory disease in the agricultural communities.'

Lara thought about Ellie's lending record from the library – all those books on cancer and oncology. She felt sure that it was related to GreenGo. She was trying to educate herself on the damage it was causing.

'And where do you come into this?' asked Lara.

'Last year, a farmer came to see me. Nick Miller, owner of Heckfield Farm. Good guy, approaching retirement. Nick was sick. Two of his farmer buddies in Woking

County had gotten sick too. Nick Miller and his friends were some of the first farmers in the state, in the country, to start using GreenGo. They were wondering if there was a possible link to GreenGo, but they didn't even know where to start looking to prove it was.'

Elmore sat back in his chair.

'I was wary about getting involved. The Campbells are powerful. Besides, any class action takes years, and I'm sixty-eight years old.'

He popped his chair back from recline.

'Still, sometimes you think *what the hell*. I had to do something. It was so disturbing. It can take decades for patterns to emerge that a certain chemical is dangerous, but with GreenGo, the time between exposure and illness seemed so quick. I had several meetings with the Millers, and encouraged them to sue, but then they went quiet. Nick died.' He held up his hands. 'I started asking around, seeing if anyone else was prepared to take on AgriCam, but I was met with silence. And then Ellie Campbell came to see me.'

'What did Ellie say?'

'AgriCam didn't launch GreenGo into the world knowing it was carcinogenic. But their crime was to ignore the data when it started coming through. When they realised that one of their products was harming their customers, AgriCam should have immediately taken the product off the market.'

'But they didn't do anything?'

'They did something, all right. They paid people off.'

'Ellie told you that?'

'She'd seen evidence of it, yes.'

'So why didn't you do anything about it?' asked Lara. 'Sue the company or tell the world?'

Elmore shook his head.

'How could I, when no one was prepared to testify?

The Millers weren't the only farmers affected. I can name thirty others who have developed lung cancer or kidney failure in a 50-mile radius. But the Campbells have been paying people off: the Millers, others, making them sign non-disclosure agreements in return for seven-figure settlements.'

Lara sat forward: the real question hadn't been asked.

'You don't think any of this was connected to Ellie's death, do you?'

Elmore looked sad.

'If it did,' he said, putting the thick file back in his cabinet and closing the door with a 'clang'. 'If someone had done something to shut Eleanor Campbell up? Well, then you'd have yourself a real scandal, wouldn't you?'

Chapter 38

'This is him?' asked Sarah, bending over the file and taking out the mug shots. 'This is the guy forensics linked to Harry Robbin's yard? He doesn't look like much.'

'They never do, said Glenn.

Sarah picked up the top sheet and read out some of the headlines from Wayne Fortune's predictably extensive criminal record.

'B&E, assault with a deadly weapon, conspiracy to commit kidnapping, theft from a vehicle, parole violation; your basic lowlife scumbag. No murder, but there's still time.'

She flipped to Fortune's custody record.

'Juvie at 12, county jail, five years for kidnapping, a two-spot in Framington for grand theft auto – not the video game. Hmm... took a plea deal on a battery charge back in last year.' She looked up. 'We got ourselves a snitch?'

'That could be useful,' said Glenn. 'Better ask him, huh?'

Forensics had matched Wayne Fortune's DNA record to the sample outside Harry's house almost immediately;

then, it had just been a matter of tracking him down. That had been equally simple:

Glenn had found Wayne asleep in a bar in Maryville, three towns over from Benedon. The barman had called the cops when Wayne refused to shift after having drunk most of a bottle of illicit tequila.

The police department's secure interview room wasn't fancy, just a boxy space with a table bolted to the floor, but then Sarah didn't anticipate that this would require much finesse. From his record, Wayne Fortune didn't strike her as a criminal mastermind.

'Sit up, asshole,' said Glenn, bulling his way into the room and evidently waking up the suspect again. 'I'd like to introduce you to Chief of Detectives Sarah Carter.'

'A woman?' said Wayne, rubbing his eyes.

'Excellent start, Wayne,' said Sarah crisply. 'Your observational skills are second to none. That will help you a great deal over the next couple of hours.'

Wayne was skinny but tough, with a drinker's florid nose and paper-thin skin wound with pale blue veins. If Sarah hadn't read his file, she would have put Wayne at around 45. Tragically, Wayne had barely limped past 30.

'Woman or no woman, I got nothing to say,' said Wayne. 'Except howyadoin' honey?'

'Then I've got a feeling this is going to go very badly for you,' said Glenn, placing his bulk between Wayne and Sarah, a looming presence that couldn't fail to intimidate.

Sarah flashed a look of gratitude to Glenn.

'Let's cut straight to it, Wayne,' said Sarah, placing her wristwatch on the table in front of him. 'You've got ten minutes to cooperate with me. By the end of that time, I want you to have told me why you broke into Harry Robbin's house and shot him on Labor Day evening.'

'Or what are you going to do?' he challenged her.

'I'll charge you with murder one, anyway,' she said.

For most people, that level of accusation would have been like a punch in the gut, but Wayne Fortune had been accused of crimes all his life and denial was second nature to him, almost a reflex.

'Murder? You got me all wrong. I don't do no murder. You've seen my record.'

'Yes, I've seen your record,' said Sarah wearily. 'And you know what I see? A violent criminal.'

'I'm a lover not a fighter,' said Wayne, then cracked up laughing. Both Sarah and Glenn just stared at him until Wayne stopped.

'Hey, tough crowd. Look, what do you want me to say? I didn't kill no one.'

Sarah sighed.

'I don't believe you had beef with Harry Robbins, Wayne. But I do think that you shot him.'

'And why would I want to do that to some Prof?' he replied.

'That's what I'm here to find out. Maybe it started as burglary. It was Labor Day. Lots of people weren't at home. It was easy pickings for a man like you, Wayne.'

'What do you think I was looking for? Books? I don't need no books.'

Sarah didn't like to concede that he had a point. It was something Glenn had brought up before too. Why break into a teacher's relatively humble cottage when there were plenty of beautiful homes in the Benedon area? Her eyes narrowed, thinking about Ros Davies again.

'Or did someone pay you to kill Harry Robbins, Wayne?'

An expression passed his face. It was as if he was

forcing himself to look impassive. Sarah was an experienced enough interviewer to know she was onto something.

'I can name at least five people who wanted Harry Robbins gone,' said Sarah, slicing her hand through the air. It was a slight exaggeration - she supposed the Campbells didn't like him, and Harry could have caused trouble for Ros's Provost election campaign.

Wayne crossed his arms. 'Before you pulled me in, I'd never heard of no Robbins.'

Glenn leaned closer. 'Spoiler alert Wayne, he's the dude you killed seven nights ago.'

Wayne sighed, trying a different tact.

'I ain't killed no-one, Detective Carter. Labor Day night, I was hanging out at home having some drinks, like most people.'

'Wayne, we have evidence that you were there,' pressed Sarah.

He slumped back into his chair and stayed silent.

'Did you wonder why we took your sneakers when we arrested you?' she asked.

'Because my feet are like deadly weapons, man,' he said, sarcastic now.

Damn, thought Sarah, rubbing her eye with impatience. He's looking at life without parole, and he's cracking jokes.

'We took your shoes because there are footprints all over the crime scene. They are an exact match with your sneakers. We also have a DNA sample match which puts you at the scene. I see you've got a cut on your wrist there. Looks nasty. Maybe your gloves weren't long enough.'

Sarah didn't mention that however compelling this evidence was, it was still circumstantial. Wayne's lawyer would claim he had been creeping about, casing the joint for a burglary, which was barely even a misdemeanour. He would almost certainly argue that Wayne was in Harry's yard later in the week. They had no evidence to say *when* he was there. Sarah's hopes were pinned on the forensics team finding fibres from inside Harry's apartment on the clothes they'd seized in their search of Wayne's apartment. But that would take time, and it still wasn't conclusive. Plus, Roscoe was already screaming blue hell over the cost, the publicity and, most of all, the implication that Benedon might be the kind of town where murders were committed. As far as he was concerned, that was the worst crime possible.

'Wayne, make this easier for yourself. Blame it on someone else. Just give me the name of the person who wanted you to take out Harry Robbins. I gave you ten minutes, but we are down to six,' she said, tapping her watch.

The hood shook his head again. 'It's not me, man. You got yourself a case of mistaken identity.'

Sarah picked up her watch.

'All right, out of time,' she said. 'Wayne Fortune, I am charging you with....'

'What? No!' Wayne was waving his hands back and forth. 'No, no, I got six minutes left!'

He looked at Glenn in appeal. 'You heard her; she said ten minutes, man.'

'Detective Carter is very strict on timekeeping,' he said. 'And I'm not sure you can tell the time, Wayne.'

Glenn began to rise, but Sarah stayed where she was.

'I ain't saying anything more without my lawyer, man.'

'Wayne, you waived your right to representation, remember?' said Glenn.

'That was before I knew you would be accusing me of murder. Like I said, I'm an innocent man. Thought I wouldn't need no rep-ree-sent-tay-shon,' he said, drawing the words out.

Sarah sat back, waving a weary hand.

'Fine. Let him call Saul.'

'I've got a lawyer,' said Wayne.

'You have a lawyer, Wayne?' said Glenn, pulling out a notebook. 'Who?'

'Jeff. Jeff Strobe.'

The door opened, and a uniformed officer stepped in. It was Brin, the ambitious young cop just out of the Academy.

'Sorry to interrupt, Chief, but I think you need to come.'

'What's up?' asked Sarah.

The officer looked over at Wayne and gave a slight shake of the head.

'Okay, Wayne,' she said, standing. 'Back to the tank. We'll pick this up when I get back. You make the most of our time together too, because you aren't going to see a woman for a long, long time.'

She paused at the door, looking him in the eye. 'You're going to jail, Wayne. Forever.'

Sarah was dismayed in the corridor to see Heather from the care home. Worry was written all over her face, and Sarah was immediately on high alert.

'I'm so sorry, Sarah,' said Heather. 'I didn't know what to do.'

'What's happened?'

'Your mom got out, just walked out of the yard. The gardener had left the gate open....'

'How long ago?' said Sarah, already moving towards the door.

'Maybe forty minutes at the most. We have a couple of nurses out searching near Beauville, but as it's you, I came straight here.'

'No, you did the right thing, Heather, thanks.'

'You want us to put out an APB, Chief?' asked Brin.

The answer was yes, but Sarah knew just how that

would go down with Roscoe, using police resources to track down a doddery old woman.

'Not yet. But we need as many people as possible to search anywhere she might be.'

Heather nodded.

'I can call the bowling gang to help look.'

'Excellent. Thanks, Heather,' she said, trying to keep her cool as panic bubbled in her chest. 'I'll check my mom's place, then take Main Street down to the campus. Call my cell if you see her.'

Sarah jumped into her car, trying her best not to break the speed limit, but failing. She at least resisted the urge to use the siren.

'Where did you go, Mom?' she whispered, taking a corner almost on two wheels, 'What were you thinking?'

The real trouble was that Sarah had no real idea what her mother was thinking. The doctor had used the metaphor of a bunch of wiring torn apart by a storm, swinging about in the wind. Occasionally some of those wires would connect and spark, and her mother would suddenly get a notion to do something. In the past, Sarah had found Colleen in the garden, digging a grave for Monty, Sarah's long-dead goldfish, tears streaming down her face. Another time, she found her mom sitting quietly on the porch, a suitcase neatly packed, waiting for the taxi to take her to the airport. Mostly these incidents were re-triggered memories, so the family home was the most likely place she would return to. Muttering a prayer, Sarah turned into the street and left her car slantways across the road, door wide as she sprinted across the front lawn. Scrabbling her keys from her purse, Sarah was surprised to find that the front screen was already open. She burst inside and came face to face with a middle-aged woman with blow-dried hair and a Chanel skirt suit that wasn't quite Chanel.

Standing behind her was a young couple, their mouths wide open.

Oh shit, thought Sarah, grasping the situation immediately.

'Leanne,' she panted. 'Sorry, sorry.'

'Our wonderful owner...' said the realtor, doing her best to make it sound light-hearted.

Sarah ignored her and turned to the shocked-looking couple. 'I'm sorry to intrude. I can explain: this is my house. Well, my mom's. Small family emergency, nothing to worry about. I'll be out of your hair in just a minute....'

She backed away into the kitchen, swiftly checking the den and the laundry room: all empty. Sarah had expected to find her mom sitting in her bedroom, but that was empty too. In fact, there was no trace of her in any sense, and for a moment, Sarah paused, looking around.

The familiar patchwork quilt on her mother's double bed had gone, replaced a hip leaf-print throw and scattered cushions. Art exhibition posters had replaced family pictures and Sarah's graduation certificate from the academy and the bedside cabinet had fresh flowers and artfully-arranged toiletries. It looked like a display at Anthropologie, which she supposed was the point. Sarah had paid a stager to put all her mom's effects into storage and to 're-draw' the house, as they put it, making it less like an old lady's house and more like something that an aspirational young couple might consider buying. The realtor had told her it was a good investment, but suddenly she felt an overwhelming sense of guilt.

Sarah retraced her steps, passing the realtor and the young couple talking out on the drive.

'Hope you liked it,' called Sarah, without much hope, jumping back into the car. 'I'm prepared to consider offers for a quick sale.'

She fired up the engine, thinking about what she had just said.

She was selling the house to liquidate funds to pay for the care home. But if she didn't find her mother, she might not need it.

Chapter 39

The cove wasn't on the map. Lizzy had said it was 'past the old pier', as if that would make the location obvious. The pier itself had been easy to find; Lara had seen it in old pictures around the college, students from the fifties in swimming caps and modest costumes jumping off the wooden jetty. But where was the cove?

Lara walked along the thin strip where cracked asphalt met scrubby weeds before joining a path weaving through the woodland clinging to the sides of Finger Lake. Between the trees, the late afternoon sunlight shone on the water, sending out dazzling golden flashes that made Lara squint. The path dipped into a dark hollow, then rose up and – finally – the trees parted, and Lara found herself in a perfect little inlet, shaggy cliffs to her left, a crescent of untouched sand to her right. As she scrambled down the rocks to the beach, Lara heard a whoop.

When Brian had sent over a PDF document, giving potted profiles of everyone at the Dean's party, Lara had messaged Lizzy, asking her if she fancied meeting up for a coffee. Lizzy had gone one better and suggested that Lara join her at the cove for a swim.

What Lara had thought was a seal floating offshore was Lizzy, twenty yards out, waving an arm.

'You coming in?'

'No! Too cold,' she called.

'Come on, Lara. Doctor's orders!' shouted Lizzy. 'You'll feel amazing afterwards. Promise!'

So far, Lara had managed to avoid the craze for cold-water swimming. The Thames was too busy with working boats once you got to Chelsea, and the coast was just a little too far. Lara's friend Stella had once persuaded her to go on a jaunt to Brighton, where the plan had been to brave the sea, but Stella had been distracted by the boutiques and cafes in the quirky Lanes shopping area, and they never even got as far as the beach. But that wasn't to say she didn't fancy it.

Lizzy started swimming back to shore with strong breast-stroke movements. She waded out of the lake, droplets of water shining on her body like crystals in the late sunshine, then wriggled into her dry robe that was in a heap on the pebbly shore.

'I thought you, of all people, might have been up for wild swimming, Lara Stone. I'm going to get you in one day.'

Lara smiled.

'How about one day this week? I would come in now, but I haven't got a costume yet, and I'm not entirely sure I want a student to see me running about in my bra and pants.'

'I get that,' grinned Lizzy. 'Listen, I'd lend you a swimsuit, but you're about three sizes smaller than I am. However, I have got coffee.'

She took a towel, lay it on the ground, and then got a flask out of her canvas bag. She poured coffee into two cups and handed Lara one.

'Congratulations on the symposium,' said Lizzy, lifting her plastic mug in toast. 'You did the college proud.'

'I just tied up loose ends and made sure it went smoothly on the day. It was all Harry's work.'

'To Harry, then,' she said quietly.

'This is a beautiful spot,' said Lara after a moment. She was changing the subject, but she meant it. The lake was still, and the surrounding hills and trees reflected on the water. The leaves were golden now, and Lara was reminded of the Robert Frost poems she loved as a teenager.

'It is lovely. Though in another few weeks, it gets too cold to swim. Once the water gets down to six degrees, it's called Baltic. You have to be fit to cope with it. But winter swimmers say they love it. It's a rush. One day I might be brave enough.'

Lara smiled. She liked Lizzy. Imagined them being friends. Part of her wanted to stay here all night and tell Lizzy about Alex. Not only did Lizzy seem fun and kind, but she was also a psych professor, which surely gave her decent judgement on the human heart and mind. But there wasn't time for that. Not today.

'Lizzy, I wanted to ask you about the Dean's party,' said Lara. 'About Harry, actually.'

'Shoot,' she said, sipping her coffee.

'Remember when we met at the Dean's party? You thought I was looking for Harry. You said that you'd seen him talking to an older lady?'

Lizzy nodded. 'Yes, they were in the library.'

'Do you know who it was?'

Lizzy shook her head. 'Never seen her before. She was in her seventies. Grey-haired, elegant. I remember thinking, 'I hope I look like her when I'm her age. Although with this hair, that isn't likely,' she said, pulling at her damp curls.

Lara pulled out her phone. Brian had done an excellent

job pulling together information on the Dean's guest list, including headshots and two-line biographies. Lara felt guilty that she'd been mildly duplicitous telling him what it was for and resolved to tell him one day, feeling sure that the gung-ho journalism student would approve.

'If I showed you some pictures, do you think you would recognise her?'

Lizzy shrugged. 'Go for it.'

She opened the document Brian had sent and started flicking through it. Most were academics or staff; a few were socialites or notables who regularly appeared on the party pages of local magazines. Lara handed her phone over to Lizzy, and she flipped through the photo stream. 'That's Nina; she's in admin... no, that's Annie Tate, Gideon's wife... I saw her at the Christmas ball last year; Daphne something? Wasn't her, anyway.'

Unsurprisingly, most of the faces were familiar to Lizzy from campus or various academic social events, but Lara was disappointed when they got to the end of the photos without getting a positive match.

'What's this for?'

'Harry must have left minutes after he spoke to this woman. I was just wondering if I should speak to her. Ask if Harry was upset or distressed.'

'And what would that solve?' asked Lizzy.

She put down her cup. 'Lara, Harry was my friend too, but he's gone. And we'll never know what pushed him over the edge, what made him feel so hopeless. Searching for reasons we can never know only leads to frustration and even deeper grief.'

'This is what I do, Lizzy. I find things out. It's the thing that I'm good at.'

'Lara, it could be displacement. If you're suffering, then maybe some counselling can help?'

'Work has always been my way through,' she said.

Lizzy gave a defeated smile.

'Wait,' she said, glancing down at Lara's phone. 'That might be her.'

She took Lara's phone and used her fingers to zoom in on a photo of the Campbells. It was a rather stiff shot of the family at some formal event.

Lara pointed to a regal-looking woman standing next to Arthur Campbell. Father Vernon had said that Eliza Campbell, Arthur's wife, no longer came to Benedon's social events, but perhaps he was wrong.

'Eliza Campbell, you mean?' said Lara, pointing.

'No, the other one,' said Lizzy, using her still slightly damp finger to touch the screen.

Lizzy pointed to a grey-haired lady standing at the back of the group. She certainly fit the description of 'elegant'. The woman had the regal bearing of a matriarch.

'She must be one of the Campbells.'

Lara took her phone back and went to Google until she found the photo.

'Cordelia Campbell,' said Lara, reading the caption on the photo site. 'Cordelia Campbell is the mother of Campbell Industries Chairman Arthur Campbell and daughter-in-law of the company's founder Sinclair Campbell.'

'She wasn't on the guest list,' frowned Lara.

'When you're a Campbell, you don't need an invitation in this town,' shrugged Lizzy. And now Lara knew she needed an invitation of her own.

Chapter 40

Alex had never seen apples that big. A basket hooked over his arm, he walked around the fruit section of the deli, marvelling at how plump, shiny and blemish-free everything was. Of course, after his visit to Maple County, the supermarket had taken on a whole different look. The bunches of identical carrots with their vivid green stalks, the polished peppers in red and orange, and even the lettuce seemed to glow with supernatural good health. Was it supernatural or chemically induced; what had been sprayed on the plants to achieve such vibrant perfection?

Alex turned away from the fresh section and walked to the chiller cabinets. After Lara had dropped him off in town before she hurried off to meet Lizzy down by the lake, Alex decided to cook Lara an intimate meal for two. In theory, it would be a farewell feast; his rearranged flight left the following evening, although he wasn't sure he could leave Benedon without finding out where he stood with Lara.

And where was that exactly, he asked himself? Where did he *want* to stand?

The truth was that he was torn in two directions: ambition or love, California or London. If he went out to LA,

Alex knew he could make a success of it; he even dreamed that he might be able to use it as a springboard to something even greater, back in London at the *Telegraph*, *Times* or the *Mail*, or one of the bigger US papers – the *Boston Globe* or hell, even *The New York Times*.

If he stayed in London, he would be professionally frustrated, but he would have Lara. He loved her. He had always loved her – he could admit that to himself now. It was why he'd never really settled down, one reason why he threw himself into work – because she was there because The Chronicle belonged to Lara's family. In his twenties, work had taken him all over the globe, but he and Lara managed to keep up a strong friendship. She was his one true north – his fixed point around which everything seemed to revolve. But looking back, when he'd been stationed in the Middle East and Asia, he'd been lucky that Lara hadn't found someone else over the years. Absence didn't always make the heart grow fonder, it made you forget. It was why he was so reluctant to move to LA now - it was risky.

He tried to think about what Lara might want. That wasn't easy. She had a world-class poker face; that was partly what made her such a good reporter, but it also made it near-impossible to untangle what she was thinking.

She had told him he should take the job in LA: she had been pretty clear about that, and truthfully, it had upset him. But was she doing what she thought was best for Alex? Or was the truth that she genuinely wasn't interested in a relationship? That night by the fire, Alex had been *so* sure he and Lara had finally woken up to the fact that each other's soulmate was right there in front of their noses. But perhaps he'd been feeling all those emotions by himself.

Sighing, Alex looked at the racks of marbled claret-coloured steaks and butterflied chicken, but to his eyes, it all looked just as tainted as the vegetables. Had all this juicy meat been pumped full of steroids or fed on carcinogenic grain? Maybe he should do beans on toast. Much more simple: and hadn't he ruined the frying pan anyway with his scrambled eggs?

He chuckled to himself, and then the smile faded.

'Alex!' he turned to see Sarah Carter running towards him down the aisles of the deli. Her face flushed, she looked in a complete state of panic.

'Sarah...Is everything ok?'

'My mom,' she panted, hands on her hips, 'She's left the care home. Just walked out. I've looked everywhere. But she's just... gone.'

At the Lobster Roll, Sarah had given Alex the full rundown of her mum's health issues, and he could see how worried she was now.

'You've tried her house?'

Sarah managed an emotional nod.

'Sure, of course you have.'

Alex had no personal experience with dementia himself, but it was a growing problem. The *Chronicle* had run a series of articles on it in the Sunday lifestyle supplement. He racked his brains, trying to recall the facts from the features he had read.

'When people go walkabout, they tend to stick to places they know. Where else might have meaning for her if she's not at home? Did she pick you up from school?'

'No, I always got the bus,' said Sarah, catching her breath.

'Any favourite restaurants?'

'I've tried them all, Alex,' she said impatiently.

'And what about...?'

Sarah held up a finger as her phone buzzed, and she pulled it out.

She beckoned to Alex as she turned towards the door.

'Thank God. The cavalry's here.'

He stood there, looking down at the empty basket in his hand, momentarily wondering if he should continue shopping. No, Lara would understand. Helping Sarah was exactly what Lara would do. He put the basket back and ran outside.

Out in the street, a white mini-van was pulling up at the curb, and a group of middle-aged Americans in leisure wear surged out.

'Alex, this is Heather, my best friend from school,' said Sarah, indicating to a woman with curly hair. Alex caught the look of pleasure that came over Heather at the description, then the woman turned to her companions.

'Okay gang, fan out,' said Heather, taking command. 'Sarah has already checked Main Street down to The Shovel, am I right, Sizz?'

'Right,' said Sarah. 'Bobby, Martha, could you check the rest of the stores down to the bus station?'

'On it,' said Martha and ran off.

'Brin and Glenn are covering the west side down to the lake. Heather, can you and Dave take the van and head back to the cinema? Anywhere she had an emotional attachment to.'

Heather snapped her fingers.

'And she used to take us there for Saturday morning movies,' she said. 'Gotcha.'

She slapped her husband on the back, and they jumped into the car.

'What about me?'

Sarah looked up as Alex spoke.

'Alex, you don't have to get involved. Seriously.'

He took a step forward. 'I want to help. I don't know my

way around this town, but I'm a journalist. It's what I do. Look for things.'

When Sarah smiled, Alex could see the relief.

'Okay, thanks', she said. 'Come with me.'

She crossed the street, and Alex followed her into a tangle of side streets.

'Mom used to be a cleaner on campus.'

Reaching the end of the street, the wide lawns of the campus opened up in front of them.

'Okay, which bit did she clean?'

Sarah grimaced. 'All of it.'

'All of it?'

It was only when looking at it from this angle that Alex considered just how big the Benedon campus was. It was enormous; it had to take up half of the east side of town. *Damn.*

'Well, I guess we'd better split up,' said Sarah, but Alex held up a hand.

'Actually, I've got a better idea.'

Chapter 41

If Fitzgerald Farm had, as Lara's research suggested, been built as a farmhouse, it must have been used to raise golden cows. The gateway to Cordelia Campbell's grand home, discreetly hidden off Lake Road, ten miles north of Benedon, was marked by white stone pillars, each topped by a carved lion. The driveway wound through wooded grounds, terminating at an open courtyard complete with a bubbling fountain, the water gushing from the mouth of a giant fish.

It hadn't been difficult to find her address. Acres of press had been written about the Campbells, and it had been easy to track it down. Lara left the car and walked up a flight of wide stairs onto a collonaded platform which was more Roman temple than farmhouse porch.

Dogs began to bark as Lara pressed the brass doorbell. They sounded big.

She saw someone approaching through the panelled front door. She braced herself to introduce herself to Cordelia, but of course, it was a uniformed maid.

'Can I help you?'

'My name is Lara Stone. I'm a fellow at Benedon College. A friend of Harry Robbins.

'Is Cordelia expecting you?'

'No, but I'd love just a few minutes of her time.'

Lara could hear footsteps in the hall. Lara peered behind the maid and saw a figure glide across the herringbone parquet floor.

'It's fine, Celeste. Lara can come in.'

The Campbell matriarch was thin, upright and slightly terrifying, like an exiled queen.

'Come through to the Orangery,' said Cordelia, leading her through the house.

'So you were a friend of Harry's?'

She no longer looked formidable. 'I'm sorry.'

'We weren't good friends, although we went to the Dean's party together last week.'

'I know. I saw you together.'

Lara looked back in surprise.

'You did?'

'Tell me, Lara, how did you end up at Benedon? I googled you. Your body of work is impressive. I wasn't sure journalists like you existed anymore. I'm glad they do.'

Lara was trying to take this all in. Cordelia Campbell had googled her, and read her work.

'I wanted a change. I have all this experience and knowledge and I wanted to pass it on.'

'Commendable,' she nodded. 'I've always felt that the fortunate have the responsibility to pay it forward. Alas, these days, I believe it's all about the accumulation of wealth and status. Even philanthropic gestures are rarely selfless. Can't an agenda simply be to 'do good'?'

'Cordelia, you spoke to Harry. What did you discuss?'

Cordelia raised her eyebrow.

'He was an impressive young man,' she said. 'Ellie was right about that.'

'You spoke to your granddaughter about Harry?' asked Lara, her surprise growing.

'I did. She told me they were working together.'

Lara knew when to wait. This was definitely one of those times.

Cordelia stood up and walked to the window, her slim hand touching a heavy damask curtain. She waited several seconds before she spoke as if she was weighing every thought up.

'My granddaughter came to see me in February; it was my birthday weekend. Ellie came to give me a gift. She was a good girl, she always did the right thing.'

She turned, her grey eyes sad.

'We had afternoon tea together, right here, in this room as we are. I could tell something was on her mind, and finally, she told me she had seen something when she was interning at the AgriCam head office. Correspondence between Beale Norris, Campbell Industries general counsel, and a farmer in Maple County.'

'Nick Miller. He had a farm in North Bend, at least until he died.'

'So you know.'

The maid came through and put a china pot, a milk jug and two dainty cups on the table.

'I know about GreenGo, Cordelia.'

'How did you know? Elmore Jones?'

Lara watched as Cordelia carefully sat down and picked up the teapot to pour from it.

'Ellie realised that there were problems with GreenGo. She knew farmers were being paid off to keep quiet. I don't think it's an exaggeration to say my granddaughter was incandescent when she found out what our family company had become.'

Cordelia took a sip of tea, and Lara noticed that the cup rattled a little as she set it down again.

'Our company was supposed to stand for good, Miss Stone. It *did* stand for good. We built clinics and libraries; we sponsored benefit dinners and Christmas lunches for the homeless. Making the world a better place was one of the founding principles of our company. The principles that my husband's father set down in stone.'

'So what did you say to Ellie?'

'I advised her to tell her father.'

She paused before she went on. 'Arthur denied it but said they would keep monitoring GreenGo.'

Something Lizzy had said to Lara at the Dean's party suddenly jumped into Lara's mind. Something about how it was significant that Ellie had chosen the Campbell Library as the location for her final swan song. 'A fuck-you to the family', wasn't that what Lizzy had called it?

As if she were reading Lara's mind, Cordelia looked at her directly.

'I don't know what happened to Ellie that night in the library any more than you do, Miss Stone. But I do know this; Ellie was angry. And she was ashamed. Ashamed of the family company and the family name.'

A tear slipped down the old woman's face, and she pulled out a delicate handkerchief to catch it. Lara wanted to comfort the woman but was fairly sure Cordelia would hate that.

'You didn't answer my question. What did you and Harry discuss the night of the Dean's party?'

The late afternoon light slanting through the leaded windows put the older woman in silhouette.

'In the weeks and months after Ellie's death, I kept

telling myself to *do something* about Eleanor's revelations. I discussed it with Arthur, over and over, but he kept denying it. He said Ellie must have been mistaken about what she saw in the office. He said that GreenGo had been through layers of testing, that it met every regulatory standard, and he categorically denied knowledge of any pay-offs.'

'Did you believe him?'

'No. But I didn't know what to do without tearing my family apart.'

Cordelia took a breath, held it, and then let it out.

'So, when I saw Harry at the Labor Day party, a solution presented itself.'

She turned a hand outwards as if producing a winning card.

'I told him about GreenGo, and I told him what Ellie had found out. I knew he'd been helping her, but she was obviously protecting him. Ellie was careful not to tell him, anyone, too much.'

Her expression turned bleak, her voice barely a whisper now.

'Harry promised me he would pick up the story and finish it in honour of Ellie.'

'Cordelia, Harry killed himself that night.'

Tears were falling unabated now.

'And I've had that on my conscience ever since.'

She paused.

'You got my note, of course?'

Lara was about to ask which note, but then she remembered the letter that had been posted under the door the day after Harry had died.

Harry knew.

'That was you?'

'Harry pointed you out at the party. Said you were his

clever new friend. When he died, I wanted to tip you off. I knew you were smart. I knew you would find me.'

'What if I hadn't come?'

'Oh, the story would have got out; I would have made sure of that. It's the only way my family can move on. We need to admit to what we did, settle this mess, then get back to our founding principles: using innovation to help others.'

Her nostrils flared and suddenly she was back to the exiled queen. But one who had done her duty.

'And now I think it's time for you to leave.'

Chapter 42

Sarah held onto the handle as she flew out of her seat, one hand raised to stop her head from hitting the roof.

'Sorry,' muttered Nathan, one of Benedon's security guards, wrestling with the buggy's wheel. 'Didn't see that bump.'

Sarah wasn't surprised; it was late afternoon and as the sun sank behind the tall campus buildings, visibility was sinking too. It was going to be hard to see anything – or anyone – soon.

'Keep heading towards the church,' said Sarah, and Nathan grunted, steering the golf buggy towards the spire.

It had been Alex's idea to get the security guards involved in the search. The little white buggies they used around campus had been utilized to ferry VIPs between the symposium venues and Alex reasoned that no one knew the campus better than the security team. When Sarah had explained the situation, the guards had been more than happy to help.

'Your dad was practically family,' said a veteran guard named Javier, who Sarah remembered from her youth. Splitting the search, Alex had sped off with Javier, and

Sarah had drawn Nathan, who was younger but had fast reactions, which was what they needed right now. Nathan hit the horn as they skidded to a halt at the chapel's side door, and Father Vernon stepped out.

'Nothing, Sarah, I'm sorry,' he said. 'We've combed the whole place, crypt to tower, we even looked in the confession booth. But I've called in some of the choir; they're going down to the off-campus student dorms to knock on doors; I don't know if your mom ever cleaned down there?'

Sarah grimaced and shook her head. 'I'm not sure, Father.'

That was the trouble: Sarah didn't know enough about the details of her mother's life. Mom was always just *there*. Sarah went off to school, her mom went to work, then when Sarah got home, Mom was back, cutting off the crusts of her PB&Js. She'd never pondered where Colleen went in between.

'Don't worry,' said the priest. 'She can't have gone far.'

Vernon was being kind: that was his job, but Sarah was a cop, and her job involved thinking the worst. It had now been three hours since Colleen Carter had walked out of Beauville. She could have been hit by a car or fallen down some stairs, she could have broken an ankle just negotiating the kerb. Anyway, Vernon was wrong about going far. Mom had always travelled by bus; she could easily have shuffled onboard unseen – she could be halfway to New York by now. Sarah shivered, and not just from the fear. As the shadows lengthened, the temperature was dropping too, she could feel it. And that wasn't good at all.

'Thanks, Father, you have my number,' she said, getting back into the buggy. Vernon stepped forward.

'Have you tried the clinic?'

Sarah nodded wearily.

'We've called the hospitals, jails and police in three counties. I even called the firehouses.'

'No, I mean the campus clinic,' said Vernon. 'It's more of a first aid station, but they have a nurse there – perhaps a Good Samaritan might have found Colleen and taken her in?'

Sarah turned to Nathan, but he had already jerked the buggy into motion, cutting across the lawn right in front of the Provost's office. Sarah gave a grim smile; those fat wheels would leave tracks across the grass, and she knew Nathan would catch hell for it, but the boy still did it to save a few precious seconds.

'Thanks, Nathan,' she said sincerely. 'I appreciate all your help.'

'My pleasure ma'am,' he said, glancing across. 'Your dad was always good to me.'

Sarah looked over in surprise.

'You knew my father?'

'Not for long. Mr Carter passed away a couple of months after I started here, but he was a real stand-up guy; helped me out when I lost my radio once. It was so sad when he...,' Nathan trailed off, realising his blunder.

'It's okay,' said Sarah. But it wasn't. None of this was okay.

She felt her phone buzz, and she yanked it out: Heather.

'What's up?' said Sarah eagerly. All the searchers had been checking in regularly whether there was anything to tell or not. They all knew how frantic Sarah was getting.

'Sorry, no news,' said Heather. 'But thought I should update you.'

Sarah bit her lip, suddenly moved by how Heather and her friends kept going, knocking on doors, refusing to give up. Every piece of bad news was like a slap to Sarah, but each one showed how ordinary people – some who hardly knew Sarah or her mom – were willing to come together to help in a crisis.

'It was a no-go at the dentist,' continued Heather. 'So we swung back by Beauville to make sure she hadn't returned there. Sadly she hasn't. Dave has also checked the whole of your mom's street and I sent Bobby down to the lake, to look before it gets dark. Nothing there either, but that's good, right?'

'Yeah, that's good,' said Sarah automatically, turning away from Nathan to hide her face. The lake. *The goddamn lake.* What if Mom had gone down to the pier and...

Sarah squeezed her eyes shut. She couldn't lose her mom too, she couldn't. The world couldn't be that cruel, she refused to believe it. Over the past year, Colleen had been slipping through her fingers like dry sand, but that had only made Sarah all the more determined to hold on tighter. But it was futile, wasn't it?

'Ma'am?'

Sarah looked up as twin lights swung across the path; she immediately recognised it as Alex's buggy.

'Anything?' called Sarah, as their vehicles drew up side-by-side.

'We've just come from the campus clinic, no one there,' called Alex above the noise of the engines. Sarah's hope dimmed a little.

She never cried, but she could feel emotion building in her chest.

It must have shown because Alex slid out and put his arm across her shoulders. He held her for a moment, then stepped back and looked at her.

'Come on. Where else can we look?' asked Alex.

'We've been everywhere,' she said.

‘Sarah, think. Has anything taken on any unusual significance lately?’

Sarah shook her head.

‘She’s just been so grouchy, dredging up everything negative from the past. She’s even been making digs about my school reports.’

‘Maybe that’s it,’ said Alex, clicking his fingers. ‘If her mind is jumping back to incidents where she was stressed or emotional, perhaps she’s not going to go to the places where she felt safe or happy.’

Alex was right, but they’d checked the local high school. And anyway, Colleen Carter had never been overly concerned that her daughter wasn’t a star student.

Then a thought struck her, and her eyes opened wide. Why hadn’t she thought of it before? She turned to Nathan.

‘Were you working on the day that my dad had his heart attack?’

‘I was,’ he said, looking embarrassed.

‘Nathan, where did it happen?’

Sarah had been living in New York, and all she had been told at the time was that her dad had ‘keeled over’ while at work.

‘It was down by the old bicycle sheds,’ said Nathan. ‘I was on the night shift that day. An EMT truck was still here when I arrived.’

‘Someone had reported a theft, so he walked down there. That’s where your dad had a heart attack. That’s where he died.’

‘What are we waiting for…’

She jerked back as the guard hit the gas, spinning the little buggy in a circle, powering back the way they had come. Sarah felt a small flower of hope growing in her chest.

The old bike sheds were near the West Gate of campus, a remote part of the college, not much there, just the post-graduate admissions building and the marketing office. The shed was a long-covered structure with racks for the bikes. Given that there were new covered locker pods for bicycles near the library, Sarah was not surprised to see just a handful of rusty cycles chained up.

Nathan slowed down the buggy, but Sarah didn't wait for it to stop before she jumped off.

It was dark now. Shadows threw shapes over the old shed.

'Colleen Carter. Are you there?' she shouted.

She heard a rustle coming from behind the sheds. Sarah ran round and saw her mother, standing quite still, next to a tree.

Sarah crossed straight over to her mother, throwing her arms around her, squeezing hard.

'We've been looking everywhere for you,' said Sarah, tears in her eyes.

'I'm just waiting for your pops to finish his shift, then we can all go home together, okay?'

'Yes, yes,' said Sarah, burying her face in her mother's shoulder. 'We'll do that.'

She put her arm gently over her mother's shoulder and led her back to the path. She was dimly aware of another buggy arriving. She glanced up and saw Alex give her a reassuring smile. Sarah nodded her thanks in reply.

'Hey, Mrs Carter,' said Javier. 'You ready for a ride down to Main Street?

The old woman's eyes lit up. 'Do I get to sit in the front?'

'Only place for the star of the show.'

Sarah sent a text to Heather and they arranged to meet at the Benedon Arch.

'Are we going back to Beauville?' asked Colleen, taking her daughter's hand, and she climbed into the buggy.

Guilt and sadness gripped Sarah's belly and for a moment, she didn't know what to say.

'Oh, I know that's where I live now, and I know why,' said Colleen, looking directly into Sarah's eyes. Her words were lucid but her expression was sad. 'I just wish it wasn't this way. I hate being like this. I just want to go back to the way things were.'

Sarah put a hand on her mother's cold cheek.

'Me too, Mom,' she said. 'Me too.'

Chapter 43

Alex looked in the cupboard: it was almost bare. The fridge had similarly slim pickings; a bottle of wine and half a carton of milk, nothing he could transform into his planned romantic meal. Besides, the most important ingredient was missing: Lara.

He had no idea where she was, or when she would be back. There'd been a single text:

Off to see Cordelia Campbell. Back soon.

And then he'd had a missed call whilst he had been helping to look for Colleen Carter. He'd let it go intentionally, fearing, 'I'm with Sarah Carter,' would not be well received. But now he was genuinely worried and Lara wasn't answering his calls. He turned as a key rattled in the lock and Lara walked in.

'You're back. Thank God.' He felt his shoulders sag with relief.

‘I told you where I was going. And I did call you, but I couldn’t reach you.’

‘I’ve been looking for someone on campus. An old lady, she had dementia. She’d left her home and gone wandering and...’

He was being deliberately vague, which he knew was not a good start for a day-old relationship. But jealousy was not something that he had the head space to deal with right now.

‘Colleen Carter,’ she said, glancing up at him.

He shook his head; it was typical of Lara to already know.

‘I went down to Benedon police station,’ she explained. ‘I wanted to speak to Sarah but she wasn’t there. They told me they’d seen her with you,’ said Lara, throwing her bag down on the table.

‘Lar, I bumped into her in the deli. She was frantically looking for her mother. What was I supposed to do?’

Lara gave him a thin smile.

‘You did what you should do,’ she said and Alex felt himself relax a little. It was silly to assume Lara would be unreasonable. If anything, he was slightly miffed that she hadn’t been more upset about him spending the evening with Benedon’s attractive detective, even if it was completely harmless.

‘So did you find Sarah’s mum?’

‘Yes, she was fine in the end.’

‘I’m glad.’

God, the day had been crazy – but all he wanted now was a quiet evening with Lara. It still hadn’t really sunk in that they together. All day they’d been behaving as if nothing had changed. But it had changed. Everything had changed and Alex wasn’t entirely sure how to behave.

‘So, I almost bought some food,’ he said. ‘I wanted to

make us dinner. But by the time I got back to the deli, it had closed so all we've got is beans on toast, which wasn't exactly what I had in mind.'

'Right now, I'd settle for a G and T.'

'That, I can sort.'

She smiled and his heart squeezed. They were together. They were finally together. If that wasn't cause for celebration, he didn't know what was. He'd went to the kitchen and pulled out bottle of gin from duty free. Expensive, Japanese, in a fancy bottle. He got two tumblers from the cupboard, poured a healthy measure in each and topped it up with tonic.

He gave her the glass and didn't know where to sit. It was hard to believe that the previous evening, they'd finally kissed, had sex, shared a bed. Suddenly he felt awkward, like the teenage Alex, who hadn't really discovered his confidence with the opposite sex until he went to university.

'So, did you tell Sarah about GreenGo?' asked Lara, sitting forward.

Ah. Alex could help feeling a stab of disappointment that she had shifted the conversation back to Harry Robbins and Ellie Campbell as if it was just another day in the *Chronicle* investigations department. And what if she was using the AgriCam scandal that was unfolding as a way of deflecting him?

'No, I didn't get the chance,' he said, 'Sarah had other things on her mind, given her mum's disappearance.'

'Of course.'

'Anyway, where have you been? Who is Cordelia Campbell? I was worried.'

'Cordelia is Ellie's grandmother.'

'I guessed that, but why did you go to see her?'

He knew how Lara operated. She could be a generous

team-player, but deep down, she was a lone wolf and when she disappeared she was generally on the hunt. As her boss, as her friend, it was maddening. The work they did was dangerous, and disappearing into the night, even to see an old woman, seemed foolhardy to someone who cared about her.

'My friend Lizzy told me that Cordelia was at the Dean's Labor Day party. She saw her talking to Harry.'

He sat and listened as Lara gave him a potted version of what Cordelia Campbell had told her: that Ellie had been investigating GreenGo, driven by what she had found at AgriCam head office. Ellie had told her grandmother, who, after struggling with it for months, had told Harry at the Labor Day party, wanting him to publicise what had happened so the company could atone and move on.

'So that's why he ran out,' said Alex when she had finished. 'To start work on the story straight away.'

Dinner was suddenly forgotten. Alex had already connected the dots. Cordelia had told Harry about GreenGo and a few hours later he was dead.

'Brave as it was for Cordelia to speak to you, we still can't prove any of this.' He wasn't arguing with her, simply switching into editorial mode where it had been his job to make sure a story stood up. The journalists at the *Chronicle* hated him for it, but as Deputy Editor it was all part of the job.

He held up his fingers to tick off the points. 'We can't prove that GreenGo is deadly because all the farmers have been paid off. Without evidence from the AgriCam office – memos or contracts with the farmers - we can't prove that AgriCam knew their product was dangerous, because they'll just deny it. And we can't prove that Harry was killed for knowing what he knew.'

'We can't prove it yet, but I'm sure that's why he's dead.'

Alex wasn't easily frightened. He had worked in the most hostile of environments; war correspondent friends had been killed metres away from him. But big money frightened him. Big money people were rich because they were ruthless and ruthless people were dangerous when they were cornered.

Ding dong!

Alex tensed as the doorbell rang.

'Are you expecting anyone?' he asked.

'No,' said Lara.

Alex got up from the sofa, crossed the room and peered through the fisheye peephole of the front door.

It was a woman he didn't recognise. A fifty-ish, expensive blonde. He'd say she had a cold, grim expression but he couldn't tell for sure through the lens.

'Did Cordelia say she would come round?'

Lara was looking through the front window onto the porch.

'That's not her,' said Lara.

Alex opened the door a fraction. She had the cool beauty of a Hitchcock leading lady. Her hair was in a flawless French pleat, she was wearing a tan trench coat and clutched an oxblood alligator skin handbag to her chest.

'I'm looking for Lara Stone.'

Lara was already beside him.

'Yes. Can I help you?'

'The question should probably be, can I help you? I'm Eliza Campbell, Ellie's mother. I believe you've just been speaking to my mother-in-law, Cordelia.'

* * *

They all sat around the little kitchen table. Lara had made more tea, but nobody was drinking it.

'I'm sorry to come to you like this,' said Eliza finally. 'It must be something of a surprise.'

Lara and Alex exchanged a look.

'I think the real surprise is hearing you speak, Mrs Campbell', said Alex. 'It was our understanding that you had a condition that...'

'Had rendered me mute? Yes. Psychogenic mutism. People like to put a medical label on things they don't understand.'

'What label would you put on it?' asked Alex.

'Grief, Mr Ford.'

Alex knew what she was talking about too. Grief was personal and hard to explain. When his mum had died a few years earlier, he'd felt as though he had been dropped into a raging river, being torn and scraped along the bottom, unable to find his way to the surface. It was the fiercest of emotions that could do strange things to a person; looking back, if Lara hadn't been his rock throughout those difficult weeks and months, he wasn't sure if he'd have coped.

Eliza paused and then looked at him as if they needed more of an explanation.

'My mutism began when Ellie died. It stopped when Cordelia came to see me this evening. I'd been told that it can end as quickly as it begins. Apparently, that's true.'

'Why have you come?' asked Lara simply.

Mrs Campbell looked down and twisted her wedding ring around her pale finger.

'It appears there are some advantages to silence,' said Eliza, glancing back up at Lara. 'After a while, people forget you're there. It was as if I had become completely invisible.'

Alex sat forward.

'What did you overhear, Eliza?' said Alex, immediately grasping her reason for coming.

'You know all about GreenGo,' said Eliza finally. 'You

know that Cordelia, my mother-in-law, told Harry about it at the Dean's party?'

Lara nodded.

'I didn't go to Ros Davies' house that night. People think I'm a freak show act these days, so I avoid social situations. But I went to sit on our terrace the morning after the party. It was early – I prefer weaker sunshine – and I'd gone outside to read. The window to Arthur's study was open and I was close enough to hear the conversations going on inside. Norris Beale had arrived. I've known him long enough to recognise his voice anywhere. They started talking about Harry Robbins. Beale said the situation had been dealt with.'

Alex felt his heart jump: the implication was clear, but he needed Eliza to spell it out.

'Harry Robbins had been dealt with?'

Eliza nodded.

'It appears that way. Arthur was appalled, furious. He called Beale all kinds of names, said he had overstepped the mark.'

'Was he specific about what Beale had done?'

Eliza looked up with her cool blue eyes. 'I don't know for sure. Beale kept saying that Arthur had wanted "the problem" to go away – and that's what had happened. He had fixed it.'

'And what did Arthur say to that?' asked Lara.

Eliza looked away, deeply uncomfortable. 'He said, "I didn't mean you should blow the guy's brains out."'

Silence descended on the little kitchen.

'Arthur just wanted the problem dealt with. He wouldn't have wanted anyone to hurt Professor Robbins.' Her voice was a whisper, her posture very upright in the chair, as if she was trying to hold herself together.

'How did you know I'd come to see Cordelia?' asked Lara.

'She came to see Arthur immediately after you'd left her house. She came to plead with him to get all this out into the open, to take GreenGo off the market. But Arthur wasn't at home. She spoke to me instead. She told me that she'd told you all about it, that the story was better off out than in. I agreed with her and knew I had to do something too. Hush money isn't a marketing expense. Killing someone isn't a PR and business strategy.'

She put her hands on her thin thighs and then pushed herself up. She smoothed down the silk of her dress and buttoned up her jacket.

'I never liked Beale Norris,' she said tightly. 'Now, I'm not sure there's much more to be said,' she said, snapping back into the haughty society dame. 'I should go.'

'Eliza, you know how serious this is? You know that the police are going to want to talk to you about it?'

The woman nodded crisply.

'When you have a voice, you have an obligation to use it. I know that now.'

She hooked her quilted leather bag over the crook of her arm and left without a backwards glance. Alex listened to the sound of an engine start and roar, and then fade away into the distance.

'This is big,' said Alex, feeling as if he was back in the newsroom, every impulse firing. 'This has everything. Society murder, corporate greed.' He put his hands over his face forcing himself to think. What angle was the strongest? What headline could they use, what evidence did they need to make it as water-tight as possible? The *Los Angeles Globe* would be angry of course. This was an All-American story – a corporate empire, a glamorous dynasty, a New England campus – and they would hate to see it run first in a British newspaper. But he didn't work for the *Los Angeles Globe* yet. He was still a Chronicle editor.

'It's time Alex,' said Lara, putting a hand on his arm.

'Time for what?'

'Time to stop treating this like a story. We're not on assignment. This isn't a *Chronicle* investigation, it's a police investigation. We need to tell Sarah Carter everything we know before anyone else gets hurt. That's why I went to the station earlier, to tell her about my meeting with Cordelia.'

Alex looked at her in astonishment. It wasn't like Lara. Last year, her best friend had been murdered, but she kept pushing and pushing, working with the police, sure. But at the end of the day, The Yacht Party was a story, and it was hers. *Theirs.*

'Last year I almost got killed pursuing a story,' said Lara, her voice s full of emotion. 'But it was worth it because I got justice for Sandrine. Alex, I don't want to go through it again. I don't want to risk my life for this. For anything. Not now I have you.'

Alex stepped forward to take her in his arms. He kissed the top of her head, and then rested his chin on her crown. The wave of love he felt for her was so strong it almost knocked him over.

'I don't want to risk this either,' he whispered into her hair.

'Come on,' she said pulling away. 'We can get mushy later. We'd better go and find Detective Carter.'

'Let's go,' he said squeezing her fingers.

Lara held her hand up and wiggled her little finger.

'And let's make a pinky promise not to tell Darius.'

Chapter 44

Sarah kicked off her shoes and rubbed her tired eyes, wondering if she should treat herself to a soak in the tub. She hadn't even had a tub at her apartment in New York, and back in Benedon, she only ever seemed to have time for a quick shower. But tonight, at the Carter family home, she knew she deserved the longest, most bubbly bath in history. Sarah was dog tired. Exhausted and stressed and still scared about how it might all have panned out that evening. She didn't dare think about what would have happened to her mother had she strayed further than the college or if the weather had been as stormy as the previous night.

Sarah perched on the edge of her bed and looked around the carefully remodelled bedroom. Even with the soft drapes, the jugs of flowers and warm lamps, the house felt cold and empty. And not because most of the Carter's keepsakes and personal items had been cleared away, boxed up and put in the loft for storage. The house felt empty without her mother. The walls seemed to echo, footsteps on the floor sounded hollow. Without Colleen Carter, it was missing its heart.

Her phone in her pocket chirped at the sound of an incoming email.

She read it, and saw it was from the realtor. Apparently, the couple from earlier that evening had loved the house and wanted to put in an offer.

Sarah had to give a soft laugh at that. The way she had barged into the house earlier that night and given everyone a shock, annoying the realtor, alarming the people doing the viewing, Sarah had thought they would all run for the hills. But no. They wanted the house. Her house. Her home.

She closed her eyes and threw the phone on the bed. Dealing with the sale could wait for another day. Was it even what she wanted? Sarah wasn't sure.

She'd come back to Benedon to regroup, that was all. Her original plan, when she had been forced out of the NYPD, was to return to Vermont for a year or so, settle her mother into a home, recover from the scandal she'd become unwittingly embroiled in at the Precinct and then head back to the city – maybe Philly or DC, perhaps somewhere with a little more sunshine like Miami or Austin. She was only thirty-nine. It wasn't too late to start over. But over the past few days, her feelings towards Benedon had changed. For so long, Windsor County had been a place she wanted to run as far away as possible from, because she wanted a bigger, more exciting life than the one her parents had lived. But what was so wrong with small-town life – friends you had grown up with, shopkeepers who knew you by name and threw you a line of credit, neighbours who would give you lightbulbs when you couldn't get to the hardware store or left books on their fence for people to take? You didn't get that in New York.

A thought hit her with such power it was like a punch in the guts. *She liked it here.* She liked Glenn, Brin and Heather and the bowling gang. She liked Steve in forensics, maybe not in the way that he hoped, but she liked the way that people would go out of their way to help you. Most of all, she liked being there for her mom.

Sighing, Sarah got up from the bed, catching her reflection in the dark windows. A bath was too indulgent. Really, she should be working on the Harry Robbins case – she had to charge Wayne Fortune or release him within twenty-four hours – but she just couldn't concentrate right now. Couldn't get things straight in her head. Ros Davies had the strongest motive for wanting Harry Robbins dead. She was married. The scandal of an affair with a junior professor would certainly stop her becoming Provost. But how was she connected to Wayne Fortune?

She was turning to go back downstairs when her cell phone chirped again. *Dammit.* She'd told Glenn to hold anything bar an asteroid strike until the morning. What now?

We need to see you. Can we come round in ten? Alex Ford.

This was why she should never give out her personal number, even to hot guys from London. Even so, Sarah was intrigued. She fired her address over to Alex and had barely had time to put her phone in her pocket when there was a hammering on the door. Instinctively, she snatched up her gun from where she had left it on the bedside table. She was still wearing her holster and slid the weapon inside before going downstairs.

'ETA ten my ass,' said Sarah, as she opened the door. Alex strode inside, Lara Stone close behind.

'You said your house had just gone up for sale,' smiled

Alex. 'There are not many brand new listings in your town. In fact, there's one. I found out the address, drove here and took a chance.'

'Come on in, make yourselves at home, why don't you?' said Sarah sarcastically as he stepped through the door.

'Sorry, Sarah,' said Lara. 'But we have news you'll want to hear.'

Sighing, Sarah locked the door and put her gun in the sideboard drawer. She walked them through to the kitchen. 'Drink?' she asked. 'And it's still Detective Carter.'

* * *

Sarah made them coffee and sat them in the front room. She was a little embarrassed as she watched them perch on the old velour sofa. Alex Ford was too polite to wince at the cheap instant coffee she had served up. He was a big-time newspaper editor and she felt sure he was used to the finer things in life, fancy apartments, smart cars, beautiful women – and artisan coffee.

She started to listen, prepared to give them five minutes of her time, until they started to describe the conversations they'd had that day. With a farmer in Maple County, a lawyer in North Bend and finally with the two Mrs Campbells.

'Harry was murdered,' said Lara Stone.

Sarah wasn't going to disagree , but everything they had told her was still hearsay. Dynamite though it was, none of it would ever get anywhere near a court of law – it was all one person's word against another. Even Eliza's revelations about Arthur and Beale were inadmissible. A grief-stricken woman with a psychosomatic mental condition? They'd laugh her testimony out of court.

'I should fill you in on my side,' Sarah said when they

had finished. Sheriff Roscoe would have a fit if he knew Sarah was sharing sensitive information with 'civilians', especially journalists, but hey, screw Roscoe. At the Lobster Roll, Alex had argued that they pooled their resources, and now she thought he had a point.

So, she told them about the placing of the gunshot wound and the coroner's doubts that it was self-inflicted. She told them about the forensic team finding DNA at the scene, and Wayne Fortune's arrest.

'But where does that leave us?' she said, spreading her hands. 'A suspect in the cell, plenty of motive, means and opportunity, but little hard evidence.'

She watched Alex absorbing it all. He was so good-looking it was hard not to be distracted. She felt a pang of envy at his relationship with Lara Stone, who was as gorgeous as he was. Sarah had believed him at dinner when he'd said they were just friends. But seeing them together now, looking at their easy rapport, the way his hand occasionally brushed hers, they were close, that was for sure.

'In an editorial meeting, we'd stress-test the theories,' said Alex looking up. 'See which ones are most likely and which we can prove.'

'Ok, continue....'

'We know that Cordelia told Harry about GreenGo. And we know that a few hours later he was dead,' said Lara. 'Arthur and Beale were both at that party. Either of them could easily have overheard Cordelia telling Harry.'

'Plausible, yes,' said Sarah. 'But it doesn't make them murderers.'

Alex shrugged.

'But according to your forensic evidence, Harry could easily have been shot by an intruder and you have Wayne Fortune's DNA in his back yard.'

'Wayne isn't talking,' said Sarah shaking her head.

'And even if he does, he could explain his blood sample being on Harry's property quite easily. He could say he was simply casing the joint, knowing that the owner of the property was dead. Forensics can only go so far. We can't date it to the night of Harry's death.'

Alex was up on his feet now.

'If Wayne Fortune did kill Harry, he was probably paid to do it.

Can we get Wayne's phone records? See if Fortune was in contact with Arthur or Beale.'

'We're working on it. We have his phone. He had a few incoming calls on the night of Harry's death.'

'What else could link Wayne to either of them?' asked Lara.

Lara was the quieter of the two, but more thoughtful, undoubtably clever as well as beautiful.

'There are no obvious links,' said Sarah. 'Arthur Campbell and Beale Norris are smart, high-society men. Wayne Fortune? No so much.'

'Doesn't mean there can't be a connection,' said Alex.

'Are they similar ages?' asked Lara.

Sarah shook her head.

'There must a twenty-year age difference. As for being local? I've been to the Campbell compound. It's so huge they have no neighbours. Their lifestyle? They might as well live in different universes.'

'But Wayne is a criminal. Presumably, he's had plenty of contact with lawyers. Beale Norris is AgriCam's general counsel,' said Lara.

Sarah nodded. 'By the sounds of it, he had his lawyer on speed-dial. He asked for him during our interview.'

That was the last thing Sarah had heard before she'd got the message about her mother going missing.

‘He’s called Jeff Strobe. I haven’t come across him before.’

‘Maybe he knows Beale. Let’s check out their history. See if there’s any overlap,’ said Lara.

Alex was already on his phone. Sarah reached over to the coffee table and grabbed her own laptop.

She felt a swell of adrenaline. Half of the cable channels were stuffed with cop shows and police procedurals. The world thought the work was glamorous, but the truth was it was gritty and frustrating. For a moment, she imagined herself in the *Chronicle* newspaper offices. Perhaps it was the sort of place she could have worked if she’d had sat down at school and studied. At least if her dyslexia hadn’t got in the way of her trying.

‘Okay, so Jeff Strobe is forty-eight,’ muttered Alex reading from his screen. ‘Works for Charter Matthews, a criminal defence law firm in Montpelier.

‘Let’s look at Beale Norris’s CV,’ muttered Sarah, tapping away at her computer. She wasn’t used to this kind of lateral thinking; in spite of what TV cop shows would lead you to believe, police work was more rigorous, slowly building a case from provable evidence. But she could also see the benefits of this throw-it-at-the-wall approach, especially when it came to homicide.

‘Fifty years old. Has worked for AgriCam for twelve years, also holds the position of general counsel for Campbell Industries as well as being on their board. Before he worked at AgriCam, he worked at Suarez Partners in Boston and before that he was at a place called Green, Styles and Hinch. According to his biog on the AgriCam website he went to Yale Law.’

‘Where did Jeff study?’ asked Alex.

‘Boston School of Law,’ said Sarah, reading his LinkedIn profile.

'From there he went to clerk for Justice Clarkson.

'Let's head to Internet Archives and see what we can find there,' said Lara, peering into her phone.

Sarah took a moment to smile – they were like teenagers.

'Okay, here are some web captures from Green, Styles and Hinch's website, from when Beale would have worked there,' said Lara, after another minute, speaking as she was researching. 'It lets us have a look at what their old site looked like, or at least certain pages of their site. Here we, go...An old blog post that Beale Norris wrote when he was a junior lawyer. And you'll never guess what he's talking about?'

'What?' said Sarah

'Clerking for a federal judge.'

'Which Judge was it?' asked Alex, but Sarah knew; they all had the answer to that one.

'Justice Clarkson,' said Lara, her eyes glittering.

'There's the connection,' said Alex. 'What's the bet that they're old friends. What's the bet that if Beale Norris needs any dirty work doing, he mines Jeff and his client list for recommendations.'

For a moment, Sarah felt the same excitement as Lara and Alex, and then her smile slipped.

'It's a link between Beale Norris and Wayne Fortune, sure. But we need to prove that Beale had actually hired Wayne. And we need more evidence that Wayne was in Harry's house, not just prowling around outside.'

'We'll find it,' said Lara, looking at her with solidarity.

She sounded so self-assured that Sarah couldn't help but get swept up by it.

'Yes we will,' she said. After all, the night was still young.

Chapter 45

The road was black ahead, save only for the glow from the dashboard and the twin yellow cones of the headlights, darkness pressing in from all sides. It wasn't far between Sarah's town and Benedon, just three or four miles, but in the blackness – farmland, broken only by the rare twinkle of a distant homestead – Lara felt they were like a ship bobbing on an endless ocean.

'You've been quiet since we left,' said Alex, glancing across. 'You okay?'

'I'm just frustrated,' said Lara, staring through the window into the dark. 'We have the whole story here in front of us. We have the scandal, we have the Campbell women confirming everything, there's forensic evidence to show that Harry's gunshot wound wasn't self-inflicted, and Beale Norris is linked to the lowlife who was at his cottage. It's all there. We just need that bit more proof.'

'Yes, and now it's up to the police to piece it all together and to prove it all in court,' said Alex.

Alex was driving, but he took one hand off the wheel to reach over and touch her thigh.

'I know but...'

'We have to leave it to the justice system, Lar. You said that yourself. And I know that's not in your nature, but we have got an amazing beans-on-toast romantic dinner to distract us.'

Lara gave a low laugh. She loved the way how Alex could make her feel better no matter what the circumstances.

'Alright, what else?' asked Alex. He knew her too well.

'It's Ellie,' she said.

'Ellie?'

She turned to look at him, his strong silhouette in the darkness of the car.

'Alex, everyone assumes that Ellie Campbell jumped from the top floor of the library. Some people say she was depressed, others that she was heartbroken, Cordelia Campbell believes it was from shame. What if she didn't jump, Alex. What if she was pushed?'

Alex glanced across.

'What are you saying? You think Campbell and Norris wanted Ellie dead as well as Harry?'

'I'm saying we should consider it.'

'Beale Norris and Arthur Campbell might be ruthless enough to kill an inconvenient professor, but do you really think Campbell would kill his own *daughter* to save a few quid?' he said, not looking convinced.

As they discussed it out loud, Lara was more and more convinced that Ellie Campbell didn't just fall.

'A few quid? This could potentially knock billions off AgriCam's valuation. Not to mention another billion more in settlements.'

She picked up her phone and started messaging Sarah. They'd exchanged numbers at her house, but Lara hadn't thought she'd need it so soon.

'What are you doing?'

'Asking Sarah if anyone checked the library CCTV footage on the night Ellie died.'

'I thought you knew the answer to that one. There's obviously no footage otherwise there would be no questions about whether Ellie jumped or fell.'

'There were no cameras on the top floor – at least, not then. But there are cameras at the entrance to the library. I've seen them.'

Almost immediately, there was a ping and a reply.

Not sure. Will ask Glenn Schultz. He dealt with the case.

'Lara, you need a card to enter the library. Beale couldn't just stroll in there.'

'Believe me, Benedon library isn't exactly Fort Knox. I was there last week and one of the barriers was just open.'

They were approaching her road. Alex indicated to turn into it, and slowed the speed of the car. Lara heard the notification for an incoming text.

Glenn said no tapes to check. Only front entrance and back entrance cameras at library.

'Alex, keep going,' she said, pointing towards Main Street. 'Get us as near to campus as you can.'

'Where are we going?'

'Just trust me,' she said as Alex kept on driving.

* * *

They parked the car outside the Main Street Deli and jogged across the road through the ceremonial gate, the one that Lara had gazed at the morning she had arrived, so full of excitement about her relaxing break as a visiting fellow. She allowed herself a small ironic laugh at that one.

'This way,' said Alex. He took her hand as they followed a leaf-strewn path across the darkened lawns towards the security office.

She felt herself shiver, and not from the cool night air. Alex's gesture had taken her by surprise. All day, they'd behaved exactly how they had always behaved. As colleagues, friends, and best friends who could finish each other's sentences and know what the other was thinking. With the exception of the tender moment at her cottage before they'd left for Sarah's, it was hard to believe they were a couple.

They threaded their way across campus towards the security office.

'I'm glad someone's been paying attention,' said Lara, looking around. 'This whole place looks different after dark.'

And of course, the campus felt different too, now they knew that there were people here prepared to kill to keep their secrets.

A thin evening mist was settling over the quad. The air felt damp, even though the storm had long passed. They hurried past the journalism school. Lara tensed as a door to their left opened and a figure stepped out, silhouetted by the light inside.

'Hey teach!'

Lara almost squeaked with relief: it was Brian Silvinski, her student. 'Brian, you scared the life out of me,' she sighed, pressing a hand against her chest. 'What are you doing on campus so late?'

Brian tapped the courier bag slung over his shoulder. 'The news never sleeps, you know that. I've been putting the latest issue of *The Ivy* to bed.' Lara saw the boy's eyes widen as he saw Alex.

'Oh wow,' he said, thrusting out a hand. 'Loved your talk, man. Really inspiring.'

'Thanks,' grinned Alex. 'I'd almost forgotten all about doing that. Seems so long ago.'

Seeing Brian suddenly gave Lara an idea.

'Hey Brian, are you busy right now?' she asked. 'I think you might be able to help us with this.'

Brian looked from Lara to Alex and back again, his eyes narrowing.

'What are you up to?'

Lara took his arm.

'Come on, we'll explain on the way.'

* * *

'Hello? Anyone home?'

A stocky man with a dark moustache peeked around the doorway of the Security Office.

'Javier!' smiled Alex, clapping the security guard on the arm. 'Good to see you again, buddy.'

'You too, Mr Alex. You need another ride?' said Javier with a slightly bemused grin. 'Mrs C hasn't got lost again, has she?'

'No, nothing like that,' said Alex.

'We just wanted to ask you about your security cameras. Like how many do you have at the library?'

Javier beckoned them into the back room and pointed to the bank of monitors on the far wall. 'We have them on every floor now. Security was upgraded after the accident last semester.'

'How many were there back then?'

'Only two in the library,' he said, sitting at the control panel and flicking some switches. Two of the monitors flickered and changed to grainy camera footage of two doorways.

'One in the front lobby. One at the back entrance. The cameras are more of a deterrent than a tool. It's a library, not a bank. What's happened? Someone steal a book?'

Alex shook his head sadly.

'No, we're looking into Eleanor Campbell's death.'

'The girl who fell from the top floor?'

'Yeah, it was a long shot, but we were hoping there might be some footage of that night.'

'Oh, sure.'

Lara and Alex exchanged a look.

'You have film of that night?' said Alex.

'It's all digital these days, Mr Alex, all stored on remote servers. We get rid of it after 90 days but that night, the night Miss Campbell died, we were told by the Provost to keep it. 'Her family are powerful,' he said lowering his voice. 'Provost said we had to keep all the footage, in case somebody sued.'

Lara looked at Alex in excitement.

'Can you find the footage?'

'Might take a while, but I warn you...' He turned to his control panel, rewinding some footage, then pressing play. 'See?'

They watched as students walked in and out of the library entrance, going about their business, but cameras gave an odd side-on angle.

'Not great for seeing faces,' said Alex.

'Faces?' said Brian, trying to peer into the monitors. 'Who are you looking for?'

'Actually, that's why I asked you along, Brian,' said Lara.

'As the editor of the college paper, I'm guessing you'd probably recognise almost everybody on campus?'

Brian shrugged modestly.

'I guess.'

'Would you recognise Eleanor Campbell?'

'Of course,' he said. 'Even from the side.'

Lara pulled out a notebook and handed it to Brian. 'Okay, we want to know what time she arrived, whether she was alone and...' She pulled out her phone. '...We want to know whether this man followed her into the library.'

Lara tapped on her phone until she found the AgriCam website, clicking through to the 'Meet The Executive Team' page. She held up a picture of Norris.

'He looks like a bad man,' said Javier.

'He is,' said Lara. 'We think he killed Harry Robbins.'

'That *is* bad. I liked Prof Robbins,' said Javier.

Brian gave Lara a searching look.

'You think Ellie's death was suspicious?'

'We're not completely sure,' said Lara. 'But if we can prove this guy Beale was there that night, then maybe, we're halfway to proving it.'

Lara turned to Javier.

'How long do you think it will take to find?

'It might take a while. The filing system ain't what it should be.'

She squeezed his arm.

'That's okay, we've got all night.'

Chapter 46

Sarah took a deep breath, then dialled the number. Just before ten at night, the chances of there still being anyone left at the forensics lab were slim. Half of her was hoping Steve Kirk would still be at his desk, and the other half of her was hoping he'd gone home so she could avoid the awkwardness. *Never get involved with anyone from work,* she reminded herself. Mike had been bad enough.

Two rings, three... Sarah was about to kill the call, when there was a 'clunk' and a voice barked 'Kirk.'

She breathed out.

'Steve, it's Sarah Carter.'

'If you're calling for a date, I'm too tired.'

Sarah laughed.

'I'm glad it's not just me.'

'But clearly we do have some sort of psychic link,' said Steve. 'Because I was just about to call you.'

'You were?' said Sarah, feeling her hope rising. 'Tell me it's about Wayne Fortune.'

'It is. Get ready to be happy, because we have another match.'

Silently Sarah punched the air.

'DNA match?'

'Fibres. In fact, your friend Mr Fortune did us a big favour stumbling about in the rose bushes. Once we had picked the mud from the grooves in the sole of his sneakers, guess what we found?'

'Carpet fibres.'

'Bingo. So now we can prove without a doubt that Wayne was inside the house first, picking up fibres from Mr Robbins' carpet, then fled through the yard afterwards.'

'Amazing work, Steve. Seriously.'

'We aim to please. But there's more; we also found particulates on the toe of the right sneaker.'

'Blood?' she said.

'Yep. You've got him, Sarah.'

'Steve, you're my hero.'

'Remember that when I call you next. But right now, I need about 12 hours' sleep. I'll send it all down now.'

Sarah thanked him again, then hung up and immediately speed-dialled Glenn.

'Hey Boss,' he said. 'I'm literally walking out the door, my shift ended an hour ago.'

'Well put in for overtime; this is worth it. Go wake up Wayne Fortune, then get on the phone to his lawyer: Wayne's going to need him.'

'Did we get the lab reports?' asked Glenn eagerly.

'Uh-huh. And someone's going to jail.'

Glenn chuckled.

'I love it when you talk that way.'

* * *

Wayne Fortune was leaning back in his chair, his face turned up towards the caged fluorescent tube as if he were lying on a Florida beach rather than handcuffed to a table in a police interview room. Next to him, looking much more pale, was his solicitor, an owlish man named Jackson. He was bending over a briefcase as if he might find answers inside and sweating, possibly from the cross-town dash to get to the interview, possibly from nerves. Sarah hoped it was the latter.

'No Jeff?' she asked pointedly.

'Wayne decided to go with a local lawyer for speed,' said Glenn, slurping his coffee.

'Hello Wayne,' said Sarah, taking a bundle from under her arm.

'Something for you to read.'

She dropped a newspaper onto the table with a 'flap!'. The front page was folded out so that he could read the headline.

HARDY SURGES IN THE POLLS
HARDLINE SENATE CANDIDATE PROMISES
'ZERO TOLERANCE'

Wayne sat forward, his eyes sleepy, picking up the paper, then dropping it with disinterest.

'I'm more of a sports kind of guy.'

'Yeah?' said Sarah, scooping up the paper. 'Well, maybe you should pay more attention to current affairs, because this one has a direct bearing on your future Wayne.'

She turned the paper over and began to read:

'Observers have seen a spike in support for Senate candidate Callum Hardy in the elections later this year. Hardy has run

his election campaign on a capital punishment ticket, after a series of violent crimes in the State. Should Hardy be successful, the death penalty could be reinstated after its abolition in 1972.

Wayne looked up, suddenly more alert.

'What's that got to do with me?'

'Context,' said Sarah, dropping a thick Manila file on the table. This time Wayne didn't move, looking at the stack like it might be a trap.

'What is this, detective?' asked Wayne's attorney, pushing his thick glasses up his nose.

'This is the forensics report, counsellor,' said Glenn. 'The results are in.'

Sarah leaned forward on the desk.

'Remember how we told you we could prove you were outside Professor Robbins' house on the night of his murder?'

'That was bullshit,' said Wayne, although Sarah noted there was none of the certainty Sarah had heard in his voice at their previous interview.

'Not bullshit, no,' said Sarah, placing one finger on the centre of the file. 'Your sneakers have a distinct worn tread and the imprints are all over Professor Robbins' flowerbeds. It's an exact match.'

'It don't prove nothing.' He looked over to his lawyer for support. 'You tell them, Mr Jackson. Mr Jackson said maybe I was just sneaking about, looking for some garden tools or something.'

Sarah held up a hand toward the lawyer.

'Wayne, those sneakers also prove your client was *inside* Professor Robbins' house.'

Wayne's eyes darted side-to-side, as if he might find a way out.

'That don't prove I killed him.'

'No, it doesn't,' agreed Sarah, opening the file and flipping through it until she came to a paper covered in bar-graph read-outs. 'This, however, does.'

'Is this a lab report?' asked his lawyer, leaning forward.

'This is a lab analysis of microscopic particulates found on Mr Fortune's footwear. Blood spray, if you want it in plain terms: tiny droplets of Professor Robbins' blood, matching his DNA exactly.'

Sarah watched it slowly sink in.

'Wayne,' said Glenn, with a sad shake of his head. 'You really should have got rid of those shoes.'

'They're Nike Dunks, man,' said Wayne. 'I ain't losing those sneaks, they're rare.'

'That's the other thing the lab boys mentioned in their report,' said Glenn with relish. 'They're fakes.'

Wayne swore under his breath.

He seemed more upset by having overpaid for his shoes than the fact he might be facing a very long spell in jail.

'Okay,' said Sarah sitting down, putting her face level with the hood's. 'Let's cut to the chase, shall we Wayne? If you're found guilty of first-degree murder, you're looking at a minimum sentence of thirty-five years, probably with no parole. You don't look too healthy to me, Wayne. Which means you're going to spend the rest of your life in a cell.'

'I ain't going down for no one,' he said, his voice increasing in pitch to a scream.

'What do you mean "for no one"?'

'I'm not the one who wanted the professor dead, man.'

'You were asked to do it?'

Jackson interjected.

'I'm recommending my client not to say anything further until we've had the chance to...'

'I'm not going down for this,' said Wayne again, stabbing his finger in the air. 'You sort this. And you send the cops round to who wanted Robbins killed.'

'Who was that, Wayne?'

He looked brighter for an instant. The opportunist sensing an opportunity.

'I ain't giving you a name, until we cut a deal.'

'Could you give me a moment to consult with my client?' said Jackson

'Of course.'

Sarah exchanged a discreet smile with Glenn as Wayne and the lawyer bent their heads together and began whispering.

Jackson glanced at Sarah, urgently shushing his client. He muttered something else, but it clearly didn't meet with Wayne's approval.

All at once, Wayne turned back to look at Sarah.

'I'm ready to make a deal,' he said, his voice shaking.

The lawyer touched Wayne's arm. 'Wayne, this isn't a good idea. I must strongly advise you that...'

'Hey, lawman?' said Wayne, jerking his thumb. 'You're fired.'

Undeterred, the lawyer put his hand on Wayne's shoulder. 'Please Wayne, let's take a moment.'

Sarah kept on pressing. 'Wayne, if you tell me who sent you round to Harry Robbins' house last week, the court will be more lenient on you. If you don't tell us, we can only assume you wanted the professor dead and that there was no-one else involved. A guy was sentenced to fifty years upstate only last week for something similar.'

'He hired me to shoot that professor. I needed the

money. He told me that Professor Robbins was scum. That he'd killed a girl. One of his students.'

'Give me a name, Wayne.'

'He was a rich guy.'

Wayne Fortune had started to sob now.

'What, like Lex Luthor? The Joker?' said Glenn.

'The lawyer,' he spat.

'Mr Jackson here?' asked Sarah, secretly enjoying the look of utter terror crossing the man's face.

'He was called Beale Norris.'

Sarah felt the triumph rising in her chest, savouring the moment. This wasn't her first rodeo: she knew there was a long way to go before anyone went to prison. But right now, it felt as if they were almost there.

'To be clear, you're saying AgriCam's lawyer Beale Norris ordered you to shoot Harry Robbins dead?'

'Yeah. Beale Norris,' said Wayne, rubbing his tear-streaked face. 'He said I should make it look like a robbery. I still got the computer stashed at my girlfriend's if you need proof.'

'Detective Schultz, would you please arrange to take Mr Fortune back to the cells?'

'Yes Ma'am,' said Glenn, uncuffing Wayne and dragging him up.

'Hey, no! I'm innocent man! This is a set-up!' shouted Wayne.

Sarah watched him go, then looked at her watch and picked up her files, heading for the door. She hoped it wasn't too late to make a house call.

Chapter 47

Alex had already ordered pizzas by the time the film began rolling. Or rather, the time stamp at the bottom of the screen began speeding forward: but the image of the Benedon library lobby hardly changed.

Suddenly there was a flurry of sped up images, so Lara clicked 'play' and they all watched as people began running in and out of the library.

'That's Sandra Mellon, she's one of the librarians,' said Brian as a woman ran to the door holding a phone and waving to someone off-screen. Minutes later, two uniformed emergency technicians ran into the frame.

'Usually there's lots of staff working at the library – but most of them go home at 7pm,' continued Brian. 'I heard a rumour that they were going to increase the staffing after hours because people have started using it to hang out, like socially. If you can't get a table at Jimmy's Pizza and your fake ID has been busted at The Shovel, there aren't many other places to go. Not since Al & John's cut back their hours anyway.'

'What's Al and John's?'

'Big diner on MainStreet. It used to stay open 'til

midnight, but the owners are pretty old now. They changed the opening hours a few months ago so it closes at 7 pm now.'

Lara nodded.

'Marjorie mentioned the library was party central.'

'Not this night,' said Alex, his eyes focusing on the screen. 'Where is everyone?'

'I heard about this,' said Brian. 'One of my friends was at the library that night. When Ellie Campbell was found, police wanted to clear the library. The medics were in the lobby, so they funnelled everyone out of the back door.'

There was a knock at the door. There was a momentary pause as everyone celebrated the arrival of four big boxes from Jimmy's Pizza.

Lara kept her gaze on the monitors. Frozen in the frame was a stretcher being wheeled into the library.

'We don't need to see this,' said Lara, trying to ignore the smell of hot pepperoni. 'We need to go back, an hour, maybe more, to see if Beale Norris came into the building.'

'On it,' said Javier, biting into a thick slice of pizza.

They watched the ghostly image as Sandra ran backwards, the doors closing behind her, the time stamp numbers running down. Then there was a blur of movement and Lara shouted 'Whoa!'

Javier stabbed the key.

'There. Is that Ellie?'

It was 8.49 PM. Over an hour before she was found.

'It's her. It's Ellie,' confirmed Brian. The camera gave a side-on view, but Lara slowed it down, frame by frame. Lara had only seen photos of Ellie Campbell, but that was enough to recognise her now. Her hair was tied back in a ponytail, a sweater casually knotted around her shoulders. Lara didn't know what everyone else was feeling, but she suddenly had a terrible sense of sadness. This was the last time anyone saw her alive. There she was, walking into the library, a bounce in her step. But roll the tape forward just over an hour and she was a bump under a sheet.

'That's late. What is she doing going into the library at that time?'

'It's pretty common,' shrugged Brian. 'Maybe she'd been in there all day. Look, she doesn't have any books with her. Maybe she popped out to go for pizza or to The Hub and was going back to study.'

The Hub was Benedon's social centre by the East Gate, with meeting rooms for societies and a couple of popular on-site cafes. Lara remembered her student days, particularly in the run up to tests or exams. She'd hog a quiet table all day, but break up her study periods with a trip to the Union or nearby Covent Garden to clear her head.

With a click, the footage rolled onward. Every few minutes someone came inside the library, sometimes a lone student, sometimes in pairs. There was no-one that looked like a fifty-year-old man.

Lara put her hands on her hips, exasperated. She wasn't sure what she was expecting to see. Beale Norris in a pantomime villain's cape creeping around the lobby?

'Alex, can you make a start on the back-entrance tapes?'

'Look who that is,' said Brian.

Lara spun around as Javier pressed the pause button on the footage. She was expecting to see a man; after all, Brian had been briefed to looked out for Beale Norris.

Instead, he pointed at a young woman who had walked into the shot.

'Who is it?'

Javier clicked it forward again, frame by frame. The girl on the screen was blonde, wearing a Varsity jacket, a phone held to her ear.

'Her name is Lisa Marks – she's a cheerleader,' said Brian. 'She's also Brandon Campbell's girlfriend.'

Lara felt her heart race at the prospect of catching a thread. She wasn't sure where it would lead if she pulled it, but it felt significant.

'This is twenty-five minutes after Ellie went into the library. Another thirty minutes before Ellie's fall,' said Alex, doing the maths.

'Stay with the tapes, Javier,' instructed Lara.

The footage rolled forward. One minute, two minutes, five, ten. Then movement: a tall dark-haired man walked into frame.

'Shit,' whispered Brian, and they all turned to watch his expression. They had all been expecting – perhaps hoping – to see Beale Norris. But this man was much younger, taller, more distinctive.

'That's Brandon Campbell,' said Brian, his eyes wide. 'It's Ellie's brother.'

Chapter 48

Beale's house looked like a hotel. A rambling two-storey farmhouse, it had wings on both sides of the main building and a wide porch running all around. Lit from inside by warm yellow light, it looked even bigger than the Campbell's place.

'Who says crime doesn't pay?' muttered Sarah as she parked the car on the gravel drive and walked up the steps, flanked by huge hydrangea bushes with balls of lilac flowers

The brass bell gave a satisfyingly deep chime, like the hour-strike of a grandfather clock. Enough to wake even the most reluctant suspect.

She was about to press the bell again when the door opened and a woman in her sixties peered out.

'Can I help you?'

Sarah flashed her ID. 'Detective Carter, Benedon PD. Are you Mrs Beale?'

A brief tremor of distaste passed across the woman's face. *Those micro-expressions again,* thought Sarah. *They never lie.*

'I am Glenda Krauss, Mr Beale's housekeeper. I'm afraid Mr Beale has already retired for the night.'

'Well, go give him a poke,' said Sarah, stepping inside. '*I'm* afraid I need to speak to him. Urgently.'

The woman wavered for a moment, and then closed the door and shuffled down a corridor. Sarah took in the grand entrance hall, with its polished flooring and velvet furniture, the marble-topped side table displaying a pair of Oriental vases. It looked like a hotel on the inside, too. She heard muttered voices and Norris Beale came striding from the back of the house. If he had gone to bed, Beale apparently slept in a shirt and tie.

'Miss Carter?' he said, frowning. 'What... is this official business?'

'I'm sorry about the late hour, Mr Beale, but I thought you would like to be informed that we are about to arrest a suspect for the murder of Harry Robbins.'

She said it loud enough for the housekeeper to hear and Beale waved a hand towards a snug sitting room.

'Murder?' said Beale, closing the door behind them. 'It was my understanding that he had taken his own life.'

'That was the original assumption, yes,' said Sarah, perching on the edge of an armchair. She felt on edge in this big house, miles from anywhere. The presence of the housekeeper gave her some reassurance but still, she was glad to feel her gun in her hip holster.

'But now we have forensic evidence that proves somebody went into the house and shot him.'

'My goodness that is... troubling,' said Beale, narrowing his dark eyes.

She almost had to admire him. She'd heard that expression that politics was show business for ugly people, but lawyers were also showmen. She'd seen polished courtroom theatrics dozens of times and she didn't doubt that Beale Norris could perform with the best of them.

She watched as he crossed to a table and poured himself

a drink from a cut-glass decanter. He didn't offer one to Sarah.

'Was it a robbery?'

'No,' she lowered her voice, looking towards the door. 'Apparently, somebody paid a hitman.'

'Like an *assassin*?'

'Not quite. A criminal for hire. This isn't *The Day of the Jackal*.'

'Still. In Benedon. This won't be good for tourism or prospective students. Ros Davies is going to be absolutely furious.'

For a moment she thought of Ros Davies, uptight and ambitious. She imagined handsome Harry Robbins calling off their affair, and a bitter Dean stopping his career in his tracks. Ros had exacted her revenge with the power that she had, but she was no murderer. Sarah could see that now.

She watched Beale's eyes glance towards a walnut desk and at the phone sitting on top. Sarah wondered who he was planning to call? Arthur Campbell? Another gunman?

'Well thank you for keeping me informed, Detective, but I don't really see how this is relevant to me.' She forced herself to stay calm. It had been foolish to come here alone. In her long career in the force, she had almost never gone out into the field alone.

'The suspect we have in custody is a man named Wayne Fortune.'

Sarah watched his face carefully. Not a flicker, but then that wasn't a surprise: Beale would have been prepared for this.

'Am I supposed to know this man?'

'Your friend Jeff Strobe of Charter Matthews represented him a couple of years ago.'

She'd got Glenn to do a deeper dive into Wayne's criminal record and court appearances. Strobe had represented

Fortune for second-degree burglary with a firearm. Wayne could have got a ten-year jail sentence but with Strobe's skill, he'd got twelve months.

Beale just shrugged.

'Is that so? Well, I haven't seen Jeff for a while and we don't discuss cases, so again I ask, why are you telling me this?'

Sarah took a breath. It was time to start turning the screws.

'So, why did you do it?' she asked.

'Do what, Miss Carter?'

'Why did you have Harry Robbins killed?'

The lawyer gave her a double-take.

'Is this a joke, Detective?'

'I am certainly not laughing, Mr Beale.'

He definitely caught her tone that time. Beale frowned at her, then glanced over the door.

'I really don't have time for this.' He began to move towards the exit, but Sarah stepped in between. She wasn't entirely sure she looked particularly menacing, but she had a gun on her hip. Hopefully, that was deterrent enough. Either way, Beale stopped.

'Wayne Fortune has named you as the man who hired him to shoot Professor Robbins. We have phone activity tying him to you.'

An exaggeration, but Sarah was sure Steve and his team could find it.

'This is preposterous,' snapped Beale.

'Actually, I agree,' said Sarah. 'I mean, your whole plan, it was so ill-conceived, wasn't it? Why kill Harry? Why not just pay him off like you did all those farmers? Why not just spread rumours about him, ruin his reputation? Oh wait – people already did.'

Beale looked at her and snorted. 'If anyone was responsible for Harry Robbins' ruined reputation it was Harry Robbins himself. No one asked him to hang around with a young girl, meddling in things that weren't his business. If people jumped to conclusions, that's none of my doing.'

'You ordered him to be shot in the head...'

Sarah saw his anger flare. She was aware she might be pushing too hard, but she needed him off balance.

'This is a fantasy,' said Beale, his lips tight. 'You can't prove a word of it.'

'Are you sure about that, counsellor? Because you seem rather agitated. I wonder if you're regretting hiring a loose cannon like Wayne Fortune. He's a lowlife, for sure, but men like Wayne are survivors and will do anything to save their skin. No honour among thieves and all that.'

Beale didn't react. Sarah hadn't really expected Beale Norris to roll over and confess, but she had imagined he would be rather more rattled by her accusations. After all, it was one thing to plan a murder, it was quite another to actually go through with it.

'You know, I've always wondered,' said Beale with a sneer. 'When you accuse people of murder, don't you worry?'

'Worry?'

'Well, if you really believe he – or she – has murdered someone before, don't you think they might find it just as easy to kill again?'

'Is that a threat?'

Beale smiled, but it had an edge.

'Simply a hypothetical question. Academic, you might say,' he added with a nasty smile.

Sarah felt her anger rising. If Beale had the arrogance to think he could intimidate a law enforcement officer, then he clearly believed he was above the law. But then this was a man who had killed a respected professor. Possibly Ellie

Campbell too. She didn't doubt that was why Lara Stone and Alex Ford were asking questions about CCTV cameras in the Benedon library. And why? Simply to protect his own social position. That was all he cared about.

Sarah pulled out her phone and made a few taps, then put it away again.

'What was that?' frowned Beale.

Sarah simply smiled at him.

'One moment, counsellor,' she said, holding up a finger.

She waited a moment and then the doorbell rang. Beale looked towards the window.

'What's going on now?'

'I would strongly recommend you answer the door.'

Brushing past her, Beale stalked out into the hallway, but his housekeeper had got there first.

Standing on the front step was a group of uniformed officers.

'What?' stammered Beale. 'You *dare* to come into my home...'

Sarah held up a hand to stem his bluster.

'Sorry,' she said, pulling out a card. 'Formalities. Normally I would do it from memory, but seeing as you are an official member of the bar in this state – for now at least – I suppose I'd better get it right.'

She cleared her throat.

'Beale Norris, I am arresting you for conspiracy to commit murder and for the murder of Professor Harry Robbins. You have the right to remain silent. Anything you say can and will be used against you in a court of law...'

Beale began to speak, but Sarah carried on.

'...You have the right to an attorney. If you cannot afford an attorney, one will be provided for you. Do you understand the rights I have just read to you? With these rights in mind, do you wish to speak to me?'

He raised his chin.

'I want to make a phone call.'

'I would expect nothing less,' said Sarah. 'But I respectfully deny your request on the grounds that you may attempt to warn your accomplices.'

'Accomplices?' he spat. 'I'm not a criminal!'

'I believe that will be for the courts to decide, Mr Norris.'

Sarah beckoned to the cops, but Beale stepped towards her, his face twisted into a mask of hate.

'Don't think your pathetic little games will have any effect, *Sarah*,' he hissed, venom dripping from every word. 'Every shred of evidence you have is circumstantial and I have friends in the highest places, even your boss, Sheriff Roscoe. I will walk out of your station a free man within a couple of hours. And I think you know what that means.'

'Lopez,' said Sarah. 'Please restrain Mr Norris.'

The big cop effortlessly pulled Beale away from Sarah, twisted his arms behind his back and cuffed him, thumping him face-first against the wall.

'You won't get anywhere with this!' shouted Beale, as the officers dragged him towards the door. 'You have no idea of my power. This is my town, Carter! *My* town!'

Sarah shook her head sadly.

'Not any more, Counsellor,' she said, 'This is my town now.'

Chapter 49

Lara's lungs were burning by the time she got to the police station, a large brick one-storey building at the far end of Main Street. In London she'd run along the Thames tow path most days from Albert Bridge to Tower Bridge and back again. It had taken months to get fit after a decade stuck behind a computer screen drinking coffee, but it was funny how your fitness levels could drop like a stone once you stopped.

She bent over the reception desk and rang a brass bell. She'd tried calling Sarah Carter, thinking she was still at home, but her call had been declined and a message sent that she was back at work.

'Remind me... why didn't we drive?' said Alex, pushing in through the revolving door behind her.

'I didn't think it was this far,' said Lara as a uniformed officer appeared from a back room.

'Can I help you, Ma'am?'

She looked up at the policeman.

'My name is Lara Stone. I'm a friend of Detective Sarah Carter. Is she at the station?'

The policeman shook his head. 'Detective Carter left about thirty minutes ago, I'm afraid.'

'Has she gone back home?'

'Can't say.'

Alex was already on the phone. He tapped Lara on the shoulder and shook his head.

'She's still not answering.'

Lara glanced at her watch. It was almost ten o'clock. She wondered where Sarah had got to; when they'd gone to her house, she'd assumed that Sarah had finished her shift. Then again, Lara knew what this sort of work was like, especially in a small town.

'We're her friends. This is important. I'm trying to get through to her on the phone but she's not answering,' said Alex to the young officer.

'Maybe she doesn't want to speak to you,' he replied, not impolitely.

The young officer sighed. 'Look, she's on police business.'

Lara glanced at Alex.

'Well, is there someone else we can speak to? This is important.'

'I figured,' said the officer, picking up the phone and speaking quietly into it.

By the time the door to the station opened, they had both caught their breath. A solid-looking older man with a moustache stepped out into the reception. 'I'm Glenn Schultz, Senior Detective. You'll be Lara Stone and Alex Ford?'

'Yes, how did you know?'

He flashed a smile.

'Detective Carter is very descriptive.'

'Good. Then we've got something that we need to show you,' she said, holding up a thumb drive.

‘It’s regarding the murder of Harry Robbins and Eleanor Campbell,’ added Alex.

‘Ellie Campbell? You’ve come to the right place,’ said Glenn. ‘Ellie Campbell was my case.’

He nodded towards the station house. ‘Let’s go have a look, shall we?’

* * *

They all crammed into the little office as Glenn Schultz fiddled with a clunky old desktop computer. Lara wasn’t convinced that they should be there. She didn’t trust Sarah Carter when it came to Alex – she could still remember the way the detective had been flirting outrageously with him under the street lamp outside The Shovel just a couple of days earlier. But Lara trusted Sarah as a law enforcement officer, which was more than could be said for Glenn Schultz.

‘So the CCTV tapes weren’t looked at during the initial investigation into Ellie’s death?’ she said, trying not to sound accusatory. Glenn looked miffed that she’d even asked the question.

‘There was no reason to suspect any sort of foul play, Miss Stone,’ he replied pointedly. ‘Besides, what would it have shown, if I had?’

The Benedon detective turned back to the monitor and grunted with satisfaction as a window popped open on the screen.

‘So what are we looking at?’ he said, stepping back and folding his arms across his chest. It was a static image of an empty lobby.

‘Security footage from the Sinclair Campbell library,’ said Lara.

'This is from the footage of the front entrance. There's also a file of footage from the back door.'

'Glenn, you worked the case that night. What do you remember?'

Trust Alex to smooth the waters with a tired cop. He'd even brought one of the untouched pizzas over from the security office, which Schultz had gratefully received.

Glenn Schultz stood in front of the screen, using the keys to run and re-run the footage of Brandon Campbell. Lara stood and watched, waiting to see how he would react. After all, she didn't know Glenn, but Sarah had mentioned he was born and raised in Benedon. Who knew what loyalties a life-long resident of the Campbell's town had? Who his friends were, who he owed? This could go either way.

'Well, ain't this a pickle?' said Glenn finally, then walked to the door of the office, calling out to a uniformed officer at a desk. 'Carmel, can you get me an address for Brandon Campbell, he's a student, so I'm guessing he lives on campus? Quick as you can.'

'Are you going to talk to him now?' asked Lara.

'Best thing, before he gets one of his Daddy's fancy lawyers involved. Of course, any decent brief will say this film doesn't prove anything, that the library is a public space and everyone is well within their rights to come and go as they please.'

Lara could have given him a squeeze.

Glenn put up a hand to rub his jowly face.

'But before they shut him down, I'd really like to ask Brandon Campbell why he lied to my face.'

'Did he?' asked Alex.

'Thinking about it, he yelled in my face, told me how I'd failed to save his sister. Didn't mention *he* was in the building at the time.'

Glenn grimaced at the memory. 'Yeah, I'd sure like to ask him about that.'

He was already pulling on his jacket.

'I'll get young Brin to go through the footage from the back door. See if we can catch Campbell and his girlfriend leaving that way.'

There was an urgent beeping in Lara's pocket and she pulled out her phone. 'Don't bother with that address, we've already found him.'

She held the screen towards the detective.

B&L both in library. Ironic.

'Who's that? Sherlock Holmes?' laughed Glenn.

'Brian. Our friend who was helping us identify the students on the film? He knows where they all hang out, so we sent him off to see if he could find Brandon.'

Glenn nodded with satisfaction.

'Well, let's go and ask Mr Campbell some questions.'

* * *

They could hear them before they were even at the stairs. Loud voices, laughter; it sounded more like a coffee shop than a library.

There were six or seven students gathered around a table on the third floor, but it looked as though the study group was just packing up, closing laptops and sliding books into bags. At the far end of the table, Brandon Campbell was still sitting with his feet up on another chair. The girl from the film, Lisa the cheerleader, was behind him, smiling and whispering something in his ear. She was wearing the same Varsity jacket she'd worn in the CCTV footage, Lara noted.

'Late to be studying, folks,' said Glenn affably as he walked across.

A pretty red-haired girl looked up. 'We all have a Spanish test first thing tomorrow.'

Glen pulled out his badge. 'Well, maybe you'd all better get home to get some sleep.'

They all exchanged concerned looks on seeing the police ID and Lara noticed that they all looked to Brandon. He just gave them a nod.

'Oh, Mr Campbell,' said Glenn, as if he'd only just noticed Brandon sitting there. 'I wonder if you would mind staying behind for a moment? Something that you might be able to help us with. Miss Marks too.'

Glenn smiled pleasantly as the other students packed up their things and left.

'What's all this about?' asked Brandon warily when they were alone.

Glenn nodded over to Alex and Lara. 'I'm Detective Schultz. This is Alex Ford and Lara Stone, they're visiting lecturers here. They have been doing some research into security on campus.'

Not entirely untrue, thought Lara.

'They came across some CCTV footage that I'd like to play to you; I think you might be able to identify somebody on the film for us.'

Lara watched Brandon; for a moment, she thought he was thinking of refusing, but instead he shrugged. 'Sure, if you think it'll help, but we are meeting some people down at The Shovel...'

'It will only take a few minutes and it would be a big help.'

Glenn gestured for them both to sit and Lara pulled out her laptop, positioning it so that both Brandon and Lisa could see it. Lara clicked 'play' and watched their faces carefully as the footage ran. *They must know*, she thought. *They must know where this is going.*

Brandon's expression was stony, but Lisa looked frightened, sick, glancing anxiously down at Brandon.

'We shouldn't be watching this,' Lisa murmured, her hand going up to her mouth. Lara didn't need to see the screen to know that was the moment Ellie had walked into shot. She was too busy watching Lisa's hand, which was trembling as it approached her lips.

'What is this?' said Brandon, his face white, 'Why you showing me this?'

'Just keep watching,' said Glenn in a voice that suggested refusal was not an option. Lisa was getting increasingly agitated now, putting her hand on Brandon's shoulder. He shrugged it off.

When Lisa's face appeared on the CCTV, she went so pale that Lara feared she might faint. Brandon just closed his eyes. Glenn reached over and clicked off the footage.

'Do you remember me?' he asked.

Brandon gave a small nod.

'And do you remember when I asked you where you were that night?'

Brandon sat motionless, his head still bowed.

'Mr Campbell?' prompted Glenn.

'Yes, I remember.'

'Well then,' said Glenn. 'It must be *my* memory letting me down because I thought you told me you were at your girlfriend's. At one of the dorms.'

He bent to read the time code on the film, still freeze-framed on Lara's laptop screen. 'I don't recall you mentioning that you were in the library. You certainly didn't mention that you were in the library – ah – ten minutes before your sister's body was found at the bottom of the stairs.'

Glenn let the statement hang in the air.

'Now why is that, Brandon?'

Finally, Brandon looked up, his eyes blazing with anger. 'I don't have to answer your questions. My father's lawyers will tear you to pieces for even *suggesting* that I had anything to do with my sister's death. This has been painful enough for our family as it is.'

'Perhaps so,' said Glenn unfazed. 'But I have not suggested any such thing. Yet.'

Lara stepped toward the girl.

'And what about you, Lisa?' she asked. 'Did you have anything to do with Ellie's death?'

The girl flinched.

'No, of course I didn't,' she said, her voice short and staccato.

'Funny', said Glenn. Lara noticed how Detective Schultz looked about three inches taller now. That pale, tired, overweight man desperate to go home was quite transformed from the officer they'd met at the station half an hour before. 'Funny, I've just got a message from my colleague back at the station. He's been going through the footage from the back door of the library that night. You see, before the emergency services arrived at the library, possibly around the same time that Ellie's body was discovered, you two were leaving the library. In quite a rush it seems. You fled the library the back way, before I came along and cleared everybody out. Why was that, Brandon? Lisa?

'As I said, Mr Schultz, if you're going to go around making wild accusations, I'm not going to continue talking to you until my father's lawyer is here.'

'Good luck with that,' shrugged Glenn. 'One of my colleagues is questioning Beale Norris right now about other charges.'

The atmosphere tensed. Brandon looked stunned, as if his youthful arrogance had been instantly sucked out of him. Suddenly they looked like two kids who felt completely alone.

'Just tell them, Brand,' whispered Lisa.

'Tell us what, Lisa?'

'It was an accident!' she said, her voice trembling. 'An accident.'

Just then, the library seemed very quiet and empty.

Glenn pulled up a chair and leaned towards Lisa.

'We just want to understand what happened that night, okay?'

'Lisa, don't say anything,' instructed Brandon.

'But I didn't do anything,' she said, starting to cry.

Brandon hung his head, rubbing his square jaw against the palm of his hand.

'My sister fell from the stairs and I should have helped, but I didn't. I panicked and ran.' Brandon looked up at Lara, his eyes pleading. 'And I'll live with that for the rest of my days.'

There was an edge to his voice, like a little boy who had learned how to get around a weak parent. Like he thought he could talk his way out of anything as long as he pushed the right buttons.

'How tall was Ellie?' asked Lara suddenly.

Brandon frowned.

'What? Why?'

'Just curious.'

'Maybe five-seven. Maybe your height,' he said reluctantly.

Lara crossed to the balustrade and pressed her hips

against it. She looked down into the hole that ran all the way through the building. It was still a long way to the cold tiled floors at the bottom. Not quite the distance from the fifth floor where Ellie had fallen from, but still, enough to break a back or even kill her. Lara took a slow inhalation of breath and stretched out her arms. Her hips were pressing hard into the smooth, hard wall that stopped her from going over. She tipped forward but the balustrade protected her. Perhaps if she were taller, much taller, like Father Vernon, she could have toppled over if she slipped, but the rail protected her.

She turned around to face Brandon and Lara.

'I didn't do a physics degree, but there are plenty of people on campus who did. If you're my height, it seems pretty unlikely that you could just fall. You would have to have jumped. Or been pushed.'

She walked back to the group.

'So?' grunted Glenn to Brandon. 'You know lying to an officer of the law is a crime too. Obstruction of justice gets you between 12 and 18 months in prison.'

'Brandon, no,' whispered Lisa.

'Shut up you stupid bitch,' he growled.

Silence shimmered between them.

'Brandon, do you know why Detective Carter is with Beale Norris?' said Alex, glancing at Glenn. Glenn nodded his approval for Alex to continue.

Brandon didn't reply.

'We have evidence that links Beale Norris with the murder of Professor Harry Robbins. Your family company AgriCam was selling carcinogenic chemicals. Beale Norris was paying off victims and Ellie found out about it. Harry knew about it too. Beale Norris wanted to shut down the story, so he got rid of Harry. Which makes me think; were you in charge of silencing Ellie?'

'*What?*' spluttered Brandon.

'No, that's not it. That's not what happened,' said Lisa, looking utterly terrified now.

'Do you want to tell us, Lisa?' Said Glenn. 'Because right now, I am wondering if you're an accessory to murder.'

Lisa gave a deep, frightened sob.

'Brand wanted to speak to his sister. He was looking for her all over campus...' she said, trying to control her emotions.

'I said SHUT UP, Lisa.' The more aggressive Brandon Campbell became, the more Lisa seemed determined to tell her story.

'I came to the library to pick up a book I needed for an assignment. I was on the fourth floor, and I looked up, and I saw her. I saw Ellie up there in the top-floor reading room. So I texted Brandon to tell him where she was.'

Lara nodded. All this fit with the CCTV footage they had seen. Lisa's arrival, then Brandon's, around twenty minutes after that. Campus wasn't huge. You could walk between most points of the college or the town to the library in that length of time.

'Brand just wanted to talk some sense into Ellie. That's all....'

'Did they argue?' asked Lara.

'Yes,' nodded Lisa.

Brandon lunged at Lisa but Alex restrained him. Although he was a football player, Alex could match him in strength and height.

'It was an accident,' he roared. 'It was an accident.'

He crumpled in Alex's arms, like paper being crushed in a fist.

Lara heard emotion stutter in his throat.

'Brandon, just tell us what happened,' she said.

Brandon was shaking his head in panic.

'Look, I heard Ellie was going to go nuclear with claims about AgriCam. She was talking to lawyers, to that professor. I wanted to talk to her, change her mind about going to the press,' said Brandon. 'That's all. I didn't want to *silence* her. She was my sister.'

He shook his head, fringe flopping.

'She wouldn't see reason, man. She was furious. Accused me of being an enabler. Lot of other names too. She walked off, not willing to listen to anything I said. I ran after her, tried to stop her. She twisted out of my grasp... The next thing I knew....'

Lara glanced over at Lisa.

'Is that what happened?'

She nodded sadly.

'It was an accident. A complete accident. But we were frightened. We ran out of the fire exit and left the library.'

Tears were streaming down Brandon's face.

'I didn't want her to die. I just wanted her to be reasonable. But she was never going to be reasonable once she'd met that stupid do-gooder girlfriend and the great Harry Robbins. She was suddenly a *campaigner*. She didn't want to work at the company, but it wasn't just that. She wanted to destroy it for everyone else.'

Lara could feel his quiet fury. She could almost see inside his brain. She believed that Ellie Campbell's death was an accident, but she could also see how their confrontation had become so charged. Ellie, so passionate about doing the right thing. Brandon, jealous of his older sister for so long, could finally step out of her shadow, perhaps even take over the CEO job one day, now Ellie didn't want it. But she could imagine how Brandon believed that his sister was trying to wreck his future, his new destiny.

'Ever since we were kids, she was always the golden child. She was the future of the company, I was just the dumb jock, only at Benedon because of family money. But Ellie never wanted the role. She reluctantly interned at the company, and nodded politely when my dad discussed business with her at the dinner table. He was never interested in what I had to say. I understood why she wanted to switch her MBA to journalism, but I never thought she'd want to bring us down.'

'Brandon, she'd didn't want to bring AgriCam down. She wanted to get GreenGo pulled off the market. She wanted its victims to be properly compensated. That's all.'

'I didn't want her to die,' he said, crying again. 'When she fell, I couldn't bear to look. I panicked, we panicked,' he said glancing at Lisa. 'We just kept running down the stairs and pushed out through the fire doors. Man, I just kept running. I don't know even know where we went.'

Lara stepped across and gently put her hand on his shoulder.

'Brandon, it's time to stop running.'

'I know,' he whispered. 'I'm sorry. I'm so, so sorry.'

Chapter 50

Sarah parked her car at the back of the care home and walked in through the garden. The path was even but meandering, weaving back and forth between clipped shrubs and well-tended flowerbeds still with pockets of colour despite the onset of Fall. A gardener raking leaves from the lawn looked up and waved at Sarah as she passed.

'Hey, looks great,' she called. 'Keep up the good work.'

On the other side of the garden, Sarah could see a nurse pushing an elderly woman in a wheelchair. They were singing some sort of long-forgotten jingle together, then laughing, hands clasped together.

No, Beauville wasn't the prison Sarah had convinced herself it would be. Colleen was lucky to be here.

'Hi Ms Carter,' said a young care-worker Sarah recognised from previous visits. 'Here to see your mom, huh?'

'How is she this morning?'

There was a downturn of the mouth, an apologetic shrug. 'She's doing OK. She'll settle.'

Another thing Sarah was grateful for; their honesty. There was no pretence at Beauville, everybody knew that dementia was a one-way trip and they didn't sugar the pill.

'By the way, I think Heather was looking for you, she's in the office.'

'Thanks,' said Sarah, walking inside the building, secretly glad to have an excuse not to go straight to her mother's room.

'Hey, look who it is!' cried Heather as Sarah walked into the office. 'Benedon's demon bowler!'

Sarah laughed. 'Only compared to Bobby.'

'Well everybody needs a bit of practice,' smiled Heather. 'And as I say to my kids at soccer practice, it's not about how many goals you score, it's how hard you try.'

Heather gave a wry smile. 'Obviously, I have to say that, because they all stink at sports.'

She pulled out a chair for Sarah.

'So, how's things? It was intense last night but we got through it.'

Sarah gave a soft smile. Heather didn't know the half of how intense the previous night had been.

'Does it get any easier?'

The other woman nodded sympathetically. 'Well, I wish I could tell you it's going to get better.' She paused. 'But I *can* tell you we've all got your back here. It's what I love about this town.

Sarah's heart swelled at the sentiment.

'I know that,' she said quietly. 'And I wanted to say thanks.'

'It's what we do,' shrugged Heather modestly.

'No, seriously,' said Sarah. 'Everyone here at the home – and you especially Heather – all your friends...'

Heather shook her head, her curls bouncing. 'They're your friends too now,' she said.

Sarah couldn't help smiling at that. The truth was, Sarah had never been very good at maintaining friendships, especially female ones, choosing to prioritise work or the occasional drink after work, to anything that resembled the cultivation of relationships.

'It was wonderful how everybody pulled together when my mom went missing. I couldn't have asked for better people around me. This place is amazing.'

'But?'

She looked at Heather quizzically.

'I can feel a big "but" coming right around the corner at me.'

'But...' agreed Sarah. 'But I'm still not sure this is the right way. Last night made me realise that. I think she needs me.'

Heather looked at her and nodded her understanding.

'You do know there are other ways to go about this don't you?' she asked.

'Heather, I *can't* look after her myself. My job is so demanding, it drains your humanity sometimes, I have nothing left for the day-to-day. I'll be honest, it's a struggle to get up in the mornings sometimes.' Sarah snatched at the tears on her face, embarrassed. 'Oh look, I never cry. Look at the big tough cop.'

Heather grabbed a tissue and handed it to her.

'I get it. I do. I've got four kids and Dave's mom to deal with before I even get here to the madhouse.' She flashed Sarah a self-deprecating smile. 'But what I meant is, if Beauville isn't right for you or for your mom, then there are other ways to handle the situation.'

'Like what?' sniffed Sarah.

'Like take your Mom home and get yourself a full-time carer. It's not cheap, but it's cheaper than Beauville. And I happen to know an amazing woman named Grace who will come to the house. She's got a beautiful laugh, but she's as no-nonsense as they come – I think Colleen would appreciate that approach.'

She leant forward and squeezed Sarah's fingers.

'Why don't I give her a call? See if your mom likes her at least.'

'Thanks Heather, yes,' said Sarah, feeling relief wash over her. 'I just get the feeling that my mom will be happier surrounded by familiar things.'

Another tear escaped down her cheek.

'And what's going to make *you* happy, Sizzle. I wonder if you need to work out where you belong too, because I tell you, you don't want to spend too long in limboland. It's not good for the soul.'

For a moment, Sarah wondered if she could remember anyone ever asking her that before. Instead she looked out of the window at the blue sky, at the yellow leaves falling from the trees. The familiar things.

'You know, when I first came back here,' she said slowly, 'I was just counting down the days, planning my escape back to the big city where I'd built my life. But coming back to Vermont, it's made me realise I didn't really have a life. I had a job, I had a badge and there was a whole squad of people with guns that would back me up.'

'That's always nice to know.'

But they hadn't backed her up, had they? With all those radios and computers and squad cars, there had been no real support network in New York; and when she had become inconvenient, Sarah had been pushed out without a thought.

'But here, people care – if you'll let them,' said Sarah. 'And I'm starting to see that maybe I can help people more here.'

Heather leant across her desk and picked up a framed photograph.

'Check it out,' she said, handing it across. It was a

picture of Heather wearing a gown and mortar board on her graduation day, the rest of the class lined up behind her.

'Is that *me?*' said Sarah, pointing towards an unsmiling girl on the far-left.

'It is – or it *was,*' said Heather, taking back the photo and looking

at it affectionately.

'I always knew you were going to leave,' she said. 'It's a small town, and the ambitious ones like you all left. But you know, if your ambition is to have a good life in a great place with good people around you, then there's a lot to like here. Life's good in the slow lane. You get to see more of the scenery.'

'And the scenery is pretty spectacular in Vermont.'

'Yes, it is,' smiled her friend.

They both stood and Heather pulled her into a hug, rubbing her back.

'You go see your mom, and I'll make a call to Grace – we'll see where that takes us, huh?'

Sarah walked out of the office and down the corridor. The door to her mother's room was open, but Sarah didn't go in. Not yet. She didn't want her mom to see she'd been crying. Didn't want her to worry any more than she already did.

She pulled out her phone: two messages, one from Glenn:

Wayne's singing like a canary. Brandon, not so much. Oh, and Roscoe's having kittens. We're running a sweepstake on the aneurysm. Want in?

And one from Mike:

Fishing's on this weekend. Want to come along, maybe cut some bait? Be great to catch up.

Sarah pressed 'reply'.

Sure. I'd like that. Call me when you hit the lake, I'll bring the beer.

Colleen Carter was sitting in an armchair looking out into the garden. 'Hey sweetheart, how are you?' she said.

'I'm pretty good,' said Sarah and was surprised to find that it was the truth.

Colleen looked up and smiled – bright and wide, just like Sarah remembered. 'Are we going for a walk later?'

Sarah knelt down next to her mother's chair.

'Sure mom,' she smiled, taking Colleen's hand. 'It's a lovely day out there. And then you know what? Then I'm going to take you home.'

Chapter 51

Alex had to sit on his fancy silver suitcase in order to get it closed. He wasn't sure why it suddenly seemed so full. He hadn't really bought anything in Benedon, just a bottle of Maple syrup and a hunk of cheese that he wasn't even sure he'd get through customs.

'You ready?'

Lara was leaning against the frame of the bedroom door. Alex felt a stir of desire he tried to ignore.

'I think you're going to have to keep the cheese,' he said, removing the giant paper-wrapped wedge and replacing it with his wash-bag.

'This is enough smoked cheddar for the entire town,' she laughed as he threw it over and she caught it.

'So Sarah just called,' said Lara.

'Oh, so you're friends now?' he said, clicking the case shut. He'd detected the tension between the two women on a number of occasions. He liked to think it was the simmer of competition over himself, but he rejected the idea as being too cocky.

Lara shrugged. 'We're going for a drink this weekend, although she's got someone coming up from New York to go fishing, so we'll have to fit it in around that. But that's not why she called; she wanted to fill us in about Beale Norris. Apparently, they got a search warrant for his house and found a burner phone in his gym bag. They can link a call to Wayne Fortune.'

'That's great. Do you think they'll make charges stick?'

Lara sighed. 'Not sure. Sarah's pretty tenacious, although money talks.'

Alex held up his phone.

'Brian has just sent his story over to me.'

Lara stepped forward to take a look.

'Is it good?'

'The kid must have been up all night. He's done an amazing job. I've sent it over to the newsroom already; Darius has even read it. He doesn't think it's front page news, at least, not in the UK, but he thinks every outlet in the US is going to pick it up. Maybe we can even make Brian some money through syndication.'

'We can't do anything until we've run it through our lawyers.'

Alex smiled to himself. Lara had taken a four-month-long sabbatical but she still used the phrase *We*. She would always be part of the editorial team even if she was 3,000 miles away. The *Chronicle* was in her blood, it was her heritage.

'True. And I'm sure they are going to take their red pen to most of it, but that's not Brian's fault, just where Benedon PD are with the case.'

He paused.

'He's a talented journalist. You must be a very good teacher.'

She waved her hand at him.

'Brian's a second year and I only had him for one

lecture. But I'm glad it's good. The AgriCam story is definitely going to get him a job.'

'Job?' said Alex with a low laugh. 'Try the Pulitzer prize.'

He paused and looked at her.

'It was good of you to give him the story.'

In all the time he'd known her, Lara had never worn her heart on her sleeve, never made big, loud gestures. People thought she was closed-off but really, she was just quiet with her emotions, and that hid the fact that she had the biggest heart of anyone he knew. The AgriCam scandal and the death of Harry Robbins was a big story, another feather in Lara's cap but the previous evening, when the dust had settled and they realised that they had a huge scoop on their hands, Lara had insisted that Brian Silvinski write it.

'He needs it more than me or you,' she said, with a shrug.

Alex nodded, thinking about all the people who had given him a break over the years and all the talented people in offices around the world who got overlooked because they didn't have a mentor, or perhaps the confidence to get noticed.

'We should give Ellie and Harry a by-line too.'

'Absolutely.'

There was a natural pause in the conversation. Alex pulled his suitcase off the bed and put it on the floor. Leaving Benedon suddenly seemed real. He was packed but he wasn't ready to go.

'So, are you coming to the airport?'

'Of course I'm coming.

'I thought you had lectures this afternoon?'

'Doug has given me the afternoon off. He said it's the least he can do.'

'You told him about Beale?'

'The whole faculty knows. News spreads as fast as Twitter on campus.'

Alex laughed and then fell serious.

'Did you tell him about Ros and Harry?'

'No. I'm not going to tell anyone. I think gossip has done enough damage around this campus. Harry knew that.'

'But can you bear it if Ros Davies gets the Provost job?'

'I'll be gone by then.'

Alex nodded. He knew what she meant. As a journalist, you got to hear a lot of things, you got to peep behind the curtain. The information you knew was often potentially destructive, but you couldn't interfere everywhere.

'There's a date for Harry's funeral,' said Lara. 'It's next week. I'm going to help organise memorial drinks. Buck said he'll host it, but I'm going to pay for it.'

Alex felt it again. A little stab of irrational jealousy.

'You cared for Harry, didn't you?'

'I liked him, yes. But I'm not sure I've been romantically interested in anyone for a long time. Not really.'

'Thanks,' he muttered. Her words were like a punch in the guts. For the past 48 hours he'd been trying to work out how she felt about their night together. Discussing the LA *Globe* job with her hadn't worked. And they'd shown little outward affection for one another since the night in the Blackberry Inn. Was that normal? Alex wasn't sure. When he'd first got together with Alicia, his last serious girlfriend, they spent the entire weekend in bed, having sex and drinking wine. Looking back, he didn't even like Alicia all that much. But perhaps that was why it was easy. It was the depth of his feelings for Lara that suddenly made everything complex, as if one wrong move, might destroy everything.

'I've not been interested in anyone because of you,' she said simply.

He felt as if a valve had been unscrewed and unleashed joy around his heart.

He crossed the room, took her face in his hands and he kissed her.

They seemed to kiss for a very long time.

'You know we've still got no food in the house,' she smiled, finally pulling away.

'We have cheese.'

'If I had any cocktail sticks, I'd make you one of those cheddar hedgehogs.'

Alex grinned. 'A party porcupine. I always loved those things. Haven't had one since my 10th birthday.'

'I thought you were a fancy canapes man now?'

'I never knowingly turn down shrimp tempura but if it's between Nobu catering and a party hedgehog, I'll take the hedgehog every time.'

'Then I'm going to make you one,' she said, squeezing his hand.

'Now?'

'Seeing as you're leaving me, I'm going to make you one as a send- off. I just need to pop to the deli.'

'And then we need to talk about the *Globe*.'

He paused and his tone turned serious. 'Lara, they're pressing me for a decision. The offer only stands until 9 am tomorrow.'

'UK time?'

'LA time.'

'That gives you time to get back to the office, talk to Darius. Talk to Charlie. Maybe they will offer you something.'

'Darius hasn't got anything to offer me.'

'Give me a reason why I should turn it down,' he said looking directly into her green eyes. *Just say it.* He pleaded. *Just say you love me.*

She hesitated and the pause seemed to go on forever.

'Alex, it's the editorship of the LA *Globe.* Journalists around the world would kill for that job. You've got to take it. I'm going to be in Vermont until Christmas anyway.'

'Exactly. You'll be coming back just as I'll be leaving the *Chronicle.* My notice period is three months.'

'They won't hold you to it,' she said with confidence.

'They might. Either way, it's going to be at least two years away from London.'

He looked away and rubbed his mouth. She wasn't going to say it. She wasn't going to say, 'stay in London, Alex. Stay in London because that's home. Our home'.

'You'd better not go running off with any celebrities. I know how much you like Jennifer Anniston and I hear she's single.

'What about you and the hunky priest?'

'This isn't the *Thorn Birds.*'

'No, but it's still a love story.'

Or at least, I thought it was, he thought.

* * *

Lara had tears in her eyes as she shut the door of the cottage behind her. Alex had been here less than a week but already she felt as he lived here now, in this little cottage. She glanced back at the bedroom window thinking about the previous night. After the drama of the day – bouncing around the state, uncovering the GreenGo story, linking Harry's death to Beale Norris and Brandon Campbell's dramatic confession about Ellie's death, they had practically collapsed onto the mattress and had fallen asleep within minutes. Lara had woken up in the middle of the night, when she'd heard Alex's breathing pattern change and she knew she was awake.

Impulsively, she'd rolled over to kiss him, and he had kissed her back too and they'd had intense, almost silent sex. She could still taste him on her tongue and she was glad; it meant she couldn't ignore the fact that they had been intimate anymore.

'Why can't you tell him how you feel? Just tell him you don't want him to go,' she said out loud, although she knew the reason why.

She was scared. Scared that if she told him she didn't want him to move to LA, he would go anyway. She wasn't sure she could handle that rejection. Not from Alex.

The job offer and the location couldn't have come at a worse time. Lara and Alex's friendship had survived long separations before, when he was stationed around the world for his foreign desk work. But now if he spent two years in LA, she would be pushing forty on his return and that would be getting late to have children.

Children.

She couldn't believe she was even thinking about it. They'd only had sex twice and suddenly visions of a suburban house and holidays with kids' clubs were flashing through her mind.

She resolved to stop thinking about it, at least until she returned home, and picked up her pace towards the deli. As she pushed her way into the store, she saw Zoe the moody barista was on duty behind the coffee counter.

'Hey,' said Zoe, raising her hand in hello. 'Can I get you a tea?'

Lara was taken aback. The prickly woman from ten days earlier was nowhere to be seen. Then again, so much had changed since Labor Day weekend.

'Tea? Not today, but I'll drop by tomorrow.'

'You do that. I'll see if I can get some English breakfast.'

Lara threw a white cabbage and some cocktail sticks

with US flags on the end into the basket, and although she couldn't find pickled onions, she reckoned that mini gherkins would be a decent substitute and bought those as well. Bagels, some wild sockeye smoked salmon lox and some cream cheese from a local creamery were also added.

Approaching the cash tills, she saw a tall, familiar figure at the coffee counter. He waved and handed Zoe some bills, putting the change in the pocket of his black trousers before he came over.

'Lara.'

Vernon's smile was wide. Lara was happy to see him but she was keen to get back.

'I heard Detective Carter found her mother,' he said, opening the door of the deli for her to exit.

'That's right. I wasn't involved in the search but my friend Alex was. Mrs Carter had wandered onto campus. She used to work here. So did her husband. She's safe and back at the care home.'

'That is good news,' he said, standing on the pavement, taking a sip of his drink.

'Which way are you walking?'

Her grocery bag was under one arm. She used the other one to point towards Montrose Street.

'Back home.'

'Then I'll take the long way back to the chapel.'

For a moment he didn't speak.

'I heard about Beale Norris.'

Lara nodded. That was something else that had been troubling her.

'Vernon, I can't help feeling it was a little bit my fault.'

He frowned.

'In what way?'

'If I hadn't persuaded Harry to go to the Dean's party, he might still be alive. Harry was killed because Cordelia

Campbell saw him at Ros's house and she told him about the scandal at her family company. If he'd never met Cordelia, things could have been so different.'

'You can't think like that,' said Vernon kindly.

'Maybe not. But it's true. The decisions we take can have repercussions beyond those that we can even imagine. It's the butterfly effect.'

Vernon was quiet for a moment.

'Harry used to tell me that he always wanted to write a big important story one day,' he said. 'Justice was important to him. At least now, AgriCam will take GreenGo off the market and that is going to save lives. Harry, Ellie, you... you made that happen. The decisions you all made have saved dozens, maybe hundreds of farmers from serious illness and death.'

'But Harry and Ellie are gone.'

'In the Catholic Church, we like to think of death as a change, not an ending. I think that thought helps at times of deep personal grief.'

He tossed his coffee cup in a nearby garbage can.

'I believe this is my way back to campus. And you look as if you need to hurry back,' he said.

'I do actually. I have to go and make a hedgehog out of cheese.'

Vernon laughed and the mood instantly changed.

'A cheese hedgehog?'

'It's a British party classic. I'm making it for Alex as a farewell breakfast. I'm a terrible cook so I thought I'd try humour rather than attempt anything gastronomically fancy. Besides, silly food always makes me smile and I need cheering up.'

'So he's going back to London and you don't want him to go.'

She almost raised a smile. Was that part of a priest's job description? It was as if he was psychic as well as spiritual.

'He's been offered a job, Vernon,' she said, desperate to offload her thoughts on someone. 'In LA. 'I'm not sure I'm going to see him for a while. A long while.'

'And how do you feel about that?'

'Sad. Scared.'

'Scared?'

Lara stopped walking and turned to the priest.

'I told you I came to Benedon to get some headspace and work out how I felt about him., but when I left London I made the assumption that Alex was going to be there when I got back. But he's moving to the other side of the world, and I just have this horrible feeling that he'll move on and forget about me when he gets there. I had my chance for so many years and I didn't take it. Two nights ago, something romantic happened between us, but then he told him about this job offer and I just feel as if I've missed my opportunity. He wants to be an editor. I hate LA. Those two things separate us. It's as if it's a sign that we're not meant to be together.'

'Does Alex know how you feel?'

'I'm not sure. He asked me this morning if there was a reason why he shouldn't take the job.'

'What did you say?'

'I told him to take it.'

'Why did you say that?'

'Because I know it's what he wants.'

'And what do *you* want Lara?'

She thought for a moment.

'I have a recurring dream. It's nothing complicated. It's just me and Alex on my houseboat back in London. We're drinking wine and reading books and it is so beautiful and simple, that when I wake up from that dream, I feel an incredible sense of contentment.'

'Lara, I will never marry and I'm not very experienced in romantic affairs. But I think I know people and it sounds to me that when Alex wanted you to give him a reason to stay in London, he was asking what was in your heart.'

'I love him. I'm madly, desperately in love with him.'

Lara felt her breath shudder as she said it. It was as if all the emotions she had felt, but hidden, for so long were suddenly coming to the surface.

'So tell him.'

'But this isn't about my feelings. It's about his career, his life. If he goes to LA, I'm not sure our relationship will survive it. If he stays, he'll resent me and so I'm not sure it will survive that either.'

'You have to have faith,' said Vernon simply. 'Faith in your love for each other. Faith that your love is stronger than any obstacles you'll face.'

Suddenly Lara wanted to see Alex. She wanted to be with him and tell him everything that she had just said to Vernon.

'I should go,' she said, turning to run.

'Good luck with the hedgehog,' he shouted after her.

Lara was almost sprinting by the time she got to Montrose Street. The bottom of her brown grocery bag felt as if it was about to give way, but she managed to make it home by the time the paper split.

The cabbage rolled across the kitchen floor.

Alex was sitting at the table hunched over his MacBook. He stood up and picked up the cabbage as Lara tried to get all her groceries to the countertop without dropping any more.

'I had a $100 bet with myself that you wouldn't be able

to find pickled onions in an American deli,' he said, handing her the vegetable.

'Alex, about the *Globe* job....'

He held up his hands. 'I've done it. Can you believe it? I've just sent the publisher an email accepting it.'

Her heart was thumping hard.

His eyebrows creased together in a frown.

'You said I should take it,' he said slowly.

Lara couldn't breathe. It was as if the room was spinning. She tried to do the maths. LA was three hours behind, which made it not yet eight o'clock on the West Coast. Perhaps the publisher hadn't opened the email yet. Perhaps Alex could recall it...

'I've asked for some conditions,' continued Alex. 'Four weeks holiday a year, which doesn't sound a lot, but it is for US companies. And I was thinking I could get a weekend place by the beach. I know you hate the city – the *Globe* is based in Downtown and I can't change that, but when you come over, we'll stay in Venice or Santa Monica, even Malibu.'

It was a done deal. She knew that now. His eyes glittered at the word Malibu. Alex had always loved to surf. He would love that beach lifestyle.

'Alex Ford, you are going to be a brilliant editor.'

'Will you think about coming?' he said taking her hand. 'Even for just a few weeks at the beginning. I don't want to do this without you.'

'I will have just had four months away from the office...'

She stopped herself.

'Then again, I guess I do own part of the company and that should allow me a few privileges.'

'Let's just see where this takes us,' he said softly, stroking her hair.

Something Vernon said earlier suddenly struck a chord.

He talked about changes, not endings. That was what was happening now. They'd been just friends. And now they weren't. It was the beginning of something else and that made her shiver with excitement.

'I love you, Lara Stone,' he whispered.

'I love you too. I've always loved you.'

'Come on,' he said. 'You mentioned something about a cheese hedgehog.'

Thanks for reading!

If you enjoyed The Last Supper, why not join Tasmina's VIP Book Club for news on releases, giveaways and events? www.tasminaperry.com/joinbookclub

Coming soon from international bestseller Tasmina Perry, a glamorous romantic thriller:

Seven Nights in Paris

Zoe and her new husband Mike head to Paris for their honeymoon. But the happiest day of Zoe's life turns sour when her husband vanishes into thin air within hours of arriving at their luxury hotel. At first, no one takes Zoe's claims that her husband is missing seriously. The police, the embassy and hotel security all think the groom simply got cold feet and has walked out on their marriage. After all, theirs was a whirlwind romance – perhaps he just had second thoughts. But Zoe can't believe that Mike would just leave her, and as the hours pass, her concerns grow.

Alone in Paris, Zoe turns to the one person she thinks

could help – her ex-boyfriend Lucas, a Parisian-based photographer who knows the darker side of the city better than anyone.

Lucas quickly discovers that Zoe doesn't know her new husband as well as she thinks and that Mike had a hidden agenda that has put his life in danger - and perhaps Zoe's too.

Set over the course of a week in the City of Lights, Seven Nights in Paris is an exhilarating romantic suspense story about secrets, love and the things we do in the pursuit of money.

You can find Seven Nights in Paris here.

Have you read the rest of the Lara Stone series?

The Yacht Party

The thrilling first book in the glamorous Lara Stone mystery series

What happens onboard, stays onboard...

Investigative reporter Lara Stone is heartbroken when her friend Sandrine is found dead, but Lara doesn't believe it was an accident. Sandrine's death seems linked to the murder of Jonathon Meyer, a secretive financier famous for hosting glittering networking parties on his Monte Carlo yacht Pandora.

What secrets are hidden onboard Meyer's yacht? What deals were brokered that were worth killing for? And can Lara get to the truth before she herself becomes just another inconvenient guest at the party?

The Yacht Party takes you from London's high society

to Paris, via Monaco and the Caribbean in this glamorous escapist mystery.

You can find The Yacht Party here.

The next in the Lara Stone series:

The Last Supper

Murder is on the menu...

Viggo Widlund is the darling of the food world and his remote Swedish restaurant Kluven is the most exclusive place to eat in the world. Only accessible by one road, there is just one communal table for 12 lucky people.

When Investigative reporter Lara Stone snags a reservation, it promises to be a night to remember, but murder is on the menu. Viggo is found dead and everyone spending the weekend at the snowy retreat is a suspect. Can Lara untangle the lies and find the killer before she finds a knife in her own back?

You can find The Last Supper here.

www.tasminaperry.com

Printed in Great Britain
by Amazon

62466106R00241